Cape Breton is the Thought-Control Centre of Canada
RAY SMITH

A Night at the Opera
RAY SMITH

Going Down Slow
JOHN METCALF

Century
RAY SMITH

Quickening
TERRY GRIGGS

Moody Food
RAY ROBERTSON

Alphabet
KATHY PAGE

Lunar Attractions
CLARK BLAISE

An Aesthetic Underground
JOHN METCALF

Lord Nelson Tavern
RAY SMITH

Heroes
RAY ROBERTSON

A History of Forgetting
CAROLINE ADDERSON

The Camera Always Lies
HUGH HOOD

Canada Made Me
NORMAN LEVINE

Vital Signs (a reSet Original)
JOHN METCALF

First Things First (a reSet Original)
DIANE SCHOEMPERLEN

FIRST THINGS FIRST

First Things First

EARLY AND UNCOLLECTED STORIES

DIANE SCHOEMPERLEN

BIBLIOASIS

Library and Archives Canada Cataloguing in Publication

Schoemperlen, Diane
[Short stories. Selections]
First things first : early and uncollected stories / Diane Schoemperlen.

(reSet books)
Issued in print and electronic formats.
ISBN 978-1-77196-070-0 (paperback). — ISBN 978-1-77196-071-7 (ebook)

I. Title.

PS8587.C4578A6 2016 C813'.54 C2015-907402-9
C2015-907403-7

Readied for the press by Daniel Wells
Copy-edited by Emily Donaldson
Cover and text design by Gordon Robertson

Canada Council for the Arts
Conseil des Arts du Canada

Canadian Heritage
Patrimoine canadien

ONTARIO ARTS COUNCIL
CONSEIL DES ARTS DE L'ONTARIO
50 YEARS OF ONTARIO GOVERNMENT SUPPORT OF THE ARTS
50 ANS DE SOUTIEN DU GOUVERNEMENT DE L'ONTARIO AUX ARTS

Published with the generous assistance of the Canada Council for the Arts and the Ontario Arts Council. Biblioasis also acknowledges the support of the Government of Canada through the Canada Book Fund and the Government of Ontario through the Ontario Book Publishing Tax Credit.

PRINTED AND BOUND IN CANADA

MIX
Paper from responsible sources
FSC® C004071

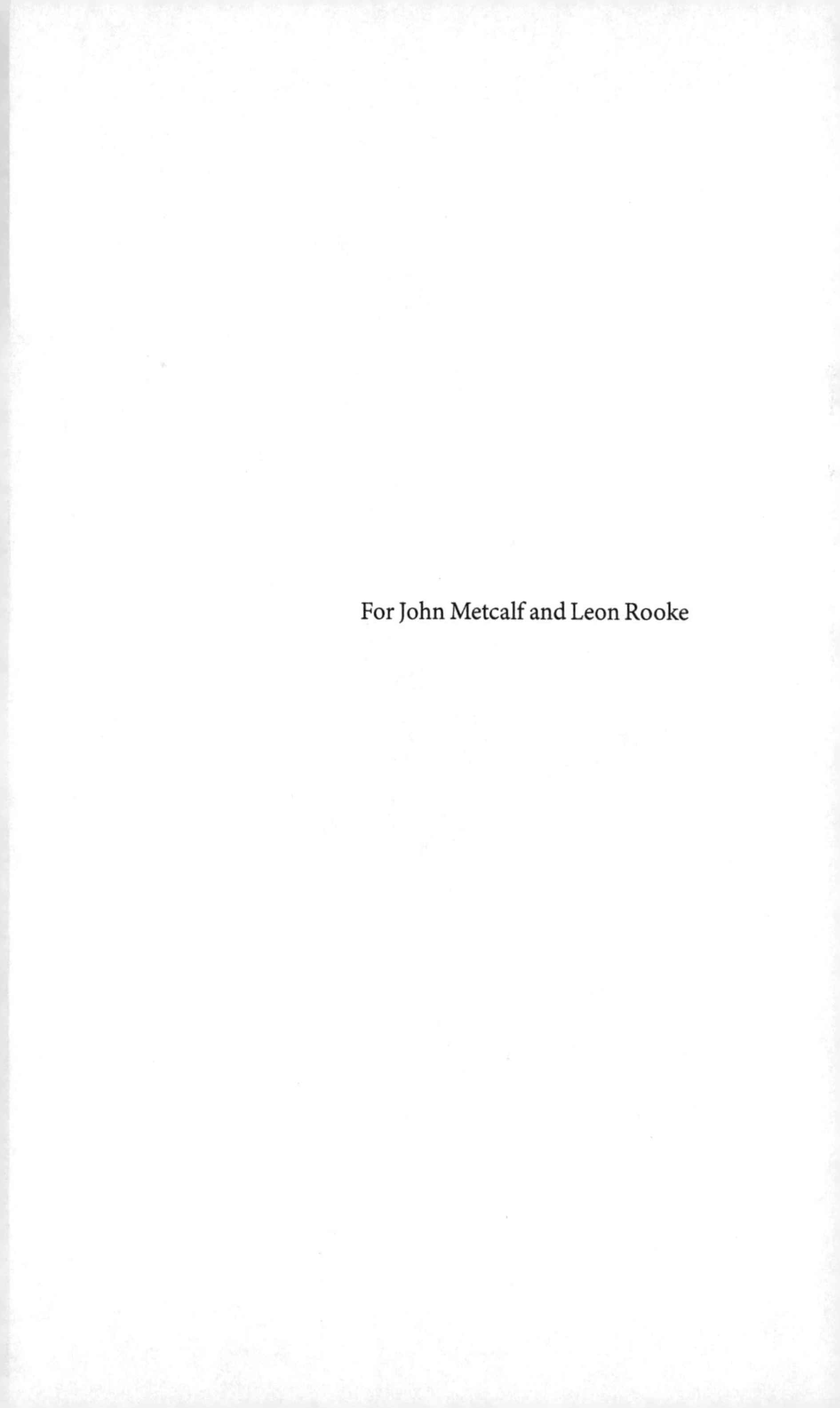

For John Metcalf and Leon Rooke

CONTENTS

PREFACE

THE FIRST STORY in this collection, "The Diary of Glory Maxwell," is my very first published story. It was written way back in 1974 when I was only twenty years old, a student with a major in English and a minor in Philosophy at Lakehead University in my hometown, Thunder Bay, Ontario. The story was published a year later in Lakehead's literary journal, *The Muskeg Review.* It has not been reprinted anywhere since—until now.

Let's go back to the beginning. In those days, Thunder Bay was a city that proudly called itself "a lunch-bucket town," its main industries being the grain elevators and the paper mill. Our little war-time bungalow, in the neighbourhood called Westfort, was so close to the mill that the smoke spewing from its giant red-and-white stack twenty-four hours a day left a fine white residue on everything: the garden, the car, the back step, the clean clothes hanging on the line to dry. Neither one of my parents had finished high school. My father worked in the grain elevators and my mother ran a post office outlet in the back of a drugstore. Other than cookbooks, the only books we had in our house when I was growing up were an old edition of the Webster's New World Dictionary that my this experience changed my life. Not only did I get to have Alice Munro as my teacher for one week out of the six, but for the first time in my life, I no longer felt quite so strange. There I was surrounded by people who were just like me, people who were interested in the same things I was and who did not think I was crazy for wanting to be a writer. Certainly back home in Thunder Bay, this dream of mine was, shall we say, *suspect.* That fall I moved to Banff, then lived in Canmore for the next ten years. I began submitting my stories in earnest to Canadian literary magazines. Many of them were rejected ten or twelve times before finding a place. I am stubborn and I persisted. Each time I received a rejection, I put that story right back into another big brown envelope and sent it somewhere else. I had taken to heart something that W. O. Mitchell often said at Banff: a writer requires an apprenticeship just like anybody else—an apprenticeship, he said, of ten years at least. In addition to all those rejections, there were just enough acceptances along the way to keep me feeling hopeful.

As it turned out, W.O. was right. In 1984, exactly ten years after the publication of my first story, Coach House Press published my first book, *Double Exposures*, a fictional novella accompanied by old black-and-white family photographs I had rescued when my mother was threatening to throw them out. As it also turned out, most of those early stories that were rejected so many times in the beginning did eventually appear in my own later short story collections.

The twenty-four stories gathered here were written between 1974 and 1990. In addition to "The Diary of Glory Maxwell," another seven of them, written mostly in the seventies, have not been previously collected. When I read these early stories now, I can see myself slowly but surely finding my subject matter, my sense of humour, and my voice—finding *myself* on the page. Sometimes it's just a line or two that jumps out at me. In the story "Prophecies" for example, written in 1978, there's this: "So what have hearts to do with love? They have no sense of humour." Almost forty years later now, I'd still be thrilled to write those lines.

I also note that, while some of these early stories were written in a more traditional manner, my fascination with innovative forms and structures was there from the beginning. There are several stories written in short sections, many containing lists of one sort or another, one modeled after a true-or-false questionnaire and another set up as a multiple-choice test. The story "Life Sentences," written in 1983, is a kind of fill-in-the-blanks interactive piece, where sometimes the missing word is obvious and sometimes not. I can't honestly say what gave me the confidence to think I could do all these different things. What made me think I could just break the "rules" of conventional story writing and do it however I wanted?

In the introduction to my 1991 collection, *Hockey Night in Canada and Other Stories,* John Metcalf wrote: "What readers must understand is that the shape of a story *is* the story. There is no such thing as 'form' and 'content.' They are indivisible; they *are* each other. New shapes are new sensibilities."

This makes perfect sense to me now but how did I know that then? I don't think I did, at least not consciously. Reviews of my work over the years have often referred to me as a writer who is "challenging the short-story form." I can assure you that never once in my life have I sat down at my desk and thought, 'Now what can I do to challenge the short story form this time?'

Most of the stories included here were written while I lived in Thunder Bay and then in Canmore. In 1986, I was invited to teach a weeklong summer workshop at Queen's University in Kingston, Ontario. This turned out to be another life-changing experience. Two months later I moved to Kingston with my year-old son, my ten-year-old cat, and a hundred boxes of books. As my life changed and moved forward in unexpected ways, I remained committed to writing. As the single parent of a small child, I remember often thinking that short stories, conventional or otherwise, were the perfect genre—because they were short.

In retrospect, I realize it was not confidence that made me think I could do whatever I wanted in a short story as long as I was telling that story in the best way possible, regardless of convention or tradition. It was that stubbornness of mine. Whereas confidence is a flighty temperamental quality that will always wax and wane, stubbornness is a good solid thing, not always wise but certainly reliable, steadfast, and dependable. Confidence is just as likely to up and leave you flat without warning just when you need it the most, but stubbornness can be a splendid thing that will never let you down.

This collection is my fourteenth book. After more than forty years of writing and publishing, I am often asked to offer advice to new writers of all ages. To them I say what I would say to my younger self:

Keep going.
You'll get there.
Read good books.
Be stubborn.
Be patient.
Read more good books.
Always remember that you have to do the first things first.

THE DIARY OF GLORY MAXWELL

(1974)

January 12

YOU'RE WONDERING about my name, aren't you? You're wondering how this pale person with the glasses got such a heroic blaze of a name, aren't you? My name is Glory simply because I am—glorious, I mean. I don't intend to sound vain—at least, I don't think I do.

Once, before she went to live with that young man who collected ships in glass bottles—once, my mother tried to explain it to me. I must have asked her about my name then, although now I can't remember doing it. She explained it to me very carefully, talking loudly, as one does to a foreigner newly come to this side of the ocean. She must have seen the foreign syllables in my eyes—she spoke very close to my ear. Her breath was hot and sweet like fresh corn. She said that there had been an argument in those larva days when I was new. An argument between my father and herself. You see: on the evening before I came to be, there on the delivery table, she had remembered a magazine story about a famous lady with beautiful legs and too many men. Her name was Lori and my mother wanted that for me. So she had named me Lori—in her mind, at least.

the words upon our minds and drawing the animal names into our flesh. He clutched at my sleeve with his new-blood fingers and cried for me to look.

"Look here, Glory. Please look at this page, this picture. Here, this is for you, Glory."

I looked. It was a picture—a photograph this time, not a diagram in black ink—but a picture of an owl. It clung to the sky in the night and its face was mine and glorious. It swooped perhaps down to the heads of the men who strained to watch its wings. But only just to their heads, never below. For an owl must never be that low—its wings need too much room. And its eyes are too bright, too glorious to watch the knees of men. I am the owl. I am glorious above the heads of man—and woman, too. I live above and my father lives there with me. We are not ready to die. There are not enough owls yet in the world.

March 18

The treatments are working well this month. But one must be very careful with the cobalt—one must understand the structure of the body to realize that. I understand and I am very careful with my own treatment of his illness. You're wondering what I, a mere girl, could do to help a man who is so sick, aren't you? You're wondering what I know that they, the doctors, many and white, do not, aren't you? Perhaps I should tease you just a little with what I know. Do you think so?

No. I will pretend that you are an animal and then I can be kind. Then I can tell you just what I know.

You see, my knowledge is new and glorious. I have pinned it gleaming to my brain only this morning and I am proud. We went together to the zoo this morning very early. The cages had not been cleaned. The metal fences were dotted with the litter of yesterday's crowd: droppings of salted popcorn pushed through the chain-links just above the sign: "Please do not feed the animals." And they had not been fed.

Many of the cages smelled bad, sour like rotten potatoes and dung. This made my father very sad. He held a small white handkerchief to his nose and he sighed.

But I wasn't bothered by the smell. It made me glad—more glad, perhaps, than wise. It reminded me of another smell—that other smell of breath and children and skin which pressed about us at the zoo. And another smell, still, of the bodies which I pass in the halls as I walk from class to class.

And so it made me glad because the animals did not mind the smell. They swept at it with their tails, but swept only half-heartedly, because the crowd expected it. And so I wrinkle my nose at the unwashed bodies that I must meet, because the crowd expects it.

The animal cages were dirty. And the animals should have sunk beneath their smell. But they didn't. Not for a minute. The lion stood up, lazy but hard. He did not bother to sniff the rancid air. He did not bother to shield the crowd from his steam-warm yawn. Rather, he stood up and yawned at them because he was king and glorious. He was strong and healthy, even though his cage had not been cleaned. And even though the cancer in my father's body has not yet been cleaned away by the doctors and their machines, he is growing stronger because I am here. And I am strong. I am the lion. And sometimes I must yawn because my flesh needs to stretch a little. I stand more easily than they, the other students, do, and I move with more grace because there is more blood in my veins: lazy and hard.

April 6

We washed the breakfast dishes together this morning. Well—I washed and dried, my father put them away. He did a fine to do it. I hate to bend so near to his face. His breath is sour and too thick. I always think to myself that that is the smell of his rotting insides, the smell of his disease. His arms aren't very strong when he hugs me goodnight, but I always feel like I am in a cage—a cage which has not yet been cleaned today. Perhaps not even yesterday.

I have forgotten how to run the new washing machine. My father bought it for me during the summer. I had told him how dull my days were now that the university had closed for the summer. So he bought the washing machine—right after the day I almost got my hand caught up in the wringer of the old one. He told me that my hands were too pretty, too smart to be squashed.

The man who installed the new machine for us explained the whole procedure to me—very carefully. And he gave me a fat booklet with thin cardboard covers and many instructions. But I think I lost it somewhere. And now I can't remember how all those buttons and dials work. I haven't been able to wash our clothes for a while now, and the beds have not been changed. But it hasn't really made any difference and my father hasn't even noticed. He sleeps a lot. He hasn't noticed.

Some people are like that—they never notice things, I mean. I often wonder what it was that made them grow that way. I know a girl like that—a girl at school. I don't *really* know her, but we did talk together once. She wanted to borrow that day's homework assignment from me. She wasn't sure that her answers were right. Perhaps she had misplaced a lung or a stomach in one of her diagrams. Her name was Janet. At first, I was going to say no because she didn't notice that my hair wasn't combed. She came and talked to me anyway. But then I stopped to think, to reconsider. Janet smiled at me while I was thinking, and her teeth were grey and soft like a row of dead garden slugs. I said:

"Yes, Janet. You can borrow it. My answers are always right."

You're wondering what made me change my mind, aren't you? You're wondering if perhaps it was her rotten yellow teeth that convinced me, aren't you? You think I'm sick, that sick. Don't worry if you do; you can't hurt me that way. Let me try and explain; it won't be easy. I am Janet. In a way, I suppose. Even though the answers are mine, their rightness is my father's. That way I am still his Glory, even though he doesn't have to know.

October 10

His skin was grey this morning and his breath did not smell. I wonder if perhaps it is because I have grown so used to it that I don't notice it anymore. I asked him if he wanted to go for a visit—an outing to the zoo. He nodded in reply, and cleaned the cobwebs of wax from his ears with his baby finger. Then he was ready to go.

He was lying on the cot in the library. I had placed it beside the shelf of books on domestic animals. He told me that he had dreamed of cows and chickens and maybe a barn door. I was glad because he cannot fly anymore and he shouldn't dream of birds. Cows are better; their feet are on the ground.

We tried to put his feet on the ground, but my arms were too thin. I couldn't lift him from the cot. The rampant cells which filled his body have made him much too heavy for my arm. We gave up soon and he groaned a little. He was disappointed, I suppose. Going to the zoo would have helped today. He could have smelled the fur and the claws. That would have helped, I'm sure.

I went out alone then. I wore a thin fur coat that my mother had forgotten when she left us here together. I did not go to the zoo, but to the pet shop instead. I bought my father a cat. It is fat and old with blurry tiger stripes across its back.

When I took it to him in the library, he smiled. That made me feel good and I flexed the muscles in my legs a little to be sure that I, at least, could still run. He told me that he was happy with the cat, happy that it was fat and old. That way, it would die soon and he would be able to dissect it—to see what it was really like. The cat switched his tail then and I bent down to touch his head with my sharp fingernails. I am the cat. My legs can still run but I'm not sure why. When I am old, a man on a cot in his library will be eager to dissect me. Eager to see how the muscles work beneath my glorious skin. I want to know what makes me run and why I have not yet changed my name.

November 21

He did not open his eyes today until this afternoon. I thought perhaps he was dead, but I couldn't remember how to find out whether he was or not. When I touched his forehead with my fingers, his skin slithered a little. I decided that was good enough. He wasn't really dead—just dying.

I read to him this evening. My mother sent us a letter today, but I threw it away. I didn't want to read that to him. Instead, I chose a book about snakes because I knew that he couldn't listen anyway. I read very carefully and perhaps a little too loudly. I could see the foreign syllables in his eyes and my mother would have liked it that way. The third chapter was about rattlesnakes and I read it twice. It wasn't written very clearly and there were many things that I did not understand. I paused after each sentence. I paused to ask him to explain just what it meant. He tried to answer me but his voice was too small and I couldn't remember what he said. I am the rattlesnake. My mind is coiling to attack and perhaps I have poisoned him with my questions and my glory. Perhaps now he can die, because there are too many rattlesnakes in the world.

December 30

His funeral was today. My mother was there, but there were other women, many women in black there, too. I couldn't be sure which one was my mother. The men dug the grave very carefully, but still it was too shallow because the ground was frozen too hard. But they buried him anyway. It had to be done.

With a sharp shovel, one man tried to murder a frozen worm as he dug. I wasn't supposed to see it but I looked anyway. The strong iron blade cut its stiff body in half. But the halves refused to die.

I am the earthworm. I have been cut in half by an axe of disease and cells. But I'm not ready yet to die. There are too many words and pictures yet to know. I am alive in halves, wiggling and blind and very cold.

BODY NO. 15

(1975)

CHARLOTTE began writing the letter early in the evening. All day she had been planning to write it but she had not planned just what to write. She did not know the young man to whom the letter would be given and he did not know her. They shared one mathematics class together that semester. She decided, as she squared the block of yellow newsprint on the desk in front of her, to let the words flow without restriction, random and free-floating. Perhaps, in this way, she could be honest and he would understand. Tucking the shapeless black strands of her hair back behind her ears, Charlotte began to write:

Dear Body No. 15,

I suppose you have a name but I don't know it; I don't want to know it. Naming is but one way used to designate, identify, a person, place or thing. In fact, it is an inferior way. You were, I would imagine, named, like most of us, by your parents—probably before you even left the hospital, perhaps even before you were born. Can you see them sitting together, alone in the evening, making lists, boys' names here and girls' names there, trying to decide who you should be? Your mother would, of course, by then be very large and round. Her nightgown would be pulling tight like cotton skin across her stomach, stretching to cover and flatten that stomach which would be one day you. Perhaps she would lie awake at night, counting the weeks and the months now past, counting them slowly upon her fingers, tapping them out in code across her stomach. She was waiting for you.

In the end, they would decide—together, of course, for they were still young then and romantic. From the paperback book which your grandmother perhaps had sent in the mail, they would select very seriously just two names—one for a girl and one for a boy. And when you were finally born—a boy—they discarded that first feminine name (it wasn't quite right anyway, was it?) and then they crowned you with that chosen One. With a name, they made you their son.

I'm sure that it's a fine name, a nice name, sounding just right with your surname. Do you like it? Probably—most people do, after a while. I won't even try very hard to guess what it might be. It doesn't matter; it could be anything—Richard, Pythagoras, Malcolm, whatever. And it could have been given to anyone by anyone for any number of foolish reasons. It may even be important to you but it cannot be part of you because it has come only from the outside.

So you see, Body No. 15, a name is a very poor way to make a person real. Once I met a cat which shared my name with me—and she was not the only one. I have an aunt, a niece, a cousin—all three are named as I am—Charlotte. But they are not me—they wouldn't want to be, not if they knew.

Charlotte put down her pen and read aloud what she had written. She trusted her ears far more than her eyes when it came to forming sentences that sounded right. She was alone in her room and the door was closed—no need to fear being overheard. She tried to imagine what the young man's reaction would be so far. He would be puzzled, no doubt, to find the blank white envelope slipped between the pages of his mathematics notebook—she would have to be clever putting it there tomorrow before the class began. Curious, he would rip open the envelope and begin reading quickly down the first page. Would he be amused by it or merely confused? Charlotte trusted the dark light in his eyes—he would understand—perhaps not right away but, yes, he would understand.

She waited a moment, pen again in hand, for the words to form themselves in her mind before she went on. She lit a cigarette and bent her head again over the paper, writing through the shadows her hair cast on the page:

> There is a better way, a much better way in the world to be known, and I have used it here. You are Body No. 15. I began in the lower left-hand corner of the classroom and that was No. 1. I always sit two rows behind you so it was very easy for me to see down to that very first row. I began counting then, One by One, until I reached you. I doubt that you even realized that you always sit in the Fifteenth seat from No. 1. You really should be more careful, more observant; for I may not always be here to tell you who you are.
>
> It shouldn't be hard for you to understand why the Number method is so far superior to any name which I could ever give you. There may quite likely be another young man in the class who shares your given name. But there can be only one Body No. 15 in the room—and that is you. You should be proud to know that. You may thank me someday.

Charlotte leaned back in her chair. She felt the wooden slats grate against her spine like corrugated steel. She thought of the gratitude he must surely someday feel towards her. She was not asking him to love her, not even to like her. She only wanted him to understand. For years now she had known how a life, every life, should be ordered and lived, yet she had never found anyone with whom to share her knowledge—until now. There were reasons, of course, why this young man should be the one, and these too must be explained:

> There are, of course, specific reasons why I have chosen to write to you. It was your hair, naturally, which caught my eye at first. I'm sure that I am not the First young woman who has told you that. I may be the Tenth or even the Twentieth—but I don't mind. I don't always need to be the First because I know, at least, that I am somewhere... But your hair, yes, your hair—are you very vain about your hair? I don't think so—you move your neck too easily, it swivels too smoothly as if on a pin. You cannot be aware of the lights and the life which dwell in your hair. Looking down at you, it is sometimes hard for me to tell just where the strands of your hair end and where your skin begins. Even the fluorescent lights of the classroom cannot force your hair to choose a colour.
>
> My own hair is brown, very dark. Many people have tried to convince me that it's black but they are wrong. Because my hair is so dark though, you would have no trouble drawing a line between it and my skin—if you wanted to. It would be easy to sketch an oval around the edges of my skin—if only to hold my face together.

Charlotte frowned and almost looked up from the page but the words were coming quickly now and she did not want to stop. She could have been talking aloud as she wrote the last paragraph but she hadn't noticed. She could have been twisting one strand of hair between her fingers as she wrote but she hadn't noticed.

> There is a problem though: sitting there behind your back, I cannot know for sure just how old you are. You never seem to turn your head so I can see your face. I can see though that you are young—you hold your back very straight—so very straight that the discs must by now have formed a ruler of bone through the centre of your body instead of just a spine. Do they grind one against the other when you bend over? I can't imagine you ever bending over. I'm being silly now, I realize. You *must* bend over sometimes—if not now, surely tomorrow or the next day. I will not be there when it happens. You are so white, so thin and I couldn't bear to see your spine come snapping open as you bend, sticking out through your skin like the broken ivory shaft of an ostrich feather.
>
> Yet still I do not know how old you are. Are you Nineteen or perhaps Twenty-One? If you would stand up, rise and leave the lecture, go perhaps down to the washroom or to the coffee machine in the basement; then I could see your ribs. I know, even without seeing them, that they must be laddered, protruding, very distinct. I could Number them just as the biologists Number the rings of a tree and then I would know just how long you have lived. It is important that I know—you will never be this old again. There is one thing though that I am certain of: you are not Twenty. You cannot be, because I am Twenty and we are not at all alike. You are a man and very thin; your elbows are sharp and the bones at the base of your neck will not be harnessed by the collar of your shirt. I am more like a series of curves. My mother has often warned me that I should go on a diet, should grow hard and thin-legged, should peel away these curves around my bones. She

does not understand that there can be no virtue, no salvation in bones and chiselled knees.

The chair in which I sit for the class we share was not made for a body like mine—I am too soft. I slide out of it unless I brace my elbows against the desk and push the small of my back through the space between the back and the seat of my chair. If I were to sit half as straight as you do, I might disappear. I cannot see your stomach from where I sit behind you but I'm certain that it's flat, tight-fitting, nailed to the bones of your hips. It does not rest upon your thighs when you lean forward to write in the pages of your notebook.

Charlotte resisted leaning forward to see what would happen. She thought instead of the days she had spent sitting in class behind the young man. She admired his concentration—not once had she seen him fidgeting, doodling, watching the clock. He paid such strict attention to the lecture that often the back of his head seemed to ripple and twitch with tension. He made her feel guilty without knowing he had—made her feel guilty for watching him instead of their professor, Dr. Hydan. She decided not to mention this right away, not wanting him to know her shortcomings too soon. She wrote instead of the class, hoping to amuse him perhaps with her quick observations hoping that he would recognize her words as the finer truth.

I have noticed that you hold your shoulders very carefully in place, much as our own Dr. Hydan does. He struts there across the front of the room, parading, yet ever careful that his shoulder blades do not accidentally come unhinged. He lounges against the edge of his desk, leaning slightly forward, eager and intent. Each day he comes to the crisis of his lecture, to the crucial point. He asks, very timid at first, "Do you understand? Does *anybody* understand? For God's sake, put your hand up if you understand!" Just at the last, his voice cracks and he hoists the bulk of his body up onto one corner of his desk. He dangles his legs like a little boy perched on the edge of a swimming pool.

He dabbles his toes against the tile and laughs because, as always, no one has put up their hand. It is a ritual which he has created.

Undaunted, the smile is deep in his face as he says, "Well, don't worry about it if you don't understand—I never did either—I still don't. Irrational numbers are impossible to understand—pure nonsense, you know that. But it doesn't matter—Mathematics is just a pack of lies anyway."

He grins and lowers his voice just a little. "Learn how to count from one to ten, memorize a couple of formulas, and you've got it beat. You'll pass the exam. That's all that counts in the end anyway."

He keeps talking, moving on to the next set of equations to be unravelled, but at this point I stop listening. Sometimes I pretend that Dr. Hydan is speaking ancient Greek—which I don't understand. It does not help for very long—I do not need to hear his voice to know what he is saying—he says the same thing every day. While he speaks, I watch all the bodies below me (all except yours) shaking their shoulders with laughter. They all love Dr. Hydan—to them, he is such a funny man; he is their favourite friend. They think that surely he must be a very good man because he laughs *with* them, not *at* them. And he is honest too, isn't he, admitting so freely that even he doesn't understand?

Dr. Hydan himself must believe that he is being honest and he is proud of himself for that—many people seem to feel that honesty is the greatest virtue, the surest way to heaven. But he cannot be honest forever about a

> lie which he thinks is the truth. There are many things beyond $a^2 + b^2 = c^2$ which young Dr. Hydan will never understand.
>
> He loves to write on the blackboard, covering it with Numbers which he does not understand. Have you ever noticed that he laughs as he writes, quite certain that they will be meaningless in the end? He coughs through them as he teaches, quite certain that it will make no difference to the universe. Dr. Hydan does not know that he should teach them from his knees, that he should pray before he speaks of the Numbers of the world. He does not know that the very word itself should be captialized like God or Buddha or the Dalai Lama. He speaks of the Numbers only in small letters and he has never stopped to think that I may have seen through his disguise.

Shaking the fingers of her left hand, clenching and unclenching them to free her cramped muscles once again, Charlotte stood up and walked around the room. She opened the window to release the built-up cigarette smoke, to refreshen her mind. There was another man whom she wished to write about but this would be more difficult, harder to explain. For a moment, she wondered if she were being foolish: why write this letter at all? Perhaps the young man to whom she wrote would be no different than that other one—perhaps he too would only laugh at her words and toss them off as nonsense. Charlotte thought, for a single breath, that she could hear that laugh and then the sound of a wad of crumpled paper, her letter, dropping into an empty metal garbage can. She dodged her own face in the mirror on the bedroom wall as she walked back to the chair at her desk.

Then the words began to come again, demolishing her doubt with their easy speed.

> Dr. Hydan is not, of course, alone in his failure to find the universe behind those chalky Numbers on the

blackboard. Once I thought I was in love with another young man much like our professor. I watched him—his name was Scottie—for several weeks before I decided that I would love him. He was, like you and me, a Mathematics major—two years ahead of me in the course. I watched him to be certain that he didn't laugh or cough as he read through the pages of his textbook. I had to be sure that he did not turn the pages carelessly, that he did not curl the corners as he read.

Scottie was a serious young man despite his name, and when I was sure, very sure, that he too was in love with the Numbers of the world, we began to see each other sometimes in the evening. Often we would study together and he would read aloud from his Mathematics textbook. But he did not understand why I got so angry when he stuttered or rushed through the words.

Sometimes, Scottie would draw Numbers for me in a white sketchpad he carried and I have never yet known another man who knew the shapes of the Numbers so well. Once I invited him to my house for the day, a Sunday. He came, of course, and he brought his sketchpad with him because I asked him to. He wanted to leave it in the back porch but I made him bring it into the living room. My mother served us tea and cinnamon doughnuts which left white crumbs in Scottie's moustache. We laughed as I helped him pick them out. Once his face was clean again and I'd made sure that his fingers weren't greasy or wet, I brought out my own white sketchpad. I too had drawn the Numbers but Scottie didn't know quite what my sketches were—not until I told him. He knew the Numbers very well, as I said before, but only by their shapes. He could not find them in my drawings at all. He wanted to discover "1," "2," "3," and "4" and he could not understand the circles and the pyramids and the universe which I had drawn. I had completed

> One Hundred sketches by then and Scottie asked me, strangely, "When are you going to stop?"
>
> I told him, "Never. Numbers cannot end." You know that.
>
> Scottie laughed and took another doughnut from the plate before he left. He forgot to take his sketchpad with him, but when he came by later to pick it up, I closed my eyes and said, "I don't have it anymore—and besides, you don't look like an artist to me."

The sketchpad was up in the cupboard above her bookshelves even now, but Charlotte did not think of that—she never looked at it anymore. The cupboard was crowded and stacked with papers and books, abandoned now beside the sketchpad. Often, lying awake at night, Charlotte thought she could hear the pages shifting and rustling into the dark.

She tapped her pen now against her forehead, trying to decide how the letter should end. The tip of the pen was silver—it felt cold against her skin. She wondered when the room and her flesh had grown so fevered and warm. Doodling her way to a fitting conclusion, she thought again of the class with Dr. Hydan, remembering something she had noticed only that afternoon.

> I had not noticed before today that you were right-handed. Perhaps, had I known it sooner, I would not have written to you at all. Tomorrow, after class, when you stand up and take your books under your arm, I'm quite certain that you, like most people, will put your right foot forward first. You will leave your left to tag along behind the rest of you very much like a careless Number left hanging down below the line. I will be watching for it and you will be making a mistake.
>
> I always put my left foot forward first. It might take a conscious effort just at first, if you are to change your

ways; but it would be well worth it. You may thank me someday. In the end, your left foot will always take you farther if you give it the lead. It will take you to forever. You must, of course, realize that this is the very reason why it has been so long neglected. The people in the world, the powerful people who decide these things, are afraid. They do not know where the left road may lead us. Have you not always been cautioned to do the right thing, to keep to the right, to proceed only when you have the right of way? The people in the world, our world, are afraid of a great many things.

That is why our Dr. Hydan so fiercely erases those Numbers from the blackboard each day as the class shuffles out of the room. Perhaps he too is afraid of what they may do if he leaves them alone for long.

Charlotte

THE CLIMB

(1975)

"ARE YOU SURE you want to do this?" Saro did not look at her as he spoke; his voice was cautious, probing.

Several yards behind him, Mae took a single step backward and focused her face upon the stretch of cliff before her. She leaned back upon her heels to see the top and the cords of her neck tensed briefly with the strain. The side of the cliff was green, vivid and uneven with a growth of bushes and small trees; the top was flat and grassy, spotted with evergreens and mud-coloured boulders.

"Yes, Saro, I'm sure."

Saro paused for a moment and then spoke quickly, "We could stay down here and go for a swim with Neil and Julie—if you want to." The last few words came more clearly to Mae's ears, as if he had raised his voice. "Or we could always go back to the camp and help Susan and Bill clean up the yard. We don't have to climb the cliff, you know." Saro did not turn as he spoke, but stood apart from her, stiff, poised for the climb.

Mae hesitated at the defensive snap in his voice and the tension which had appeared in his shoulders. "No, Saro, we don't have to do it—but I want to." Mae watched his shoulder muscles relax in relief—that was what he had wanted to hear.

He had given her one more chance, one last chance, to back out. She had refused it just as he had hoped she would. Perhaps he had known all along what her answer would be, but Mae ignored the emptiness which might have underlied his gesture. Afterwards, if she should complain about having to climb all that way, Saro would be able to toss her own words back at her in self-defense.

"Well, okay then; let's go." He turned to her now and smiled; he pulled away to begin the climb. The decision had been made: they would make the climb. And, as Saro had wanted, Mae had made the final decision. Mae could not yet understand this need in him to be absolved, this need to feel self-righteous, his refusal to be responsible for what they chose to do together. Was he thinking ahead to some unforeseen catastrophe for which he could not afterwards be blamed? Mae wondered but the question remained unspoken and unanswered.

"Well?"

"Yes, yes, let's go. I'm anxious to get started. Very anxious to begin." Mae spoke quickly, moving forward in an effort to close the gap of grass which still lay there between them. She needed to repeat the words to assure him that she was sincere, that her impatience was equal to his own: she did want to climb the cliff.

Saro spoke suddenly, as if he had not heard her: "Too bad the rest of them wouldn't come. We could have had a picnic at the top." His words seemed to come from somewhere near his right shoulder and they reached her ears in faded waves. Mae nodded her head in agreement, concentrating now upon the first few feet of the climb, forgetting that he could not see her face. She knew that his regret was genuine, but her own was a lie: she was glad that they had come alone. She supposed that Saro did not realize this but she was not anxious for him to know.

Before they left the cottage to come down to the cliff by the lake, Saro had invited the other four, but they had all refused, laughing deep in their throats. Neil had asked, "What do you want to climb the cliff for? There's nothing up there—it's not worth the trouble."

Mae had started to explain that there was something about climbing, something about the rising motion of her body and the pulling muscles in the backs of her legs there in the midst of so much unanchored air . . . something that drew her breath more deeply back into her lungs, that forced her eyes to see much more clearly, to see so much more.

Saro cut off her voice with his own: "To prove something, I guess."

"What?" Neil asked.

"I don't know." Saro grinned and turned away. He looked out the window of the cottage, pretending to be intent upon the lake where an orange motorboat hopped across its own waves like a rabbit.

Mae grabbed at the quick note of shame which shadowed his words: a pungent tenderness rushed in, choking away the initial disappointment she had felt at his ambiguity. Saro was painfully vulnerable to what they thought of his ideas, yet they did not realize how he needed their approval, if not their adoration, to continue. Mae knew that the three young men had been friends for several years; she had known Saro for only a few months—why did she see so clearly that which they had not yet noticed? A granite grain of violence hardened in her stomach and the muscles of her arms. She wanted to push them away, all away, back from his feelings too easily shown. She walked stiffly to the door and jerked it open, waiting for the violence to wash through and out of her body—she knew that it was too fierce, too private to remain within her for long. She waited for Saro to come to the door and step outside.

Yet still he held back from her, as if determined to answer them. Proding him into action, she said, "Come on, Saro."

He turned his face towards her, angry. His eyes were cool and appraising, gliding up her smooth white legs, up to her tightly held smile. For a moment, Mae understood that he hated her for rescuing him.

Once outside, walking across the wooden porch, Saro brushed his palms across his denim thighs and began to whistle. He walked ahead of her, thinking now only of the sun and the climb ahead. Mae heard chipmunks rustling beneath the planks of the steps; although she could not see them, she believed in their little brown bodies scurrying away out of reach at the hollow sound of their footsteps. She wanted to call out to Saro, to make him return to her side and be still, to force him to listen to the sound of the little round lives beneath them.

But Saro was out on the road to the lake now. He scuffed his feet through the gravel as he walked. The sound of his shoes grating on the dry stones warned her to hurry, not to speak. She knew he would not wait. His arms swung at his sides and the wind blew his hair back from his face. Mae saw that his temples were pale, much lighter than the skin across his forehead.

Coming up beside him, Mae tried to catch his hand in her own, but Saro did not notice. Instead, he put his arm around her waist and pulled her up hard against his side, jerking her off balance effortlessly. Placing her palms flat against his chest to keep herself from falling, Mae was pleased to feel his heart thudding slowly through his shirt, beating into her hands.

Mae stretched one arm up and pulled a handful of leaves from a birch at the side of the path. She pressed them into a damp tight ball in the palm of one hand and threw them then at Saro's back. The green wad landed on the ground just behind him. Saro could not, of course, hear them fall for they were only leaves, very nearly weightless. For him, they had not been thrown; they did not exist. The leaves came apart in crumpled bits upon the grass as Mae stepped over them. Her hands were sticky and stained with green sap; she rubbed them across her bare thighs. She might have sighed.

Ahead of her by several yards, Saro could not have heard the sigh—if it had been truly a sigh—but he chose this moment to turn and ask, "Are you tired yet? Do you want to stop and rest for a while?"

Pleased that he had thought to ask, Mae could then say easily, "No, no thanks. I'm just fine. Let's keep going." She smiled gratefully but Saro had already turned back to the stretch of trail ahead. He did not see her smile and Mae hoped that he was watching the undergrowth, watching for a glimpse of some small animal instead.

Saro spoke again, not stopping this time: "This part of the climb is the easiest. The slope here isn't bad. But up ahead, it gets harder. Much harder further on." He seemed to relish the prospect of danger yet to come. Mae did not answer him.

She too had found the act of climbing easy. She had not had to strain in order to negotiate the gentle slope. They followed a path worn by other feet, by unknown feet. There was even an occasional tire mark as if someone had made the trip on a trail bike. The trees on either side of the path—birch, mountain ash, pine and spruce—were small and unmarked. Mae was relieved; she had been afraid that someone might perhaps have stripped off the bark in ragged curls to carry home like a scalp, a grisly souvenir.

Watching for patterns etched in the bark of the trees, Mae climbed more slowly than Saro. She could have caught up with him and matched his stride easily but she preferred not to. The trees were laced with new growth and the bark of the birches was white, almost perfect white. Mae stopped beside one older tree to trace around the black lines which ran through the white like tangled hair. The lines were rough and ridged beneath her fingertips and she wondered how long she could rub them before her fingerprints would be forever changed. She tried to imagine a face or a figure outlined there in black but she could see only a map, a map of a land which she had never seen. She began to climb again.

Ahead of her, Saro kept strictly to the trail which was even now becoming less smooth, its edges more overgrown with scrambled underbrush. Behind him, Mae watched his muscles moving beneath the tight yellow of his shirt. His heart would be beating more quickly now than it had been when she pressed her palms against it. A stray brown branch hung caught in the back of his hair; Mae waited for his arm to reach back and pull it out. Saro did not know that it was there. He kept walking, ever moving forward, sometimes rhythmically clenching and unclenching his fists.

The path ended. Saro called back to her happily, "It looks like everyone else who climbed this cliff turned back here. This must be where the going starts to get really rough." He laughed and pointed ahead, turning back to be certain that Mae was looking forward with him. He stopped and frowned, lowering his arm: Mae was still several yards down the path behind him.

When she reached him, he said, "Can't you keep up with me? You'd better stick close behind me from now on so we don't get separated. The path ends here. See?" He pointed to the ground between his feet. Mae looked down and nodded seriously. "So don't go falling behind or wandering away. I'd hate to lose you in all this bush."

His last words should have sounded tender and concerned but he said them too quickly. Mae looked down again at the spot where the path faded away, as if marking the place firmly in her mind. "I'm sorry, Saro. I like to look around me while I'm walking. I've been looking at the trees, finding patterns and maps in the bark. And they said there was nothing here!" A sudden guarded look on Saro's face warned her not to go on.

Instead, she said, "When I have to hurry past the bushes and the trees, I feel as if I were back in another time, a time when I was much younger, really just a child. My family took a drive in the country every Sunday after church. I would be dressed in my best outfit with white knee socks and a crinoline; my father, wearing his black suit, always drove. My mother had learned years ago and really was the better driver, but, still, Father always drove. He always drove fast, so fast that all I could see was a grey blur at the side of the road. My best friend's family always went for Sunday drives too—everyone did once, didn't they?—and she told me she had seen a baby moose once feeding at the side of the road. I wanted to see one too but my father always drove so fast, so fast that I could never see anything."

Saro snorted and shook his head at the trust she placed in him each time she spoke—the fine trust that he would make the necessary connections which her words never quite revealed.

"So?" He had not intended that the single word should sound so sliced and chopped across the end. He was not attuned to forming his own connections. His affinity was with explanations, clear and logical, fully formed and reasoned.

Mae's face was warm; she grew flustered. The comparison was too elusive, perhaps too private—she must not attempt an explanation, its aptness would have been destroyed by Saro's pointed dissection of the meaning of her words. "Oh . . . just never mind. Go on ahead."

Instantly she regretted her hasty anger and reached to touch his shoulder. He withdrew beneath her fingers. Physically, he had not moved but Mae could feel his muscles coiling away like spools of copper wire. She understood that he had not meant to hurt her. She was suddenly afraid that he would realize that she had, however, meant to hurt him in return.

"Don't worry about it, Saro. It was just a silly thought," she said, urging her voice into silky smoothness and looking at him guilelessly, clearly, so clearly that it seemed almost coy.

Saro was satisfied—this was an explanation of sorts. He bent and kissed her damp forehead, dismayed to discover that a trick of the sunlight had scattered freckles in clumps across her face. Often he had dreamt of her milky white skin stretching smooth across her bones.

"You don't have freckles, do you, Mae?" he asked, running his fingertips roughly across her left cheek as if he wanted to feel the spots receding at his touch.

Mae laughed breathlessly, child-like, grateful for his silliness. She felt that he wanted to reassure her that her thoughts were no more foolish than his own could be at times. She ignored the rough pressure of his hand upon her cheek. It was a roughness which might have told her he was serious if she had allowed herself to acknowledge it. "No, of course I don't!"

"I didn't think so. Should we go on ahead now?" Saro said abruptly, peering up through the trees to the top of the cliff. The trees were larger here, the bark blacker, as if the upper half of the cliff were much older than the base, as if the cliff had sprouted out of the beach like human hair, the base surrounded with frothy new growth, the farthest tips already dry and dying.

"Yes, let's go on." Mae began to push forward through the undergrowth but her feet slid uselessly through the damp grass. The smooth leather soles of her moccasins had grown slick with having crushed so much grass beneath them as she climbed. Mae grabbed for Saro's hand to save herself but he was just out of reach. She fell easily to the ground. She felt a rock scraping the flesh from her knee. It stung but there was no blood.

Laughing at her own clumsiness, Mae held one arm up to Saro. He did not help her up. Saro prided himself upon his own physical grace, was repulsed by awkwardness in those around him—just as another man might have been repulsed by menstrual blood or the sound of someone being sick in the next room.

"What did you wear those things on your feet for? You knew we were going to climb the cliff today. Those shoes aren't made for climbing, you know that. What if you fall and break a leg or something?" Saro stepped around and past her as he spoke, shaking his head in disbelief. "If there's one thing that I don't need. . . ." His voice spiralled away from her and Saro did not see that she still sat there on the ground, just there where she had fallen. Mae thought of a day in her childhood, a winter morning when she had run out into a snowbank in her flannelette nightgown, barefoot—wanting to know if the snow would squelch up between her naked toes just like summer mud. Mae opened her mouth to tell Saro of that day and of her mother coming after her, her hair in curlers, with just her housecoat on, barefoot—but her throat snapped shut upon the words.

Mae jumped up suddenly and hurried after him, not bothering to brush away the grass which clung to the hollows in the backs of her knees. She was smiling now: she had known this day would bring them nearer, nearer to—what? Nearer perhaps to being real with each other. Or nearer perhaps to drawing back the curtain which hung between the two of them and the rest of the world, the beauty of the world.

The climb quickly grew more difficult and Mae kept her eyes now hooked to the ground. She found much to look at there, as much as she had found in the trees along the path below, more perhaps. She stepped carefully over a white feather standing upright between two long blades of grass which grew like careful hairless fingers. A bird flew overhead, squawking down through the trees at the tops of their heads. Mae thought that perhaps it had lost this single feather and was now searching for it; or, having found it, was now keeping tenacious watch over it. Perhaps the birds do understand, she thought, that the key, the key to it all, must lie in little things, in bitten-off pieces of creation set down in a new panorama. Perhaps the key lay even now in a single white feather lost in the grass but ever watched and guarded, or perhaps in the map in the bark of a tree someone might be passing even now. Mae was confident that such a key did exist, was needed . . . but where it would be discovered and what it might lead to ... she could not be quite certain. Not yet, not in this minute.

Mae knew that she must keep her eyes always open to the subtleties, the misplaced things, the objects which passed through the world unnoticed and unchecked. Someone must keep track of these things—her own eyes were very keen, sharp, the lenses finely trained. She would not be asleep when the moment came, the moment of knowing everything at once. Nor would she be greedy—she would tell, tell it all, but only to the one who shared its onslaught with her, only to the one who would be able then to see the myriad connections which her own mind was making. Perhaps, she thought, if Saro could see the same things she was seeing at the very moment that she saw them ... perhaps then he would need no explanation. Mae trusted that he would understand for he could see as well as she and when the moment, the epiphany, the truth did finally come, she knew that it would be simple: one of those little lost unnoticed things. There could be no need of explanations for then there would be nothing left.

Perhaps when they reached the top of the cliff, this cliff which was itself but a little thing set down here in the panorama of the lake, which was itself but a little thing set down here ... perhaps when they reached the top of the cliff ... they were almost there now ... perhaps there at the top, perhaps there from the brim, they would be able to see—

"Do you want to rest for a while?" Saro was kind again, solicitous, caring of her needs. "If you're tired, Mae, we can stop right here."

Mae smiled brightly at him, hoping that her mouth did not look as false and brittle as it felt. Her calves were burning and her spine ached and grated with the strain of leaning into the increasing slope of the cliff. "No, no, keep going. We're almost there now—almost there now—almost at the top." Her words, like her breath, came in brief hot bursts and her lungs felt full of soap and bubbles.

"Okay then: right, two, three, four; left, two, three, four," chanted Saro, tilting his head at an angle he would have called "jaunty." He wanted to show Mae how happy he was to be climbing, still climbing, without yet showing the strain. He was sweating; he could feel his cotton shirt sticking damply there just between his shoulder-blades. But it must be from the sun, just from the heat of the sun—this climb was nothing to him. If he had stopped to think that the climb might have a meaning for him, words like "test," "endurance" and finally "conquest" would have come into his mind.

Saro flexed the muscles in his thighs as he marched, still clowning, up the slope. He was proud of how well and easily his legs responded to his commands, to the power of his will. He was lost for a time in a surge of muscles knitting closely to firm white bones, of strong elastic lungs sucking back just enough air for one single breath: no flesh wasted, no air squandered. Saro imagined Mae struggling a little perhaps as she climbed there behind him in those foolish shoes at the ends of her foolishly, thoughtlessly naked legs. He imagined her behind him marvelling at the ease with which his body fitted itself into the slope of the cliff at just the right angle. He smiled to think that she might be envious of him.

Saro was annoyed to hear her voice, suddenly shrill and excited, calling him back to where she crouched at the foot of a tree: "Saro! Come here! Come here and look what I found!"

Saro retraced his steps and felt a gentle push of tenderness at the sight of her crouching there like a child, with her shoulders hunched and secretive and her eyes yet eager to present what she had just discovered. "What is it, Mae?"

Mae pointed to the ground beside the tree. The roots erupted through the grass like old knuckles; around them, in lazy circles, grew a cluster of mushrooms, colourless against the vivid grass.

"I bet you don't know what this is called!" Mae's voice was triumphant, fiercely proud that she herself did know. Not waiting for a reply, she explained, "This is called a Fairy Ring—you didn't know that, did you? No, I didn't think you would. Come on, kneel down, Saro, and look with me."

Saro knelt beside her, smiling and curious—not so much about the mushrooms themselves as about why Mae found them so enticing, obviously so important. He reached out to touch one and the spongy cap flipped off between his fingers.

"Oh, Saro, be careful!" Her distress was strangely extravagant. Saro stood up, startled and annoyed.

Needing to be cruel, he asked, "Why? What difference does it make?"

Carefully, Mae ignored the tone of his voice and answered, "You must be careful not to disturb them."

"The mushrooms?"

"No, the fairies." Mae was laughing beneath her words, laughing to let Saro know that this was just a fantasy. She did not believe in fairies any more than he did—but she wanted to. "They must come here at night, late at night, dressed in little red waistcoats and spats—they come to plant the mushrooms so carefully in little rings. Perhaps, one night, one laid down to rest just here, here at the foot of this stem—he pulled his cap, green cap, down over his eyes, just to rest for a moment or two. But the morning came and with it came the light. He woke up, rubbing his eyes—they sting in the sun; it is so big and his eyes are so small. Now it is morning and the Fairy Ring is not quite finished yet, not quite round, not yet circled and tight. But the fairy knows that he must leave—the light, the light is too strong. He promises himself to return the next night with more spores, promises to return and finish the ring. When the next night comes, he cries to think that he has forgotten where, just where—oh, where did I plant that Fairy Ring?"

Mae's voice was rising, hovering in circles, almost chanting. She stopped—she had not meant to let herself believe—not here, not now, not with Saro standing stunned beside her.

"You don't expect me to believe that, do you?"

"No. No, I don't. I was just dreaming, dreaming out loud. Pretending that fairies are real—I know they're not." Mae was embarrassed, as if she had been caught telling lies to a child. "Let's go on ahead, Saro. We're almost there." She rose from her knees slowly, in stages, stretching her arms up above her head. She held them there extended for a moment so that Saro might be reassured that she was a woman and real, not a child and foolish with dreams.

The final few yards of the climb were the hardest—Mae wished now that she had worn her hiking boots.

Saro reached the top first and leaned backwards, reaching back for her hand. His arm was very steady. Mae was struck by its strength and by how large Saro was, leaning back towards her, leaning back unafraid of the fall; how calmly he flirted with the space between the brow of the cliff and the ground. Her own breath came in gulps as she paused before taking his hand.

"We did it! Yes, we're here! Right on top." Saro was proud, so proud that the muscles of his body had not betrayed him, had not given way. He picked at the front of his shirt, soaked now with sweat, pulling it damply away from his chest. He felt the black curling hair stretching away from his skin, caught in the wet fibres of his shirt.

Mae agreed, "Yes, we did it," thinking, No, don't talk now, not yet. Let me look first.

She walked to the edge of the cliff, not so close as to frighten her own aching legs, but just as close as she needed to be—to see the lake below. It pulled itself across the ground in waves like a monstrous amoeba. Mae could see the ripples beginning somewhere out near the middle of the lake but she could not see them dying on the shore. The beach was hidden by the slope they had climbed.

At the sound of a motor choking into life so faintly far below her, Mae held her breath, afraid that it would now come flying out from the shore which she could not see and break the lake in two. Nothing happened. The boat did not come and

BRIGHT WIRE

(1975)

ELIZABETH stepped into the glass foyer of the University Centre. Her fingers went to her neck, suddenly aware of the autumn air against her skin. It was cold and she couldn't find her scarf. In her mind, she tried to locate it—a heap of coloured squares left perhaps upon the dresser at home or maybe dangling somewhere from a metal desk in an empty classroom. She did not go back inside to look.

"It doesn't matter," she thought. "Let my neck be cold. The house will be warm when I get home."

A girl walked past the glass doors where Elizabeth stood. She watched her moving by, thick and girdled in a sealskin coat. With her knees always bent, only the muscles in her calves appeared to move, solid and round like grapefruits inside her stockings. She walked as if watching for a place to pause, to crouch down and rest. Elizabeth swung one long leg easily, from the hip, so she could feel the denim move against her skin.

The girl moved away from the door, almost out of sight. She paused, looking down at the concrete sidewalk. Elizabeth followed the line of her glance but she could see nothing. The broad furred back of the girl blocked her eyes, Elizabeth wondered if she had dropped something—perhaps a diamond ring, a gold fountain pen or the silver key to a red sports car.

The girl stepped back abruptly, curling her lip up close to her nose. She turned, jerking her legs as she hurried away.

Something lay there on the sidewalk. Elizabeth could see it now—a small mound, black against the concrete, very round and still. The door behind her opened with a squeal of metal on cold metal; she stepped to the left, out of the way, A group of students rushed past her, laughing and pushing their voices ahead of them into the foyer, out and down the steps. Elizabeth moved closer to the glass, watching as they circled the mound on the sidewalk.

A young man in a yellow jacket bent from the waist down close to the ground. The dark mound jumped as he probed it with a wooden ruler. He drew back sharply, smiling and surprised. He moved as if to bend again until one of his friends threw a boisterous arm around his shoulders and pulled him away. Elizabeth could hear his voice, muffled and distanced by the glass.

"Come on," he said. "Let the dumb thing alone. We'll miss the bus if we don't hurry up."

There was no one on the sidewalk now. As if prodded by an electric wire, the black mound moved across the concrete in caterpillar spurts. One long leathered wing flopped out onto the sidewalk. The bat dragged itself to the edge of the grass.

Elizabeth left the lobby, striding down the steps, across the concrete to the edge of the sidewalk where the bat lay limp on the yellowed grass. One wing still hung angled out from its body. Its thin-fingered joints flexed but the wing flopped back again upon the ground.

Kneeling down, Elizabeth stared into its gargoyle face. The bat was not black after all, but very brown, and its eyes were drooping small like the eyes of a newborn child. Elizabeth felt them looking at her.

"You're not really blind, are you?" she thought. "It's just a game you play. To keep the old wives telling tales, to keep the scientists lying awake at night, trying to figure out why you can fly without being a bird."

The bat jumped again away from the sidewalk. Slipping off her jacket, Elizabeth covered the bat very gently, folding the broken wing back against its body. She was pleased to think that the lining of her jacket was black; she knew how bats love the dark.

Straightening up, she cradled the bundle against her chest. She smiled as the bat squirmed against her palms.

"Don't worry, little bat, You'll be all right. I'll even give you a name. Erebus."

As she walked, Elizabeth held her shoulders very straight, feeling solid and broad behind the bat. Often she turned and walked backwards down the roadway just to keep the wind at her back, away from the bundle in her hands. Walking backwards was difficult but it left her exhilarated with not knowing where the next invisible step might lead, not knowing upon whom or what her body might come to rest. She hummed as she walked. Her voice grew louder and deep every time the bat shifted its weight in her arms. She wasn't sure if bats could hear but she knew that singing was good for babies and now even for plants, so the gardeners said—so a little song probably wouldn't hurt the bat either.

She passed into the field between the university buildings and the road. No one who passed her had noticed the bundle in her hands. Or if they had noticed, they pretended not to wonder what she carried there between the folds of her jacket. Elizabeth thought of the things it could have been—a stolen camera; a Grecian vase from the days of the Dionysia; a plastic shrunken head like the one that hung by a red string from the mirror of the Pontiac that passed her.

It pleased her to think that no one could have known it was a bat. During the past two years of university life, she'd met numerous people who were sure, so sure, that they could always know whatever was yet to be known. But this time not even they could know that she was carrying a bat.

Elizabeth felt the bat jerking under her jacket. She wondered if perhaps its broken wing had come unhinged again. A sound came out of the bundle—a squeak, short-pitched, electronic like the beeping message of a department store signalling device.

Elizabeth started at the sound. She hadn't known that bats had voices—a voice without words, yes, but still a voice. She was glad to have this, another point of contact made.

She was close to the main road now. Unprotected by the brick walls of the university, it was colder in the open field and the wind whipped the leaves around her feet like lost eyelashes. A blue vein stood out in her forehead.

As she turned into the street, a car passed her, then slowed down and stopped. It backed carefully down the gravelled shoulder and came to rest beside her. It was a family car, a station wagon, brown and dusty with shining bumpers and rusted rocker panels. Elizabeth walked beside it carefully, without raising her eyes from the road and she could not help but brush her hip up against the chrome door handle. There was a pattern of rusted dots spreading across the door.

"Dot-to-dot. I wonder what they would make," she thought. "The face of a man, the back of a dog, maybe a leafless tree?" Finding patterns and objects in such places—on a rusted car door, on the water-stained ceiling over her bed, in a clouded sky ready for rain—was a game she often played. She'd yet to meet a person who could outdo her.

The car window rolled open and a brown face smiled out at her.

"Want a ride?" His voice, pulled from the shadows of the car, was loud and young.

Elizabeth did not answer, She walked on, in front of the car now, unafraid as the bumper eased closer to the backs of her knees. She knew that he would not run her over. There was nothing in his face to fear.

"Want a ride?" He was calm, refusing to grow impatient with her silence or the thin indifference of her back. He would wait until he got an answer. He knew she would say no.

"Want a ride?" he asked again. The tone of his voice did not change.

Elizabeth laughed but she did not turn around. She wanted to keep the wind at her back. She wanted to say, "No thanks, my bat's not house-broken yet."

He accepted her laughter and pulled away from the shoulder of the road. The gravel spun out from under the tires—a gesture of habit, not anger. The car spurted past her. He might have persisted if he'd seen her vague smile.

Elizabeth walked more quickly now, pressing the bat closer against her ribcage. Her purse slid halfway down her arm and she juggled the bat in one hand as she pushed the strap back into place on her shoulder. She pushed her legs forward with more force than usual and kept the corner of one eye trained upon the road beside her, cautious that the tires of the passing cars did not come too close to her feet.

Close now to the house where she lived, Elizabeth waited on the curb until the light changed. As she started to cross, a car turned right at the corner. Its tires broke a puddle into runaway brown beads that splashed up against her legs. She crossed the street slowly.

A lost yellow dog wandered past her through the afternoon street, mirroring the pavement in its silver tag. It sniffed at her heels and whined.

In sudden panic she wondered if dogs eat bats. Nursing the bat closer to her, she pushed at the dog with her foot.

"Go on. Get lost," she shouted hoarsely. "Get away from me." The dog slid back to the edge of the road. Its ears drooped down across the sides of its face.

The house in which she rented an apartment was third from the corner. The yard was circled by a hedge of roses that had never been pruned. Only the top floor of the house was visible above the madly tangled hedge. The narrow sidewalk that led to the front door was almost blocked by the branches. Passing between them, Elizabeth was careful that a stray bough didn't hook the bat from her arms. One branch caught at the back of her head and she jerked away in panic. Several dark strands of hair remained dangling from the branch, quickly homogenized by the bushes.

The sidewalk was broken up, its edges overgrown with loops of grass and energetic weeds. Elizabeth wondered if the moss that grew between the blocks would die during the winter. She remembered a sunny afternoon in summer when she'd come out with a knife and a cake tin full of water to collect several clumps of the moss. She planned to make a rock garden but the moss grew quickly water-logged and mouldy. She threw it away a week later and never did make the garden.

She folded her jacket back from the face of the bat and held it out in front of her.

"Here's your new home, Erebus. I live up there on the top floor. Three rooms all to myself. You'll have plenty of space to mend your wing." She thought the bat really did look up to the top of the old brick house. And she thought that its face had curdled with disappointment for just a moment—quickly hidden so as not to seem ungrateful.

Elizabeth smiled, "That's all right. I know what you mean. I used to wish there were turrets on top. Turrets and maybe a spiral staircase. And the bricks are shedding their mortar, growing slowly bald like an embarrassed old woman. But you can't put a wig on a house, now can you? I tried though—see how the drapes are bright-flowered and purple?"

The double doors were made of dark wood, no longer polished but still dignified. Elizabeth had loved the doors at first, but one day in the spring one of the oval windows was shattered by a baseball spun from the bat of a little boy. Broken glass covered the hardwood floor of the foyer. Elizabeth wanted to cry but she remembered just in time that it wasn't quite right to cry for a door or a broken window. And it wasn't quite right to love them either.

"Here, wait a minute. I've got to find my key." She set the bat down on the top step and groped through her purse for her key ring. She had two keys to the house because each door had its own separate lock. But somehow the brass knob of the left door had disappeared. She had tried to write a poem once about the missing doorknob, about the black eye-hole it left. But it wasn't a good poem and she threw it away the same afternoon. The next day she stuffed a small square of white cloth into the hole because she knew that no one would care or dare to write a poem about a little hole full of cloth. She'd always believed that the essence of a hole was its emptiness—so she filled it up.

"Here it is, Erebus—come on." She passed no one on the stairway up.

It was near suppertime and, thinking of food, she wondered what the bat would eat. There was some cat food in the cupboard—three or four cans left over from the days when she was feeding a stray cat that wandered into the yard. The cat disappeared before all the food was gone.

"Cat food for a bat?" she wondered. Maybe not—the cans were poultry and beef and she could not imagine a bat catching a chicken or a cow to make its evening meal.

She decided that bats must eat like birds—on the wing. That meant insects. She was sure the bat ate meat, even only insects, because its teeth were sharp and pin-headed. The flies were crawling indoors now, lazy with the oncoming cold, looking for the warmth. They would be easy to catch.

She unlocked the door of her apartment and pushed it open with her foot. She carried the bat across the room to the chesterfield. Placing it gently upon the middle cushion, she unwrapped it and sat down on the floor in front of it.

"I won't turn on the lights just yet, Erebus. I'm sure you've had quite enough sunshine for one day."

Although the room was small, it was almost empty. The single window was draped with purple curtains which dipped the room into muddy light. A reclining chair, inherited from a previous tenant, perched in one corner. The cracked vinyl upholstery sprouted wads of white cotton stuffing. Elizabeth had patched one large rip on the seat of the chair with black electrical tape. The chesterfield was old, third- or fourth-hand, and carelessly covered with a blue blanket.

"Well, Erebus, you certainly can't live the rest of your life in the middle of the chesterfield. Where am I going to keep you? Wait—I know,"

In the bedroom, she groped into the darkness under the bed. Sausage rolls of dust clung to her damp fingers. She brushed them off against her sweater, leaving little white balls of fluff in a streak across her breasts. Stretching out flat on her stomach, she twisted her head back and forth, trying to see back to the wall. She gripped a large brown box by one corner and worked it gradually out from under the bed.

Sitting on the floor in the middle of the living room, she held the box between her knees and ripped it open. Inside was a brass bird-cage built with thin strands of wire. The ends of her hair caught in the bright wire of the cage as she bent over it, checking to be certain that the clasp of the door still locked.

She padded the bottom of the cage with an old white towel and placed a saucer of water in one corner. There had been a red plastic water dish which fastened to the wire but she couldn't remember where it was.

Leaning back against the wall, she balanced the cage on her knees. The bat huddled in the corner opposite the saucer, struggling to fold its broken wing back close to its fur.

Elizabeth plucked a yellow feather from the wire of the cage. It had once been used to keep a canary, yellow, singing, even once laying a small blue egg that never hatched. A young man from the university had given her the bird and the cage, explaining that no, it wasn't a special occasion—he was just "the generous type." Elizabeth didn't know him very well. She'd met him once in a bar where she sat growing heavy-headed with wanting to know the names of the trees before they were tables, now lacquered and sticky with ice and cigars. She did not want to have to speak to him and explain.

His name was Kevin. Both he and Elizabeth were majoring in Ancient Philosophy. Kevin clung to the idea that they went well together because they both loved minds and theories and Aristotle. Elizabeth agreed because she had no reason not to. Kevin would have been disappointed if he knew that she often fell asleep over all those ancient words.

Kevin always talked. His body was full of a liquid noise which poured out in laughter and famous names. To Elizabeth he was like a man eating fire and glass just to prove that his tongue wasn't easily shocked, but was instead padded and coarse, like the tongue of that cat that used to come to the house for food. Kevin too lived his life out of paper and smiles just as the cat lived his adventures out of tin cans instead of jungles and green-feathered birds.

Elizabeth did not give the canary a name. It was too yellow, singing too loudly, brash and monotonous every evening. When Kevin asked about the bird, she told him it had died. A lie—she'd given it away to a young woman she met one day at lunch in the university cafeteria.

"I kept the cage," she told him. "I hope you don't mind—but it was so pretty that I hated to give it up."

Kevin soon stopped sitting behind her in every class they shared. She hoped he'd found somebody else to give canaries to.

Elizabeth now put the cage on the bookshelf beside the chesterfield. She looked up at the painting which hung beside the shelf. An original watercolour, she had chosen it from a university exhibition. Her father paid for it, easily ignoring the price.

She'd chosen it because when she first saw it, it brought one word to the surface: "light-hearted." It was a landscape with mint-green trees, turquoise waves, and sailboats popping up from a yellow horizon, She seldom looked at it now but when she did, it made her wish for purple, black or navy blue. She came to hate the artist even though she usually couldn't remember his name—he'd been unfair to the spectrum, having so neglected its darker side. The picture had no balance and it was too light-hearted after all, with nothing to stop it from floating away like a lost canary feather or a yellow balloon.

"Now I know what to do with it," she said, jumping up and hurrying into the kitchen. She rummaged through the cupboard over the stove where she kept a child's set of paints. Her mother had bought them for her once but she'd never allowed Elizabeth to play with water in the house. And so the watercolours were never used.

She carried a cup of water into the living room. It spilled over the edge, leaving a pattern of dots on the floor.

She climbed up onto the chesterfield. Her feet sank deep into the stuffing and the upholstery stretched as she searched for a solid place to stand.

Posing with the brush in her hand, she measured the painting with her thumb and one eye. She placed a small black dot exactly in the centre of the scene. She looked down at the face of the bat in the cage and she started to paint.

Several minutes passed and then she backed away, straightening her shoulders, easing the muscles in the back of her neck.

"There, that's much better, isn't it?" She jumped down from the chesterfield and ran to the opposite wall to admire her work. Yes, there was balance now. The face of a bat hung in the middle of the horizon, lapping the points of the sailboats with its chin, severe against the pastel yellow sunrise.

"Yes, much better." Satisfied, she went back to the kitchen and deposited the paints and the glass in the sink with a pile of assorted dishes.

Returning to the living room, she sat down in the chair beside the bookshelf and said, "Do you want me to read to you for a while?"

She moved the cage closer to her chair. She peered at the books on the shelf, dismissing those with bright paper wrappers and turning instead to a thick volume bound in black leather. She pulled it from the shelf. It was a Bible. She knew that there would be no yellow canaries, no young man named Kevin, no girdled girls in sealskin coats in those onionskin pages.

She spread the Bible flat against her palms. Gilded and curling like bright wire, the letters on its cover shone through her fingers.

She curled one thin leg beneath her as she read and the other hung down to touch the floor with just her toes. The bat hung upside down from the wire bar in the middle of the cage. Its broken wing flopped down to brush the bottom of the cage with just the ends of its long-fingered joints.

WAITING

(1976)

One: Dory

AFTER A TIME even the sound of the television stopped. Dory couldn't tell how long she had lain awake listening to it. The voices of women had come to her for hours perhaps, woman voices with no words, soft and sudden, as if they were talking in their sleep. Soon Dory stopped listening for them and listened instead for those other voices, deeper voices.

Man voices. Making little waves that roll right through my belly, not my ears. Like water waves. Just like when my dad sat me down in the sand at the beach. Just like that time and the waves came up over my belly.

Just before the silence came, Dory heard familiar music coming through the bedroom wall and through the woollen blankets tucked up tight around her ears. Dory held her breath, straining and hoping to hear. She caught and remembered the song just in patches. It made her think of plywood and big blackboards and chalk. All of these things became tangled up in the song.

What song? Throats singing fast, yes, too fast, and slowed down then by some other throat. Grown-up throat wearing a wool suit and nylons and green high-heels. That throat with no first name. Only "Miss" and last name "Burns." Miss Burns singing this same song and she leads the room by its throat through the notes with her pointer. Fingers made of chalk and chalk on her cheeks too. Cheeks that move up and down and sing this song . Calls it "anthem."

The song was the signal for another day to begin. And once it had been sung, she could sit down at her plywood desk and wait to be told to open her books for the day. And Miss Burns, standing up at the blackboard, would always call her "Doria" and she would sit up even straighter then, trying to make the full name fit. But none of this could happen until the song had been sung. Until it had been sung by everyone all the way through to the end, time and the day could not begin to pass. But now Dory could not sing: the song had lost its words somewhere and Miss Burns wasn't there to rescue her. Without Miss Burns' throat to push the music into line, there could be no song.

The silence came with a click. Dory could picture that girl out there in the living room turning off the song before it could end. And now time could not pass. That girl out there turned off the music, not wanting the evening ever to end. That girl who came over only when Dory's parents were going out for the evening.

"Estelle" they call her. Or "the babysitter." She means they've got to go. Her face at the front door makes them leave. Why leave? House too small maybe. Not room enough for all of us here and so then they leave.

You're just being silly.

I know.

The screen door had closed tight and fast on their backs when they left early that night. Dory's mother was still saying goodbye when it slapped shut.

Now another sound came into Dory's room. Another sound somehow familiar, everything from out there seemed to sound familiar from inside her room. This sound was soft and shuffling. Like wool and slippers.

Yes, that girl has feet with slippers on. Wool with pink puff-balls stuck to the tops of her toes. Good for walking on floors in the winter.

Dory rolled over in her bed and the covers rolled with her. The sheets twisted up around her legs, close and tight like drying skin. She looked up through the darkness to the ceiling and discovered a new game to play with the porcelain light globe. Looking straight at the spot where she knew it hung she could see nothing. But if she turned her head and let her eyes sidle slowly up to the spot . . . there it was. At least it was there until, in her slow sidling, she was finally looking straight at the spot again. And then the white globe was gone. The game kept Dory amused for some time. But then came the sound of the back door opening and closing.

The door is locked. No one home. No one? That girl is gone now. And only I am home.

In her bedroom with the door shut, Dory could not know that the back door had been shut and then locked from the inside. She could not know that Estelle was stretched out on the sofa, already falling asleep. Dory's parents would not be home until the next day. They had gone to spend the night at a neighbour's camp. Dory was left at home because there would be snowmobiling ("Too dangerous," her father had said) and then liquor and lots of ribald jokes ("Hardly the thing for little girls," her mother had said).

Dory lay awake now waiting for their homecoming sound, for the sound of their car outside in the street. When it came, the sound would spread itself out flat in the street like new snow.

Headlights grazed the bedroom ceiling, laser beams of light. And then the same darkness drew back deeper into the room. Dory undid her legs from the bedsheets, unravelled her flannelette nightgown from where it had spun itself around her shoulders.

The house was quiet. To Dory, the silence simply proved that she was alone. Her feet felt for the floor.

Floor is wet? No, just cold. So cold it sticks to my skin. Like when my tongue got stuck to the car door handle. Cars went by and I cried there stuck. And my dad laughed while he undid me.

And then?

Blood and my mother made me drink warm milk. Silly girl, she said. And I felt silly too. I cried and she smiled. So silly.

Dory crouched down in front of the bedroom window. Her fingers gripped the wooden sill with little peanut knuckles. The sound of the car outside continued. She could see it now. But it wasn't their car. This one was too small, kneeling down, there beside the snowbanks and the garbage can. Theirs was bigger and blacker.

The door of the car opened and a girl climbed out, nursing her purse close against the cold. She walked away from the car without looking back, as if it were no longer there, as if she no longer thought at all of the one she was leaving behind.

Leaving? Must leave. Not room enough for everybody in that little car. She doesn't care. People leaving never care, do they? No, and the ones who're left, they don't care either. Neither do I. Everybody smiles through goodbye. Smiles? Yes, because they'll come back. They? That girl, Mom, Dad, family, me. We all smile.

Cold now, like the tile, Dory's feet slid across the floor as she groped her way back to the bed. She heard the car drive away.

After a time, Dory stopped listening for them. And listened instead to her breath and to another breath which seemed to come from the back side of the door. It was, she decided, the breath of the house.

And who will sing my house to sleep? Not me. No one. It will just sit and wait. Maybe it can't ever sleep. Never? No, and I won't again either.

Dory was not afraid. She had not been alone often enough to know that there might be a reason to be afraid. Her parents did not come home.

Why not? I don't know. Forgot maybe? Well, I won't forget. Won't go to sleep either. Keep my eyes open. Open? Yes, but just let me close them for a minute. Hurt from looking at nothing for so long. Nothing? Well . . . at the dark then. And that's nothing.

Just let me close them for one more minute. One more little minute. Just one more . . .

Dory could not have known when she fell asleep.

Afterwards, she wouldn't even know for sure whether she had or not.

Two: Caroline

Caroline resisted the impulse to turn on the television set. She sat in an armchair lodged in one corner of the room. The throw cover had slid down the high back and lay in a bunch at the small of her back. Annoyed, she leaned forward. A spring bounced up hard beneath her.

Rearranging herself to avoid both the throw and the spring, Caroline stroked the uncovered arm of the chair.

Stroking: such a comfortable motion. Stroking everything back to passivity. Passive like passion. From the same word. And we're in love so passively, letting its moments enfold us, and we are passionate together. But passive apart. When apart? Now. Alone for a time and in love. How long in love? Forget now when it all began. Like Christmas Eve that way. On Christmas Eve there is no past. Only future. And waiting for the morning. Waiting now for Matthew to come home. Will come. Before the morning. Long before.

A freight train shunted cars on the track which ran parallel to the house. Somewhere in the kitchen a dish rattled and the metal kettle shuddered on the stove.

My ears and the room fill up . . . with? Sound in simple waves. Like the ones that get caught up in a seashell. Remember that day on the beach and I found a conch when the tide went away.

Listening to the sea inside it: I felt just like this. Will tell Matthew when he gets home. But no. Remember what he said about the conch: not the sea, silly girl; logical explanation for this common phenomenon. And everyone knows that science has taken the sea out of seashells. Silly girl.

A novel lay open on the table close to her chair. Caroline picked it up. She read one more page, skimming. The floor was vibrating slightly under her toes.

Vibrating. Like waves in the wind. No, not waves again. Just a simple freight train. Or maybe just the rhythm of these written, rewritten words. Catches at my veins. Beating them back into shape. Hammer on tin. I wish I'd been the one who wrote these or some other words. Lots of words all laid out in lines. Laid out on pages spread out flat on Matthew's lap. He could take my words with him then. When he couldn't take me. There would be no forgetting then. And he does forget me, yes, when I'm not there. A door closes on my face and he is walking away and forgetting. Fast. Like now.

Caroline put the book down in her lap and stretched her arm out long before her. The deep pull of her muscles made her yawn.

The hours spun away on the clock-face. Caroline's confidence dipped away at random intervals. And anxiety filled up the space.

What if . . . an accident? Out there somewhere away from me, forgetting me and the car steers itself off the road. Into the ditch in silence. Why silence? Shouldn't there be metal ripping and white bones bruising, burning black? No. I'm not there. No sound with no ears to hear. No sound? Well, maybe just sad singing. From the sky or maybe from this mouth, my mouth, here.

She hummed a tune out into the room. But her lips were dry and sometimes the song sucked in the silence instead of displacing it. She hummed her way through every nursery rhyme she knew, tying the notes up in ribbon with her cigarette tongue. The ashtray balanced on the arm of the chair was bulging with butts. Caroline frowned at it.

Like squirrels. With wrinkled brown tails and acorn cheeks fat with waiting for winter that day. Walking that day together through the bushes and trees way out there. Past the city limits somewhere. And Matthew wondered when the squirrels gathered up those nuts and when the trees sprouted all those leaves. We never saw them do it. Only talked. Talking our way around so many trees—some were dead—and he told me things. All those forest things he'd read about in school.

Caroline stood up and crossed the room to the window. Her hair hung down her back in two thick braids. No one thought this unusual for a woman her age anymore. All her friends kept their hair short and curly but they'd grown accustomed to her braids. She pushed open the drapes which had become warped and slightly discoloured with this constant habit of hers. Even when the drapes were closed now, an uneven oval of the outside showed through.

She watched the street and tried to pretend she wasn't alone.

And when I turn my back to the window again he will be there. In the chair, reading the book, the one with the blue binding. The one I've been reading. My book for now. Can share the same words anyway. And smoking too. He will be smoking like I was. And I'll see the smoke poking holes in his hair and I'll laugh when it gets in the way of words. The smoke seduces me and the words do too.

Caroline turned from the window. Of course the chair was still empty. And the only smoke in the room was not curling up through the air but lying in layers instead, stale and thin and dry.

He'll come home when he's done what he's got to do. Has to see some people first. Faces, just faces, no names. His friends, not mine. Work faces, the ones he spends the day with. Saves the nights for me. When we are together, they're left alone. But before that can happen, some things must be done.

Matthew buys them drinks and then he drinks some too. With them. Cheers. Being friendly. What does that mean to him? Buying drinks and food. Rare sirloin steak and mushrooms and salad. No sour cream on my baked potato, just butter, thanks. Smells good. Tastes better. He buys more food when somebody new joins the group. He is somewhere out there in a room full of little round tables and three-legged chairs and music and drinks full of ice cubes and hot food and faces and fresh smoke and walls without windows and legs arms hands teeth.

Caroline looked out the window again, watching the world through well-polished glass. The red brick bungalow directly across the street was brightly lit and six cars were parked against the curb in front. Their roofs were littered with yellow wet leaves that dripped steadily down from the birches on the boulevard. She pictured a cluster of shiny-skinned people laughing into the bright little rooms.

This time the spring did not jump when Caroline fit herself back into the armchair. She leaned her head up against its high back.

It's early yet. It's early yet.

She chanted the lie to herself in a monotone, believing that this combination of words would work magic, would work her a spell that would make it all true.

She thought that when Matthew did arrive, she would cry, just at first, just when he came in the door.

But not now. My tears are no use when there's no one here to catch them. Catch them? Yes, with his fingers imported fresh from the world. Fingers factory-sealed in new leather gloves, vacuum-packed.

Just in case she fell asleep before he arrived, Caroline left the back door unlocked. He might have forgotten his key.

And yes he will come. And open the door and carry his love for me inside with him. A carefully obedient love. Kept on a leash, three paces back, with a choke chain. It will heel on command. And it even plays dead.

She leaned back further and deeper into the chair. The buttons on the back felt round and large, protruding like somebody's eyes.

Matthew did not come home. Caroline let herself fall asleep and she missed the sun just starting to rise.

Three: Hannah

It was a Friday sometime in March. Or it might have been Thursday and it might have been in April. Hannah reached for the little cardboard calendar—Courtesy of Your Friendly Neighborhood Bank: We Care About Our Customers—on the chest beside the bed.

Surprise. Wrong again. All wrong. It's a Monday in May. Which means? Nothing in particular. Or it might mean warm rain and children slopping through puddles in plastic yellow rainboots. Making waves in the oil-skinned water. Waves and they shine. Means there should be sun. But no, it's night now. Means darkness moist like breath.

Hannah strained to put the calendar back in place on the night table and almost missed it in the dark. The flesh of her upper arm hung like raw bread dough. She thought about her arm, her body.

Belongs to this house, this room, these covers too. Something's coming soon to catch it up and go. What something? Morning maybe . . . or? You know. No, tell me. But you already know. Maybe, but I want to hear you say the word. All right then: death.

Oh.

With the sound of an electric typewriter driven too long, drops of rain broke against the metal awning outside her bedroom window. It was a familiar sound and Hannah was quite calm with the waiting.

Waiting here for the end. It will come. Of course. No more illusions. Old women all die, always. I'm not afraid. Not eager either. Just waiting.

Hannah was well-prepared. Her will was made, her estate was in order, the house was neat and uncommonly clean. She'd spent all afternoon washing and waxing and dusting just to be ready for this company that she knew would come. Both the front and back doors were unlocked.

Today will be the day. Because it's a Monday in May and there's no better time than right now. Today is the very last day. I have decided. I'm ready.

She waited without wondering what it would be like to die. Long ago she'd realized that it wouldn't be like anything. It would just be. There was no sense then in wondering about death, let alone worrying about it, as so many of her younger friends had. Most of them were dead now anyway.

She began plotting her meal for the next day. This was a ritual, the only foolproof way to find sleep. Breakfast came first of course. She prided herself on always following the natural order of things.

For breakfast then? Porridge. Just the thought makes me gag. But must have it. Cannot endure those plastic teeth first thing in the morning. Need to come at them from behind sometime later on in the day. So they can't come bouncing down shut on my tongue. Would they? They just might. You can't be too sure.

And lunch? Salad maybe. Yes, with lettuce and celery and those cute radish roses that new paring knife does up so well. But no. Stomach will provide a hundred instant replays of those radish roses. All day long. Free of charge. They only taste good the first time around. No radishes.

Hannah snickered into the room.

No need for all this. I won't need to eat tomorrow. No instant radish replays and no pink plastic gums. When he comes, he brings his own food. And when we get to where we're going, meals are included in the package price. But who is he? You know.

The bells of the church at the end of the block tolled three times.

Who rings them at this time of the night? Never thought of that before. Who then? I don't know. Maybe they work on faith. Like remote control without the wires. But religion doesn't work that way, does it? Sure it does. They've got that man with his finger on the switch. Name is God and he sits on a stool in white robes. In front of the switchboard and closing his white eyes and pushing all those coloured buttons. We all jump then. When our button gets pushed. Everyone's marked with a name. Or maybe just a number now. Waiting for the finger of God to find it. The finger named . . . what? Death, maybe. God's right-hand man.

Hannah grinned into the dark and settled back into the mattress, letting its cotton-coated fingers work their way up to her skin. She folded the blankets back neatly across the middle of her chest, like a paper napkin neat on somebody's lap. She counted the seconds between each breath, evening it out till it was five every time. Hours passed.

He will come. Who? Death. Didn't your mother tell you that everything comes to those who can wait? I can. And he will.

And what to do about the funeral? Well, I want flowers of course. Lots. Every kind the florist can find. And a coffin grey like seagull wings stuck to rainclouds. Strong wings to bear me up. Gained a few pounds over the years. The wings had better be the heavy-duty brand. Guaranteed for life.

And of course there's the music. Never could make up my mind about that. So many details to fuss around about. So this is how a life ends, is it?

The pillowcase under her neck was growing damp, almost sticky. She pulled it out from under her head and turned it over, cool side up. She cautioned herself to relax, determined that she would not let herself become impatient.

Must make a good impression. Don't push too hard.

A short sharp pinching at her scalp reminded her that her hair was still in pincurls, wrapped up in a pink and green scarf.

Must take them out. Must? Yes, he's coming tonight and metal messes up the machine that finds the bombs and the machine guns. Just a routine Security Check, ma'am, they'll tell me. Nothing to concern yourself about. And we've all got to pass the Check before we can get on the plane. The plane? Well, how else do you think we're going to get there, silly? And I've got to pass the Security Check or he'll leave me behind. He might be insulted. Just might not come for me again. And then what would I do?

Must take these pincurls out right now. Well . . . in a minute.

Hannah reached for the lamp on the night table. Her hand brushed just the edge of the shade. She did not flinch at the crash, pleased by the so-loud noise in her so-empty house. She closed her eyes for a minute to wait.

A minute. A minute.

How many minutes?

Again she heard the church bells. She counted eight rings.

Eight? How can that be? Morning.

The sun shone in through a split in the curtains. Hannah yawned. Unravelling the covers from around her legs, she stood up and yawned again.

Poor sleep last night. Those damn bells would wake up the dead and my lamp fell on the floor. Broke. Now who could sleep through all that?

Breakfast was simple: porridge.

I'll fool you, damn dumb plastic teeth.

She prepared the porridge while still in her nightgown, forgetting to put on her housecoat and slippers. Walking to the back door to bring in the milk, her feet made dry sucking sounds on the floor.

The door was unlocked.

My God.

Hannah steadied herself against the door frame.

What if? What if somebody had broken in? What if somebody, something, had just walked right in and helped themselves? To me.

She slammed the door.

Locked.

The oak panels were strong and safe with no knots.

Locked.

She covered the keyhole with the palm of one hand.

Locked.

TO WHOM IT MAY CONCERN

(1976)

Monday, April 26
Dear Mom:

All last week I was meaning to sit down and write you but just couldn't seem to get around to it till now. I know it's been over a month, and probably closer to two, since I got your last letter. I hope you haven't been worrying about me—even though I know without asking that you have. Everything here is fine now. Well, not really *fine*—but I'll get to all that in a minute.

First things first: are the leaves on your new philodendron still turning brown at the tips? While I was sorting through some of the old things in the cedar chest, I came across a book on the care of foliage plants. Possible causes of brown leaf-tips: soil too dry (water more frequently and more thoroughly); soil too high in salts (leaching is the only answer); or air too dry (buy a humidifier or maybe hope for rain?). Take your pick, I guess. And by the way, the rubber plant that Stewart bought me for my twenty-seventh birthday, the one I named Ulysses, has collapsed. Mental exhaustion perhaps? Do plants have nervous breakdowns?

People do. But don't worry—I won't. But I'm getting a little ahead of myself now.

The real reason why I'm writing this letter (and why I've been putting it off for so long) is to tell you that Stewart and I have separated. For good. The divorce is in the works.

After six whole years, after only six years. Maybe you were right. I know you never liked him much, even though you never told me why. Maybe I never asked. But do you remember what you said when I told you we'd set the date? You said, "Well, Vera, you're the one that has to live with him, not me." According to all the movies and TV commercials that I'd seen, you didn't get your lines right. Maybe you've forgotten this by now. But I never have.

And yes, I did have to live with him. And maybe now I've got some reasons of my own for disliking him. He must have gone through three new picture tubes (coloured, of course, and nothing but the best) all by himself. And I've just had the chesterfield reupholstered for the second time—nobody yet has invented the miracle cleaner I needed to get rid of those grease stains he left after so many evenings lying there sweating with no shirt on. Eating buttered popcorn or Spanish peanuts. His mother taught him years ago never to wipe his fingers on his pants so he used the couch instead.

Are you surprised by the separation? I know I've never mentioned how very many nights there were when one of us didn't come home. (I always stayed with my friends on those nights but I don't know where Stewart stayed—can't say that I much care now and I can't remember why I never asked him then). But then maybe you aren't surprised. Maybe I underestimate you. Maybe you've been reading in between the lines of my letters all along—although the letters and the lines were few enough at that. So maybe you've just known it from the start.

When you write to Thelma and Jessie and all the other relatives (I know I can count on you for that), please don't insinuate that I just gave up. It's not true, not true at all. I've forgotten now how many schemes I cooked up in hopes of "saving" our marriage (or at least of salvaging something for scrap and old scrapbooks). I was so damned determined to make it work, maybe just to prove to myself that you were wrong. I tried staying at home and crocheting afghans and cooking gourmet meals and cleaning out the toilet bowl at least two times a week. I tried working as a volunteer, an office clerk, a newspaper reporter and a barroom waitress. Through it all, I took evening courses in psychology and conversational French. I tried writing a novel and painting a still life of garlic bread and grapes and I even tried giving Tupperware parties just like all my happily married friends did. And I made sure that we had sex at least four times a week. But nothing worked.

Stewart tried too—despite what you're thinking right now as you read this and nod your head in sympathy with me. He sent me flowers when it was nobody's birthday, took me dancing, helped me with the dishes every single night, made sure that we had sex at least four times a week.

So you see, he wasn't quite the villain that you were/are sure he was/is. There will be no blame-laying here. We grew apart, away. We lost the need to talk and smile and dream out loud and spend lunch hours together in crowded cafeterias with just our knees touching under the table. And I've almost forgotten now that the question "How are you?" can have any answer but "Fine." We stopped asking and explaining and now we've even stopped asking the questions. It was all just too much trouble after all.

Last month we redecorated the living room—new upholstery as I've already mentioned and stacking tables, three of them, and a swag lamp with a tassel at the end of the pull-chain and even a new group of pictures for the west wall, all in matching metal frames, of course.

It didn't help though. And now the carpet doesn't match.

Stewart left two weeks ago yesterday. I had a shower while he finished packing up his things. But the water ran cold and

I had to get out before he had time to be gone. I'll always see him now, just going, going, never really quite gone. I guess I need new luggage now. All I've got left is the old cardboard case that you bought me when I left home for college. How many years ago was that anyway? Never mind; don't count.

There are lots of things now that I just don't count, no longer keep track of. Like how many bathtub rings I've cleaned and how many ashtrays I've emptied and how many jobs I've gone through and how many diets I've started and how many of my old friends have been divorced and how many are getting remarried this summer. It makes it somehow simpler just not knowing,

It's starting to rain. I can hear it on the awning. I've got some clothes out on the balcony. I tried washing my new wool suit. Hope it doesn't shrink; it cost me fifty dollars. No alimony arrangements have been made yet.

Please don't ask me to come up and stay with you. The kitchen needs painting. I guess I'll get to learn how to use a roller after all. Never thought I would. There were always advantages, I suppose. But do write soon. Or maybe call—collect. I'll be able to afford it if my income tax cheque comes in this week,

Love,
Vera

P.S. Maybe I should have phoned to tell you this. But I never thought of it till now. And my voice always sounds so much better on paper than air.

Tuesday, May 11
Dear Mr. and Mrs. Burgess:

I hope the two of you enjoyed your wintering in Florida. I am sure that you are both very brown and fit and well-rested. I am beginning to wonder if the sun has decided against coming this far north this year! It has been raining off and on for the past two weeks here.

I am writing this letter to the two of you just in case Stewart has not done it yet himself. We all know how he feels about writing letters, don't we? I am writing to inform you that your son and I have separated. We are planning to be divorced as soon as possible. I regret that I cannot let you know where Stewart is living now—I don't know myself. Probably you will hear from him once he gets settled in at a permanent address.

I don't mean to insinuate that Stewart has "deserted" me. The end of our marriage was not nearly as drastic or dramatic as all the things that word implies. We reached the decision together—rationally. Stewart never did go in much for dramatics. You both know how very logical he always is—so clear-eyed, far-seeing and diplomatic. Even throughout all of our difficulties, Stewart managed to remain on an even keel. I do not think that the break-up has changed him at all. He would never let it.

The reasons for our separation are not particularly dramatic either. It has nothing whatsoever to do with adultery or cruelty, not even of the mental kind. Our marriage simply has ended. I cannot even truthfully say that it "fell apart"—it merely faded away, came slowly undone. We were not "torn asunder." None of the standard phrases seem to fit what has happened between Stewart and I. We just stopped being together even when we were sitting just the two of us in the very same room.

Stewart was always very tolerant of my needs and always much too polite and self-controlled to laugh at my moods and emotions. I am sure you taught him all this even as a child. He always listened when I demanded that we talk about "us"—even though he afterwards contended that there was nothing to talk about because there was nothing wrong with "us." And I realize now that he was quite right after all, although I could not see it at the time—there wasn't anything to talk about because there wasn't really any "us."

He took me out wherever I wanted to go whenever I asked him to. But once we got where we were going, he never failed to inform me that he really had not wanted to go, had in fact agreed only in order to humour me. He is such an honest man as I am sure you both well know. But he never would tell me what *he* wanted to do. When I complained that he made me feel guilty because I always seemed to be getting my way, he quite calmly and clinically assured me that he had nothing to do with it, that I made *myself* feel guilty. He was always so blameless and guiltless and maybe he was heartless too—although you may think my choice of words a little too harsh for your only son.

He let me have as much time as I needed to be by myself. He let me go out for an occasional evening with "the girls"—as long as we kept to our shopping and knitting and recipe-swapping, of course. He let me buy myself a new gown for every wedding that he ever took me to. He let me take night courses at the university too—maybe he thought they would expand my horizons and make me that much more interesting to come home to every night. But then he did not come home every night. But then neither did I.

Oh yes, we had an equal marriage—at least that's what Stewart told me to believe. He even let me have my very own chequing account with personalized cheques and everything. His generosity astounded me and did you teach him that as well?

Do not think that I am especially lonesome without him. The apartment is small and some of his hair is here still clogging up the bathroom drain. I know it's his because it's brown and I am still a blonde (even thought you were so sure my roots would grow in black).

The only time I really miss him is on Monday nights. He always put out the garbage then just before the late night news. He never missed a night. And oh, how the neighbourhood ladies must have envied me as they came trudging out with their garbage bags and cans! And now we smile and call to each other across our new-mown, unraked, Monday night lawns.

After Stewart left, I cleaned the attic out and I am sending you a parcel of the things he saved through the years: a tennis racket needing to be strung (he always kept in shape), a double-breasted suit with too-wide lapels (he always kept in style), a shoebox full of pictures and postcards and old swizzle sticks (he always kept in touch with memories and moments that we didn't share). These things meant nothing to him—he left them here with me. But knowing the two of you as well as I do, I am sure that they'll mean everything to you.

Vera

Sunday, May 16
Dear Therese:

For weeks I wondered, Is this the end? Hoped not, hoped so, hoped not, hoped so. Wished I had a daisy to help me to decide.

But now I know that yes this is the end and I am happy and I am hurt and I am happy and I am hurt and the door slammed oh so good, so loud and I wanted his ears to hear it again and again and striding out to the car he forgot for once to worry about tripping and falling and ripping his pants and ruining this moment and I heard the car door open good but quiet and no one screamed goodbye and the tires did not spit up gravel and hate as he left. They simply rolled away.

For a week I lay awake not sad but so afraid that he might return for revenge with a gun burn down the house love someone else on our front lawn kill himself with the car but then I wasn't losing any sleep anymore and this is the end and he will not call and I only slammed that door behind him because he couldn't get mad about the things he should have and he will not call and I've figured out at least a dozen ways to get around without a car.

Today is Sunday and now I'm more sorry about that than the fact that Stewart is gone because Sundays make me maudlin because Sundays make me think.

How is your eczema and what about your sister, the one who flew to Europe right after her divorce? The weather here has been, is, and will be, wet. The wind in the night makes my bedroom awning squeak. But then the covers get so heavy on my skin that I can't help but be safe. And I am sleeping better now than I have for our six years.

Therese, are you wondering what went wrong with us? I am. It started as a simple song, song with no lines and no words, only movements and motion and my hands gesture up round and ripe like grapes and who'll pull back the skin and swallow up the seeds to help me understand?

The things that I wanted were simple enough but my words wouldn't work for some reason and who had the ears or the hours to listen to me anyway? I felt like blisters were breaking up under my skin. I promised the world that I'd not give it words because already there are enough. So I tuned up my throat and I wanted to make a new sound, my sound, not his sound, not our sound, but my sound, my, mine. I wanted to push the world one more step, one solid step closer to wherever it is we are going. In my mind I heard the sound and it had no name because that would mean words and then it came out.

But the ears it broke through to were his ears and old, not old like with cobwebs and rust, no, not that old. But they were just familiar old with too much use and expectation. They were just filled up with all the sounds that every body makes sometimes: maybe when they're being born or making love or dreaming of someone who has not and will not ever be born. There was no room and no reason for me and my sound. He always wanted a reason. But before I could teach it to heel, my mouth started talking, explaining, discussing, reaching for reasons instead of the sky.

And that was all he ever wanted anyway.

This morning on my way to buy another quart of milk (the other one went sour and curdled in my coffee), I saw a bird's egg broken on the sidewalk. It was blue, a robin's egg. And does this mean that someone next year won't get to see their first red-breast of the season? For that person, it won't ever be spring and why do I hope that it's Stewart?

Who's fault is all this anyway? Why, I have to say it's his, of course. Because he couldn't learn to listen and now that he's gone, I've finally remembered how to cry again. Just not too much or too often because what if my tears all run out? I can even cry again at sad movies and the Sunday night reruns of *Lassie*.

I don't know where Stewart is and it's too late to teach him how to wash and iron his shirts. He asked me once to show him how but I said no because I wanted there still to be something that I could do for him that he couldn't do for himself. It helped me know he needed me. And he won't wear a single shirt that's wrinkled or a day away from clean.

Last night I just forgot and set the table up for two. Cleaning up, I dropped the plate that wasn't used and why was I so sorry that it didn't break?

There are still a myriad of things that need to be done—my lawyer calls it "tying up loose ends" and I've been there at least a dozen times, signing papers and changing the beneficiary of my insurance policy and signing some more papers. I'm beginning to enjoy it all—it must be time to leave. My lawyer always sighs and says how lucky we are that there were no children involved and he's constantly admiring how very adult we are being about this whole damn thing,

Yesterday a deaf-mute came around the neighbourhood selling helium-filled balloons. I bought a yellow one for fifty cents. I left it for a while just to stick light-headed to the ceiling but then I took it out onto the balcony and gave it away to my favourite neighbourhood child: the sky. It went at first just cautiously up. Did it know this was one ceiling that it would die trying to reach? I want to believe that some of me is fierce and brave enough to go with that balloon.

How many times have you and I shook our heads so sadly and in unison when we got the news of another divorce? Funny that now I just can't be bothered to shake my head at this one—can you?

My mother, of course, wants me to come down south for a while, to spend a month or maybe two getting a tan and a man. Why can't I make her understand I don't want either one?

I'm coming out to visit you instead. Don't panic though: I don't intend to move in on you or anything. I'll find my own apartment and a job and maybe I'll even learn how to drive. I'll be thrifty and mobile and quite comfortably alone. I'll be there in about two weeks. Don't meet me at the station—I can find my own way home.

Love, Vera

P.S. It must be summer after all. A ladybug is bashing its brains out on the light globe over my head. The sound of its wings on the glass is like flames.

Monday, May 31
To Whom It May Concern:

I realize that it isn't common practice for a former tenant to leave a note for the unknown future tenants—but there are certain things I feel that you, whoever you are or will be, really ought to know. I am taping this note to the fridge door so you can't miss it and maybe so the door won't look so empty now that it's given up being a bulletin board and a calorie chart (at Stewart's suggestion, of course).

No, the roof doesn't leak and the taps don't drip—although you do have to turn the bathtub hot water tap at least two good cranks before it comes on. There are electrical outlets in every room. The bathroom light switch works backwards. This is not a mystery (too bad)—we put it in ourselves. Merely an amateur's accident.

Don't plug in the toaster while you're ironing. Garbage pickup is *early* Tuesday morning. The grocery store at the corner does deliver, does not give credit. Use the stairs whenever you can—the elevator tends to get stuck on the roof.

I hope you can arrange your furniture to cover up the worn spots on the rug and that stain in the corner too—once we had a cocker spaniel named Babe for a week before the landlord found out. And maybe you can use a picture or a plaque or a high-school diploma to cover up that dent on the west wall. It's only a remnant of the day I threw our hand-carved granite ashtray (a wedding present from my aunt Thelma) at Stewart's forehead. The dent, I guess, is my fault because I threw the things. But his fault too because he ducked.

AN EVENING IN TWO VOICES

(1977)

MONTHS and months after that evening, I have ways of remembering it. Special ways, my own ways, which end up being always the only ways.

It happened in April. Everybody agrees with me on that at least. Maybe it was documented somewhere by some demented scribe. I don't know. But now it's common knowledge that it happened in April. A fact. It can be proven by the rest of the world. And what else are friends and calendars for anyway? They help you keep your dates straight if nothing else.

It was in April. No question about that.

And there was a thick fog that night. I remember walking up the front steps to Doreen and Gerald's house, almost believing that I could feel the fog parting around my nylon legs, like that Bible lake parting for the children of Israel. Fog brushing and rushing away at the force of my skirt folding around and over and under the air.

Doreen insists that it wasn't foggy. Not foggy at all. "Clear and cool," she says adamantly. She swears her memory is correct. And I don't try to argue her out of it anymore. People who are perpetually (and purposely, perhaps?) wrong don't know how to give in with grace.

It was my evening anyway. So naturally I remember it more clearly than anyone else. Naturally. Surely that makes sense. It's simple enough, isn't it? I remember it being a foggy night and it *was* a foggy night. David was holding my hand when we walked up the steps so close together—virtually leg-in-leg, I guess you could say if you wanted to be humorous or coy. Gerald opened the front door and welcomed us in.

It was still getting dark early then. After all it was only April. Everyone agrees with me on that. I can't remember now (oh yes, I admit it, I'm not perfect, there are pale patches in my memory, patches sewed on with binder twine or dental floss perhaps) how David's hand felt around mine. Or how it felt to have my hand nursed along in his. It was such a familiar feeling then—one that I had no reason to remember, I suppose.

Yes, Gerald opened the door to us. That rectangle of light with Gerald spread out stark in the middle of it sticks in my mind now. A bright rectangle marked off from the night by just the thin straps of the door-frame. Rectangle bright with electricity and friendship and cozy conversation and plenty to eat and drink. The light and Gerald welcoming us in through the fog. No, I will not say that he was haloed by the healthy house. That would be much too clichéd and my memory may be many things but it's most certainly not clichéd.

Doreen insists that she answered the door that night and that the kids were screaming in the background because they wanted to stay up for the party too and Jeanette, the youngest one, couldn't get her pajama bottoms on right and they were binding up around her legs, cutting into her just-bathed skin. Doreen says she was screaming back into the room at them instead of saying to us graciously, "Well, hello, do come in. Come on in and let me take your shawl, Estelle. You're looking so lovely tonight. My goodness. Do come in."

And Doreen says her hair was already coming down, running in stray strands down over her damp forehead (damp with steam from the stove and sweat from the screaming) and that new style had cost her ten whole dollars just that afternoon. Already it had wilted with the crises of kitchen and kids and hostesshood happening all at once.

She says David wasn't holding my hand either. That he was just standing there on the step with his arms folded over his stomach. She says he wasn't even looking at me—or her either, for that matter. That he was gawking off somewhere behind us to where he'd parked the car.

"Likely wondering if some drunk would come around that damn sharp corner and slam right into him and push him up over the curb into that rotten old elm," she said. There's no need for sarcasm but she never seems to realize that.

I know she can't be right anyway because David never worries about things like that. He has too many other things, splendid things, going on inside his head. No room left in there for the trivia that troubles all the rest of us. And he has such good luck anyway that he never needs to worry about such things—they just wouldn't happen to him anyway. He leads a charmed life, oh yes. And I always believed it would rub off on me too. But somehow it never did. Not his fault though, more likely mine for not being patient or secure enough, or maybe because I didn't listen enough or pay enough attention to the way he'd long ago learned to live his life as if nobody mattered. I just never got to that state somehow, never stopped needing the rest of the world. Because after all he was part of the rest of the world too, wasn't he? And I couldn't ever reach the state of not needing him. Couldn't even imagine that then. And when I can't imagine myself into a situation anymore then I know that it will never be. I trust myself.

Doreen insists that David didn't even look, let alone smile, at her when she invited us to come inside.

And no, of course, he didn't. Because it was Gerald, not Doreen, who answered the door.

And Gerald was so very gracious. Just as he always is. He took my shawl from around my shoulders without even needing to ask. And he unwrapped it so very well, his easy muscles slipping it down off my slim shoulders. Oh yes, they were slim. Maybe even almost sharp around the edges. And I'm sure everybody would agree with me on that though I've never thought to ask. It's just one of those facts that never need to be verified. And Gerald unwrapped me without getting his fingers caught up in the holes—crocheted holes, I mean. They're supposed to be there. Not like moth holes or old holes. These were fashionable holes. And he folded the shawl then over one arm, holding the other out to guide me into the living room.

But not before he'd made David welcome too, shaking his hand hello. Gerald always was such a God-damn gracious man, gentleman. So very good at making me feel so very good. It comes to him naturally. He is well-versed in all the subtle social graces. But they aren't just pinned onto the outside—they just seem to happen. So very elegant, well-mannered, in such clean control.

Once I even told Doreen that she should be happy to have such an exceptional man around the house all the time.

She said, "What do you mean by that?"

I explained to her so patiently about that particular evening and how good he had been at greeting us and asking all the appropriate questions without even needing to think about it. Making us feel that he'd no doubt been sitting right there in the living room for hours on end just waiting for our arrival. He seemed so eager for our company. Not fumbling school-boy eager, but elegantly eager. Which must be a hard thing to master; eager elegance, I mean.

After the explanation, Doreen just laughed at me. I guess I must have looked puzzled at her reaction because then she took to explaining:

"Gerald? Elegant? You've got to be kidding, Estelle. Gerald doesn't know the meaning of the word. He never answers the door for company anyway. And I've told you before that he didn't answer it that night either. Honestly, Estelle, you talk to me about that night like I wasn't even there. But I was there. I know what really happened. You don't have to pretend with me, Estelle.

"Gerald was sitting there with his feet up on the coffee table after I'd spent half an hour waxing the damn thing. And with his shoes on too. Of course. And nowhere near being ready for company. No tie, his shirt all unbuttoned so his paunch could stick out all over the place. Probably had a beer in one hand and a cigar in the other. Not moving a muscle when the doorbell rang. Except to holler, 'Hey, Doreen, get that damn door. You deaf or something?' And me rushing around trying to get the kids to bed and none of the food ready yet and I couldn't even get him to zip my bloody dress up for me. He was just too busy with some stupid movie or some dull documentary on Hawaiian volcanoes or East Indian art or something."

She paused then. For breath perhaps. Or maybe in complete exasperation. We were talking on the telephone—fortunately. I jumped in and said there was somebody knocking at my door—which there wasn't, but then she didn't need to know that. There could have been someone at the door. It could have been the paper boy or someone with a telegram or just a neighbour dropping in for a chat and a quick cup of coffee. So I just said there was somebody at the door.

And Doreen said, "Oh." Sounding so deflated. But I didn't let her make me feel guilty. Not this time.

"Bye," I said.

I don't see much of Doreen anymore. We can't seem to agree on anything lately.

As a matter of fact, Gerald did have a drink in his hand when he showed us in that night. But it was a martini, with a one-eyed olive marooned on the bottom of the long-stemmed glass. Not a beer. And he didn't have a paunch either.

He showed us into the living room.

"Have a seat. Can I fix you a drink?"

"Yes, thanks. I'll have a martini."

"Me too. Dry."

"Two martinis coming right up."

And he already had a whole tumbler all mixed up. So well-prepared. So in control of the evening. I sat down on the chesterfield because that way David could sit right beside me. He wouldn't be stuck away across the room all evening. I guess you might say I was feeling especially intimate that night, although "intimate" doesn't seem to be quite the right word. But it'll have to do. Seems that the words for so many of the things I'd like to say just haven't been invented yet. I mentioned that to David once but he must have missed the point because all he said was, "Words aren't invented, silly. They just happen." So there, it happened again—the words weren't quite right and so he couldn't quite hear what I was saying.

David sat right beside me and I remember thinking it was such a long long chesterfield, the kind with four cushions instead of only two or three. And our thighs were touching. He does love me, I thought. This is proof—all the proof that I need to be sure.

He smiled at me then and patted my knee. As if he knew what I was thinking. It's possible, you know. We were that close. And so maybe he knew what I was thinking and just wanted to let me know that I was right.

I couldn't help but lean the side of my body up against him just the slightest little bit. His weight made a valley in the cushions and how could I help but be drawn down towards him? I wonder now if he felt the pressure of my arm against his. No, he didn't move away. Yes, I'm sure he felt it. And liked it too.

Doreen says David sat across the room with both feet up on the footstool. I can picture it there growing out of the plush shag carpet like a toadstool crusted with tweedy brown fungus. But David's feet weren't on it.

Doreen says his arms were folded across his stomach. All of his body folded carefully, compact, closed, as if he'd rehearsed the position just before. As if he wanted to be sure invasion was impossible from any angle. I laughed when she told me this but she just shook her head at me—comment closed. But I didn't care. She always was too caught up in trivia to suit me.

It must be months now since we got together. We did exchange Christmas cards though, one last remnant of our friendship. But maybe that's what Christmas cards are for anyway. I signed my card simply "Estelle." She wrote "With much love from Doreen and Gerald and Jeanette and Darryl and Donny" and somehow it was all too careful and neat to be done out of anything but a sense of duty. Duty is neat; love is not. And I wonder if she stacks all the cards up in front of her on the kitchen table and signs each one exactly the same and then passes them over to Gerald who stuffs them into the envelopes and addresses them in alphabetical order from a long list. And maybe Gerald passes them on to Donny then (he's the oldest child so I'm sure he must contribute to Christmas too by now) so he can lick the flaps and stamp each envelope. Yes, I'm sure it must have been Donny who did that because the stamp was on upside down.

Theirs was the only address I didn't need to look up when Christmas card time came. You see how well my memory serves me.

Why can't I convince Doreen of that? I've stopped trying now.

There were bald spots in that evening—long lapses in the conversation. But they weren't gropings or awkward angry spaces. No, not at all. They were comradely silences, simply elongated moments between our words, commas in our conversation.

When Doreen brought around that tray heaped with hors d'oeuvres, for instance. There was no need to speak then, no need at all. Better simply to observe the orchestration of ovals, pentagons, squares, and circles. And on top of all those aesthetic crackers so many kinds of cheese and pâté and parchment pickles and (could it really be?) caviar.

Doreen laughed when I happened to mention the caviar once. "I've never served caviar, Estelle," she said. "You really are imagining things, you know. Have you ever thought of seeing someone about these delusions of yours? You know what I mean. Going to see a. . . ." She never finished the sentence.

But no, I didn't know what she meant. I know now though. I've figured out all her insinuations now— including this one. And I have to wonder what ever made me think she was my friend. How could a real friend make such a rash statement, such a complete misjudgement?

And Doreen says she didn't serve crackers that night either. But potato chips and cheesies and the fattest pretzels she could find downtown. She says she remembers it well because she had to keep everything hidden from the kids all day so there'd still be some left by the time we arrived.

I cannot help but feel a little smug with knowing she's quite wrong. Yes, of course she's wrong. How else to explain the satisfaction of a cracker fitting right on my tongue, gradually releasing bits of flavour into my throat? The memory is too vivid—I couldn't have made it up. I remember David commenting on them too. Something about how much trouble Doreen had gone to and she really shouldn't have but he was damn glad she had. Such a witty man when he wanted to be, when the situation seemed to demand it. He was always so very sensitive to such things. He could always be depended on to fill in the blanks.

I remember Gerald discreetly refilling the tray and smiling proudly at how much we were enjoying ourselves in his home.

Doreen says he just glared at her when she turned off the TV in the middle of the show.

"Glared at me and grunted," she said. "And grabbed another bunch of pretzels and tried to shove them in his mouth all at once until the salt was falling down his chin and sticking to his shirt."

We didn't talk much while we ate the hors d'oeuvres. But I remember David sinking down a little deeper into the sofa, pushing his legs out in front of him, sighing and easing himself into the evening as if he wished it would never end.

I wish it never had.

Doreen agrees with me about the sigh at least. But she says it came when she pulled the drapes shut and David could no longer see the street going by and the cars and the city changing shape in the dark. She says he must have been wishing he was somewhere out there instead. I don't know where she gets these silly notions. David always liked the sunshine so much more than the night. She never knew that though. She didn't know him like I did. He was not an easy man to get close to. I was patient though and I finally did. She never tried, I suppose. And why should she?

It was such an easy evening—all four of us knowing our lines and our places, leaving the room only at opportune moments. And who could ever say who conducted the evening so well? The air was ripe with ambience and there was never any need to scramble through our respective days in search of a new topic of conversation. One word flowed out of and into another. There are patches in the evening now where I can't remember who said what, who nodded, who sighed in agreement. But it didn't seem to matter much anyway. We were all in such accord that we could have spoken for each other. Perhaps we could have carried on the whole evening without words at all. Yes, we were that well-attuned. I tried to tell Doreen about that special kind of conversing that needs no words, that special kind of relationship based on questions that need never be asked and answers that need never be spoken. That perfect relationship where neither partner needs to speak—not because they have nothing to say to each other but because they have everything to say to each other and words are now just overcoats donned solely for the benefit of others.

Doreen shook her curlers at me and said, "There's no such thing. How can you expect me to believe all that, Estelle? You're just rationalizing away the fact that you and David had run out of things to say long before that night. Or maybe you're just trying to romanticize that sad state everybody seems to get to. Gerald and I reached it a long time ago. That state when you know somebody so damn well that you can't convince yourself anymore that anything about them will ever be new again. You don't give a damn anymore and you're just as happy if he keeps his damn mouth shut for once and lets you get on with the things that are needing to be done."

I didn't know how to respond. I pretended to understand but I didn't and I still don't. There just isn't that much cynicism in me—no, not even now. So I humoured her. She seemed to need so much to be bitter, to suffer something just a little bit every day, just a little bit *more* every day so at least she could feel she was getting somewhere.

I listened to her and then I said, "It really was an easy evening though."

She blurted out a laugh and started to bring up sample moments she remembered. I must have been out of the room to have missed so much. It doesn't make sense. She said David was especially quarrelsome. She said he disagreed with me on almost everything and even suggested that I was talking too much for my own good, telling Doreen and Gerald personal things that were no one's business but our own.

And Doreen said she could still hear him muttering, "I suppose all your friends know how often I change my socks and how short I cut my toenails. Honestly, don't you have anything better to talk about? But then I suppose you don't, do you?"

No, David would *never* speak to me like that. Not even when we were alone and certainly not when we were out with friends. But I could not make her believe that she must have misunderstood. Maybe he did say something like that but I'm sure he was only quoting something he'd heard. Maybe telling a story or making a joke.

But I know he would never speak like that to me.

Doreen says he was even arguing with Gerald. About hockey, religion, football, politics—all those things that they'd always agreed on before. I cannot imagine David and Gerald ever disagreeing. They've spent too many magic masculine hours rewriting the world and bouncing the bottoms of their brains off each other, making a whole new world out of what remains of this one.

Doreen says that the disagreement with Gerald started it all. She couldn't remember what it was all about, which only proves that her memory isn't nearly as reliable as she likes to think it is. But then Doreen always was one who could convince herself of anything if she really wanted to. She says David started talking about wanting to make a change in his life, that he was tired of hearing all the same old arguments for and against all the same old things. And he was getting so tired of doing all the same things all the time and going to all the same places, all the same bars and restaurants and theatres. Doreen says the despair in his voice then made her forgive all that had gone before.

And yes, I do remember him saying that. And he had said it all before. I knew how he felt. It came as no surprise to me. And as always he included me in his plans too. Naturally. Said I should get out more, take up some new hobbies, keep my mind active and stimulated. And the more he talked about it, the more enthused he got and, as always, the more enthused David gets, the more enthused I get. And then I was all fired up with his plans and making them my own already and believing that, yes, I'd been thinking that all along, that I was just needing to get it all out in the open.

And I remember thinking, "This is so damn much better (and so damn much cheaper too) than therapy—primal, transactional, gestalt or otherwise." And then I was ready to change my life with him.

And then he said it. Oh yes, I remember.

"I'm leaving town," he said. No, I wasn't surprised. He'd talked of it before. We'd talked of it. "Got myself transferred clear across the country, to a place I've never seen." My heart jumped. Not out of fear or surprise, but out of happiness because we were leaving and we would learn how to read a new place together and there would never be an end to the new things we could experience there. And already my mind was making moving pictures of what it would be like.

Doreen disagrees.

"No, Estelle, it wasn't like that. He wasn't enthused. He was grim and determined and he didn't look at anyone when he said it and he certainly didn't look at you. He wasn't even trying to pretend that you were part of the plan. I remember thinking how cruel and dishonest he was being, doing such a thing to you in front of us, even if we are your best friends."

Silently, I rewrite the "are" to "were."

David and I didn't discuss it on the way home. I suppose we were both too pleased with our news, too busy making dreams and plans. When David dropped me off at my apartment, the smile was on his face, not just on his lips, and I couldn't sleep for wondering what to take and what I'd have to buy for the move.

He left in less than a week.

Two days later, I got a telegram saying that he'd already met the new boss and things were working out even better than he'd planned and he knew I'd understand because I always understood—that was one thing he had to give me credit for.

Doreen says I tore the telegram in shreds and threw it in the fireplace. She might be right there. I can't seem to remember.

PROPHECIES

(1978)

I ONLY WANT TO SAY that I already know we won't last. First night together: new man, first night, feast night. After we made love last night, at least you didn't ask, "How was it for you?" I appreciated that, but your red beard will never match the pansies on my pillowcase. You clash with my constructed atmosphere. The colour red makes me jumpy, especially first thing in the morning. And I can't ask you to shave it off. Not because I think you wouldn't but only because I've never known how to ask for the things that I want. Oh, I know how to *get* them all right; I just don't know how to *ask* for them. How do you ask for a piece of cheese, a ride downtown, a voice or a hand in the dark, a friend, a lover, silence? I was in Grade Six before I ever asked to leave the room. I can't ask, I don't know how. So I just keep on taking instead, and hope that all the questions have been understood.

I'm sure now that we won't last. I couldn't sleep last night with your body in my bed. Became hopelessly entangled in disjointed dreams of robust thighs and facial hair. I have no intention of becoming marooned in a mess of sleepless nights. Your absence will never cause them, but neither will your presence. I've always valued my sleep.

Which is not to say that last night won't somehow find a way to survive. For every day, there's always a last night. It may or may not be remembered though, may or may not separate itself out, like a piece of sludge in suspension, from all the other nights. I might not remember your words but I will remember mine. I might not remember where we went but chances are that I'll remember why. But that's not so strange—after all, we don't make the places where we go, we just make their reasons for being there. I might not remember what day of the week it was (by this time next week, I'll probably already be having trouble with that one) but I'll remember that your mouth was already wet before the wine reached it. And I'll remember how well you went with the weather. Burnished autumn early evening. Autumn has always been my favourite season. But maybe now that I've met someone who fits the season so well, I'll change my mind. Thinking of it now, I find I much prefer the world in winter: black and white and needle-edged.

I only want to say that I seldom remember the things that other people actually do when I'm with them. Cannot afterwards recall how many people were there or how you got stuck in a traffic jam on the way and how mad I was because we were ten minutes late. Cannot remember the anger afterwards, cannot conjure how it changed the feel of the upholstery or the taste of my cigarette or the shape of the streetlights. I'm angry only when I really am, cannot be angry when I think about being angry. That's just thinking, not anger. I seldom bear grudges.

I will remember things like an auburn eyelash or a sprout of sweat on your left temple as it grinds against my cheek or your eyeballs rolling up and back into your head when you laugh (not a pretty sight). Memories will dive back at me just when I mean to be making new ones instead. I will not remember your favourite song or the jokes you tell me or your birthday or the directors of the movies we may see together. I will remember where we sat and how that man beside me watched the movie (what movie? I won't remember) while wheezing his way asthmatically through to intermission and then pawing through his tweed jacket for a wad of Kleenex and a plastic vaporizer.

I can remember a sentence caught once years ago through an open office door: Why haven't you told your husband yet? But I won't remember your sentences, will quickly and smoothly lose your voice in between theatre seats, night music, cigarette smoke and the shower curtain. I might remember your beard twitching with unshed tears over *Lassie* reruns, sad movies, and my indifference to hemorrhoids, low back pain, inertia and unemployment. But I will remember this only because it will make me wonder why you persist in pretending.

This is only a warning, not a threat. There is a difference. Simply a temperate warning—one of the rituals of romance, a step in the toe-dance we all do. So free with your attentions, hoping that someone, the right one, will intercept your advances. But the right one never does. The others notice though and think it's all for them. They stake a claim on your cow-eyes and will not let themselves admit that they were accidentally misdirected, deflected in mid-dance. Somebody keeps running interference, taking more than they are given. You need so much to believe, not wanting to know the truth and my real name and what will or will not be remembered afterwards. You are not organized for afterwards. Do not get carried away and give all your old clothes to the Salvation Army.

You talked last night about the right one (your judgement, not hers), orbitting around you, spinning, always spinning away. But here you are again, with me this time, giving yourself up to become quite caught in the magnetic field. Unable to remove yourself, to pretend it isn't true, unable to reverse the poles. I am not the right one (my judgement, not yours). You will make yourself believe that your hands are tied. Don't think for a minute that I know a thing about knots. After a while you will not let yourself remember the dreams you had in California, the memories you should be keeping instead of laundering away, the plans you made and wish you hadn't, the need to eat when you're hungry, the faith of family and friends.

And I, according to my own pattern, will by that time want my freedom. Will want my freedom *back*. But how do I ask for that when I didn't even know it was being taken away? I choose to make room for friends, but lovers just force their way in. I'm not sure how long it will take me this time to remember that I don't have to ask for something that was mine to begin with. And I won't have to say, Thank you very much, either. Not if I don't want to. And I won't.

You were transparent with your preprogrammed evening of candlelight and flowers. Who made them mean romance? Candles go out, burn down careless houses, make funerals holy. They don't make love. And flowers die, breed bugs, make homes for bumblebees. They don't make love either. Hearts and flowers aren't much of an improvement. Hearts are pumps and red cinnamon candies on Valentine's Day, are transplanted by nimble hands. So what have hearts to do with love? They have no sense of humour. If the choice of emblems had been mine, I might have picked typewriters and crayons, or white-tailed deer and transport trucks, or Christmas lights and roosters. I could make almost anything mean love if I really wanted to. I have my doubts about red beards though.

You already have no place in the words and the lines that come to mind. You've already told me that I don't seem to make much sense at times—I'll probably remember that. You will never be comfortable just walking through the woods with me. You'll try, of course, but you won't leave any footprints beside mine in the snow. I want to make nursery rhymes but you won't understand—nursery rhymes to be preserved by little girls in white ankle socks skipping rope in the school grounds. You wouldn't see the value of white ankle socks, I'm sure. And I never did learn how to skip double dutch, couldn't practice at home because I was an only child and there was no one around who would turn the ropes for me. You won't be able to show me the ropes.

You see, I'm looking for answers just like everybody else. But for me the looking is the important thing. The finding comes like a gift, like Christmas or birthdays or weddings. And the best gifts are always the ones you buy for yourself because only you know what you really want. Do not buy me an orange lampshade with a silk fringe all around, a granite ashtray, a plastic parakeet, or a moose paperweight.

Enough—no more lists. Let me make light rays instead. Laser beams can kill but not if you don't believe in their power. It will hurt you to see me with my arm around another man but it's bound to happen. Because after all, it's my arm and I'll put it anywhere I want to. But it might not hurt if you don't let yourself believe in me too much. But I see already that you aren't like me, cannot convince yourself of virtually anything just because you want to. Truth only comes with the telling. It will hurt at the time but afterwards you won't remember the pain.

Don't call me a pessimist. I want to hear violins just as much as anyone but I twirl in the silence too well. I persist in making always the wrong songs, will never remember how to harmonize. Harmony is for choir-boys and barbershop quartets.

Within a certain space of time we'll be so very honest with each other. We'll be able to tell lies only to ourselves, never to each other. We'll never believe that the simple answers just might be the right ones.

You cannot hear harmonica notes without trying to play the blues. You cannot understand that I will give up reasons for Lent, will rewrite your semantics, will stop asking for reasons and start asking for long explanations instead. And smiles. Oh yes, you are already so greedy for my smile (if only because yours comes so easily, with a little bacon grease just around the edges) but I don't give it out for free. One night I will sit with my teeth all brushed up and waiting for you to phone, believing you will smell them white across the wire. But no, you don't phone and you must be out drinking again with the boys from work and oh, you think you're so unique. But don't you know that all the wayward men on afternoon TV stop off at easy bars for beer before they go home to those pretty wives busy giving birth to Chicken Fricassee and Pineapple Surprise?

There will be Sunday just-after-noon phone calls.

I will say: Good morning, how are you?

You will say: Lousy.

I picture bugs in your beard but my answer is noncommittal: Oh?

I've got this crummy headache and I slept in too late and I've got nothing to do. I'm bored. God, I hate Sundays.

Oh.

Well, what do you want to do today?

I have my fistful of suggestions ready: Maybe a ride? Or we could go to the library or for a walk by the lake.

Nah. What else do you want to do?

Well, we could go for a walk or—

You said that already. What else?

We could drop in on Harold and Jean or we could go for an ice cream cone, chocolate mint.

Nah.

What do *you* want to do then?

Whatever you like.

But I just told you what I'd like.

Whatever you'd like besides those things then. What about supper?

I haven't planned anything.

Oh.

We could go out to eat.

Okay. Where do you want to go?

We could go to the Waterfront, they've got good seafood.

Nah, I don't feel like seafood.

What about that steak place on Knight Street?

Nah, too expensive.

And then I will say: Let's go wherever you want then.

But I won't mean it. Do not make a note of the things I say to you. I won't remember your reply and my words may or may not be true.

THE GATE

(1978)

WE'RE ON OUR WAY to Mapleside.

Our new station wagon—my father calls it "the suburban"—is black and my mother, fanning her face with a magazine, says for the fourth time, "I don't see why you had to have a black car, Roy. Black just absorbs the heat. I can't stand it!"

My mother's name is Natalie and she's a hairdresser. Her short dark hair, coated with hairspray, is perfect. She never touches it. I'm not supposed to tell anyone that she dyes it. As if I would.

The inside of the suburban rises around me in white folds: front seat, dashboard, doors. My father is driving too fast but I'm not worried. I'm reading all the road signs to him as they pass. The prairie unfolds around us and we're all sweating.

Up ahead, the broad-shouldered asphalt is liquefied by the sunlight. I'm expecting the car to fall off when it reaches that point where the highway seems to spill into the sky. I know it won't really—it doesn't—and I try not to be disappointed. I am twelve and I don't want to go to Mapleside today anyway.

We've already been driving for two hours and the windshield is covered with bug guts. I think I can smell them. My father swerves onto the shoulder to miss a dead skunk lying in the middle of the road. The smell makes my eyes water. My mother says, "Tomato juice. You have to use tomato juice to get the smell out." I try to imagine washing the whole car with tomato juice.

Around the next corner, there are red flashing lights and a policeman stops the traffic with a flag. We have to wait five minutes while another policeman directs a tow truck backing up to a transport truck which lies upside-down in the ditch like a giant silver beetle stuck on its back, legs waving, helpless. My mother says, "Look the other way, Sylvia. Just in case." Is that blood on the road?

Further on up the highway, my father guides the car left across the oncoming lane and pulls in past two green gas pumps.

"What are we stopping here for?" I ask.

"This gas station's the last before Mapleside," my father says. "Thought you might have to—"

"—freshen up a bit," my mother finishes. Her voice is sudden in the car—I'd thought she was asleep. "I think we could all stand to get out and stretch our legs a bit, don't you?" she continues gaily, feeling for the door handle with one hand, smoothing her dress down over nylon knees with the other, and looking back over her shoulder meaningfully at me.

I think briefly of refusing to get out of the car but realize it would be futile.

I clamber out of the back seat, my bare legs peeling off the hot upholstery like a Band-Aid. My father, lifting the legs of his suit pants and shaking them, stands beside the car and admires it.

"Do you want a pop, Syl?"

I wish he wouldn't call me that.

"No thanks, I'm not thirsty."

I am too.

My father strides purposefully away and my mother says, "Come on, Sylvia. The ladies' is over here, around the side."

I step carefully over the black tube which runs from the gas pumps to the building like a leash. I follow my mother around the side where we find a green door marked LADIES. Below the word is a painted figure, armless, with a white triangular skirt and one thick leg. This is much the way I feel in my new pink dress. My mother made it.

Inside, she runs the tap till the water comes out clear and cold; smelling of must and metal. The porcelain sink is stained brown around the drain. Holding me by the chin, she dabs at my greasy forehead with a wet lace handkerchief.

She says, "I want you to look presentable this afternoon."

I stand there obediently, concentrating on the wall over her shoulder. A hard-backed beetle inches up the tile and disappears through a hole under the wire-covered window. Lucky.

My mother keeps on talking. "Now Sylvia, this is your first funeral." As if I didn't already know that. "Your father and I have discussed it and since you'll have to go to one sooner or later, we figured it would be just that much easier on you if it was someone you weren't really close to—I know how sensitive you can be. You've only met Old Isaac once or twice and he's just a distant relative—the perfect choice, we decided." Her explanation makes me feel resentful and grateful both at once.

She lets go of me, rinses out her handkerchief, and leans close to the spotted mirror, inspecting her own face, which, of course, isn't nearly as dirty as mine.

I wait near the door, watching her draw new red lips on her mouth. The film of water on my forehead evaporates, leaving my skin feeling cooler but tight across the eyebrows. I can feel my white socks sagging around my ankles.

"There we go, we're all set," my mother announces, smacking her lips. She turns to me, smiling, and her front teeth are pink.

"You've got lipstick on your teeth," I say.

She walks past me, opens the door, and says, without looking at me, "Your socks."

As I climb back into the car, my father holds out a bottle of Orange Crush. When my mother isn't looking, I press the cold rippled glass against both cheeks.

A few minutes later, we turn right off the highway onto a gravel road. I am studying the back of my father's bald head, tracing the line between his sunburn and the smooth white dome of his skull. Being an important businessman at home in the city, he almost always wears a hat. But now, in the prairie heat, it's perched on the seat between him and my mother, white straw with a navy band. I keep thinking it will collapse like an angel-food cake. I don't really know what my father's job is, but he's always making appointments and long-distance phone calls.

My mother pulls a magazine out from under the hat and starts reading. But from the way she turns the pages so fast, licking her thumb every time, I can tell she's only looking at the pictures, which all seem to be of well-polished women and cars. Her fingers leave damp rings on the glossy pages. I try to look over her shoulder but she slaps the magazine shut and puts it back, face-down, under the hat.

My father is still driving too fast and we're leaving a cloud of dust behind us. I roll down the window and stick one arm out into the warm wind. I imagine that my skin will be instantly coated with colourless dust just like the brown weeds straggling all down both sides of the road. The wind rushes into the car.

"What're you doing back there?" my mother says, turning in her seat. By now I've got my head halfway out the window, holding my mouth open to the wind.

"Sylvia! You close that window this minute! I don't want all that dust getting in here. Don't you forget we're going to a funeral—this isn't a picnic, you know." We never go on picnics anyway.

I close the window, look at my father, and roll my eyes. Watching the road ahead, his face is sweaty and blank. But I know that once we're alone, he'll shove my shoulder and snicker, saying, "You sure know how to get your mother riled up, little girl."

I turn my back to her and look out the rear window. She probably thinks I'm sulking. Let her. She fiddles with the radio but, impatient, gives up easily and the radio snaps back into silence like a rubber band.

I read the sign: MAPLESIDE—ONE MILE. My mother was born in Mapleside and my parents often go back for weddings, funerals, christenings, and sometimes just to visit. I seem to be related to half the town. The residents of Mapleside, all 816 of them (that's what the next sign says), have always seemed old to me, sand-coloured and dull. I can't imagine them ever living anywhere else. Even their babies look used.

The last time I was in Mapleside was two years ago when we came for the wedding of one of the cousins whose name I can never remember. My father got drunk so we stayed overnight with some more cousins—Ed and Betty Overing and their only daughter, Colleen, who live on a farm west of town.

My cousin Betty Overing is the fattest person I have ever seen. She is the daughter of this Old Isaac whose funeral we're going to this time. But he was still alive then and lived with them on the farm.

Betty's husband, Ed, was still alive then too, for a few more months anyway. Ed was a dairy farmer and always wore a dirty red bandana around his neck. I think he slept in it.

Colleen Overing was ten then, the same age as me. I had to sleep in her room. She kept putting her hands in my hair and whispering, "Pretty, pretty, you're such a pretty." She was always scratching herself and there were little round scabs all over her legs, some still bleeding. For weeks afterwards, I was sure she'd given me lice and I would wake up one morning bald like my father, with all my pretty hair just lying there on the pillow beside me.

That night, when Colleen and I were getting ready for bed, she pushed a chair in front of the door and said, "I have to show you my collection." Which turned out to be a lot of old black-and-white snapshots in a shoebox. She went through them all, one by one.

"This is my dad in the war." A much-younger Ed was standing with four other soldiers in front of a big sign that said: DANGER: DO NOT GO BEYOND THIS POINT: VENEREAL DISEASE. They all had their arms around each other and around a black-haired woman laughing with no shoes on.

"Funny, eh?" Colleen said, poking me in the ribs. I laughed and had no idea whether it was funny or not.

"This is my grandpa killing a pig." Old Isaac had one arm stuck halfway up the pig's rear end. What?

"This is my mom chasing a chicken for supper. That's before I was born. See that bulge there? Well, that turned out to be me. Funny, eh?" Hilarious.

Before we left the next morning to go back to the city, Colleen took me out behind the chicken coop to show me the slough where her father drowned the barn cat's kittens.

This time, before we ever left home, I decided I wasn't going to let her scare me.

My father parks the suburban in front of the Mapleside Anglican Church, my mother puts on her little white gloves, and we go single-file through the churchyard gate. The church had been redone that spring in bright white clapboard and the townspeople had planted red peonies around it like a wreath.

Inside, the sunlight streams milk-coloured through new opaque windows and there are ranks of new blond pews, each with a small brass plaque nailed to the aisle end. We're ushered into a pew near the back by a bony young man whose pants are too short. His forehead is peeling with sunburn or acne. I smile at him just in case he's related but he doesn't smile back. He's no one after all.

The church is packed and people are still coming in, standing three-deep along the back wall. The whole town is here, rustling, sweating, and clearing their throats. My mother leans across me and whispers to my father, "Isn't it lovely so many people turned out?" My father's bald head nods amiably.

The congregation falls silent when the minister steps up to the pulpit. His bushy white eyebrows twitch and he's sweating too. Cocking his head like a dog, he looks out over everyone's head and seems to be talking mostly to the clock on the back wall. I can't hear him for the hum of an electric fan mounted on the wall at the end of our pew. Under the fan is a bouquet of red snapdragons and blue forget-me-nots wilting in an old jam jar of yellow water.

The woman sitting next to my mother keeps shifting around, adjusting a baby in her lap. I can't tell if the baby's a boy or a girl because its face is all scrunched up. We're all waiting for the baby to cry but it falls asleep suddenly and the mother relaxes, smiling gratefully at my mother.

A strange animal howling begins near the front of the church. The minister's mouth just keeps on opening and closing, so I decide this must be part of the funeral, something that happens all the time, one of those things my mother was trying to protect me from.

"That's Betty," my mother whispers behind her gloved hand. "You remember poor Betty." Betty has been "poor Betty" for a year and a half now, ever since her husband, Ed, went out behind the chicken coop one morning after milking and shot himself in the head.

I squirm forward, trying to get a look at her. She's still fat, maybe even fatter, and the rolls at the base of her neck wobble when she cries. I'd expected that grief would somehow make you hollow. Her shiny black dress is pulled tight across her shoulders and her bluish flesh bulges out around her sleeves. My mother pushes me back into my seat.

A faint smell of cow dung drifts back to me from the man in front. His head is nodding and I can't tell if he's sleeping or agreeing. A blue fly lands on his neck and just sits there.

Then everybody stands up and sings clumsily, picking their way through an unfamiliar hymn. My mother is singing too, her throat tight and muscular like a fist. My father stands up but doesn't sing. I've never heard him sing. At the front, all the women in the choir look bloated in their royal-blue robes. One warbling voice stands out above the other average singers. They're all singing with their eyes closed. The congregation slurs along behind them like boys in hip-waders.

From where I'm standing, I can just see one corner of the coffin. It takes me a minute to figure out that's what it is. Cool grey like seagull wings, its sides are studded with silver scrolls. It's closed and I'm disappointed because I thought I'd finally get a chance to see a real live corpse. Then again, my mother probably wouldn't have let me look anyway.

At some clandestine signal I seem to have missed, everyone starts to leave. Betty is still crying into a red bandana squashed up under her nose. Her other hand flutters at her black lace collar. Colleen is walking right behind her.

Outside, the congregation stands around in loose bunches. They're all shifting from one bunch to another or from one foot to the other in the heat. The women are talking and the men are batting at flies. Some are already making their way to their cars for the mile-long procession to the cemetery west of town. A knot of black-suited boys is moving towards the back of the church. Betty stands on the steps with Colleen and the minister, who is patting both of them alternately. Colleen stands sway-backed, watching the boys go through the back gate and out behind the church. They're all patting their pockets, looking for matches. Betty is managing a smile for the minister. I'm trailing my mother all over the yard.

"Come on, Sylvia," she says, steering me towards a circle of women who are all wearing loose flowered shifts and sensible shoes. "We have to be sociable at least. Your father's already gone to the car." I can tell she feels slighted by this.

As we approach, one of the women backs away from the group and exclaims, "Why, Natalie, I didn't see you in church. And is this your little Sylvia? My goodness, how she's grown! Dorothy, come and look at little Sylvia," she calls to one of the other women, as if I'm not really there or can't hear what she's saying. The other women draw more closely around my mother, delighted with her blue city suit and dyed-to-match peau de soie pumps. I feel proud of her.

I can see Betty and Colleen alone on the steps now, the minister circulating through the yard. Betty is gazing around vacantly while Colleen peers up at the bleached sky as if watching for rain or geese. Her black sateen dress is gathered in tight at the waist under a glossy red sash and a white paper rose. Her yellow hair is piled in uneven bunches at the back of her head. My own dark hair is curly and short because my mother doesn't believe in long hair on children. I feel clean and neat.

Colleen sees me watching her as they come single-file down the steps.

My mother moves away from the women and says, "There's poor Betty. We must go and give our condolences, Sylvia." Betty and Colleen stop, as if they're waiting for us.

"Oh, poor Betty dear, I'm so sorry," my mother croons, pressing one cheek up against Betty's. I wonder how long it will be before she dares take out her handkerchief and wipe the dirt away. "Your father was such a good man, Betty, so kind, we all loved him. His death is a blow to us all." No matter what happens, my mother always knows what to say.

"But Betty dear, we really must be going now," my mother says cheerfully. "Roy's waiting in the car. We'll drop by the farm before we head home. Will that be all right? I've brought you some things, a carrot cake and some bread-and-butter pickles. I'll see you then, dear." Betty sniffs and nods vaguely. Colleen ignores us both.

Before my mother can get to the gate, another group of women—younger relatives this time, some holding prune-faced babies and all of them smiling—has surrounded her.

"Natalie, how are you?"

"Natalie, what a lovely suit!"

"Natalie, your hair, I love the colour! I wish George would let me . . ."

I start back to the car alone.

"Hi, Sylvia." It's Colleen, and her voice is an unmistakable challenge. She never did like me. I just knew it.

She stands on the gravel walkway and puts both hands on her hips. Her hair is coming loose, hanging down her back in loops.

I am very polite. "Hello, Colleen. How are you?" My mother would have been proud of me.

"How's yourself?"

"Fine, thank you."

"What are *you* doing here?"

"Well, I'm here for the funeral—just like everybody else." But I know that's not quite what she means.

"He was my grandfather, you know," she says, jutting out her chin. This is some kind of accusation or dare.

Before I can think of an answer, she tells me, "He lived with us for years and years, you know, all my life. Every morning he sat across the table from me, eating porridge 'cause he had no teeth, just gums. They were always bleeding. He said he didn't need teeth. I have pictures of him when he was young—lots—in my collection. I always knew he would die."

Frightened by her outburst, I have no idea why she's telling me all this—she doesn't even like me. I suddenly hate my pink dress. It should have been black. Why didn't my mother tell me funerals only come in black?

"Did you cry in there?"

I shake my head. No, I didn't cry. I wasn't even listening.

My mother calls to me from the car. "Come on, Sylvia. Hurry up or we'll lose our place in line."

I start towards her but then I stop to dig for a nickel I think I see half-buried in the sand below the gate. I sift my fingers through dust, dead grass, and little stones. My mother calls again and I reach up to brush off the dirt. There was no nickel anyway. In circles I rub the sand in. The dust drifts brown down the front of my dress.

When I get to the car, I can see Colleen behind me, swinging on the gate.

NOTES FOR A TRAVELOGUE

(1978)

IT'S RAINING the morning we pull out of town. We stop at the grocery store to buy juice and fruit for the first day of our trip. The usual Saturday shoppers haven't been put off by the weather. Husbands shrug their jackets up over their heads and run recklessly towards their cars, aiming themselves with keys held outstretched in one hand. Mothers scoop up their babies like footballs and jog across the street to the cars which are now ready for them, doors open, motors running.

We drive all day, passing through the rain and out into the sunshine. Actually, my husband Grant does the driving and I do the passengering. At first I feel guilty about not even offering to take a turn at the wheel, but what's the point? It's his car and he never lets me drive it far anyway. Just as well. Whenever I'm behind the wheel and he's there beside me, the car sputters ominously, convulses, jerks, stalls. My feet get tangled in the floor mat. Grant just sighs and sweats.

We've never had a holiday together before, even though we've been married for nearly two years now. Grant usually goes off alone while I stay behind, patient, understanding, watching for postcards and drawing red and blue felt-pen lines on the map he leaves me. He once admitted that he likes to think of me alone in the house with nothing to do but wait for him to come back home. I didn't contradict him. We have no children.

Some people have a baby to try and keep their marriage together. Other people buy a new house, build a rumpus room in the basement, put blue wallpaper up in the bathroom, buy a pair of his and hers snowmobiles. We're going on a week's holiday together.

The landscape we pass through is all new to me and I discover that cactus and rattlesnakes do grow in this country after all. Some teacher years ago in public school told me it could never happen here. My husband smiles at me in smug congratulation—I've finally figured out what he, of course, has known for years.

Once it gets dark, we pull into the first campground we come to, breaking away from the hypnotic bracelet of bright tourist towns strung up and down both sides of the highway. The place feels large and vacant as we pitch our tiny tent in the dark. Waving the flashlight around and shivering, I know I'm not being much help, but if Grant is annoyed, at least he doesn't say anything. Maybe I'm being too hard on him.

Morning reveals a white Winnebago squatting just down the way, fat with sleeping strangers. There seems to be ten or twelve of them, with interchangeable heads, emerging one by one in various states of half-dress. The children race down to the lake in a pack while the adults put the coffee on. Then they holler blindly back and forth at each other through the tree cover—warnings, discoveries, the breakfast menu. While I'm waiting my turn in the fibreglass outhouse, a white poodle licks amiably at my ankles. Grant pumps up the Coleman stove and breaks eggs seriously into a metal bowl.

We continue driving west. Fruit stands sprout up lopsided on both sides of the highway. The lakes here are slender and smooth, like legs, and the hills are lumpy, in multiple shades of burnt-out brown.

Grant would drive all day without stopping, I think, even though we began this trip determined to take our time, dispense with schedules (I didn't even bring my wristwatch) and dabble in the countryside as we went along. When I ask though, we can stop for photographs, lunch, a Coke, a toilet. While he waits for me, Grant kicks all four tires to check the pressure and picks dead bugs off the headlights.

For the last fifty miles there are cars on all sides of us, gathering us up, willing or not, into their desperate push onward, forward, ever forward, lemmings to the sea. The line of cars, four abreast in the rain, is like a train, unable to travel anywhere but on this track on which it's been set down.

We take the early evening ferry across the strait. The vibrating drone of the engines overpowers the motion of the water below us. I, who have never been on a ferry before, marvel at the seasoned sea commuters who space themselves courteously along the olive green benches, sip coffee, read the paper, play solitaire and hearts as if nothing is happening. Their kids and their cars are all waiting faithfully on the far shore. The boat pulls its way through the black water and I stand out on the deck till I'm soaked. This amuses Grant who hugs me pleasantly and leads me back inside.

We set up our camp that night in the middle of a twilight cedar forest. Grant scrounges around for dry wood and manages to build a respectable fire. We drag two stumps up as close to the flames as we can bear. Through the smell of smoking cedar, Grant with shining eyes says, "I don't know what it is about campfires, but they sure are hard to take sometimes."

No matter what happens next, we will always have this. No matter what I do, my husband, it seems, won't quite assume the villain's role the way I think he should.

We spend the next day exploring the forest, after discovering that all the edges of the ocean are owned now, and cannot be reached by the uninitiated. We cannot get down to the sea and content ourselves instead with admiring the rotund trees, moss dangling like green sleeves from their branches. The trees at home are skinny and vicious—they creak and come down in the wind, smashing windows, high wires and car roofs.

It's October and there's nobody else around. The spongy ground is quilted with maple leaves. It's hard to tell when the rain has stopped because the trees still spit down water like bird droppings when we brush accidentally up against them. We hold hands without thinking.

I've never spent seven straight days and nights with my husband before and I'm not sure yet that I like it much. Here there aren't the normal spaces furnished by his going off to work every day, by my going out to the grocery store or for a Sunday afternoon stroll with my friends and their babies, by my getting into the bathtub before bed and lolling around till I'm all wrinkled, all relaxed. Here there's no routine, here we have nothing to go on.

I don't think Grant wants to get rid of me exactly, but I sense him expecting something from me, a suggestion, a decision, a show of independence.

I guess I'm supposed to say,

"Come back for me in an hour or two, I'm just going to jaunt up this little mountain here."

Or,

"Come back for me in a year or two, I'm just going to fly up to Baffin Island and find myself."

But even when we go into town (Blue Hills, it's called) to pick up more eggs, some back bacon, milk, a green pepper, I trail around the grocery store behind him, afraid somehow of letting him out of my sight. Afraid for him or afraid for me? I don't know. If I told him this fear, he would say,

"Sharon, you're neurotic."

And I would say,

"No, I'm not, I'm not, I am *not* neurotic."

And he would say,

"Now you're getting hysterical."

My husband thinks I'm always on the verge of something—hysteria, neurosis, tears, breaking down. He calls me "the wife" when he thinks I'm not listening.

Late the next evening, we take a drive through the town of Blue Hills, sucking on the ice cream cones we waited in line to get and speculating about the lives of the strangers we see framed by their yellow-lit windows, caught in suspended animation with the curtains still open as we cruise through the rain like spies.

The main street of Blue Hills has all the shops and businesses down the west side, the strait on the east. Ragged wooden docks poke into the water like tongues. There are lights further out, another island. I think I see two people on the very end of the longest dock, dangling their feet in the water, but then again they may be only shadows.

I'm convinced that our extended silence is the comfortable kind common to marriage until Grant says,

"This isn't working out. Let's head for home in the morning."

This is something I already know, but not something I want to hear. I have to agree with him though.

We decide to spend our last night in the only motel in Blue Hills—it is, in fact, named "The Only Motel" in blue and white neon. Grant will not admit that he enjoys the idea—maybe he doesn't, who knows? He goes through the whole procedure of checking in, unlocking the room, dragging our wet packs and tent inside, as if it were some final, shameful concession to weakness, as if being in the motel instead of the tent proves we just aren't strong enough to suffer enough after all. I, for one, am glad to be here. I think my socks were starting to mildew.

I've stayed in a motel with my husband once before and already know there is nothing intrinsically erotic about motel rooms. We go to bed early and watch coloured TV. Grant keeps jumping up to fiddle with the fine tuning and then falls asleep while the news is on. The sheets and pillowcases are yellowed and smell reassuringly of industrial-strength laundry soap.

In the miniature bathroom there are many little bars of odourless soap, glasses in white paper bags, enough gold towels for ten people, and a strip of paper across the toilet seat that reads, "For Your Protection." In the morning I shower first and the water runs cold on Grant. He is an unlucky person.

I suppose we will stay together a while yet, my husband and I. But the end is inevitable, if only because he thinks so. He wants the end to be graceful and friendly, generous. He has his fantasies too—I can see that now. I suspect though, that we will hang onto each other until the alternatives have all been tried and the complications have set in. For now though it is simple. But Grant will never let me walk away feeling broken, self-righteous and sad. He will not let me sacrifice myself or anything else for this love, he wants me to be strong. He wants me to walk away from him silently, with a faraway but pleasant philosophical look in my eye.

Driving home will take longer than leaving. Anxious to arrive, I will pass the hours wondering how much mail is waiting for us, conjuring the sheets, tablecloth, drapes, new carpet, cat purring deep back in her throat like a pigeon, everything occurring and recurring in safe clean patterns. Grant will drive on steadily through the rain.

When we finally get there and the door is unlocked and we are inside, I will say,

"Why did we come home so soon? There's nothing for us here."

Wanting only for my husband to tell me that there is. But he, being a clumsy liar, will say,

"I hate to see you disappointed, but I knew you would be, Sharon."

I cannot find the energy to unpack, will rummage uselessly around in my pack while the cat winds herself around me in an excess of emotion. Without water for a week, the plants have all gone dead and brown on the ends.

This is not unpleasant because I'm already starting to know what I'm going to do.

CRIMES OF PASSION

(1979)

JACK MARSH didn't like parties much but he went to this one anyway because he'd been out of town, working up in Edmonton, for two weeks and because Benjamin Kozak was his best friend. When he got to Ben's, late, everyone was in the living room dancing, drinks in hands, in front of the picture window. Most of the dancers were women. Leaping and bright-coloured, their reflections were like flames in the glass. Beyond them, outside, it was snowing thickly. The snowflakes were like moths around the streetlights.

Ben's new house wasn't finished yet and, without curtains, baseboards, or carpet, the room looked raw. Jack thought Ben would never get the place finished now that his wife, Carol, had left him. Jack thought of Ben as a soft, slow-moving man whom Carol, with her loud voice, plush body, and gourmet cooking, had quite consciously spoiled, mastered, and then abandoned. Now Ben was always giving parties, filling up the unfinished house with young women and beer.

Ben, who seemed to be dancing with all the women at once, caught sight of Jack and wiggled his beer bottle at him, gesturing towards the kitchen.

Jack found Emily Lipton in the kitchen.

He supposed it was inevitable that they would keep meeting like this, at parties, on the street, in the grocery store, for years to come. They'd been together, in one form or another, for three years and he assumed their lives would always be connected somehow, if only by coincidence. Even when they'd first split up two months ago, he didn't think, Now I'll never see her again. Aurora was a small town and they had all the same friends and it never occurred to him that one or the other of them might move away someday. Jack thought they'd be good friends when they were old.

Emily stood with her back to him, looking out the window. Jack couldn't tell if she was trying to see out or was merely admiring her face in the glass. He knew that her new lover, Tom, lived right across the back lane. Carol had told him.

He said, "Carol told me you'd be here."

Without turning, Emily said, "She told me you'd be here too."

Jack helped himself to a handful of pretzels and a slippery cocktail wiener. On the counter, there were also ripple chips, a bag of Oreo cookies, and a green tin of dill chip dip. He couldn't help thinking that if Carol was still around, they'd all be having yogurt dip with chilled fresh vegetables, camembert and brie, liverwurst and lox. Carol used to give great parties. People just naturally gravitated around her and she thrived on it. If Carol was still around, the party would be in the kitchen. She was always cooking something that smelled good and would feed everybody. Along with the food, Carol dispensed advice, recipes, backrubs, and the perfect wine. She was always the centre of everything. The house organized itself around her whether she was there or not. And when she wasn't there, Jack thought, everyone seemed to be expecting her to arrive any minute now.

"How is Carol these days?" he asked. He and Emily always talked about Carol. She was the buffer zone between them. Jack leaned against the stove.

"Doing very well," Emily said. "She was sorry she couldn't make it tonight but she thought it was too soon."

Carol Kozak was Emily's best friend. When she left Ben three weeks ago, Carol had moved in with Emily temporarily. Whenever Jack and Ben talked about being left (which was seldom), they were both always looking for someone else to blame. Usually Ben blamed Emily and Jack blamed Carol, but sometimes they switched it around.

Emily finally turned to face Jack. She was eating a banana.

"You're eating a banana."

She looked down at it.

"Emily, I just don't understand you."

She was still looking at it.

"You never ate bananas when you were with me. Emily, you *hate* bananas." This was some kind of accusation. They were always accusing each other of something.

"Oh, Jack. People change, you know."

"Well, I haven't." He was proud of this, proud to think that his life was just the same without her. He saw no reason to change. He thought this proved something but he hadn't figured out what yet.

Emily was angry now. She said, "Jack, this is ridiculous," and threw the banana peel in the sink. But then she was already smiling at him again.

Her moods were changing too quickly, shifting like sand so Jack couldn't keep track of them. Jack had no patience with moods, his own or other people's. He admired consistency, not eccentricity, which made him uncomfortable because he could never be sure what would happen next. This was something new about Emily too. He used to know exactly how she'd react to anything he might choose to say. He liked to think he'd never intentionally used this to hurt her. Jack thought of himself as a noble man and he wondered why they couldn't have a casual conversation anymore. He thought of the last few months they'd been together and how every day there'd been something else, another emotional complication, one more layer to add to the pile. Now there were more things they *couldn't* talk about than things they could.

He stepped towards her, reaching awkwardly across and behind her, feeling for the light switch. This was the closest together they'd been since she left him and he regretted it instantly. He was afraid she'd touch him. Emily had always been the one to touch first, kiss first, touch again, rubbing the same spot on his back until it went numb. Jack was afraid that if she touched him now, even accidentally, he would pull away and she would be hurt. He thought he didn't want to hurt her. But she didn't touch him.

Jack flipped on the overhead light and retreated back to the stove. They'd been talking in the dark and suddenly it had reminded him of being in bed with Emily and she always wanted to talk before they went to sleep and he would be too tired and she would tease him, saying she'd had a deprived childhood because she was an only child and she had no sisters to talk to in the dark. Sometimes she was laughing and petting him while she talked. But he would fall asleep anyway, sometimes right in the middle of a sentence, and then she would be mad and go sit in the living room and smoke cigarettes for an hour or two. Once, she went out for a walk at three in the morning even though she was afraid of the dark, but Jack was sleeping and he never knew until she told him and then she never did it again.

The fluorescent light was comforting. Jack looked at Emily more closely. She was sipping her beer and concentrating on the music or something else. She would never again, Jack realized, make things easy for him. She was wearing a baggy cream-coloured blouse and a long billowing skirt, dark blue patterned with intricate flowers and leaves, made of that puckered cotton that always made Jack think of incense and wheat germ. She used to wear plaid shirts and jeans. Whenever Jack thought of Emily, she was wearing a red plaid shirt and faded jeans.

Sometimes he used to tell her how much he admired women who looked like *real* women. Emily never seemed to know what he was talking about so then he would point out certain women on the street as examples. These women were always wearing summer dresses, gold earrings, sheer nylons, and high-heeled sandals that made their calf muscles stand out like plums. Sometimes Jack imagined how it would feel to have a woman like that walking beside him, her perfume coming to him in subtle waves, her nylons rustling as her high-heels clicked on the concrete. But really Jack thought these women were too good for him. He thought of them as "queens." Emily and most women were what he called "utility grade." This second group was much larger than the first. Queens were women he wanted but was afraid of. Utility grades were women he didn't want very badly but they were, he thought, friendly, manageable, and grateful.

Jack used to say, "Emily, I want a real woman, a feminine woman. You could be one if you tried." He didn't understand why this made her so mad.

He meant it as encouragement, not insult. Emily seemed so unsure of herself, of how she wanted to be—he figured she was just waiting to be shown. He thought of Emily as the kind of person who was always being given advice just because she always looked like she was asking for it, whether she was or not. This still felt true.

Now it seemed like Emily was still wanting him to have an opinion of her. The long skirt clung to her thighs, her arms and neck were naked. Maybe now she wanted him to admire her from afar.

It had only been two months but Emily's hair looked much longer, falling loose and tangled down her back like dark vines. Jack had always liked it long (it had been that way when they first met) so he said, "I like your hair. New clothes too?"

"Yes, and I made the skirt myself." Emily turned half around to make the skirt spin out and then drape around her legs.

Jack fished around in the fridge and came up with two more cold beer. He opened them and handed one to Emily, resisting the urge to point out the fact that she'd never sewed when they were together. He pictured her hunched over the sewing machine, pins in her mouth and yellow threads in her hair, teeth clenching and unclenching as she jammed the fabric through. This, he remembered, had something to do with her childhood too. Emily and her mother, Fern, who could sew everything perfectly, were always fighting about it. There was some long, involved, and emotional story about a brown jumper that he couldn't remember anymore.

Jack didn't know what to make of Emily's parents, Mr. and Mrs. Lipton. The summer they came from Ontario to visit Emily, it was hot every day for two weeks and Mrs. Lipton sat out in the back yard with her feet in a bucket of cold water because her ankles were swelling with the heat. Arthur Lipton was just quiet and nervous all the time. Emily was always telling Jack how wonderful her parents were, but when they were all together, they never seemed to get along. Jack couldn't understand any of this.

He thought his own parents were perfect. They lived in Edmonton and were quite well off. Mr. Marsh was a lawyer and owned three large apartment buildings. Jack couldn't understand why Mr. and Mrs. Lipton, who certainly weren't rich, were always spoiling Emily even though she'd been away from home, living in Alberta, for five years. They kept sending her money and big boxes filled with fancy towels, canned lobster, and electrical appliances. Jack's parents never gave him money or presents anymore, except at Christmas. They'd brought him up to be an independent man. Whenever he had to work up in Edmonton, he stayed at their house but he paid daily room and board and did his own ironing. Mr. and Mrs. Marsh didn't like Emily and their opinion was important to Jack.

Now he said, "It's a pretty skirt, yes, very nice," but he thought it didn't suit her.

A round woman in black satin pants walked between them. People kept coming into the kitchen like this, getting more beer, more pretzels, or just passing through on their way to the bathroom. It was, Jack thought, like being on a train and he and Emily were talking only because they'd happened to get on at the same stop.

It wasn't that Jack wanted Emily back. It was just that he didn't want her to change. He wanted her to be always the way she had been when they were together. He didn't want to think of her going out and buying bananas, yards of blue cotton, a sewing machine, all these things that had nothing to do with him. The changes in Emily made him think the woman he'd known somehow wasn't true anymore, never had been. He couldn't decide which Emily was the real one and he still needed to know. Sometimes he thought she'd been putting on an act for three years but other times he thought she was putting on an act now. There was no way of knowing her anymore.

"How does Carol like her new job?" Jack asked. Carol was always starting a new job. This one was with a travel agent. The last one had been with a firm of lawyers and the one before that with a real estate agency. Carol's jobs never lasted more than six months. She always quit. Jack thought she was irresponsible, not exactly shiftless, but sadly careless in shaping her life. He and Emily used to argue about Carol. He would say Carol was a bad influence and then Emily would defend her fiercely, ending lamely with, "Well, she's my best friend, you know." To which Jack would reply, "But that doesn't make her a good person." He thought this was obvious but sometimes it made Emily cry.

Jack's opinion of Carol, however, didn't stop him from confiding in her now and pumping her for information about Emily. He would inspect and analyze his feelings out loud for Carol, knowing full well that she would, in turn, relay them on to Emily. Once he said to Carol, "If she'd given me half a chance, I might have married her." Later Carol said that Emily, when she heard this, said, "What's that supposed to mean?"

Emily was looking out the window again. It irritated Jack that she wasn't paying attention to him, even though what he was saying wasn't really important at all. He wondered if she'd always had this habit of drifting in and out of conversation with him.

"How does Carol like her new job?" he asked again.

Ben came into the kitchen for another beer. He was rumpled and damp from the dancing. "Does Carol have a new job?" he asked.

"She's working for a travel agent now," Jack said.

"She thinks this job will take her somewhere," Emily said.

"She always thinks that," Ben said gloomily. "What she can't understand is that no job and nobody will take her anywhere. She just has to get there all by herself like the rest of us."

Jack hated this new philosophical tone of Ben's. He was seeing a psychologist once a week and sounding more and more profound after each visit, more serenely sad, more proud of being so hurt. Jack believed that there are some things that should never be said out loud because they give too much away.

Ben had his back to them as he rummaged in the fridge. Emily raised her eyebrows at Jack who instantly resented her attempt at conspiracy. She was always doing this, drawing people to her with promises of intimacy and secrets. She did this to everyone, especially other women. Jack thought she had no sense of discrimination.

When they used to go grocery shopping together on Saturday mornings, Emily was always stopping to say, "Hello, how are you?" to somebody. These other shoppers were mostly women, Emily's own age or older. They almost always had something attached to them: shopping carts, strollers, shy husbands, assorted children. One woman, her name was Betty Champagne, kept her little boy on a leash. She said he was hyperactive. Another woman, Laurie Dorion, was pregnant with her fourth child. She always said, loudly, "I'll sure be glad to drop this thing. Never trust an IUD or a man either." Laurie had red hair and was always wearing a green sunsuit. She looked like an olive. Jack would wait beside the cart, sighing and folding and unfolding his arms, while Emily conducted these capsule conversations between the Corn Flakes and the Kotex, whispering and gossiping and making lunch dates.

Now Jack, by way of refusing Emily's invitation to take a side, said, "Oh, you know Carol."

"Where is she tonight?" Ben asked, emerging from the fridge.

"I don't know."

Jack could see that Emily was still a lousy liar and he thought it served her right to be uncomfortable. She'd changed everything for all of them. Once they'd all been friends together, he and Emily, Carol and Ben. But now they were all sleeping in different camps. He was sleeping alone, Ben was sleeping around, Carol was sleeping on Emily's couch, and Emily was sleeping with Tom. Carol said Tom had a waterbed.

A sharp-breasted girl in a pink sweater came into the kitchen and jiggled all around Ben until he went back into the living room to dance with her some more. As he disappeared again into the music, Ben winked back at Jack who raised an eyebrow at Emily who smiled harmlessly at the fridge and said, "Her name's Marlene."

Somebody turned up the music and Jack could see more dancers galloping around the living room. Everybody seemed to be wearing fewer clothes.

Jack turned back to Emily and looked out the window with her. Tom's house was all in darkness.

"He's not there," Jack said.

"I know."

"Where is he?"

"I don't know."

Emily had been seeing Tom for just over a month. Carol kept Jack informed. Carol thought Emily and Tom were perfect for each other.

Emily and Jack had never talked about Tom but Emily had a clever way of slipping in his name at random moments of conversation. Jack never knew if she did this to hurt him or to assure him that she was all right. He also never knew which way it made him feel.

Jack knew Tom to see him but that was all. Tom was an accountant and that meant he was always wearing a suit—brown, grey, blue, a black one once, with colour-coordinated ties, shirts, and shoes. Although Jack expected that women should just naturally spend all their money on clothes, he was suspicious of men who might be doing the same thing. But Tom drove an old yellow pickup truck and Jack liked the truck.

"How are things with you and Tom?" It seemed all right to ask this question but Emily looked surprised.

Carol said Tom was good to Emily. There was some suggestion of a drinking problem but Tom was trying to get on top of it. Carol said one time Tom was in a car accident while he was out with an older woman named Joan. Tom was drunk and he drove off the road and into a tree. They walked six miles home on the highway because Tom was afraid the police would find him. Joan was only wearing summer sandals and Tom took off his mitts and put them on her feet. Carol said, "Some women are just never prepared for anything." Carol said Emily went back with Tom the next day to help pull the truck out of the ditch. And then she went with him to the police station and told them he'd hit a patch of glare ice and missed the corner.

"Good, we're really good," Emily said now. "We're talking about taking a trip to Mexico. I applied for my passport already. Tom's been there twice before, he has friends there now, and he says I'll just love it."

That wasn't what Jack was asking.

Emily went on. "He's colour-blind, you know. And when we go shopping for things for the trip, he's always hollering across the store at me to come and tell him the colours of everything. He laughs about it but I always think that even when I do tell him a shirt is brown, he still doesn't know what I mean. He'll never be able to see what we see."

Jack said, "I can see your car at his house from my back window." Jack lived just around the corner, half a block down. "Sometimes I drive by that way just to see if you're there. And then I'm disappointed if you are and if you're not."

Afterwards, Jack would try and remember how many beer he'd had because he would think that he had to be at least half drunk to admit such a thing.

Emily said, "One night at Tom's I couldn't sleep, I don't like waterbeds, and I was just lying there watching car lights on the ceiling. I sat up to look out and it was your car going by."

In a while, when Emily went to the closet for her coat, Jack went too.

She said, "You don't have to do this anymore."

"What?"

"Leave when I do."

"But I want to."

"All right then."

Jack realized that they'd missed the whole party. They'd always been this way at parties. Emily used to accuse him of never having figured out how to have a good time.

He waited outside on the porch while Emily put on her boots and scarf. Tom's house was still dark. The snow was so heavy it made the darkness look white.

When Emily came out, Jack said, "He's still not there."

Emily said, "I thought he'd be home by now."

Jack was watching the snow fall on her dark hair. He would have given her a ride home but she didn't ask. There had been something earlier about her car getting a new muffler. He knew she was afraid of the dark but there she was, smiling and waving and walking away from him anyway, and he was already feeling better. In the morning he would go skiing.

HISTORIES

(1980)

ANNE and Peter Dickson used to live in southern Ontario. Then they went west to Alberta, just like a lot of other people. They settled in Lairdmore, a small town in the Rockies. Peter said Lairdmore was a boom town where there would always be work and they would always be happy.

Peter, who was a carpenter, built them a house in the new subdivision at the south end of town. In this part of Lairdmore, all the streets were named after indigenous birds and animals: Porcupine Place, Fox Avenue, Sparrow Street, Marmot Boulevard.

Anne and Peter lived on Cougar Crescent where all the houses were new. The street usually smelled of fresh paint and of wood burning in all the new stone fireplaces. Most of the houses were either white aluminum siding or white stucco and had a sled, a stroller or a German shepherd parked in the front yard. In the winter, each yard was bisected by a precisely shovelled sidewalk. Often there were small children playing on the snowbanks and the snow would fall back onto the sidewalk in chunks. The families in these houses were all young and they all knew each other. They compared their mortgage payments, their children's report cards, and their grocery bills.

One or another of the wives was always having a dinner party, an affair, or a minor operation. They all appeared to be more or less content.

Soon after they moved in, Anne sent a photograph of herself and Peter standing in front of their new house back to her family in Ontario. Her mother mailed back a batch of recipes and wrote, *Annie, you're so thin, so thin I wouldn't know you. The house is nice though.* Nobody else except Peter called her Annie anymore—Annie was obviously somebody else, a much fatter person.

In Ontario, Anne had worked for a small commercial photography studio, Eberhardt and Associates. They shot weddings, postcards, family portraits and baby pictures. When she and Peter moved to Lairdmore, Anne decided it was time to try a different approach. Peter teased her about wanting to be an artist. (All the aspiring artists they'd known in Ontario were convinced they could become "real" artists if only they were given half a chance. "Half a chance" usually meant being spared the need to earn a living, cook hamburgers, and clean the toilet.) But Anne knew that Peter was proud of her.

She carried her camera with her everywhere. She thought there would never be an end to the number of things in Lairdmore that should be photographed. She took up cross-country skiing because she saw it as a way to get closer to what she wanted to see. She could not have explained precisely what it was that she was after, but she assumed that it, like most things of value, would never be found by ordinary or easy means.

At first Anne limited her skiing to several afternoons a week on the Lairdmore Golf Course. After two weeks she felt competent enough to attempt something more challenging. One morning just after Peter had left for work, Anne packed herself a lunch and put on her new down parka, her grey wool knickers, and a pair of thick red socks. With her black hair spurting out from under a tight yellow toque, her head looked like a fat sunflower.

Carrying her skis, poles, and a small backpack which held ski wax, her lunch, her camera and extra film, Anne left the house and headed for the far edge of town. The morning cold was solid and extreme, like a capsule forming itself around her body. The snow crunched under her boots like broken shells and her scarf swooped out behind her in the wind.

It was still early and the streets were quiet. In most of the houses Anne passed, only one or two rooms somewhere near the back were lit, kitchens in the morning, warm yellow squares. All the furnaces were on, waving flags of white smoke. Frosted-up cars, still plugged in, were warming up in the driveways, disappearing inside their own exhaust clouds.

Walking backwards against the wind, Anne watched thin clouds unravelling around the mountains, shredding on the high peaks. The snow and the immaculate morning light brought out every formation of the rock, outlining each crack and knob in precise detail.

Lairdmore sat in an oval-shaped river valley, tightly ringed by mountains on all sides. Sometimes, when Anne could no longer imagine a road actually coiling its way through all that rock, she thought of the valley as an island with no way to get off. This was not an unpleasant feeling.

In about fifteen minutes, Anne had reached the far edge of town. Close to the coal mine that had brought Lairdmore into being a hundred years before, there were no sidewalks and no street names here. The houses, which were owned by the mine and leased to the miners, were all made of wood, improvised, unstructured—jazz music. The yards were full of assorted accumulations—gutted cars, old tires, a bathtub still up on legs and filled with tin cans and rusty gears. Anne thought she could smell something like kerosene and bread mould mixed together but then decided she was only imagining it.

She walked past one house with two green wooden lawn chairs still sitting out in front, mounded with snow and frozen to the ground. She stopped to pet a round black cat that came rubbing around her ankles, purring, its whiskers stiff and white with frost. It looked like a walrus.

The miners' houses were black with coal dust, another accumulation, one they would never be able to get rid of now. The windward sides of the trees were black too and the miners' children might grow up believing that trees everywhere were supposed to be black on one side. The mine itself was out of sight, around the corner beyond a dense group of evergreens. A square blue engine pulling twenty coal cars behind it was switching from the main track onto the spur, squealing on the cold rails.

Just beyond the last house, Anne stopped to wait for a ride up the gravel road to Bridgetown.

Peter disapproved of her hitch-hiking. "You never know what you're letting yourself in for, Annie," he'd warned several times. "I really wish you wouldn't. It's not safe, or smart either. There's a lot of sick people in this world." Peter expected nothing but the worst from strangers.

He also disapproved of her skiing alone. When she'd told him several days before of her plan to ski up to Bridgetown, he said, "What if you fall and break a leg? Or you could get lost, you know. I'd never find you. And there are wild animals up there too, you know, bears. I'd worry about you, Annie, out there all alone." Peter expected nothing but the worst from solitude.

He would disapprove of this day altogether.

He didn't disapprove of *everything* she did—only, he said, of those things that caused him to worry. (Peter seemed to think that all this busy worrying was something you just naturally took on when you got married.) The things that caused him to worry were numerous. His fear for her was sequential and cumulative. He stock-piled new dangers and flashed them out at her triumphantly. It became remarkably dangerous to go to the laundromat alone at night, to leave the house unlocked when she went out to the post office, to be friendly to strangers and stray dogs.

In Ontario, Anne had been afraid of everything too. The fear had been a gauzy vague discomfort and the bad dreams were persistent. In them she was always hiding, running, crying, or dying in unnatural and imaginative ways. The dreams had not recurred in Lairdmore. They might just as well have belonged to somebody else.

Anne turned her back to the wind and pressed one mitten to her left cheek where a patch of skin the size of a quarter was growing numb with the cold. Two or three cars passed by without stopping. Finally a lop-sided pickup truck pulled over and stopped. The truck was mottled black and primer red, burning oil in a dense blue cloud behind.

The driver pushed open the passenger door as Anne ran towards the truck, her ski poles banging against her shins. "Where you heading, miss?"

"Up to the Bridgetown Road," Anne said, leaning into the warmth of the cab and juggling her skis.

"Well, hop in then," the old man said amiably. "I'm going up that way myself. Just throw your gear in back."

Anne slid her skis and poles up over the tailgate which was green and tied shut with a twist of rusted baling wire.

She got into the cab, slapping her black leather mitts together like a seal. "Cold," she said, ducking her chin down inside the collar of her jacket.

"Cold, damn cold," the old man agreed vigorously. He was packed in tight behind the steering wheel in an army green parka. His breath had condensed in beads on the bright orange scarf that was wound several times around his neck. It might have been holding his head on. "I'm Herb Murchie," he said.

"Pleased to meet you, Mr. Murchie. I'm Anne Dickson."

"Oh, just call me Herb. Mr. Murchie's my pa and he's been dead twenty years now. I'm just Herb." He let go of the steering wheel to shake her hand. Wrapped in a double wool mitten, his hand felt like a pile of old socks. "You must be new in town."

"I've been here for over a year now," Anne said. But she knew that to the old-timers even families who'd lived in Lairdmore for ten years or more were still "the new folks up the road aways." And the old-timers were all tangibly proud of the position they held in Lairdmore, which was quickly becoming a community of newcomers, most of them wandering in from Ontario and other parts east.

"Myself, I been here for seventy years," Herb said. "When I was a kid, weren't more than twenty houses here altogether. Just that, the mine and the company store. My pa was mine foreman and my cousin Jake, he ran the store. Stole licorice from old Jake. Never amounted to much of a thief though, I was always getting caught with black teeth and a stash in my sock drawer." He laughed and offered Anne a sticky peppermint from a bag in the dash. "Still got a sweet tooth though."

Herb smiled shinily with perfect teeth and gums of an unlikely peach colour. He sucked hard on two peppermints at once, clicking them against his teeth.

They were silent as the road lifted them up out of the valley and crossed a fresh avalanche chute. The passageway that had been chopped through the snow was just wide enough to admit one vehicle. The compacted snow on either side stood in solid six-foot banks mottled with boulders and branches.

"Nice trip, the ski up to Bridgetown," Herb said. "Still do it myself, the odd time. Mostly though I just like to drive up and take a look around, like I'm doing today. But the place is nothing now. When I was a kid, must have been five hundred people lived up there."

Bridgetown, like Lairdmore, had been a coal town. The mine had chopped streets out of the mountain like steps and put up over a hundred houses for the workers and their families. The Bridgetown women put in big vegetable gardens behind the houses and chickens ran loose in the yards. All the men worked for the mine.

Since coming to Lairdmore, Anne had read several histories of the area. Many of them were actual journals kept by explorers and settlers who'd first come to the mountains. She also bought a book on mountain flowers, a field guide to rocks and minerals, and a full-colour catalogue of mountain wildlife. The books settled themselves around the house . . . Flowers in the kitchen, Wildlife in the bathroom, Explorers on the top of the digital clock-radio on the bedside table. She propped Flowers up against the kettle and studied the identification key while she washed the supper dishes.

When Peter first noticed the new books straying all over the house, he said, "What do you need all these books for anyway?" Peter assumed there must be a reason for everything.

"I like them," Anne said.

"Is that the only reason?"

"Well . . . I suppose they're educational."

Peter said, unconvinced, "I suppose." He believed that Anne never did anything for the obvious reasons. Once he'd told her he was proud of the fact that she wasn't a simple woman. As if, Anne thought some time later, that meant nobody could expect him to understand her anyway.

The road narrowed to a single lane and disappeared in a tight curve to the right. Herb pounded the horn twice to warn any oncoming traffic. On the right, the road hugged a sandy embankment so steep that it was completely bare of snow. On the left, there was nothing but a small pull-off space in case of emergencies. The road was icy and even at ten miles an hour the back tires of the truck began to spin uselessly. Anne stared nervously over the edge, willing the truck around the corner, but Herb never stopped talking about Bridgetown. It was as though, Anne thought, he wanted to be sure she knew both where she was going and what she'd be missing when she got there.

He'd gone to school in Bridgetown. "We fed the elk right out the window," he told her. "They'd eat right out of your hand, slobber all down your arm. Aunt Mary Margaret, she was the schoolteacher, brought apples for them. But she's dead now."

The whole mountain seemed to be riddled with his relatives. Most of them were likely long dead by now, but no less a part of the family for that.

Anne smiled and nodded but Herb needed little encouragement to go on. "In those days," he reminisced, "Bridgetown was quite the place. There was the smithy and Ike Bacon's drugstore where he sold liquor out of the icebox in back and the big general store with everything from long johns to playing cards and duck eggs. My cousin Gertie, she gave piano lessons in a room up over the drugstore. There was even a whorehouse, course I wasn't supposed to know about that. The two churches, Presbyterian and R.C., they were always fighting back and forth to see who'd have Friday night bingo. I won a turkey from the R.C.'s once but my ma, she wouldn't cook it seeing as how we were Presbyterian."

Anne imagined Bridgetown's terraced streets perpetually filled with bingo players and buggies and apple-chewing elk.

"Here's the turnoff now," Herb said, pumping the brakes and guiding the truck onto a road to the right. "I'll take you in to the first bridge. Can't go no further with the truck though, road's not plowed past that."

Anne pulled off her toque and shook out her hair which was damp and curling with sweat. Herb jiggled the knob on the heater but nothing happened. "Stuck wide open all year round," he explained, shaking his head and untying his scarf.

Anne was glad to stay and listen that much longer. Herb knew all the histories of the valley, remembered everything, piled up stories and years one on top of the other like layers of rock. But he didn't seem to think of the things he remembered as history, didn't appear to structure time the way other people did, in a straight line from past to present with three dots at the end for the future. There was something circular in the way he spoke of all those years. They were all of a piece, a single sphere enclosed by the continuity and the limits, birth and death, of his own life . . . a crystal globe looking in all directions at once. The space of time between then and now was curving in a great arc which would join back to itself in the end. Herb spoke as though he saw no reason why anything should have changed in the first place and no reason why it shouldn't all change back again one day.

Anne thought of her own family back in Ontario. None of them, not even the old aunts and the great-uncles, told stories like Herb did. Maybe they didn't have any, maybe they'd always been just the way they were now. Anne could only remember being told one story, the one about Uncle Amos being struck dead by lightning on the Hallsey Golf Course one Saturday afternoon. His nine-iron was welded into his hands. And that story was only told at weddings and funerals. The rest of her relatives had lived quietly without taking notes and then died quietly without making a fuss. In Anne's family, eccentricity was considered impolite.

Peter came from a large family too but his relatives turned out to be no more entertaining than her own. There was one woman, Aunt India, who'd suffered what the rest of the family called "a nervous experience" when she reached menopause. She'd sold her house in Lashing Heights and moved to Paris with an easel, a box of oil paints, and a Lhasa Apso pup named Chin. In the eyes of her family, the worst thing of all was the fact that she soon began to make a lot of money from her painting. If she'd failed, they could have loved her again and sent her the airfare home. The lives of all the other Dicksons were quite straightforward and Peter was just like them—his life persisted in falling neatly into place around him. Other people's life crises were simple decisions for Peter.

He'd passed through public school without undue trauma and through high school without undue study or stress. He'd gone on to university because it seemed appropriate at the time. He'd majored in Social Work because he liked people and thought he could help them simplify their lives. He'd dropped out in the middle of his third year because one day at lunch he realized he wouldn't be able to save the world anyway, with or without five years of education. He'd taken up carpentry because he was good with his hands and a man with a trade could always find work. He'd married for love. He was the most untortured person Anne had ever met.

Herb, who seemed to be following Anne's train of thought, said, "I even met my own true love in Bridgetown." Anne smiled encouragingly, wanting to hear more.

Herb went on. "Effie MacKay, her name was. My brother Leonard, we were mountain guides together then, he introduced us. Went to the dance every Saturday night just to see her. I took her a corsage every week for months just so she'd dance with me. Still wouldn't marry me though, corsage or no. She'd say, 'I'd rather be an old maid than a widow, Herb Murchie. You're going to kill yourself up there one of these days. I'm no fool,' she'd say. Then she'd flounce off and dance with somebody else. A hard woman, that Effie," Herb said, with fond admiration. "Course this was all before the bad times came."

The bad times for Bridgetown had begun with the 1928 explosion. Ten miners were killed and the town began to turn against the company. The men who survived refused to go back down inside the mine. They organized a strike for danger pay and better safety measures. After the Crash in 1929, the company could only afford to work the mine during the summer months. The people started packing up and moving down the mountain to Lairdmore where the higher quality coal meant year-round work. In a year and a half the Bridgetown Coal Company was bankrupt. They burned down the tipple and sealed up the shaft. They tore down all the houses and Bridgetown was gone.

Anne was still wondering about Effie. "What happened to her when the town folded up?" she asked.

"She came down to Lairdmore too then and took a job teaching at the new school."

Anne imagined Effie, a stern young woman in a black bonnet, walking away from the town and down the mountain with a suitcase in one hand and a corsage in the other. There were men in black business suits tearing down her house behind her. The mountains were set in monochrome all around her, white snow, black trees like bristle brushes. Of course it was a cloudy day. Effie kept walking away, a hard woman with her suitcases (cardboard) full of tablecloths (linen) and silverware (sterling).

Herb continued. "Wasn't long before she up and married Ulysse Paquette."

"I'm sorry," Anne said. She'd been hoping for a happy ending.

"Oh don't be," Herb said, grinning. "She ended up a widow anyway. Ulysse, he died in a fire at the hotel he owned. Not the kind of thing you could lay odds on beforehand." Anne found it hard to smile along with Herb at Ulysse's misfortune.

"By then I was working in the Lairdmore mine, I was forty-five. Effie and me, we got married the next year. She wore a grey suit and an orchid. Never did figure out why she thought my being down inside the mountain was any safer than being up on top of it!" Anne was relieved to discover that it had all worked out in the end. There was some kind of basic reassurance to be derived from other people's happy endings. She felt like applauding but put on her toque and mittens instead. They were at the first bridge, where Herb would leave her. In the narrow road, he turned the truck around in little jerks until it was aimed back down the mountain towards Lairdmore. He got out and helped Anne lift her gear over the tailgate.

"Enjoy yourself," he called as he drove away. "Bridgetown'll always be the best place around these parts. You'll see."

Anne propped her ski poles up against an evergreen and positioned her feet on her skis, snapping the bindings shut with the tip of one pole. She could still hear Herb's truck grinding back out to the main road.

The bridge was made of logs, several of them rotted away now, forming dark crevasses in the snow. It was the first of three that had given Bridgetown its name. The creek below it flowed slick and garbled over the rocks, moving too quickly to freeze. Anne skied across carefully, her eyes tearing in the wind. She imagined the first explorers, the ones she'd been reading about, coming this same way . . . coming to this unnamed river in flood which must be crossed somehow if the pass was to be found and the country pushed through to the other side. They were all still here somehow.

You could only hear river sound rushing, a monstrous new pulse in your ears. The water came up to your neck, roped around your ankles. Food and clothing, three guns, swept away. Horses screaming. You might never be dry again.

Anne pulled her camera out of her pack and composed a shot of the bridge. She fitted her skis back into the fresh track and continued on. The track carried her forward, turning each corner in a smooth arc, leading her on like a map. If her skis slipped out of the track, they would sink deep into the new powder on either side.

You had nothing to go on, no trail, no map, no guarantee. Even the Indians didn't come this far, knew these mountains had nothing to offer but magic and myths. They were afraid. They had no names for the Shining Mountains. The rock was all one, no distance measured, no time either. No way to get through in miles or hours. The rock existing in a single dimension: space. You were pygmies.

The track went steadily uphill and Anne was beginning to sweat inside her parka. She loosened her scarf and unzipped her jacket a few inches to let in the cool air. She started to hum and then stopped, the little insect sound nervous and impossible in this place.

The trail took a sharp turn to the left. Slowing down abruptly, Anne lost the rhythm of her stride and struggled to stay in the track. Around the corner, the trees were thicker and more tangled, dead ones propped up against live ones, creaking under the weight of the snow, rotting away from the inside. The branches, which did not appear until several feet up each trunk, were growing blindly into each other. Anne photographed just the trunks, dismembered torsos, bodies without arms or legs, so many, so thin. But there was nothing horrible about them here. It was only carried away in the camera, spread out in the darkroom, hung in a frame on the wall, that they would become alarming or ridiculous.

You must have thought this an unfortunate land. Candelabra pine trees can only be beautiful once they no longer need to be journeyed through. They were the same trees, smaller then than now, but no less impossible. This place would not even be pleasant for another fifty years.

In some spots the trees were so thick that neither the sun nor the snow could get through to the ground. Here the grass sprouted like meagre hair through the frozen dirt.

Your crazy battered horses could never find enough grass to fill up their well-bred bellies. Ranging farther and farther, their hooves skidded on the wet rock. One dappled mare fell over the edge without crying out, still chewing.

The trail opened out of the trees, following the rim of an undercut cliff. Trying to plant her left pole, Anne jabbed first empty air and then a large chunk of snow and dirt that came loose and bounced down the cliff.

Her left knee, the closest to the dropoff, began to vibrate uncontrollably. Her thigh muscles clenched up tight and would not push forward. Her image of falling was large but not vivid, not extending much beyond the thought that Peter would disapprove if she died away up here when he didn't even know where she was.

The hardships were always borne. You never seemed to doubt that they could be, and you never seemed to be afraid of dying if they couldn't. Sewing-machine legs on the ledge sent pebbles like bullets over the edge. Your courage was genuine: you had no choice.

Anne pushed harder, leaning more on her poles, hauling herself up with the whole length of her arms. The trail rose more steeply, up over the second bridge and around a pile of boulders that had slid onto the old road. She'd imagined herself strong and severe on this mountain, taking the miles with ease and determined grace, but now her lungs were like bricks in her chest. She paused to wipe the sweat from the back of her neck and then leaned on her poles to rest, breathing deeply.

You thought of the old women back home serving high tea and teaching the little girls to embroider. Rock of Ages in cross-stitch. They had already stopped thinking about you. There was no way to reach you, too much rock in the way.

The trail dipped down to the third bridge. Anne brought her arms in close to her sides and pushed forward. She did not think about falling or stopping—either choice was more or less impossible.

A young woman—what was her name?—came with you, would not let her new husband go off alone this time. He was embar-

rassed and proud, you expected nothing but the worst . . . fainting, falling, complaints, she was bound to turn back after ten miles. But she tricked you all by being strong, silent, pregnant. The boy was born in a cave like an animal with no fur. Happy and howling, the two of them. You could do nothing but wait there three days while she healed (you were outraged by this indecent pain which you were supposed to be protected from) and nursed him and sang. It was hard to look at her because you knew she was braver than any of you.

Anne stopped on the last bridge, changed the lens on her camera, and focused far back into the trees.

This is a photograph of you, woman . . . see there, behind the big tree. No one will believe your stories. There is no way of knowing that you were ever here. The land closed up behind you like a mouth.

The trail took her into a large clearing. On the south side of the meadow, snow-covered terraces mounted the slope. Bridgetown had clung naturally to the mountain like a goat.

Still wearing her skis, Anne climbed awkwardly up to the third terrace and focused a long shot back down the slope.

This was a photograph of no one.

Still climbing, Anne watched the ground carefully, expecting artifacts, some archaeological sign just under the snow . . . a horseshoe maybe, or a broken dish with flowers painted in the bowl . . . discarded bits of lives like fingernails. But there was nothing. A promising lump in the snow turned out to be a dead squirrel.

On one of the upper streets she discovered one side of a concrete foundation still standing. It had been a large building, a church or maybe the school.

Even Herb Murchie's memories weren't real here. Effie wasn't here either, she was dead beneath the valley floor, her name and two dates like bookends carved in the granite. In the summer there might be red peonies on her grave.

There had been children born here. They were all in nursing homes now or dead, and the place on their birth certificates did not exist. They would always be children in Bridgetown, adults only in some other place. Anne tried to imagine families passing through high-ceilinged rooms on their way to dinner, school, the mine, cousin Gertie's piano school. She tried to imagine couples making love and could not put them into a big feather bed, but only onto the meadow, brushing away branches and pine cones before they laid down. Hard women, loved. Woman served up on the rock, bruises in a string down her backbone.

She climbed back down to the meadow and ate her lunch sitting on a bare rock in the sun.

It was almost dark by the time she got home.

She and Peter are eating supper at the blonde maple table which Peter built when they first moved in. The white dishes are like coins on the blue tablecloth. Two of Anne's photographs hang on the wall behind them but they aren't looking at them.

The first photograph is just above Peter's left shoulder. In it, an old man and an old woman are out in the backyard shelling peas. The white enamel bowl is wedged between their straight-backed wooden chairs.

Her dark dress is spotted with tiny colorless flowers like scars. His home-knit sweater is sagging brown and blue. Their faces lean together, rapt with green peas dropping into the bowl like beads from a broken bracelet.

They are stationed in front of a rock face which there is no reason for them to pay attention to.

The rock after rain is like some shiny metal.

The man and the woman cannot climb anymore . . . too old, too easily broken and bleeding . . . wingspan too short.

They are pretending there is nothing behind them but sky. The woman's hand reaches down to ease the bandage around her tree-stump leg.

They look like crows but are not.

The second photograph is just above Peter's right shoulder. In it is an empty house which was torn down by the time Peter first saw the photograph. He couldn't remember where it had been.

White clapboard lists to the left, shedding overcooked shingles like flakes of sunburned skin.

There could have been a dinner table still there inside, set with white and silver for roast beef and carrots and lemon meringue. Anne doesn't expect Peter to be able to see inside because he still believes in the inherent solidity of walls.

There is no glass in the window frames which are peeling off in strips like cellophane tape. A blue curtain is flapping out through one of the holes. You can see right through the house. It has no intestines. You can see right through to the mountain behind.

There is rock in the frames. Rock like frost would have been on the pane, or faces steaming on the glass.

"What did you get up to today?" Peter asks, mopping up the gravy on his plate with a chunk of bread.

"Nothing much," Anne says, sucking on a chicken wing.

It would take too long to explain. She will tell him eventually. And he will believe, mistakenly, that the day had been too unimportant to mention at the time. She will tell him one day, inadvertently.

FIRST THINGS FIRST

(1980)

NEXT TIME, if I get the chance, I'll ask more questions first. I imagine some kind of questionnaire. A snappy little quiz to hand out at the bedroom door. It seems there are always some subjects you just never get around to until the whole situation is pretty far advanced. And then it always turns out that those were the important things. The ones you should have known about right from the start.

First things first.

QUESTION ONE:

Are you allergic to cats?

I come from a long line of cats. I was only five when I made the major discovery that, at any given time, there are any number of stray cats just roaming around out there free for the taking. My mother, I realize now, withstood this barrage of skinny furry (and probably wormy) creatures remarkably well, and we always had at least one cat around the house. Occasionally she tried to talk me out of it by explaining how maybe some other family owned the cat and they would be missing it terribly and crying. But I was young and had no sympathy for people who lost things.

When I figured she was getting fed up with me and might give me trouble, I would run home from school carrying a cat under one arm like a football, toss it in the back door, and keep on running. I went down the street to the park where I would swing furiously for half an hour while the cat, I hoped, was making itself at home. If, when I did venture back to the house, there was a dish of milk by the fridge and my mother was talking to the cat while she started supper, I knew we were all set. My father was always the one who got sent out for more kitty litter.

But all my cats were short-lived. The world, it seemed, was rife with things that killed cats. Dogs, fish-hooks, rotten meat, distemper, and speeding cars that didn't stop. Finally, my mother decided that neither of us could take much more of this. So my father rigged up a leash on the clothesline for the next cat which turned out to be a big orange tom I called Punky.

One night that summer I slept over at my friend Ellen's house. It was too hot to sleep so we spent the whole night with a flashlight under the covers reading *True Story* and touching ourselves. Ellen stole the magazines from the drugstore where my mother worked. When I got home in the morning my mother was sitting on the back step crying and my father was watering the garden, something he usually never did. My mother said the cat was dead, had hung himself in the maple tree while trying to catch a bird. Instinctively I knew this was some cruel and unusual punishment for the feeling that came from reading *True Story.*

Right now I have only one cat because I live in a miniature basement suite. Her name is Jessie. Sometimes I call her Liz Taylor. She's black, fat, and very sure of herself. In the sunlight her fur shines blue. Some people say I'm neurotic (or at least very odd) about my cat but I don't care. There have been so many times when she was all I had. So now my cat collection consists mostly of cats on calendars, cats on posters, and cats hand-painted on little ceramic boxes. I also have Polaroid pictures of Jessie taped all over the fridge door. Love me, love my cat.

Last April I met this guy James at the horseshoe tournament. Half the town was there with all their kids and all their dogs, no cats of course. Cats never get to go anywhere.

James started talking to me during the ladies' final. He said he'd been wanting to meet me for weeks.

And then he said, "Joyce, do you ever think you're more clever than your friends?"

I thought that was very perceptive of him because maybe, just maybe, sometimes I do. So I started paying more attention to his good brown skin, his curly black hair, and the long muscles in his thigh. He told me he was reading *War and Peace* for the third time.

James kept bringing me more cold beer from the ice-filled bathtub in the garage. Another woman, Lana, kept bringing *him* beer and hovering, but he just kept touching my arm and asking me who my favourite writer was. It was all wonderfully tense. I must admit that sometimes I like that sort of thing. But only if I'm winning.

Later it turned out that Lana was his lover right before me. But you can't always know these things at the time.

When it got dark, those few of us who were still hanging around went into the house and arranged ourselves on and around a sagging old couch. I remember it was the colour of dried blood. Lana sat on one arm and it fell off. We all laughed warmly to let her know such minor disgraces didn't matter to us. James played the mandolin and sang. There were also some guitars and pretty soon we were all singing. I thought about how James and I could be together and talk about music and books all the time. Sometimes we would play backgammon and have liqueurs in our coffee. I would show him some of the stories I'd written and then he would sing to me. A Bob Dylan song.

When I finally got tired of waiting for something more to happen and got up to leave, James said, "Joyce, I want to start seeing more of you." I was ready for anything.

He started phoning and coming over to my apartment, sometimes for supper. I quickly discovered that he favoured romaine lettuce, baked salmon and seedless green grapes. I suspected that he'd never once succumbed to the glory of greasy french fries. When he was fasting, which was at least once a week, he drank gallons of ice water and nothing else. I admired his willpower but had no particular use for it myself. He lent me his favourite book, a scathing exposé of the eating habits of North Americans.

He was working extra shifts at the sawmill and never had much free time. He started coming over late at night without warning. I had no idea when to expect him. Sometimes when he arrived I was already in bed, reading or asleep with the cat on my chest. Other times I sat at the kitchen table until two in the morning, all dressed and casually keeping the coffee warm. Somewhere I'd already learned or been told that phoning a new man too often or asking for more information was unpleasant. And I already knew that expecting too much from James was risky; he couldn't take the pressure. I was always perfecting my technique of biding my time.

When James did appear at the door, he'd start grabbing at me as soon as he could get his work boots off. He smelled like freshly cut wood. (Afterwards, I wondered if maybe it was really some racy new aftershave designed to make women drool for the I'm-a-labourer look.)

He never actually pushed me into the bedroom but he was always spinning me around and pointing me in the right direction. Pin the tail on the donkey.

I just assumed that we'd get around to all those other things, the music and the books and the all-night discussions, soon enough.

But there was a problem with the cat. Every time we had

sex, first I had to lie in bed waiting and trying to look voluptuous while James gobbled four or five antihistamines and gagged. Jessie always sleeps on the bed no matter who else happens to be in it. Then, the whole time, while I wiggled around underneath James looking for the right spot, he snuffled and choked and cursed the cat. Afterwards, he had to get dressed right away and go home before his eyes swelled shut. He told me I'd have to get rid of the cat. Jessie, of course, adored him.

One night when he was trying to get my nightgown off, something occurred to me. I said, "What makes you think you can come over here and climb into bed with me anytime you feel like it?" He'd run out of antihistamines that night anyway. And I wouldn't give my cat away for anybody.

James, I suppose, was one of those guys that afterwards you can't imagine what you ever saw in him and you feel like a damn fool. And your friends all tell you they never liked him anyway but they didn't say anything before because they didn't want to hurt your feelings. And you wonder why nobody ever tells you the truth until it's too late to save you.

QUESTION TWO:

Do you sleep on the couch every night after supper?

When I lived at home, the same thing happened every night. While my mother and I were still sitting at the table having our second cup of tea, my father would head into the living room aimed at the couch. He snored while we cleared up the supper dishes. Some nights he slept there right through till the eleven o'clock news. We were all in the living room and I was reading something for school and my mother was sewing or working on her stamp collection and watching TV at the same time. My father slept on the couch in his white t-shirt and green work pants, snoring with his mouth open, bubbling a bit, and heaving around. I couldn't even look at him.

My mother often said she hadn't slept in the daytime for years. From that I figured women were just naturally better than men because they didn't need to sleep so much.

Last August I met this guy Dean at a party. I remember thinking he looked a little tired but I didn't see that as a serious problem at the time. He fell asleep at the party but then we'd all had quite a bit to drink and he wasn't the only one. He looked like a child when he was asleep. It wasn't until later that I discovered this is true of many people and is not an accurate measure of one's character.

Dean came over for supper twice the first week. He arrived right after work, armed with a bottle of good red wine and a new shirt. He seemed so hurt if I didn't kiss him passionately at the door and then rush right off to open the wine. I thought this was substantial proof of how much he loved me already. I served the wine in my good crystal glasses. Long-stemmed, they made me think of roses.

After supper then he wanted me to lie down with him but it wasn't for sleeping yet. I liked that (he called it "dessert") but it wasn't always so much fun on a full stomach.

Once, at exactly the wrong moment, he said, "Don't make so much noise."

After that I couldn't work up as much enthusiasm anymore.

Dean talked a lot about moving back to Ontario where he owned sixty acres and building a house together. He said it could be done for $5000. I thought he was being overly optimistic but it wasn't until later that I felt compelled to point this out to him. He said we would have chickens, a cow, a big garden, and some babies.

I began to indulge myself in sunny fantasies. It was always summer on our farm but if winter ever did come, we would spend the evenings reading by the fireplace, making popcorn, and touching each other every now and then. I imagined working in the big garden, pregnant in a long flowered dress weeding the potatoes with a smiling little round person (male or female, it didn't matter which) crawling down the row behind me. Someone I know now would arrive for an unexpected visit and go away in a week quite miserable with envy.

By the third week, Dean was coming over every day at five-thirty on the dot, wondering what was for supper. He still got a passionate kiss at the door but he didn't bring me the wine anymore. (I can see now that I wasn't paying enough attention to detail at the time.) I didn't mind the cooking every night. I must admit I like to cook. Dean's favourite food was spaghetti. Somehow all that chopping and spicing and tasting convinced me that I loved him as much as he loved me.

By the fourth week, he still wanted my spaghetti but now every night after supper he would flop down on the couch and say, "I just need to relax for a few minutes." Sometimes he even asked for a blanket. Then he slept for three or four hours. I can't say as how I found this very entertaining.

One day he went to sleep on the couch *before* supper and I realized he'd been lying to me all along—he slept so much that he'd never have time to do anything, let alone build a house and help me in the big garden too. I also remembered that I didn't like farms.

I kept stirring and tasting the spaghetti sauce until I could hear Dean snoring. Then I switched everything off, left the pasta to congeal, and walked over to the ballpark. There was no game that night. I sat at the very top of the bleachers and spit sunflower seeds all over the bottom seats. The base lines had been freshly chalked, the infield raked, and the backboard repainted. There was a district tournament coming up on the weekend. The mosquitoes were bad but I sat there until it got dark and then I took my own sweet time strolling back to the house.

Dean was still sleeping, the cat was outside, and the whole house reeked of garlic.

It was something of an anti-climax. I was looking for a fight.

QUESTION THREE:

Do you still talk about your mother and/or your ex-wife all the time?

Some people have heard all about my mother too. Back in high school, I went out for a while with a guy named Ted. He was the first boyfriend I had who owned a car. On Friday nights, after an hour or two at Country Style Donuts, he'd drive me out to the airport parking lot, our industrialized version of the old lover's lane. While he kissed me and tried to put his tongue in my ear, I gabbed on about my mother. Instinctively I knew that even by proxy, her image could protect me from doing something I didn't want to, something which it was no longer necessary or feasible to refuse on strictly moral grounds. Winter was coming and we had to leave the car running. I knew this was dangerous too. One night, after a few weeks of this, Ted suggested we go over to his house and take all our clothes off. He said we would sit around in the nude and drink hot rum toddies. I had no idea what I would talk about while sitting in the nude—certainly not my mother. Maybe we would compare scars. I never went.

Just after Christmas last year, I went out with this guy Larry who, as it turned out, was always talking about his wonderful mother and his awful ex-wife.

I first met Larry when he was singing in the Landmark Lounge here in town. That very first night he struck me as being kind of soft and sad, nervous but pretending not to be. I must admit that sometimes I go for that type. I have occasional spells of wanting to be somebody's mother.

Larry was wearing blue velvet pants and a silk shirt embroidered with blue fish. He was very thin. His hair was pale red, long at the sides and thinning on top. Under the bright stage lights, his face and hair were all one colour. He was attractive though, with a gravelly voice and acrobat fingers on his electric guitar. All the other women in the bar were obviously admiring him so I did too. Pretty soon he was looking right back at me and I imagined he was singing those sweet songs to me. I sent him up a rum and Coke and he came right over to my table when he finished singing.

Pretty soon Larry was staying at my place whenever he was singing in town, and phoning me every other night when he was out on the road.

Sometimes I drove out to spend the weekend with Larry wherever he happened to be playing. Usually we could have a free room in the hotel. These rooms were all the same, the sheets were always yellow, and the toilet was always running.

On the Saturday we would go out in the afternoon and wander through these strange towns, shopping and taking pictures of old buildings. Larry took pictures of everything, especially me. On the Saturday night I'd go down to the bar where Larry was singing and sit all alone, nursing my Scotch and concentrating on looking cold and mysterious. I liked to watch the young girls all admiring him up there on the stage. I smiled serenely while they sent him up drinks and little notes scribbled on paper napkins and empty cigarette packages. He saved the notes and read them to me later in bed. They were so in awe of him and offered phone numbers, drinks, kisses, true love. We made fun of their fantasies. Only I knew he was wearing his white Stanfields under his velvet pants. He collected the notes in an old spiral scrapbook but I never doubted him. Usually we spent Sunday lying around the hotel room, admiring ourselves and feeling safe and smug.

Beside Larry, I became tough and large. I wanted to look after him, save him from suffering anything ever again. This included colds, TV dinners, and another broken heart. He adored me. Once he said, "Joyce, there's not one thing about you that I don't like." With a rush of recognition, I understood that I'd been waiting to hear that from someone for years.

He told me first thing that he'd been married before. His divorce had become final a month before he met me. For a long time he didn't call her by name, only "my ex-wife" or "that bitch." She'd left him without warning, taken the kids and moved back in with her parents who were rich and lived in a monstrous mansion in North Vancouver. Larry said it was all their fault, they'd never liked him and they turned her against him. They wouldn't let him see his own kids. He made it sound like a conspiracy.

He often said, "I gave her everything she asked for and then she left me anyway."

This was supposed to make me feel sorry for him and sometimes it did.

But he thought his mother was perfect. Her name was Irene. In various anecdotes, Irene was wise, beautiful, patient, understanding, strong, and she made the world's best scalloped potatoes. I just knew I was never going to turn out to be that good. I was doomed.

Of all the things I ever cooked for him, the only thing Larry ever paid attention to was the scalloped potatoes. I vaguely recall some passing remark about a big pot of meatless minestrone (we were dabbling in vegetarianism then, exploring the secret world of lentils, eggplant, and crunchy granola) but I can't remember now whether he did or didn't like it. Larry was the most timid eater I've ever met. He picked through each meal like he was looking for little bugs or hairs. He chewed like a rabbit, only with his front teeth because his back teeth were rotten.

This was because, when he was a kid, his mother didn't have enough money to take him to the dentist. She raised Larry all by herself because her husband had turned out to be a rat and a petty thief who left them when Larry was just a baby. Larry made their poverty sound splendid. About his father, he said, "We never needed him anyway, we were better off without him." And I could see that he hated him.

Larry's ex-wife's name was Janet and pretty soon she was getting blamed for everything that went wrong. Whenever I criticized Larry, he said, "It's all Janet's fault, she made me that way."

Whenever, in a rush of guilty affection, I told him he was the best man in the whole world, he said, "You'll have to thank my mother for that, she made me that way."

Between Janet and Irene, I couldn't figure out who I was supposed to be. He already had one woman to hate and another to love. What did he need me for anyway? Perhaps he thought of me as a captive audience.

Over the years, he'd built himself up a whole bank of debits and credits. On the one hand, he would stroke lovingly for me the acute memory of his mother waiting at the comer to walk him home from school every day. They couldn't afford to move to a safer section of town. On the other hand, he would relive vividly for me the time he came home from two weeks on the road and found Janet in bed with his best friend. "In *my* bed," he wept. In the final analysis, this trespass seemed the worst part of it.

Once, feeling a little drunk and perversely intimate, I attempted to reciprocate and confessed to him my entire love life thus far. He never forgave me.

One night when Larry was out on the road, I went to the lounge and got drunk and spent the night with a guy named Sam. The next morning, changing the sheets, I realized I could be just as unlovable as the next (or the last) person. I'd always felt obligated to be a good person. The realization that I didn't have to be was maybe not something you'd especially want to know, but it was a relief just the same. I gave up trying to feel guilty and went to the laundromat.

Larry came home a week later and I told him about Sam. I knew that, as far as Larry was concerned, I'd already done the worst thing possible and there was no turning back now.

He punched the wall and cried while I flew at him like a bird against a picture window. Finally I said, "Now I can see why your wife left you." I guess I'd always known I'd be able to use that on him one day—just because he was always using it on me. He'd always acted as though that was the only interesting thing about him—the fact that Janet had left him and so, naturally, he was scarred for life.

THE FOURTH AND FINAL QUESTION:

If you're not looking for love, then what are you looking for anyway?

It seems that nobody wants to believe in love anymore. Certainly nobody wants to admit that's what they'd really like to find out of all this rushing around. I wonder how everybody got to be so afraid.

I used to think it would all get easier as I got older. But I can see now that it only gets harder. And so many of the things you discover about people just by wanting or trying to love them turn out to be things you were happier not knowing. Too much water under the bridge. I used to think I would die without love. Now I know that's not true. Usually this knowledge reassures me but sometimes even now I catch myself wishing I still believed it. Wishing my heart would stay broken just once. Broken and bleeding, a stain to scare strangers away.

But I know now that love can't keep you alive.

I was still in high school, cultivating a crush on a boy named Don who was three grades older than me. I knew he had a girlfriend who went to a school across town but I figured I could work around that. One day Don skipped school to go fishing with two friends at Indian Lake. They were drunk in the boat and when it went over, Don drowned. The other two lived. One moved away to Winnipeg with his family and I heard that the other one rushed right out and married a girl I never liked.

There was something shameful about dying when you were skipping school and drunk too. None of us talked about it much. Death by drowning was no distinction. It only meant that I could never dream about Don anymore without having silver gills appear somewhere around his ears. And it also meant there could never be a reason to stop loving him.

Anyway, I guess you might think from what I've told you that I'm not very good at this sort of thing. I don't think it's my fault though. It just seems that all the men I meet start out one way and end up another. Next time, if I get the chance, I'll ask more questions first.

THE LONG WAY HOME

(1981)

MARY phoned Ruth one Saturday early in June. It was two in the morning Ruth's time in Alberta, four o'clock Mary's time in Ontario.

Once Ruth came awake and determined that no one had died, Mary said she had two weeks' holiday starting next Monday and would be taking the train to Calgary to be matron of honour at her cousin's wedding. She wanted to get a bus out from Calgary and spend one night in Aurora with Ruth. So they made arrangements for a week from Wednesday.

Then they talked about their parents, other relatives, mutual friends, anybody they could think of. According to Mary, everyone back in Hastings was fine, just fine, or at least the same, still the same. The dramatic crises which had fuelled their high school years had, it seemed, mysteriously dried up as they all grew older. Ruth figured this must be either because they were all too busy now and weren't paying attention, or because those destined for early death, suicide attempts, and botched abortions had already fulfilled their fates, leaving the rest of them to muddle along unspectacularly. They didn't talk much about themselves because they hadn't seen each other for five years, not since Ruth left Hastings and moved away to Alberta.

Ruth described her apartment in Aurora and Mary described their new house on Elmwood Crescent so they could picture each other while they talked. Ruth was in the big corner chair in the dark living room, curled up naked inside the afghan her mother had just sent her for her twenty-seventh birthday. The chair was brown and the afghan was every possible shade of blue. Mary said she was sitting at the kitchen table in her bathrobe, smoking low-tar cigarettes and drinking cocoa because she couldn't sleep. The bathrobe was green and the major appliances were harvest gold.

Ruth's new lover, Steve Schroeder, came out of the bedroom and splashed around in the kitchen getting a glass of ice water. The fridge light came on, milky blue on the ceiling. Mary said David was upstairs asleep, had been for hours, Lee-Ann too. David Barnes, Mary's husband, used to work at the grain elevator in Hastings but he'd quit last September to go to university. Now he was in first-year Psychology. Mary was supporting the family now, working for a real estate firm where she was always getting promotions, bonuses, and complimentary steak dinners for two because she sold so many houses.

Ruth had only met David once and then just long enough to discover that he was a chronic and vicious Monopoly player. She imagined him now, dreaming of Boardwalk and Park Place, twitching. She'd never seen Lee-Ann, their three-year-old daughter, and tended to picture her as a pink-coloured pupa with no teeth. Being an only child, Ruth never had much contact with babies. Her mother assured her that a shortage of maternal instinct was hereditary on her side of the family.

Then Mary asked, "Are you still writing?" People always asked Ruth this even though, as far as she was concerned, there had never been any possibility of her stopping.

Ruth gave her stock answer. "I have to keep writing, I don't know how to do anything else." Which was probably true and usually good for a laugh at dinner parties.

When Ruth went back to bed, Steve was asleep. He left for Edmonton first thing Sunday morning. His band was playing at the Macdonald Hotel for two weeks. In the familiar confusion of his packing and promising and kissing goodbye, Ruth never did get around to telling him about Mary.

She'd been with Steve for four months now and for over half that time he'd been out on the road with the band. In her mind, Mary's visit was already shaping itself into one more anecdote she could rehearse, file away, and then retrieve to entertain Steve with when he got back. He always stayed at her place when he was in town.

The next Wednesday, just around suppertime, Ruth started cleaning the apartment. She assumed this was still a prerequisite to having company from out of province. Mary was to arrive at eight. Defensive in advance, Ruth decided against changing her jeans and brushed her teeth instead.

The bus, for once, was on time.

At the front door, Mary hugged Ruth hard into her shiny sweet-smelling hair. They kissed each other, laughing. Ruth realized this was something they'd never done before, not even once in fifteen years.

Mary took Ruth by both hands and held her at arms' length, saying, "Just let me look at you."

Mary was beautiful and Ruth understood that this was not at all what she'd been expecting. She'd probably been feeling sorry for Mary for years. She noticed first, and then felt guilty for noticing first, that Mary's skin had finally cleared up, even the pock marks were gone. Her thin blonde hair was still long but now curled softly around her face like leaves. And she had contact lenses, blue ones. Her dress was blue too, running down into a complicated print of turquoise and yellow parrots at the hem.

Mary could have been, Ruth thought, one of those women she invariably saw on the Eighth Avenue Mall in Calgary, one of those women who was always wearing red lipstick, a pastel linen suit, high-heeled sandals with no pantyhose, and who was always just on her way into or out of some tall glass building, amiably ignoring the nice young man in the three-piece suit who was always holding the door for her. She could have been one of those women who always made Ruth want to get contact lenses and a perm.

Mary said, "You haven't changed a bit."

That's what Ruth was afraid of.

In the kitchen, Ruth offered coffee first but Mary said she'd prefer a drink. Ruth stood on a chair and got the bottle of rye down from the cupboard over the fridge. Mary settled herself at the kitchen table, crossing her legs and arranging her skirt. She took a pack of cigarettes and a slim gold lighter out of her purse. Her hands, creamed, manicured, and remarkably still, were perfect.

When they were younger, Ruth recalled, they'd never questioned the fact that they would one day pass magically from gritty adolescence to lustrous womanhood. The change, they were certain, would be sudden and magnificent. With its arrival, they knew they would at long last be released from all fear and unhappiness and so would enter together into a lifelong state of serenity and self-satisfaction. They would never again be sick, lonely, mad, or silly, and could not be punished by anyone for anything. They seemed always to have known that innocence was a dangerous and ridiculous condition to find yourself in for any length of time.

While they were waiting to be transformed, they discussed the way they would style their hair, the clothes they would buy, the meals they would cook, and the parties they would give for each other's birthdays. They studied sex in a library book and were disturbed to learn that newlyweds are likely to have sex every night, but agreed that by then they would be able to endure anything.

Now Mary was sipping her drink and complaining pleasantly enough about the long boring train ride and the plans for the wedding. There were five other bridesmaids and Mary couldn't understand why anyone should have to subject themselves to bright blue velvet in this heat. And who did Debbie, the bride, think she was fooling with that expensive white dress?

Whenever Ruth thought of weddings, there seemed to be something smoky about them. This had to do with diamond rings compared in the girls' washroom during the last year of high school. Right after Christmas vacation, the new diamond rings returned to classes in a herd. Girls who'd hated each other since Grade Nine became bosom buddies on the strength of getting engaged on the same day, either Christmas morning or New Year's Eve. They would assemble in the washroom between classes, sit around on the floor, and discuss wedding dresses while smoking hot butts with stiff left hands. The butts sizzled out and unrolled in the toilets when the bell rang.

In Aurora, it seemed, weddings had fallen into disuse. Ruth had only been to one in the five years she'd lived there. It was an informal gathering at the couple's apartment but even then, the guests all seemed slightly embarrassed until the groom brought out some beer and turned up the stereo. The whole idea of marriage was something Ruth sneered at, they all did, and yet there they were, toasting and kissing and congratulating the happy couple who'd been living together in that apartment for years. Ruth couldn't imagine the feeling of wanting to marry someone who was also wanting to marry you back. Afterwards she was depressed for days, failing to find the expected satisfaction in thinking that no one had ever, at least not to her knowledge, felt that way about her.

While Ruth mixed two more drinks, Mary admired the apartment which was compact and crowded with second-hand furniture, big coloured pillows, photographs and posters, and hundreds of books. Ruth often thought that one of the finest pleasures of living alone was being able to watch all your belongings spread out around you and no one else could complain or rearrange them. Mary said, "It's just like you, Ruth, just the way I imagined it would be."

Ruth thought Mary had it all now, that combination of power, self-control, and stylishness they'd been so impatient and so prepared for when they were younger. She couldn't imagine Mary being afraid of anything anymore.

Ruth, on the other hand, was still waiting to feel like a grown-up. She was still prone to eating pepperoni pizza while having slobbering hysterics at four in the morning. She had yet to get anything besides sore knees out of washing her kitchen floor and she'd never seriously considered waxing it. Babies still intimidated her, laundry depressed her, clothing stores made her cranky, and she bubbled with resentment when she ran out of soap in the shower and found that her mother wasn't standing right outside the bathroom door with another bar. Sometimes she still wished she could go back to the time when she was living with her parents and going to university, gorging herself on literature and logic and her mother's rare roast beef. Her parents were proud of her and she'd been safe then, not yet needing to be strong or cynical or organized.

Mary took a picture out of her green leather bag. It was Lee-Ann on her third birthday, smiling out of the lace collar of a frothy white dress with little red hearts on it. She was born on Valentine's Day. Her hair, blonde and straight like Mary's, was tied up in pigtails with two red ribbons. Ruth thought she looked happy, pretty, and very bright. Mary said she was looking for a baby brother. "Maybe next year."

Lee-Ann was with her grandmother while Mary was away. Ruth wondered why David couldn't look after her. Mary said, "He has a hard enough time babysitting the nights I have my yoga, never mind for two weeks straight," as though it were obvious and rather lovable, to married women and mothers at least, that there are some things you just can't expect of men because they just aren't capable of doing them. Ruth nodded as though she too understood and approved of this principle. "Besides," Mary said, "Mom just loves having her, the only grandchild so far, you know."

Mary had four brothers. Ruth had always thought this should mean she was spoiled, but instead she was ignored. Mr. and Mrs. Yurick seemed to assume that, being a girl, the worst problems Mary would ever have were acne and myopia. Mrs. Yurick, Ruth thought even then, never expected much of anything, good or bad, from Mary. It was the boys who needed to be looked after, protected from drugs, alcohol, wild girls, and fast cars. They were all still in Hastings, the four of them saved now and sensibly acquiring steady jobs, nice wives, and brand-new houses.

From what Mary said, it appeared that Mrs. Yurick found her more interesting, more likeable even, now that she was married and a mother herself.

"How's *your* mother?" Mary asked.

Ruth still envied those chummy mother-daughter duos she would see having afternoon coffee at the Aurora Café, chatting and gossiping, exchanging advice and complaints about husbands, helping each other on with their fur-collared coats, just like they were old friends. Ruth was sure that she and her own mother would never manage that. Ruth figured her mother would never consider her an adult person until she either published a book or got married, preferably the latter.

For years Ruth's mother always told her, "Just live together, don't bother getting married, it's not worth it." She also said she had no great burning desire to be a grandmother anyway.

But lately, as Ruth passed twenty-five and kept on going, her mother had started asking pointed questions. She kept bringing up the married cousins back in Hastings who were all expecting a second child by now but were still decorating their new houses all by themselves, and the unmarried cousins, also back in Hastings, who were all getting diamond rings for Christmas and registering their china and crystal at McCartney's. She had some trouble keeping the names in Ruth's letters straight and was always asking about some man Ruth hadn't seen for two months.

Ruth's father, who seldom expressed an opinion on anything not political or automotive, declared that he would still love her anyway, no matter what she did, and to hell with what her mother said.

After the picture of Lee-Ann, Ruth felt they weren't talking enough and she thought it was her fault since they were, after all, in her apartment. So she came up with a picture for Mary, an old one which, for reasons she had never contemplated, she still carried in her wallet.

In the picture, they are standing, five girls, in front of the Hastings Airport, squinting into the sun. The humid August heat is somehow palpable, emanating perhaps from the burnt-looking sidewalk or the swollen grey shadows behind them. Mary recognized it immediately as the day she and the other three left for school in Toronto. Ruth was the only one staying behind in Hastings where she would begin university three weeks later.

Mary handed back the picture, shook her head and said fondly, "You're so different, Ruth, you were always so different."

In the picture, Mary and the other girls, Doris, Shelley, and Sandra, are all wearing their summer dress pants, white or pale or blue or beige, with matching short-sleeved flowered blouses on top. Sandra has a white cardigan folded over one arm. Doris and Shelley are standing arm in arm. Mary, on the right, is holding one hand to her forehead, shielding her eyes from the sun. Ruth is on the far left, wearing the baggy blue jeans her mother hates and the purple Indian cotton shirt she bought that summer at the fair. All down the front of her shirt there are embroidered flowers and little round mirrors which are flashing in the sunlight.

Ruth supposed that Mary was right—she had been different, still liked to think of herself that way. But sometimes now she suspected a change in tone, some modification in herself that she couldn't quite get at. On bad days, she wondered if being different might have stopped being her natural condition and become instead a set of precious irregularities which she practised and used as a talisman against the rest of the world, flashing it into people's eyes to disarm and then charm them, like the mirrors on her purple shirt.

Ruth thought Mary was distressingly conventional, something which she never allowed herself to be. Occasionally though, she would surprise herself in the act. Like that day in the laundromat when the hum of the machines lulled her into a picturesque fantasy of herself folding some nice man's shorts with the baby propped up, gurgling, against the orange laundry basket. She stopped herself but not in time to keep some kind of energy, some secret hope, from washing down through her arms and legs and then out, a greasy smear all over the linoleum. It was the same feeling she got when she thought of all those young couples sitting inside their new cedar houses on a cold snowy evening, and she could not imagine what on earth they might be doing, and she suspected that no one would ever tell her and she would never know how to do whatever it was two people did together to pass the time.

They were just getting ready for bed when Mary, who would spend the night on the couch, discovered the old high school yearbooks on the bottom bookshelf. She flipped through the pages of pictures and called out familiar names to Ruth who was in the bathroom washing her face. "Marjorie Hicks, do you remember Marjie? Lionel MacKay, didn't he die or something? And Jeanette Labelle, you wouldn't know her to see her!"

Ruth made a pot of tea and they looked through the yearbooks for a long time, sitting on the floor with the books spread open between them, Ruth in her flannelette nightgown, Mary in the green bathrobe. They hooted at their former selves and groaned at their former heart-throbs and tried to outdo each other with silly memories and imaginary fates for the people they'd never liked. They laughed so hard they had to pound the floor and hold onto their stomachs or sometimes each other. Ruth realized she hadn't considered the possibility of actually having fun with Mary.

Pointing to one picture, Mary asked, "Do you ever hear from Allan?"

"No, I don't."

Mary said he'd married someone else a year after Ruth left Hastings, some woman she didn't know but who was reportedly cruel and beautiful. Allan was working at the Hastings City Hall now, something to do with building permits, issuing or inspecting them. Mary said, "I never understood how you could spend three whole years with Allan and then not marry him. Didn't you feel like you'd wasted your time?"

Ruth couldn't begin to explain it all now. She'd just never looked at Allan as someone to marry. But after the last five years of relative silence, broken only by Christmas cards and the occasional newsy note, she didn't know how to retrace for Mary the complications, the reasons, the decisions that should have been difficult but weren't. After five years, they had only the facts to go on.

The first three years had been chronicled in fat late-night letters and the odd phone call, while Ruth went to university in Hastings and Mary quit school and sampled a variety of low-paying jobs all over Toronto. Ruth graduated and moved to Alberta about the same time Mary brought David home to Hastings and married him. Soon they were both too busy for letters. Ruth had a good government job in Aurora and a singular, unhealthy relationship with a man named Jim White. Mary had Lee-Ann, took the real estate course, and went back to work. Ruth left Whitey after three years, quit her job to write full-time, and began a long series of short but educational romances.

"Where's Bart these days?" Mary asked abruptly. Bart was one of Ruth's old lovers. She'd been with him at Christmas and, feeling optimistic at the time, had mentioned him in all her Christmas cards. Between Bart and Steve there'd also been Don but Ruth skimmed over him because he'd only lasted a week and she was anxious to get to the good part, the past four months with Steve. She could just imagine how it all looked to Mary—the same way it looked to her mother, no doubt—a parade of penises with no prospects.

She told Mary all about Steve, every romantic detail she could think of—the songs he'd written for her, the impulsive weekend at Calgary's best hotel, the roses for her birthday, the way he jumped up every night and did the dishes so Ruth could just relax and read the paper. She wanted Mary to know she was all right now. She wanted Mary to envy her.

"I have the best of both worlds," Ruth said. "All the advantages of living alone when Steve's away, and all the advantages of living together when he's in town. All the advantages with none of the disadvantages. This arrangement suits me fine."

She'd used it before, this vision of secure independence, used the same words to draw women to her, to dazzle them and then make them see how discontented they really were. Mary quarrelled with the word "arrangement" which she said sounded mercenary.

Ruth showed her a picture of Steve. Mary admired his brown eyes which looked deep and warm in the picture. But Ruth was angry because he hadn't called her for over a week so she said they didn't look that good in real life. But then she felt guilty and kept working his name into the conversation so Mary would know they were serious about each other.

Just after they'd gone to bed, Mary called out in the dark, "Did I tell you Andrea says hello? She's fine, just fine. We talk on the phone every day."

In high school Andrea Gray has been the other, less committed member of their trio, serving mainly as a handy alternate best friend whenever Ruth and Mary weren't speaking to each other.

When they were all seventeen, Andrea tried to kill herself with Aspirins. Ruth had since wondered why they weren't surprised and why they just assumed she'd done it for no particular reason. Ruth and Mary went to visit her in the psychiatric ward and afterwards Mary said, "How could she let us down like this?"

Two months later Andrea met and married Earl Burnett. They rented a house in the country. They had to go on welfare and whenever Earl got angry, he would throw his supper at Andrea's head. She got pregnant and the baby, a boy, was born dead. Ruth and Mary went to visit her in the hospital and were outraged to think they'd kept her in the maternity ward with all the happy mothers and their pretty babies.

Then Andrea had an affair with Earl's best friend, John Jackowski, who rented their spare room. Everybody knew about it except Earl who left her when he found out. Andrea married John, who came from a wealthy family, and they built a ranch-style house on ten acres of land. Andrea got pregnant and had a nine-pound baby boy. Earl went to visit her in the hospital and apologized for everything so Andrea named the baby after him. John became a teacher. Andrea got pregnant and had a girl this time and then she got her tubes tied but almost died from an infection. Earl married a girl named Louise so Andrea, John, and the kids all went to the wedding. By then, Andrea was twenty-two, Mary was back in Hastings with David Barnes, and Ruth had just moved to Aurora.

But now Andrea was fine, Mary said she was fine.

Ruth lay awake in the dark for a long time, wondering how Andrea could ever be fine, how she could possibly have come through all that and still end up just like everyone else. Ruth imagined that her skin must still be the same even now, the humid colour of sliced mushrooms, vanilla-scented. What was the point then of going through and surviving such pain if it did not leave a mark on you?

The next morning Ruth got up late after lying there for nearly an hour, mostly awake but sometimes dozing in and out. She listened to Mary in the kitchen, opening all the cupboards in search of the coffee, boiling some water, opening the fridge for the milk, turning the pages of a magazine. It was comforting.

When Ruth came out of the bedroom, Mary was sitting at the kitchen table in her bathrobe, reading a magazine Ruth has shown her the night before, the one with her new article in it.

"Good morning."

"Morn." Ruth had always been inarticulate in the morning.

Mary kept reading and then said, "You're so lucky, Ruth," with a broad gentle gesture that took in everything—the bright yellow cupboards, the blue countertop, the magazine, the floor-to-ceiling bookshelves in the living room, the oak desk, the filing cabinet, all the other books piled on every flat surface, and Ruth in her nightgown, too.

Ruth didn't know Mary well enough anymore to tell whether she meant it or not. She didn't think so though. Afterwards Ruth would wonder why she found it easier to believe that Mary pitied, rather than admired, her.

She couldn't make out Mary's mood but she gave her stock reply anyway, trying to make her laugh. "It wasn't luck at all, just good birth control." Ruth thought she wanted to hear what was on Mary's mind so she added, "You're not doing so badly yourself, are you?"

Mary brightened up and started talking about Lee-Ann and the good daycare centre she'd just discovered.

Then she started talking vaguely about a girl named Lisa whom, Ruth remembered, she'd mentioned several times the night before. Ruth had assumed she was someone Mary worked with but now it seemed that Lisa was David's friend, not Mary's, a fellow student in the Psychology course. Lisa, as it turned out, was in love with David and they were having an affair.

Mary did not suggest a reason for the affair, but seemed to take it for granted, speaking of it in the same way she spoke of marriage: as a foregone conclusion.

Mary knew all about it because David told her everything just the way he always had. Mary said, "He knows I understand him. If he couldn't talk to me about it, then I'd be worried." She was very calm and Ruth didn't have to say anything.

Mary knew all about Lisa, she'd even met her once at a student party although she wasn't sure if they were already having the affair then or not. Mary said Lisa had long black hair and lived in a single room not far from the university. She rode a motorcycle in the summer so David bought her a new bell helmet for her twentieth birthday which was in March. Every Thursday Lisa and David went for pizza after their night class and then they went back to her room. He never spent the whole night with her though. Mary said, "Poor kid, she thinks he'll leave me for her. But I'm not worried, things like that don't happen anymore. I know he doesn't love her, he can't live without me."

She was talking quickly now, with her head down, eyes focusing on the edge of the table, her feet, on the floor. Her elegant hands, fluttering up to her throat and then flopping back, palms up, into her lap, were like pigeons.

With a ballooning sense of horror, Ruth imagined the two of them, Mary and David, sitting at the dining room table after supper, having their coffee or maybe a cozy liqueur, discussing "the problem." Lee-Ann, in pigtails and miniature denim overalls, was shovelling an artichoke from one side of her plate to the other. Mary and David were making fun of little Lisa. David might mimic her walk or her silly snorting laugh. Mary would laugh then too and pat his hand across the thousand-dollar oval teak table. They would sabotage the girl's thin hopes with their generous conjugal maturity. Ruth didn't feel sorry for Mary because Mary was making sure it was clear there was no reason to.

Ruth went into the bedroom to get dressed. Mary followed her, still talking, coffee cup in hand, and sat down on the unmade bed. She admired the sheets, which were brown with orange flowers and green leaves.

Ruth rummaged around in the dresser for a clean t-shirt. She felt uneasy undressing in front of another woman. It reminded her of being in the girls' locker room after Grade Nine gym class and they were all wearing baggy blue gym suits with their first names embroidered across the back and Ruth was silently suffering her lack of noticeable breasts and the smell of her own sweat, while the other girls, and Mary too, bounded around the steamy room, snapping each other's bra straps and admiring themselves. She thought now of turning her back to Mary but decided it would be childish.

Mary was saying, "Do you remember how we always agreed that if our husbands were ever unfaithful, even just once, we would leave them and go live together in a nice apartment with our kids and some cats?"

Ruth remembered how often this prospect had sounded more appealing to her than what they would have to do if their husbands were true-blue.

Mary said cheerfully, "It was a relief to find out that's not what you have to do after all. It really hasn't made that much difference to me, I know it's only a physical thing." Ruth wondered why married women liked to dismiss sexual attraction as trivia, forgetting how it could make everything in the world that you'd ever took pleasure in—books, music, mountains, lobster—seem pale and foolish, merely a series of distractions to help pass the time until you could lie down beside him again.

"I'm not afraid of Lisa," Mary said. "I'm not afraid of anything anymore . . . It's David who's afraid now, he's afraid she might kill herself if he stops seeing her. I try to reassure him though, I tell him it's not likely that anybody would love him that much. I tell him real life isn't like that."

Just around noon, Ruth walked Mary to the bus stop which was actually the drugstore on Main Street. The upper storey of the building was being renovated and raw planks stuck out through the window holes like severed limbs. Someone dropped a hammer from the upper scaffold; there was much imaginative cursing from down below but no injuries.

All the businesses in Aurora were assembled on three blocks of Main Street, which was crowded now with cars, dogs, and people all busy with the intricacies of summer. Ruth imagined people all over town tanning, bicycling, sweating, buying briquets, and wishing for convertibles and cold beer. Their children by now were probably pickled in pink lemonade.

The heat was already building. There would be a thunderstorm when the sun went down. The mountains ringing the river valley in which Aurora sat were hazy and blue, flat with no shadows, no shape.

"It's like a cradle," Mary said enthusiastically. Which was true enough, but not something anyone who lived there would ever have said out loud.

A group of people stood in a knot outside the post office, gesturing at each other with postcards and phone bills, paying no attention to the mountains. They all, Ruth knew, kept their private counsel with the mountains, took from them what they needed, did not presume to discuss them beyond admiring them when they went pink with the sunrise in summer or avalanched and killed tourists in the winter. The mountains, they knew, were not merely surfaces, were rock all the way through. Parts of them, stratified intestines, had nothing to do with seeing at all.

The bus to Calgary was late so Ruth suggested they wait in the Aurora Café across the street. On the sidewalk in front, a German shepherd lay stretched out on its side, sleeping or dead. Two women with baby strollers and bags full of groceries sidestepped the dog without looking down.

Inside, the café booths (obligatory orange vinyl patched with black electrical tape) were all filled with workmen on their lunch hour, wearing hard hats, dusty denim shorts, and yellow steel-toed boots. Ruth and Mary found two stools at the counter. Doreen, the waitress, cook, and dishwasher, stood behind the counter filling salt shakers and humming a modified version of "Onward Christian Soldiers." Her white uniform was splattered in odd places with mustard and ketchup.

Mary was once again wearing her blue sundress and two or three of the workmen stared at her, not being rude, just curious. Ruth knew some of them and smiled. Tomorrow they would ask her, teasing, "Where's your friend?"

Over coffee and grilled cheese sandwiches, Mary asked Ruth, "Do you think you'll get married?"

Ruth misunderstood, thinking it first a rhetorical, then an irrelevant, and finally a nosy question.

She thought of her cousin, Denise, back in Hastings whom she had always been told had married late in life. For years, the whole family had treated Denise with a hopeful sympathy, as though there were little else she could be expected to do at such an advanced age besides marry a widower or keep working forever at the Bank of Montreal. Ruth had recently figured out that Denise actually got married at twenty-eight. Her husband, Howard Machuk, was a gynecologist who'd never been married and he gave her everything she could possibly want, including a dishwasher for her thirty-first birthday. So the family had finally relaxed, except for the fact that Denise kept working when she didn't have to anymore, and they would never have a family now because it was too late.

Mary simplified the question. "You and Steve, I mean." She picked through her sandwich and pulled out two dill pickle slices.

Steve Schroeder, who was thirteen years older than Ruth although he didn't look it, had been married twice already and had two complete families living in British Columbia, a son and a daughter in each, both with new fathers now. Ruth had never looked at Steve as someone to marry. Mary said she could see her point.

"Oh, don't worry," Mary said. "You'll get married some day, everyone does. It's so nice to get all that high romance stuff over and done with, to have everything settled for once and for all, to know you don't have to be alone ever again."

After all that Mary had told her, Ruth wished she was joking, but she wasn't.

The bus arrived and Mary got on, calling back promises to say hello to everybody back in Hastings for Ruth.

The next night was Friday so Ruth walked over to the bar. She put on a skirt, pale green with pink wild roses, and a white halter top because it was too hot. Being the only bar in town, the Aurora Hotel, decorated with barn wood and antique sepia photographs, was where everyone went to meet everyone else on Friday night.

Ruth sat with some friends and drank beer and then Scotch, which was her favourite. Mostly she talked to a man named Martin MacDougall whom she'd met at a barbecue the weekend before. He was an ex-high school teacher from Prince Edward Island who was now a divorced carpenter living in Aurora. Picking up where they'd left off at the barbecue, he told Ruth the rest of his life story and bought her a couple of drinks.

When Martin got up to leave just after midnight, Ruth went with him. They walked to his house which was just two blocks from hers. He took off his shirt in the kitchen and got out more beer. He wasn't talking, and he didn't seem to notice or, if he did notice, he didn't find it strange that Ruth was silently crying.

When they went into the bedroom there were no curtains on the window and no sheets on the bed. He said he'd just done the laundry.

After a few minutes, Ruth sat up and retied her halter top. At first Martin wouldn't let go of her hand and then he got angry and started swearing and shaking his fist at her. At first she felt sorry for him but then she laughed to herself at how foolish he looked lying there on the bare mattress with his pants down around his ankles and his skin showing white in the darkness. Her own bare feet looked like wax on the tile.

She didn't give much thought to Steve who hadn't called her for two weeks anyway. It was something of a relief to discover that she didn't care whether either one of them liked her or not. She'd often wondered why women spend so much time doing things to make men fall or stay in love with them, while the men all expect to be loved just the way they are. There was a certain freedom in not wanting to fall or be in love. Ruth figured she could probably do just about anything now.

Putting on her sandals in Martin's back porch, she thought maybe she hadn't really gone there planning to have sex anyway. But she quickly gave up trying to convince herself. There was, she supposed, some tacit agreement between two people who left the bar together after midnight on Friday night. She knew this was true in Aurora anyway. She didn't know what rules other people in other places might have made for themselves.

There were no lights on Martin's street. The night sky was so densely black that Ruth would never have guessed there were mountains inside it if she hadn't known better. She started walking home, then turned back and cut across Martin's yard to the next street which was the long way home but well-lit. She was glad to think there was no one at home that she would have to tell the whole story to, complete with insightful suggestions as to what this might or might not have to do with Mary, and humorous remarks about still being afraid of the dark at her age.

WHAT WE WANT

(1982)

We could be anything.
We could be wives.
We could be terrorists.
We could be artists.
We could be wizards.
We could be women but we're still dressing like boys.

What we want is a change in style.

* * *

PENNY AND PAT are secretaries. There's nothing wrong with that. All week long they're typing and talking on the phone for hours, mostly to other secretaries, sometimes to each other. Evenings they're watching the sitcoms, rinsing out their pantyhose, ironing a skirt for tomorrow. Penny and Pat have been friends for years.

One wants kids, the other one doesn't.

One's been married, the other one hasn't.

One wants to get married, the other one doesn't.

Guess which one?

They both live in the mobile-home park. They're paying for their trailers, adding on a spare bedroom, a sundeck, what about a greenhouse, trying to make them look like real houses instead of like trains.

Saturday afternoons they get together for pots of drip coffee and a piece of pie at one trailer or the other. All morning they've been grocery-shopping, washing clothes, vacuuming, polishing, and dusting, and they're sure ready for a break. They deserve it.

They're over at Penny's admiring her new blue linoleum and figuring out how much it'll cost to repaint yellow in the spring. Then they're talking about the summertime, next year, last year, they'll be having barbecues, playing baseball, working on a tan. Winter is no fun. They might take a night course: Chinese cooking, volleyball, or beginners' photography. They're tired of rug-hooking. But some of the things that get planned will just never get done. They're like dreams that way, plans, potent at the time but quickly shed.

The men that Penny and Pat live with are truck drivers. They've gone downtown in the 4 x 4 for a beer with the boys. They'll be talking about gravel and unions by now, smelling like diesel fuel. Men.

It's cold and the trailer cracks. White smoke streams straight up from all the other trailers, drawn in together like covered wagons. Penny and Pat assume they're filled too with warm women in clean kitchens, drinking black coffee and spilling their guts, saying, How true, how true, it's all true.

They make perfect sense to each other.

Last week I was ready to throw him out.

Me too.

But things are better now. We have our ups and downs.

Us too. Ups and downs, well yes, how true.

You won't believe what he did.

Never mind, listen to this.

Well, he came home drunk again last night.

Him too?

I've never seen him so drunk.

Me neither.

He passed out at the supper table. Put his head right down on his plate. Chicken pot pie all over his face.

Do they ever laugh. Some things are bearable only because you know you've got someone to tell them to later and laugh.

More coffee and the conversation goes like booster cables between them. Sometimes they're saying the same things over and over again, three times, four, just to be sure they're getting through.

He's a good man though.

Yes.

A good man, yes.

Yes.

He's so good to me.

Yes.

He treats me like a queen.

A good man, yes.

When the boys come home with a pizza, the girls are still sitting there putting a little rum in their coffee and laughing their fool heads off. The cat goes smugly from lap to lap.

* * *

Sometimes we want what they tell us to want.

We want a gas barbecue and a patio to put it on.

We want younger-looking hairless skin and a mystery man to rub it against.

We want a Hawaiian holiday, sun-drenched, and a terrific tan that lasts all year round.

We want fur and a dishwasher too but we don't expect to ever really get them. This gives us something to dream about, something harmless to hope for.

Promise us anything but give us an American Express card.
We're not as bad as you think.

What we want is original as sin.

* * *

Evelyn is a photographer. She's also divorced. So which came first, the chicken or the egg? She wants to be famous and fairly rich. She may be already famous, already rich (fairly), but artists are just never satisfied. She wants to be all the rage in Paris. After dabbling desultorily in landscapes, living rooms, and freaks, Evelyn does mostly portraits now, self-portraits, vegetable portraits, some fruit too.

She's living alone in an elegant studio apartment over some old warehouse down by the docks, of course. It's an unsavoury neighbourhood, yes, but the apartment inside is perfect. One big room, high ceiling, green walls all covered with her own work. She's meeting herself every time she turns around, first thing in the morning, last thing at night. Evelyn thinks it may well be the best place in the whole world.

Her first piece in this vein hangs now over the king-size bed. It's called: *The only thing worth caring about is food.*

There's Evelyn in bed in a cheap motel room nursing a cracked WATERMELON which has leaked red sticky juice all over her belly. Arranged in piles on the lumpy sheets are PARSNIPS, CELERY, ZUCCHINI, and ten copies of *The Joy of Cooking.* Her stretch marks are like slugs. Some people have said this piece is too obvious. What do they know?

Evelyn's best-known piece is called: *I spy with my little eye something that is edible.*

It is a series shot in Safeways downtown and it stars Evelyn and six of her friends, life-size. There they are, each curled up in a shopping cart holding up flash cards that say:

BROCCOLI
BRUSSELS SPROUTS
CANTALOUPE
LEAF LETTUCE
CALIFORNIA GRAPEFRUIT
STRING BEANS.

Evelyn's flash card says:

BUY ME.
I'M A NUTRITIOUS
AND DELICIOUS
LITTLE PEACH.

The critics usually admire Evelyn's courage, her sense of humour, her technical ability, and her vast and brutal talent, quote, unquote. Evelyn has been alone for years and she figures it's probably just as well, saves having to defend herself and decamp. She cuts out the rave reviews and sends them to her ex-husband, Gerry, who is still writing a bad novel in Michigan and never replies. He has stopped sending her money and Christmas cards. She could care less.

This afternoon Evelyn's working on something wonderful called: *Portrait of a woman wearing metal.*

She sets up the camera in the kitchen, takes off all her clothes, and climbs into the stainless steel sink, which has been polished like a mirror in preparation. She puts the colander on like a helmet, one CARROT sticking straight out the top. She poses patiently in the hysterical heat, sweat trickling down her sides, back, nose, and into her mouth.

Later in the darkroom she will decide that her baggy SWEET POTATO breasts are far more expressive than her face, which is too pale, too bland, an ordinary old POTATO.

Evelyn knows that she's not getting any younger, she's closer to forty than thirty now. She could care less; in fact, she's kind of relieved. Youth, it seems in retrospect, was nothing more than a damp guilty invasion of privacy. And marriage was like when she worked in that bank one year—a misguided attempt at being, if not exactly normal, at least ordinary.

Now she's well-seasoned with furious secrets.

She wants to be admired from afar by those heavenly young curious men who come to her shows and want to buy her a drink or a vegetarian pizza afterwards. They never have enough money to buy her any of the things she really wants. And so sometimes they're all falling in love with her just when she's walking away.

* * *

When we can have whatever we want, we want Beaujolais in crystal, good to the very last drop. It makes us feel silky and smart.

When we can have whatever we want, we want rich red food, the kind that's hard to come by:

lobsters with claws
succulent berries and cherries out of season
steak tartare dripping.
It makes us feel bloody and wet.

When we can have whatever we want, we want a crystal chandelier for the dining room. It makes us feel vicious and spoiled and it will cut you when it falls.

Some people say we're already vicious, already spoiled.
Not spoiled enough.
Not vicious enough.
When we can be whatever we want, we want to be exquisite.

What we want is deluxe.

* * *

Sandi goes out shopping almost every afternoon. Her man Stan's on midnights at the mine, he's working, always working, bringing home the paycheque, bringing home the boring old bacon. He's sleeping all day and Sandi's just got to get away. I don't want to disturb you, sweetie. And besides, his humid snoring bulk in the bedroom drives her up the wall. She can't sing, she can't dance, she can't even vacuum.

She puts on some more makeup and runs for the bus that'll take her way across town to the mall.

Once there she walks up and down for a while, just looking in the store windows, admiring the shoes, the anorexic double-jointed mannequins, and her own reflection in the glass. She sits down for a while and has a smoke which she butts in some potted plant. She recognizes some of these young punks who are just hanging out, they're here every day too. Why aren't they in school? Why isn't she? They're always eating buttered popcorn and footlongs, slouching around the record store, stealing the odd little thing. That girl with the pink hair must be some kind of freak.

Sandi tried stealing once too, a pair of fake gold earrings shaped like zipper heads. But it was no big deal. Buying things is more fun.

She has a toasted bacon-and-tomato sandwich and a hot fudge sundae (which gives her pimples and courage too) at the lunch counter in Zellers.

She likes to look at everything. I'm in no hurry, just passing the time. Just looking thanks, this stuff is junk. She likes to buy barrettes, mascara, pantyhose, shampoo, and a zodiac key ring, Cancer.

She's looking half-heartedly at wee frilly baby clothes. She knows she's too young yet for a baby. Some people said she was too young to get married too, just seventeen. But that's different. You can always get rid of a husband if you have to, but you can't divorce a kid if you decide you don't like it after a year or two. The two people in the world she would like to talk to most right now are her mother (who's gone to Hawaii for the winter with her new husband, Bert, who's better than the first two anyway, richer) and Linda Ronstadt.

She's trying on ten pairs of shoes because the salesman has nice big eyes behind those silly glasses and he's rubbing her arch, well sort of, and admiring her ankles, well maybe. This is something like Cinderella but sexier.

She's trying on a purple sweater shot with gold threads through and through. She's trying on that new brand of jeans that everyone's wearing, they're all the rage, they're the ones you see on the side of the bus. They look better on the bus. She's trying on five purple t-shirts with different sayings on the front. Purple is the greatest because it means something. Purple is like orchids and eggplant, exotic.

Sandi's standing in her old blue ski jacket in the pink dressing room thinking that she's naked, bony, and nippleless like those bald-headed mannequins and the shoe salesman stands there staring. He's never seen anything like it. She just wants him to see her, she's not sure what will happen after that. After that, it doesn't really matter.

She just wants him to stop thinking she's dumb and half-dead just because she's so young and so married. That's only the way she looks, not the way she feels.

She wants him to know what she's really like.

She wants him to know every single thing about her that there is to know.

She's going to get one of those black velvet paintings, either the one with the bullfighter or the one with the big eyes crying one tear, for over the couch, and good old Stan, he'll just have a fit.

So let him.

* * *

Picture this:
Our eyes are like bruises.
Our legs are like milk.
Our breasts are like magnets.
Our hips are like instincts.
Our teeth are very cultured pearls.
But our hearts, our hearts are sweet, sweethearts.

What we want is a new disguise.

* * *

Lillian dreams about surgeons. She used to be a nurse.
She's on the table in the operating room
blinking in the bright light
waiting for the cocktail party to end.
Everybody she knows is there
sipping dry martinis
eating little crackers
sucking their thumbs.
Her daughters are drinking tequila and swinging.
Somebody plays a piano poorly.
The surgeons come at her from all directions
like bees
kissing through their surgical masks
tickling her with feathers or forks
mental as anything. They take her apart like a puzzle
painless bloodless
pass her thighs around on a plate
bite-size delectable lox.
There's nothing to fear.
There's nothing to fear, dear.
She knows there's nothing to fear.
When they put her back together again

she's a new improved model
deluxe lovable wise and her breasts are perfect.
Only trouble is sometimes they get too drunk
forget how the puzzle fits
leave her spread out all over like that
one arm dangling from the door knob
smelling fishy.

Lillian's husband Hank is a half-crooked new- and used-car salesman. Lillian's twin daughters are half-crazed teenagers but she's not sure how crazy because they're never home anyway. They might be out getting pregnant, addicted, or arrested right now. You never can tell. What the twins say they're doing is visiting the museum, studying at the library, or attending an afternoon of chamber music. Do they really expect her to believe that? They do it on purpose, they want to be unnatural, they want to annoy her, they think they want to be writers or something.

This family lives in a happy beige house with a view, a verandah, three bedrooms, and a two-car garage. Lillian's in the kitchen right now whipping up hundreds of cookies for Christmas, rolling them in finely chopped walnuts, topping each one with a clot of raspberry jam when they're cool. The whole house smells like a TV commercial.

Hank's out in the garage changing the oil or something. Lillian's waiting for the last batch to bake, licking her fingers, and flipping through last month's *Vogue* or the numbers on the television dial. Outside, the wind is coming up grey, bringing snow at last.

Oh good, it'll be a white Christmas after all.

What's wrong with this picture?

They sniff at her all day like dogs, the dreams. She wants them, doesn't, wants them, doesn't, wants them, doesn't, does. It does not seem possible or necessary to tell anyone or do anything about the surgeons. What you don't know won't hurt you.

* * *

We want.
We sing.
We like.
We scream.
We see.
We say.
We can say it without saying a word.
We can be cunning.
We can be brave.
We can be lazy.
We can be maidens all in a row, singing the postpartum premenstrual brand-name blues.
We can be dragons too.
We've got personalities we haven't even used yet.

What we want is a fight.

* * *

Mitzi May is a tricky kind of gal. She keeps a room in some rundown hotel, the kind you see from the bus, with steamy little windows lined with ketchup, milk, and beer bottles. There was some woman died down the hall one time. It was the smell that finally brought them around. The room when they broke down the door was filled with bird cages. Worse than the death was the sadness. But Mitzi isn't sad, Mitzi doesn't worry, Mitzi's just rolling along.

One time she met this funny old boy in the alley and he's telling her, You've never seen life. He's trying to catch some broad who's crawling away from him, puking. And Mitzi just smiles up one side of her face and takes off after the guitar player from The Deadbeats who's taking her to a big party tonight. But she never forgot either.

She comes out at night like a dew-worm. The city this summer is stuck on hot, new wave, heat wave, swollen. The high-rises radiate silver sluggishly. She's not afraid of anything, this one, no one can hurt her, no one can touch her now. She's getting on her best dress, all silver like armour. Her breasts are like badges or the poke of a gun in your ribs.

She cruises the all-night donut shops, checking out the fifty-eight varieties, baked every day, fresh coffee too, one free refill only. Everything's fresh here, country style.

Mitzi wears black lipstick just for a laugh and talks all night about her new tattoo.

Baby you're not listening.

The guy at the next table slumps deeper down into his fresh cup of that fresh coffee.

Honey what you want?

He's looking around for the waitress who's supposed to come and save him. The guy's a simple insomniac, innocent, listening to country music on a portable tape player. Help me make it through the night. This is just too corny to pass up.

Sweetheart let me help you. I could make your dreams come true how true.

Sugar I could do things do some things for you make your blood boil over make it run ice-cold.

When the cops come in on their nightly rounds, the first one says, Hey Mitzi, what's a girl like you doing in a nice place like this? Ha ha ha.

They're both smirking at her, wiping their foreheads with the backs of their hands like bus drivers. But even they're afraid to touch her, she's so excitable, this one, she's a real lizard, this one.

She's really something, that one, the other one says as sulky Mitzi sashays away, packing a purse like a suitcase, and singing The Rolling Stones.

She's pretty snappy-looking tonight, this one. She thinks she's going to some pizza palace where the coffee's better and they've got wild music on the jukebox. She thinks she's going dancing.

* * *

We want to be dangerous.
We want to be wicked.
We want to be enormous.
We want to run rampant.
We want to get savage and leave the whole sad world behind us, hanging by a thread.
Boom.
Boom.
Boom.

What we want is a getaway car.

* * *

We could be anything.
We could be wives.
We could be terrorists.
We could be artists.
We could be wizards.
We could be legends in our own time.

What we want is a change in style.

LIFE SENTENCES

(1983)

THEY'VE KNOWN each other, this woman, this man, ever since they were kids, healthy, wealthy, and (   ). For all their young lives, they lived in identical ranch-style homes side by side on West (   ) Avenue. Both their fathers were important energetic men in the (   ) Company downtown and their mothers were (   ) housewives, lazy and slim.

They were both only children, growing up smoothly with a strong sense of their own (   ) power. Everywhere they looked there was money or signs of it. Money was not something they ever had to (   ) about. They lived comfortable lucky lives, exclusive (   ) lives. They knew nothing of pain or suffering, danger or (   ). Such things did not seem (   ) or possible.

As adults, they share (   ) memories of lavish turkey dinners, shiny bicycles, picnics at the cottage on Lake (   ), and washing the Cadillacs with their dads on Saturday afternoon in the sunshine. Their moms are sitting in one kitchen or the other, slopping up brandy until they come outside angry and squinting and (   ), refusing to cook. These kids don't care, they don't know any (   ).

They were innocent together, this girl, this boy. They have no sense now of having met; they might as well have been (   ), that's how close they were.

One day in high school the young woman looked (   ) at the young man and saw that he was remarkable. She knew then that she wanted to spend the rest of her (   ) with him and only him. There was no reason to think that she wouldn't. She'd always got what she (   ) before.

They did everything together in those halcyon days and their parents thought they were (   ) and cute. They went to movies, dances, and football parties, holding (   ), smiling and kissing in corners. They made (   ) love in the back seat of the car the young man's parents bought him for his (   ) birthday. The young woman loved it when he put his (   ) in her (   ). She was filling up her hope chest with crystal, fine linen, and (   ). She just naturally assumed that the young man (   ) her as much as she (   ) him. He certainly (   ) as if he did.

Of course their parents all approved. Their fathers were talking about retiring early and buying a condo in (   ), which was all the rage at the time. Their mothers were still drunk half the time and now these two kids understood that such behaviour was (   ) and likely to drive them to the same psychiatrist in later years.

After high school, the young man smashed up his car and walked away without a (   ) to some fancy college in (   ). The young woman stayed behind and sold novels in a bookstore while she (   ) for him to come home. Her rich parents said this lousy job was (   ) for her.

They wrote letters back and forth, this young woman, this young man, long letters, (   ) letters, unsatisfying letters. It was only after the young man came home for Christmas the second year with a (   ) gypsy girl that the young woman realized he might not (   ) her after all. Some men when you (   ) them, you know that somehow, slowly, they're going to defeat you. She was (   ) but he wasn't paying attention anymore. So she pretended to be (   ) and succeeded. He was (   ) fooled.

The man and the gypsy were married the next summer in his parents' backyard. The woman was invited of course and had to go just to show him she wasn't (   ).

But the young woman still (   ) the young man. She got fat, fat, fatter, sad, sad, sadder, and her broken heart was driving her (   ). So her worried parents sent her away to Europe for a little (   ). She came home much thinner and much (   ). She hated the young man now, which was much easier than (   ) him.

In a few years, the young woman, who was no longer feeling young, married a doctor who (   ) her desperately and bought her a mansion filled with wonderful things right on (   ) Street, the best part of town. Her parents didn't really like this doctor but they figured he was better than (   ). So did the woman. She didn't really (   ) this doctor but figured she'd learn to in time. The young man was (   ) and didn't make it to the wedding. He sent along a Cuisinart instead. The young woman's parents thought that was the end of that. Not likely, not by a (   ) shot.

Shortly afterwards, the young man's father (   ) himself tragically in the head, his mother promptly (   ) herself to death, and the young man inherited everything, through no (   ) of his own. He had so much money then, he would never have to work again. It was all very (   ).

As it turned out, the mansion he bought for his gypsy wife happened to be on the same street as the mansion of the woman and her doctor husband. He said it was an accident, purely (   ). By now he had a set of gypsy twins and another (   ) on the way. He was always buying new Cadillacs and smashing them up, a ridiculous habit that nobody (   ) seriously. He was just like a cat with (   ) lives, extended lives, flaunting them. The woman had become a writer of (   ) poetry and no longer found it necessary to (   ) the man. She was writing about other things now anyway. Absence makes the (   ) grow (   ). They were both getting older and (   ), in spite of themselves.

So they decided to become friends again, (   ) at first and then (   ). Pretty soon, it was as though they'd never been (   ).

The man teaches the doctor how to (   ) and, in return, the doctor teaches the man how to (   ). They have many things in (   ), the two men discover. They love the same restaurants, the same sports, the same (   ). After a while, they even begin to (   ) alike.

Sometimes the woman babysits the gypsy twins and the new baby, who is a (   ). She has never liked kids but it seems the (   ) she can do for that (   ) woman. She and the gypsy go shopping together, drink (   ), laugh about (   ), and talk about (   ). Everyone thinks the two women are (   ) friends and in a way they are too.

The woman and the man are glad to be (   ) again after all that's happened. They tell each other (   ) and they kiss in corners on New Year's Eve. Once or twice the doctor accuses the woman of having an (   ) with the man but of course that isn't strictly true. Still though, he says she just wants to have her (   ) and eat it too.

One day at lunch the man confessed to the woman that his marriage was (   ). The woman was hardly surprised—indeed, this seemed in retrospect to be exactly what she'd (   ) all along. The gypsy said the man was a (   ). The man said the gypsy was a (   ). They would never be (   ) again so there was no use trying. It was nobody's fault.

Not long afterwards, the doctor announced he was in (   ) with the gypsy. Everybody was surprised but there was (   ) to be done about it now. The doctor said the woman had never really (   ) him. The woman said that was true, (   ) but true. There was no one to blame. They were all very civilized people, unlucky maybe, but (   ).

After the divorces, which were unfriendly but (   ), the man and the woman stuck together. It was the (   ) thing to do. They (   ) each other.

The woman soon sold her mansion and moved all her furniture down the street. The gypsy's furniture was (   ) anyway, so they sold it. The woman wanted to burn it but the man said she was being (   ).

By this time, the woman's parents had moved down south to the dream condo in (   ) and she was glad she no longer had to face them. Her psychiatrist had helped her understand that she would never be able to (   ) them, no matter what she did. It was the curse of only children that their parents were never (   ), never satisfied.

This same psychiatrist had also helped the man realize he would never be happy either and his trouble with those Cadillacs was a (   ) wish. They were working on their problems (   ), this woman, this man, and it was no wonder they had so many, considering the way their monstrous mothers had (   ) them.

The man and the woman had all the same friends as before and nobody seemed to (   ) that the doctor and the gypsy had disappeared. It was as though those other two had never been much (   ) anyway. There was no need to get married now: once bitten, twice (   ). Besides, they were too old to have (   ) now anyway—it was too late for some things, lots of things, (   ) things.

Their lives, twin lives, discoloured, go on and on and always (   ). They still like to (   ) and (   ) and (   ). They still love the same (   ), the same (   ), and the same (   ). The man is still buying Cadillacs and the woman is still writing poetry. She knows that they're supposed to be (   ) at last. What more could they (   ) for? But her poems are all about (   ) and the man just wrecked another one.

Today the man is out in the driveway washing the Cadillac. The woman is thinking that if she has to watch him do this one more time, she will (   ), just (   ). She's in the kitchen drinking (   ) and getting meaner and (   ) by the minute. She knows this drinking is a (   ) habit. She knows she's just like her (   ). How depressing, how (   ), how true.

It seems that there are only two more things she can do in her life: stay with this man till (   ) freezes over or (   ) him. He'd be better off (   ) anyway.

Either way, she knows she will never be free of him. This man does not (   ) her, she knows that now, she's sure he never did, she's sure he never will. He knows her too well, all too (   ). Familiarity breeds (   ). She keeps wishing he'd drive the new Cadillac over a cliff and be (   ) with it. She can just see the flames, she can just hear the (   ), she can almost taste the gallons of (   ). The one thing she has never been in her life is alone.

She goes through all the ways she could do it, one by one. The possibilities are (   ). She thinks that (   ) would be best—bloodless, tidy, and (   ). No one will ever know. She's sure she'll get away with it—she's led a charmed life. No one will even (   ) her. She is above suspicion, though not above (   ).

The clouds are (   ), the ill wind is (   ), it looks like it's going to (   ).

Life, it seems from this vantage point, tends, intends, to go on for a very long time. There is no one to blame, no one to thank, no one but (   ).

TRUE OR FALSE

(1984)

MAVIS SINGER is sitting out on the back patio reading *The National Enquirer* just for a few minutes while there's no one around likely to catch her. Waiting for last night's supper dishes to cool off in the dishwasher, she's letting the June sun dry her hair. It's grown back some now but it's still pretty short and shaggy looking, which, fortunately, is the style this year. Purple is the colour this summer so Mavis's sundress is purple. In this position, stretched out in the canary yellow (last summer's colour but passable this year as well) canvas lawn chair, Mavis looks pregnant but isn't.

The house behind her, financed largely by the insurance money, is breezy looking, a curious cool blue with white trim. It is an old house made over inside and out, as is the emerging pattern in this part of the city. Everything around her is brilliant and acute—geraniums, greenhouse, garbage cans, picket fence, colours blatant and blazing in the heat. It's nearly noon but there's nothing to get in a hurry about—she's got all day. It's Wednesday. The neighbourhood kids are coming home for lunch all up and down the block, zipping through the alley on their bicycles, rearing up on them as if they were stallions, glinting electrically in the sunlight.

Suddenly one boy, who is carrying a big bag of peaches under one arm, rides his bike right into the side of the garbage truck which has been lumbering from house to house and is now directly behind Mavis's place. She leaps out of the lawn chair and runs to the boy who lies curled on his side, half on the gravel and half in her backyard. The peaches are rolling away in all directions like marbles or pearls from a broken strand.

TRUE OR FALSE?
FALSE.

Mavis leaps out of the lawn chair and runs into the house, into the kitchen which is modern and cool. She squats down in front of the refrigerator, leaning her forehead against its cold green door, holding her stomach, praying, hating herself but praying for forgiveness just the same. Bravery, she realizes, is admirable but no longer possible.

Mavis looks pregnant and might be. She isn't really worried one way or the other. Where she comes from, these things are, if not exactly taken for granted, then certainly taken in stride.

* * *

For as long as Mavis Clay could remember there was always a summer fair in Indian Mound. It was held the last weekend of August in the open field just east of town which must have been owned by somebody but was never used for anything else. The dilapidated barn in the middle became the exhibition hall, crammed full of Indian Mound matrons in flowered dresses fanning themselves with newspapers and examining the prize-winning beets, pies, peach preserves, and afghans. To the right of the barn, where all the cars were parked, the little kids could play horseshoes or go for free pony rides. To the left were the smaller livestock barns and the performing ring.

Mavis went to the fair every year just because it was something to do for a day at the end of the long hot vacant summer. That particular summer, when Mavis was fifteen, she went to the fair alone and ignored everybody she knew. She hadn't been home for a couple of days but she figured the family probably hadn't missed her much, there were so many of them. They were all there (except for her oldest brother, Jack, who was already in jail) plus a whole parcel of relatives, some from out of town even, come to make their annual visit to Indian Mound, rather like paying your respects. But Mavis ignored them all, even her little sister, Beth, who clearly adored her and kept waving madly in her direction.

Mavis stood with her back to all of them where they sat, squinting and sweating, ranged in lawn chairs and on upside-down milk cans along the side of the pig barn. She was watching her best friend, Molly Florence, on her horse, Starr, in the first round of the barrel racing. She was sucking on an ice cream cone in her new blue short-shorts and her white sandals. Her hair in a ponytail straight down her back felt silky in the sunlight, her skin in the heat felt succulent.

Suddenly two German shepherds ran into the ring, snarling and chewing at each other's throats. Starr pranced sideways and then reared up, throwing Molly to the ground. Snorting and bucking, the horse came right at Mavis who did not move a muscle. Some man grabbed her by the hair, snapping her head back, and yanked her out of the way just as the horse plunged headfirst screaming into the dirt right where Mavis had stood. Molly lay curled in the middle of the ring as the two dogs rolled around in the mud beside her and people came running from all directions.

Mavis wandered away across the field, past the barn, and perched on the hot hood of somebody's car to watch the little kids riding around in circles on those gentle fat ponies. As it turned out, Molly wasn't seriously hurt—a broken leg was all. Mr. Florence shot the damn horse.

TRUE OR FALSE?
TRUE.

Accidents will happen.

For Mavis, it was the kind of day that later you go over and over again in your mind, looking for clues, and still later you find yourself running face first into parts of it, patches or chunks of it, at inappropriate moments. It was the kind of day that has nothing to do with anything else but itself . . . the kind of day that marks both the end and the beginning of something . . . the beginning of living dangerously, yes, but the end of what?

* * *

Just after lunch (herbed cream cheese and Hungarian salami on a toasted bagel), Mavis Singer walks the four blocks east to Murphy's Corner Grocery. She is careful to lock and double-check the door behind her. There are starting to be more and more burglaries in the neighbourhood and Mavis is afraid of being robbed, afraid of losing all her treasures again. The back alley is empty, unchanged, as if nothing has happened. Maybe Mavis can believe that nothing did.

Usually Mavis goes to the Safeway at Chesterfield Mall but she only needs a few things today. To tell the truth, she secretly prefers Murphy's anyway, partly because her best friend, Tess Berry, shops there and partly because of the store itself, which is dimly lit and jumbled, in an old-fashioned way, aromatic, with the barley, brown rice, and other grains stored in big red barrels in the back corner. They do not carry Kraft Dinner, Sara Lee cakes, or Coke. Murphy, if there is such a person, is long gone—to the country, Mavis assumes, the grave, or the bank. The clerks and the stock boys are all foreigners, transplanted from tiny humid overpopulated countries, striking Mavis as loyal, sincere, and happy to be here.

TRUE OR FALSE
TRUE.

Mavis is secretly overwhelmed by the vast selection at the Safeway and when the cute little checkout girl says, "Have a nice day!", Mavis only nods grimly, knowing that she says the same thing to everyone and wanting to tell her to suck eggs.

* * *

When Mavis Clay was sixteen, she was involved in a serious single-car accident on the Old Post Road one August night. She and Molly Florence were cruising the countryside with two Indian Mound brothers, Zack and Bub Hammer, Mavis in the front seat with Bub and Molly in the back with Zack, a mutually satisfactory arrangement the two girls had decided on in the Rainbow Café before ever getting into the car.

The car went out of control for no apparent reason, rolled three times, and came to rest on its roof in an irrigation ditch. Molly and Zack were shaken up and bruised not badly hurt, so Zack ran back down the road for help while Molly stayed with Mavis and Bub. They had both gone through the windshield and lay crumpled together in the rotten water, the single intact headlight shining right on them and the radio still playing. Molly got down in the ditch with them and held their heads and sang silly songs in a crying, crooning whine until the ambulance came. When the police arrived, there was some question about drinking and driving but, as it turned out, Bub Hammer lost the sight in his left eye and that, it seemed, was punishment enough—no charges were ever laid. Both he and

Mavis were in the hospital for weeks. The doctors assured Mavis that the scars on her face would disappear in time. They said she was damn lucky to be alive.

When Mavis Clay was sixteen, she nearly died.

TRUE OR FALSE?
FALSE.

This is a carefully constructed story that Mavis Singer wants her new friends to believe because she thinks it makes her somehow more valuable, more precious to them.

What really happened was that Mavis got disgustingly drunk at Molly Florence's sixteenth birthday party and fell or walked through the picture window of Molly's parents' house. She lay face down on the lawn in limbo until somebody found her and drove her to the hospital. The blood and the dew on her face were both wet, one warm, one cool, both wet, the same only different. And Bub Hammer lost his left eye in a barroom brawl.

When the bandages were finally unravelled and removed, Mavis was, more than anything, surprised. The disfigurement wasn't that extreme, not grotesque or repulsive or anything like that. She thought she could even grow fond of the scars someday, take a kind of perverse pride in them eventually. They were like trophies, tangible proof of something . . . pain, survival . . . mortality or immortality or both.

The scars did fade with the years, as the doctors had promised, and now they are like lace or slugs, depending on the light and her frame of mind.

* * *

When the phone rings the first time it is Molly from Indian Mound, who lives in the city now, too, in a low-income housing project with her husband, one-eyed Bub Hammer, and their two kids. She works sporadically as a bun-wrapper in a bakery downtown. Molly and Mavis used to write back and forth a lot when Molly and Bub were still living in Indian Mound but they seldom see each other now. Molly, who has always been a loyal sort of woman, is constantly calling to suggest they get together for lunch, coffee, bingo, but Mavis always puts her off. Today Molly wants to go over to the Chesterfield Mall and shop around. Mavis, who is defrosting the fridge and feeling mildly irritated, says, "You wouldn't know me if you knew me now," and rips the telephone out of the wall, for once and for all.

TRUE OR FALSE?
FALSE.

This is what Mavis, who really is defrosting the fridge and feeling mildly irritated, would like to say and do. Instead, she says, "Oh, I can't today, Molly, I'm expecting the TV repairman this afternoon," crossing her fingers behind her back. The TV set works fine—for a thousand bucks it should. Then the two women talk affably for a few minutes about the transit strike, their folks back in Indian Mound and, of course, the indecent heat. They talk just long enough so that Mavis can hang up gracefully and not feel guilty about it.

* * *

Mavis Clay could usually count on running into Danny Singer at the Rainbow Café. She and Molly and the rest of the crowd hung out there all summer, pumping coins into the table-side jukeboxes, slurping up milkshakes and chips and gravy. Usually Danny would slide silently in beside Mavis in their booth. Sometimes he parked his convertible right in front of the café and he and Mavis would go out and lounge against it for a while. This was when Molly would disappear—she wasn't stupid, she knew when she wasn't needed or wanted around anymore. She knew when to leave them alone, those two ... Danny in his cowboy boots and jeans, a pack of cigarettes stuffed up the sleeve of his black t-shirt ... Mavis in love.

Danny was quite a few years older than Mavis and worked pumping gas at the Indian Mound Esso. His family had a pig farm just west of town but it was never really clear where Danny lived. He was liable to turn up anywhere in that wonderful car, drinking a beer. Mavis knew that sometimes, when the weather was bad, he rented a room for a week or so upstairs at the Indian Mound Hotel. She suspected that the rest of the time he slept in the car. She loved this about him, this unanchored itinerant quality. He could go anywhere, do anything; he could take care of himself.

To tell the truth, Danny Singer was the only guy that Mavis had ever really wanted. Secretly, hugging herself, she thought of him as "forbidden fruit" ... something tropical, succulent and potent, slightly bruised, possibly poisonous. He was a vagabond living just this side of the law. Mavis had no reason to suspect that he would ever change.

TRUE OR FALSE?
TRUE.

How was she supposed to know that Danny Singer would gain weight, lose his tan and some of his hair, take up bowling and stamp collecting, quit drinking, send his aging parents to a retirement village in Florida, fall in love with mowing the lawn, trade the convertible in on a station wagon? How was she supposed to know that Danny would mutate into the perfect husband, the perfect father, the perfect Little League baseball coach?

* * *

When the phone rings the second time it is Tess Berry, Mavis's best friend. She teaches the watercolour class which Mavis attends every Thursday night at the art college and is, of course, tall and slim and intense, with long, curly black hair and wild-looking eyes. Having travelled extensively, now she dresses in elegant, inspired outfits picked up for a pittance on other continents—Asia, Africa, South America. At various times in the past, Tess has experimented with photography, body-building, and cocaine. Now she writes poetry, plays the mandolin, raises doves, sculpts, and grows her own herbs. Except for Mavis, the crowd Tess travels with is composed exclusively of painters, playwrights, sculptors, poets, actors, and musicians. Her husband, Russell, is an actor and a good one at that. They do not plan to have children.

Today Tess and Mavis make plans to drive to class together tomorrow night. Afterwards they will go for a couple of drinks at The Black Cat, a jazz club, one of those new hybrids, the deli/bar, which are springing up in the more fashionable neighbourhoods around the city. Mavis finds such clubs convenient because now she can say, "I'm going to the deli," when what she really means is, "I'm going to the bar," a more determined and dangerous announcement somehow, one more likely to meet with resistance.

Mavis prolongs the telephone conversation as long as is casually possible, telling Tess about the accident in the alley, how the peaches went rolling every which way, how she ran out to help that poor careless child. Mavis is flattered by this friendship with Tess who, she imagines, has no doubts about herself and no secrets either. Tess is everything that Mavis wants to be.

TRUE OR FALSE?
TRUE.

Tess is everything that Mavis wants to be now.

* * *

Mavis Clay and Danny Singer were getting more and more restless while everyone else in Indian Mound got more and more sluggish, lazier and lazier as that relentless suffocating summer wore on. Existing for weeks in a sulky state of perpetual excitement, they were looking for adventure, whatever came their way, planning their escape in endless and abundant detail.

Mavis only went home when she felt like it, to grab a change of clothes or a half-decent meal, home where they usually said, "At least you're not pregnant," or "At least you're not in jail," and then went on about their business. Mavis's parents had other things to worry about, what with that tribe of hellions they'd managed to bring into the world. Mavis figured that another body more or less in that zoo didn't make much difference and she was probably right. Every time she did go back to the farm there was a different brother or sister sleeping in her bed anyway. Most of the time she stayed with Danny, in the car or in his room at the hotel.

One morning Danny said, "I can't stand it one more minute," so they packed up the convertible and drove to a public beach about forty miles west, Deadman's Point, where they spent the afternoon in and out of the shallow water, drinking beer and collecting shells. It wasn't until the next morning, after spending the night at Deadman's and then heading west again instead of turning around and going back to Indian Mound, that Mavis realized they were really doing it this time.

They made their way across the prairies, pretending to be tourists, sleeping in the car, sometimes in a cheap motel. Mavis had no idea where Danny got the money and she didn't like to ask. They ended up in Euclid, Alberta, because the place where they stopped for gas needed a mechanic.

Pretending to be married, they lived together in two rooms in back of the station, sleeping on a mattress on the floor and cooking their meals on the grill in the restaurant out front. Mavis helped out in the restaurant when it got busy, dishing up endless pork chops, mashed potatoes, and hot rhubarb pie to punks and truckers. Some of the girls who came in tried to make friends, but Mavis ignored their overtures, figuring that she already knew enough people to do her for a while. She and Danny kept to themselves. These girls struck her as too innocent, too eager anyway, and certainly untrustworthy. She was always feeling crabby and her feet were just killing her but she made better tips if she smiled and winked and bent over a lot when she cleaned tables.

By November Mavis knew she was pregnant but she figured that if she just ignored it, it would go away by itself, like the flu or a mosquito in the bedroom in the dark. Mavis wasn't stupid, she knew this couldn't really happen, but still . . .

One day she took all her tip money out of the jar and caught the bus back to Indian Mound. The driver dropped her off at the side of the highway because the town was too small to be a regular stop. She was scared to death.

TRUE OR FALSE?
FALSE.

Mavis was bored to death. Euclid by this time had become just like Indian Mound, except that it was hillier and she didn't know anybody there but the kind old couple who owned the station. Once they'd got there it seemed as if Danny's sense of adventure had just dried right up.

The gossip stirred up by Mavis's return to Indian Mound alone was scant substitute for the initial intoxication of their escapade, but it was better than nothing. Even that didn't last long though, as the townspeople quickly forgot about her and got busy with Christmas. Only Molly was interested in all the juicy details.

* * *

When the phone rings a third time, it is probably either Molly again, the doctor calling about Mavis's Monday appointment, or a wrong number. Mavis, who is cutting back the spider plant, just lets it ring.

TRUE OR FALSE?
TRUE.

Mavis lets the phone ring and ring until the fool on the other end finally gives up. This makes her feel gaily indifferent and powerful, too.

* * *

Danny Singer was no dummy: he went back to Indian Mound, too, but not for another month or so, until he'd given Mavis some time to think about it.

Mavis and Danny were married in a simple ceremony in the Indian Mound Church in January. Molly Florence was maid of honour and one of the bride's older brothers, John Allan, stood up for Danny. The bride wore a knee-length white dress which caused a minor flurry of interest. Both sets of parents disapproved of the marriage but had resigned themselves to the fact that there was nothing else to be done. The wedding dance was held in the Legion basement and everybody had a good time in spite of themselves.

With Danny's savings (which were far more than Mavis or anyone else would ever have guessed), they bought a small old house on Main Street. Danny got his old job back at the Indian Mound Esso, where he was quickly promoted to head mechanic. Mavis fell easily into the role of young housewife, spending her days sewing curtains and slipcovers, fixing up the nursery, planning a garden, and cooking good nutritious dinners for Danny every night. Danny bought Mavis a blue budgie for her nineteenth birthday, to keep her company, he said, until the baby was born. Mavis, who would have preferred a fluffy white kitten or a horse but didn't like to complain, named the bird Julie. The baby, a girl they named Amy, was born in June, barely six months after the wedding, thus satisfying everybody's suspicions. They were making improvements on the old house while saving up their money to buy a new one and Danny was nursing his dream of owning the Indian Mound Esso himself someday.

For a few years, Mavis, Danny, and little Amy Singer lived quietly and happily in the little house on Main Street.

TRUE OR FALSE?
TRUE.

For a few years, the young Singer family threatened to live happily ever after and disappoint everyone.

* * *

Mavis Singer is having her afternoon nap, a secret indulgence she feels guilty about but just can't give up yet. In the dream Amy is riding a black horse on a beach. The horse bursts into flames and runs into the water which is a hundred feet deep. Danny is trapped under somebody's car and can't save her. Mavis is afraid of fire and has forgotten how to swim. In the dream there is no sound.

TRUE OR FALSE?
TRUE.

The dream disturbs Mavis for the rest of the day.

* * *

One morning just before Amy's fifth birthday Mavis took $100 from Danny's sock drawer (she called this borrowing, not stealing, because after all they were married), got Amy all dressed, and caught a bus back to Euclid, Alberta. The old couple who owned the gas station was still there and Mavis got work in the restaurant again. The suite in back was occupied so Mavis took a room in a boarding house just until she could afford something better.

Back in Indian Mound, rumour had it that an older man, a married man named Joe Fletcher, was involved. Joe had disappeared at about the same time, went out for a loaf of bread and never came back.

TRUE OR FALSE?
FALSE.

Joe's disappearance at the same time was just a coincidence. He went east, not west, and, as it turned out, came slinking back to Indian Mound three months later, tail between his legs.

Danny Singer was no dummy and when he tracked Mavis down back in Euclid, she was at the laundromat, folding clothes and reading *The National Enquirer* while Amy played with her dolls on the floor.

* * *

Mavis is out working in the garden, sweating and hacking worms in half with the hoe.

TRUE OR FALSE?
TRUE.

Mavis hates worms, even though she knows they're good for the soil. Mavis hates the garden, which was not her idea in the first place, because it reminds her of Indian Mound and the old house on Main Street. There are some things that can no longer be thought about.

* * *

Back in Indian Mound, Mavis and Danny began saving their money in earnest. They'd had about all they could take and wanted to buy a house in the city. They went in most weekends all through that boring summer, just checking it out, and by the end of August they knew exactly what they wanted, which is more than most people can say.

Danny was working all the time, ten or twelve hours a day, six or seven days a week, and Mavis was spending a lot of time over at Molly's, who was married now, too, to Bub Hammer, and living right across the street. They had coffee together most days, at one house or the other.

One afternoon, after Mavis had put Amy down for her nap, she wandered across the street to Molly's just for a few minutes. This day it was too hot for coffee, too humid to sit inside that little hotbox of a house, so they were having a beer in the backyard, admiring the garden and the gladiolas and whining about the heat, when all of a sudden the fire siren went off, freezing activity all over town, curdling Mavis's stomach just like it always did. The one thing she was most afraid of was fire.

It took Mavis only a minute to realize that it was *her* house that was on fire. She was up and running, screaming, and before anyone could stop her, she was inside the burning house, inside the flames, flailing through the smoke to Amy, coming back out through the picture window that had exploded, her hair ablaze and the child lying limp in her arms as if she were already dead.

TRUE OR FALSE?
TRUE.

The house was reduced to a smoking black skeleton, faulty wiring, all of their accumulated treasures lost. Poor Julie, the budgie, was cooked in her cage, so much roast meat, and all of Mavis's beautiful hair was burnt off. The insurance money would enable them to move to the city sooner than anticipated but, of course, they weren't thinking about that yet. Mavis knew that she and Amy both were lucky to be alive. Afterwards, when people went on and on about her bravery, she felt hazy and surprised. Brave is not something you think of yourself as being.

* * *

Mavis is in the kitchen starting supper when Amy gets home from school and Danny gets home from work. Amy's books and lunchbox, Danny's boots and coveralls, all drop in a heap beside the back door. He is co-owner of a garage down on East 27th now. He's handing Mavis a peach he found lying in the backyard so she tells him the story of the accident, the true story. Danny is understanding, comforting, he puts an arm around her shoulders, rests his cheek on the top of her head. He knows everything about her by now. There are no secrets, no surprises, between them. Anything can be discussed, examined, dealt with maturely. Amy is in the living room, watching reruns of *Mister Ed, The Talking Horse.*

After supper, the Singer family will have a quick game of Old Maid which is Amy's favourite. Then Mavis and Danny will do the dishes, she washes, he dries and puts away, and talk about Amy's eighth birthday party coming up on Saturday. Amy has already invited all her little friends from school. Mavis decides that a barbecue, just burgers and dogs, would be the best idea. Danny will go out and mow the lawn while

Mavis helps Amy with her homework, runs her bath, and then tucks her into bed. Then Mavis and Danny will watch the early movie and go to bed right after the news.

TRUE OR FALSE?
TRUE.

After supper, all of these things will happen and the Singer family will sleep peacefully all night long in their cool blue house, as if they've been doing it all their lives.

TRUE OR FALSE?
FALSE.

After supper, Mavis Singer will go down to The Black Cat Deli/Bar with Tess Berry and pick up some young guy in leather pants and spend the night at his place.

TRUE OR FALSE?
FALSE.

After supper, Amy Singer will accidentally electrocute herself with the curling iron in the bathtub.

TRUE OR FALSE?
FALSE.

After supper, Danny Singer will go and visit Molly Hammer from Indian Mound, with whom he is having an affair.

TRUE OR FALSE?
FALSE.

After supper, Mavis Singer will go and visit Bub Hammer from Indian Mound, with whom she is having an affair.

TRUE OR FALSE?
FALSE.

After supper, Danny Singer will stroll down to Murphy's Corner Grocery for a loaf of bread which Mavis forgot this afternoon (silly woman) and never come back.

TRUE OR FALSE?
FALSE.

After supper, Mavis Singer will ask Danny Singer for enough money for a one-way ticket back to Indian Mound.

TRUE OR FALSE?
FALSE.

After supper, the Singer family will live happily ever after.

SHE WANTS TO TELL ME

(1985)

YOU'RE SITTING THERE like a bouquet of flowers, pastel, perfumed, and conspicuous. You want to tell me your whole life story. You also want another drink. How can I refuse you either? How can I refuse you anything?

You say, "Your geraniums are lovely."

It's that special single hour on a late summer's evening when the light has gone all sentimental, the birds are singing dementedly, and way out in suburbia, some beautiful virgin boy is mowing his mother's lawn, flexing his thighs, and dreaming he's the singer in a rock and roll band.

"I've never had much luck with flowers myself," you tell me. "I find it easier just to let some man buy them for me."

Here our downtown birds are ratty old pigeons, circling aimlessly, preening and cooing at nothing. Our downtown boys in their black leather jackets are always playing video games, flexing their fingers, hooked, and I can't imagine what they might be dreaming. Most of them will survive.

"They always die on me."

You sniff the breeze, which is supposed to smell like berries or white sand, but in this neighbourhood is mostly exhaust. You massage it into your bare arms anyway, stretching your legs, kicking off your shoes (which are perfect) and settling in. The soles of your feet are dirty and smooth, like a child's.

"The flowers, I mean."

Our ice cubes are melting. I'll go in and get some more. I wish I had an ice bucket, a silver one. You do. You must.

"Expensive feet, I've always had expensive feet. I can only wear Italian shoes. It gets to be like a curse. I had to search the whole city to find such marvellous shoes."

And here I sit, me with my plain old peasant feet, domestic feet propped up on a flower pot, swelling and smelling in the heat.

I get more wine. Also domestic. But you are, I imagine, too well-bred to notice.

"It hardly smells like summer anymore," you observe. "The nights are getting cooler, longer. Where does the time go? It seems to pass so slowly but always carries on, and then in the end, it's nothing but gone. This wine is delicious."

You think you're in Italy, Paris, on the Riviera or the Virgin Islands, anywhere but here, examining your fingernails, tucking your hair behind one ear, pulling up your lacy white skirt to catch the last of the sun. You think that I'm just like you—which is flattering but nerve-wracking. I'd hate like hell to disillusion you.

"In the beginning I just loved this building. Being up in the air like this, I thought I was on top of the world."

The balconies on either side, above and below us, are like blinkers. They are cluttered with various junky but revealing accumulations: gas barbecues, an exercise bike, water skis, a baby carriage, underwear and pantyhose draped over the side, red geraniums and a sleeping bag—these last being mine. I like to sleep out here when it's hot. The bugs don't bother me much.

"But sometimes now I feel like a little girl up in the attic playing dress-up, clomping around in my mother's high heels."

There's a siren in the street. I can almost hear the crowd converging. But we're up high enough here to be immune. At least we like to think so.

"All dressed up and no place to go."

Directly across is another high-rise, higher, with offices inside—doctors, lawyers, psychiatrists, I suppose. The windows are all copper-coloured, like those expensive pots and pans you always see hanging around magazine kitchens.

"Other times I get to thinking about all those people below me, layers and layers of them, doing whatever it is that normal people do—watching TV, making popcorn or love, putting their babies to bed. They don't know that I'm walking around on their heads. They don't care. But sometimes," you tell me, "sometimes, I can feel their hard little skulls under my bare feet like pebbles."

You were out on your balcony, right next door, when I came out here onto mine. Leaning against the railing, you were shielding your eyes with one hand and peering up at the sky. No, more like into it, deeply. Watching for something, a flock of fabulous birds, an alien invasion by air, or maybe a sign from God. Your balcony is empty, tells me nothing.

"Hunter says I'm starting to sound crazy again. He says, 'Marguerite, you're losing it.' But maybe I'm just fooling around."

Finally you turned towards me and, ordinarily enough, waved across. I beckoned you over with my frosted glass, wanting to share the wine so I could dispense with feeling guilty about drinking alone.

"I met Hunter in a tavern in Toronto. He was there with his buddies for a beer after work, watching the strippers and pumping the pinball machine full of quarters. I have no idea now what I was doing there. Hiding. Finding him in a dump like that made him seem more real than the rest. I still thought falling in love was an acceptable practice. For a few months anyway, I took Hunter to be an ordinary man, normal, decent, and dependable. Which was what I thought I wanted. That was then."

Next to you, Marguerite, Hunter is *ordinary (lots of men these days wear earrings—I know that), so ordinary that he could be almost anything to you: lover, husband, best friend, second cousin twice-removed. It's hard to tell. He's too dark to be your brother. There is about the two of you none of that aggressive self-insistent happiness which marks newlyweds and people who are together when they shouldn't be.*

"We came here by accident, more of an experiment than a decision, the transplant of something vital into something else."

I was glad when you moved in. That apartment had been vacant for months and I'd pretty well given up on the people on the other side. They're an old foreign couple with a pack of little rat dogs over-running their apartment. Their grown-up children come over on Sundays with casseroles, pies, and flowers done up like wreaths—as if they've already died and gone to heaven. Maybe they think they have.

"I never dream about him anymore. Mostly now I dream about babies, having them, losing them, buying them. I also dream about trains, catching them, missing them. Sometimes they're coming right into the bedroom. If you dream about a dead cat, what do you think that means?" you ask me.

"Hunter holds me when I wake up crying but it doesn't help anymore."

I've been listening to the sounds from your apartment but all I get is the usual: vacuum cleaner, sometimes rock and roll music turned up too loud, the bed banging against the wall, the occasional argument in the middle of the night but I can never make out the words and there are no dishes breaking.

"You know what I mean."

Somewhere over the years, I have become the kind of woman other people feel compelled to confide in. Time and again I've kept my big mouth shut on all sorts of serpents and secrets, justifying their faith in me.

"You're so easy to talk to."

But other times too, I've come home from an evening with friends, half-drunk, tender and sobbing with the sheer weight of knowing so many things about so many people. They give me too much credit, they forget that I'm a person, not just a receptacle. I can spill things too. The beans. My guts. The wine. I can be dangerous too, not always just vicarious.

"My first husband's name was Frederick."

I've always hated that name. Makes me think of a beagle with slippers in its mouth.

"We met on a Mexican beach where we had both gone to recuperate—from different things, of course. I was just out of the hospital and he was just out of a miserable marriage in Vancouver. He'd lived there all his life, brilliant and crazy, always wanting to dive off a high-rise into the sea. I wanted to meet a genius. I wanted to meet a maniac. Frederick was the man of my dreams. In that warm water we were like swordfish, supple and salty and tasty. We were young. Six months later we flew back to Mexico and were married on that very same beach. My bridal bouquet burned up in the sun. More wine please."

We're well into our second bottle now. It's a good thing I keep a supply in. You just never know when you'll need another drink.

Now that I've got you here, I don't want to think of you jumping up and running away.

"Back home, marriage was nothing like Mexico or swimming, nothing at all. I told him what I wanted but he wasn't listening, or maybe he was down by the sea."

You're talking in code and assuming, in the way of unhappy young women, that I know much more or much less than I do. You're right either way.

"I want them to know I'm a person, not just a place."

I'm wanting to believe everything you're telling me. I'm willing to listen to anything. Nothing about you can surprise me.

"I nearly drowned once when I was a child, but I got over it. I'm a superb swimmer now, so they tell me."

There is no way of knowing if what you tell me is true. But that, I suppose, can be said of most people. The truth, like old wooden houses in the winter, is always shifting, cracking, settling back down in some other season, some other place. Nobody wants to admit that truth, like time, can never stand still. It is always a becoming, always a changing, always a staying-the-same.

"I was already sick by that time and was supposed to stay in bed all day. I was happier then than I've ever been since. I always kept the curtains closed. One wall was filled with floor-to-ceiling bookshelves. I read with a flashlight so I didn't have to open the drapes. The other wall was covered with dolls and stuffed animals, hung from little hooks by little strings around their little necks. Their bulging faces only frightened me when I was delirious from the drugs or the pain. The rest of the time they were quite friendly. But still I can't sleep if there's any part of me, even one toe, hanging off the edge of the bed."

I can't sleep in the bed at all. In the summer I sleep out here. In the winter I sleep on the couch. Nobody knows this about me. I sleep alone.

"There was one doctor who said there was nothing wrong with me. He said it was all in my head."

You know what they say: Two heads are better than one.

"We got rid of him."

It was all in his head.

"Everything I wanted came to me before I even had to ask for it. Silent nurses relayed tray after tray up the stairs. They would slide into my room, sighing and patting my hair, spoon-feeding me sometimes, bringing me whatever I cried for: icing sugar, jelly beans, lemonade, pink mints."

More wine.

"My tutors were all handsome young men who seemed to be hiding from something. My favourite was the one who taught me how to play the banjo and five-card stud. About everything else, he couldn't care less."

Me neither.

"I just naturally assumed this was how all little girls were treated. And if they weren't, they should be. I thought everyone was just like me. Or wanted to be."

Some things never change.

"Once I saw a man beating a little dog in the gutter with a baseball bat. When I tried to stop him, he swung at me too. This was either in Mexico or Toronto, I forget which. This was later."

It's as if you're wrapped in something. Valium or some vague aura, mysterious but convincing. The sunset, the wine, your slack voice, all are equally potent, and I am captured by the puzzle, the pieces you offer me, one at a time, like grapes. Everything is going wine-coloured around me, especially your hair, with the sun going down all through it.

"My father was a diplomat, whatever that means. It was never really explained to me and I never thought to ask. It was enough to know that he was someone important, always dressed in a three-piece suit, talking on the telephone, bringing home presents, buying black cars, always going away again."

My father was an alcoholic, whatever that means.

"Most of the time he ignored me, which was comforting."

Comforting enough.

"He's retired now, my old man, still handsome and lolling around exclusive hotels, sending me postcards that I stick on the bathroom wall. He never interested me much anyway."

I picture the old man lounging in a hot tub, sucking on crab legs, white grapes, the succulent oiled shoulder of some ripe debutante. He drinks dry martinis all day long. He beckons for a pen, dashes off something slightly witty, slumps back into the water, his fatherly impulses stifled or satisfied for now. Having a wonderful time. Glad you're not here. You never interested him much anyway.

"My mother's funeral was a discreetly grand affair. Nobody asked the uncomfortable questions and only her old black maid, Maisie, was primitive or generous enough to cry. There were thousands of flowers, white lilies mostly, her favourite, like snowbanks on the altar. I wore the most gorgeous blue silk, raw silk—everyone loved it."

The more you drink, the more your accent goes southern. Imagining you in front of a white pillared mansion becomes irresistible. In ten starched crinolines, you're waving and weeping till your eyes are like bruised peaches and the tops of your breasts swell and pulse. Two blue peacocks, dazzling and heartless, strut stiffly around you. An old yellow dog lies on the lawn, sleeping or dead. Your man is going off to war (Civil) and we all know he'll never come back. Sad, so sad, this scene is so sad it should be on the cover of a romance novel. Somewhere in it there are also magnolia blossoms, in your hair or scattered around your feet.

Oh shit. Frankly Scarlett, I don't give a damn.

"My mother had no influence on me, none at all."

This cannot, is not, will never be true.

"Once I thought she never really wanted me."

Once I thought I could see the future but it was only a coincidence.

"But then she left me a fortune."

Fortunes. I collect them, the kind that come in cookies: You will have good luck and overcome many hardships. For better luck you have to wait until autumn. You will receive a gift from a friend. Good news will come to you from far away. *I figure if I keep them long enough, they're bound to come true.*

"When I was a little girl, I wanted to be a fortune teller."

And what are you now? Don't you dare start reading my mind.

"My second husband, Max, was killed six months after the wedding. It was his own damn fault. That was when I decided I would never get married again. There's nothing sure in this world."

I'll drink to that.

"Hit by a bus."

The nerve of some people.

"Just that morning, we'd bought tickets to Spain. I went by myself but it wasn't the same. I'd forgotten about the bulls."

I'm afraid to imagine the sound.

"Once I saw a chicken with its head cut off running by the side of the road. That was in Spain too."

Once I chopped a chicken's head off with an axe. The axe was dull and it took a long time. That was on the farm. Then we made soup for supper.

"The thing about travelling is you're always thinking that the next restaurant, hotel room, city, or country will be the perfect one, the one thing you've been searching for all your little life. I could have been a gypsy if I'd wanted to."

Even your purse is like a suitcase, lumpy with eccentric items, I imagine—a hammer, a box of sugar cubes, and a syringe.

"In a hotel room in Paris, I found a photo album stashed behind the bed. Everyone in it looked happy and French, black and white. There were all combinations, young and old, men and women, with statues, horses, dogs, hugging each other. Everywhere there were trees, flowers, windows, rocking chairs, lace. There was a whole series of women clowning in white face for Hallowe'en or a play, doing mime in the street. Every little thing looked French. This is my favourite."

In the photograph you hand me, four young women are lounging around a fountain with flower beds. They're dressed in loose long skirts and sandals, resting their heads and hands on each other, lovingly. They're carrying things, paper bags, purses, a sweater. They're going somewhere, shopping, home, or out of the country. They look quite beautiful and intense, yes, very French. If they could talk, I wouldn't know what they were saying.

Why are you carrying these handsome anonymous women around in your purse as if they were good old friends?

"I want to be just like them. I want to be in the picture."

What you tell me is like marbles, those clear glass ones, green that you can see through if you hold one up to your eyeball. Marbles, the big ones, hard and flawless, no avenue in. They hit off each other in the dirt, spin away in tangents, out of reach altogether.

"When we moved into this place, I found a hundred dollar bill behind the stove."

What are you doing always looking behind things, beds and stoves, looking for other people's treasures or castoffs, finding them too? I found a diamond ring once but I sold it.

"I thought it was a lucky omen."

I thought you were perfect.

"Sometimes, just to cheer myself up, I use some of the money to send myself flowers. And then I pretend I don't know who they're from."

I thought you were going to teach me something, maybe how to swim.

"All I want to do is sleep."

You're no longer emotionally charming.

"The worst thing about being in jail that time was having to phone home and explain why I wouldn't be there for Christmas."

You're too young to know so much.

"I've never liked Christmas much anyway."

Too bad.

"I thought it would be different."

It is.

"Everything, I mean."

Are we drunk yet?

"It wasn't my fault."

I'm just feeling bitchy.

"You'll see what I mean when I tell you."

I'll try.

"All my lies are white ones."

There he is now, just in time, Hunter on the next balcony, waving "Hello" and "Come home" in one simple gesture. He's so graceful for a man. You gulp down your wine, gather up your purse, your perfect shoes, rush off barefoot and unsteady. Why are we looking so guilty? He's so powerful for a man.

You're off to your apartment which, I imagine, is laid out just like mine and furnished finely but starkly. Vivid white walls, old wicker painted black, pink vases, and pillows scattered around strategically. These are called accents. No plants—they would die. No dirt—of course not. There may be a red stain somewhere on the white rug but it could be anything. It could have been there when you moved in. There is also an aquarium, full of flowers instead of fish.

You're off now to perform unimaginable acts: making filet mignon, juicy and rare; overseas phone calls; love.

I'm just going to sit here awhile and finish my wine. As soon as I lie down in the dark, I'll be trying not to listen. You're not quite a stranger anymore, an intimate one if you are. I know too much now to invent you.

I want to tell you my whole life story.

HIS PEOPLE

(1987)

HOLLY met Nick for the first time in the shared driveway between their two houses. She was backing out the door Monday morning with the car keys in her mouth and a wicker basket full of dirty clothes in her arms, heading for the laundromat. She was also talking to herself: "And don't forget to put out the garbage, dummy."

Nick was coming down the driveway. "Morning," he said.

"Oh hi, and here I am talking to myself," Holly said, blushing. It was a hot day already and Nick was undeniably attractive in his little white shorts.

"Taking him to daycare," he said. His small son kicked up the gravel behind him. "Stop that, Nicky. Right now. Three last month."

"Laundry," Holly said, gesturing at her dirty underwear with her chin, which was narrow and rather pointy, a part of herself she'd never really liked.

"Hear you're from Alberta." Nick motioned towards her red-and-white license plates which had expired two months ago, but you had to pass the safety check in Ontario before they'd give you new plates and Holly was still getting around to taking the car in. "I was there once, went to pick him up.

Cost a fortune to fly there, what a place. You're lucky to be out of there. His mother was no good. Cherie."

Holly already knew that Nick was divorced, lived with his grandmother, and was just out of jail. He was looking for work. He spent whole weekends sitting on the front porch with his feet up on the iron railing, watching Nicky play in the driveway. Holly admired his patience with the boy, who cried a lot and seldom did what he was told.

Throughout the month of July, Holly noticed, the whole humid city seemed to spend the evening on the porch. Up and down the block, her neighbours hauled out the straight-back kitchen chairs, drank lite beer and wine coolers, fanned themselves, and swatted mosquitoes with the newspaper. Cars passed occasionally, ferrying children or dogs with their heads hung out the windows, or teenagers playing their car stereos full blast so everyone would notice them and know they were cool. In the park at the end of the block, the children were calling back and forth, pushing each other around in the wading pool, or swinging violently, trying to work up a breeze.

Next door, Gran fanned up her skirt and Nick took off his t-shirt and wiped his face with it. His hairless chest shone and he was studying the oiled torsos in a weightlifting magazine. The day before, Sears had delivered a whole set of barbells which Nick set up in the garage. Then he spent two hours with his cousin, Frank, on the punching ball he'd rigged up in the backyard. The sound was like slapping or tom-toms.

"Worst summer in twenty years," Gran called across to Holly on her porch, having another beer, and reading *The Dead and the Living,* poems by Sharon Olds. She'd be taking classes at the college in the fall. "It's not the heat, it's the humidity'll kill you," Gran said in her gravelly voice. "Hard on them." She nodded towards little Nicky, who was riding his tricycle madly up and down the driveway, whining. "Quit that.

Hear me? Hyper. I never seen a kid can't sit still for a minute. Heat's hard on them."

Nick ignored her and the boy both.

"Nick, you make him stop that. Leg's bad today." Gran propped her foot up on the railing, patting a deep circular scar around one kneecap, which protruded like a burl.

Nick yanked the tricycle away and put it in the backyard while Nicky screamed.

"What a kid," Gran said, massaging her knee. "Hyper. And he's even worse since *he* come back and now he's even worse since she come back, Viv." Nick's mother, Vivian, and her new husband, Walter, who was in the armed forces, had just returned from Germany, where he had been stationed for three years. Nick's father, Lloyd, was Gran's son. "But we weren't having none of ours brought up by the likes of her," Gran said. "So him and Lloyd went out west and brung him home. She got three other kids anyway, who knows where *they* come from."

When the daylight faded, Holly put down her book and went inside for another drink. She turned up the radio in the living room so she could hear it outside.

Nick appeared on her porch with a bug light. "She's gone in to put him to bed, she wants to watch *Mike Hammer.*" He hooked the bug light to the iron railing and plugged it in. "Been trying to get up my courage to come over here. Thought you might be needing this." The bug light glowed a humming blue-violet, snapping when the mosquitoes hit. He pointed to the green mosquito coils Holly had arranged around her front steps. "Those are no damn good." He sat down on the bottom step, leaned against the stucco wall, and slapped himself vigorously. "Allergic. See this." He twisted around to show her a large red welt on his lower back. "Swell up like a grapefruit, scratch for days." He stood up and sprayed himself front and back with a can of Off. "Here, let me spray you."

"They don't seem to bother me much," Holly said, but stood up anyway and pirouetted slowly while he sprayed her all up and down. "Would you like a chair?" she asked.

"I'm fine."

"Would you like a beer?"

"Don't drink. You're always reading, what're you reading?"

She handed him the book and, by the bug light, he studied the cover photograph: a man and a woman nude, her front, his back, *Adam and Eve* by Frank Eugene.

"Never heard of it," he said.

"This one," Holly said, opening the book and leaning into the mauve snapping light to read:

THE ISSUES
(Rhodesia, 1978)

Just don't tell me about the issues.
I can see the pale spider-belly head of the
newborn who lies on the lawn, the web of
veins at the surface of her scalp, her skin
grey and gleaming, the clean line of the
bayonet down the center of her chest.
I see the mother's face, beaten and
beaten into the shape of a plant,
a cactus with grey spines and broad
dark maroon blooms.
I see her arm stretched out across her baby,
wrist resting, heavily, still, across the
tiny ribs.
    Don't speak to me about
politics. I've got eyes, man.

"I only read the facts," said Nick.

"What?"

"You know, *National Geographic* and Matthew, Mark, Luke, and John."

"What?"

"You know, the Bible. I'm studying it every day. The priest come to see me, he give me the books. Do you know the world?"

"I don't think so."

"I think you do. The Lord He says if you know the world, it'll hate you."

"Well, yes, sometimes I think the world does hate me," Holly admitted. "And I wonder why."

"All you gotta do is give yourself over to the Lord and He'll show you the Way."

"Oh, I just love this song," Holly cried, jumping up and running inside to turn up the radio. She sat back down, casually closer to Nick, and sang along with Fleetwood Mac: *If I live to see the Seven Wonders/I'll make a path to the rainbow's end/I'll never live to match the beauty again,* thinking of the man she'd left behind in Alberta but it never would have worked out anyway, she knew that. She was lonely and wondering if Nick would kiss her goodnight.

There came the sound of sirens close by.

"Fire," Holly said.

"Cops," Nick said. "Once they found a dead body in a house around the corner, you know."

Just then his father, Lloyd, with his new wife, Freda, pulled up front in his immaculate maroon Pontiac Parisienne. "He's taking me over to the mall tomorrow, buy some clothes so I can go to church from now on. Nice clothes and a fishing rod, going to do some fishing too," Nick said as he was leaving.

"Gimme a ride to the mall?" Nick called from his open kitchen window. Holly was out in the driveway washing her car. "She wants to rent a steam cleaner, do the rugs. Might as well do yours too while I'm at it. Missed a spot there."

He hopped in. "You're up early. Some days I'm just crawling out of bed at noon and there you are in the kitchen window all dressed and everything already and I think, Wow."

Walking from the car to the mall entrance, he said, "Sometimes I just hate coming to this mall."

"Why?" Holly asked, thinking with a thrill that there was someone inside he didn't want to see, someone from his criminal life, or maybe he'd broken into one of the stores (which one? Radio Shack, Big Steel, Birks) or shoplifted something (what? pearl necklace, suede coat, a gun) and got caught.

"'Cause this is where the fat people shop. You know, from Willow Ridge, the suburbs."

And the two women coming out of The Bay as they went in were bulging and jiggling in their terry cloth shorts sets, laughing and licking on chocolate ice cream.

When they got the steam cleaner, Nick discovered he'd forgotten his wallet, so Holly showed her I.D. and counted out the twenty-five dollars.

"Are you two together?" the clerk asked suspiciously.

"I guess so, yeah," said Nick.

"What were you in for?" Holly finally asked him. They were watching fireflies in the grass. There was heat lightning in the west but the rain never came.

"You know?"

Holly nodded but of course he couldn't see her in the dark and looking away like that to the park where some kids were drinking beer around a picnic table, a case of twenty-four stashed behind the wading pool.

"Suppose *she* told you."

"Frank."

"None of his damn business. Watch him, he'll steal you blind get the chance. Just no good even if he is my cousin. She'll be sorry letting him come around here. Going to get some smokes."

Holly watched him striding across the park, past the mound of rocks in the middle which he'd told her was an Indian burial place. "They're talking to me sometimes, the skeletons, the spirits," he'd said. "You don't believe me, do you?"

He stopped to talk to the kids drinking beer in the park.

In ten minutes he was back. "Those kids, this one kid," he was laughing, "says he just got out this morning, they're celebrating. So I says, You're stupid, kid, you got no sense. Here, I got you a popsicle."

The next morning Holly saw that the picnic table has been left balanced carefully on top of the Indian rocks.

Nick thought he had a job cooking down at Mr. Pizza Patio but then when he showed up for his first shift, they said forget it because they had found out he'd done time. "The boss, the jerk," Nick told Holly, "he goes, When did you get out, so I go, Yeah and when'd you get off the boat, buddy?" Holly swore she'd never order pizza from that place again.

Then he did get a job, pumping gas at the 24-Hour Texaco out by the 401. His mother, Vivian, bought him a 650 Yamaha to get back and forth to work. "He's got money to burn," Nick said, meaning Walter, his mother's new husband. "Got a state-of-the-art German stereo and an $8,000 wall unit. Porsche. Gonna get Nicky a real jungle gym."

Nick and his cousin, Frank, who only had a ten-speed, tinkered with the motorcycle endlessly. When they weren't taking it apart or putting it back together, they were washing it.

"Lend me some money?" Nick asked Holly one night on her porch.

"How much? What for?"

"Insurance. $150. Can't drive it till I get it."

Holly hesitated. She didn't like lending money to men because it seemed only to create complications.

"Well?"

"I don't know."

"Pay you half in two weeks when I get my cheque. Other half next cheque. I'll mow your grass, change the oil in your car, and who's gonna shovel your snow this winter?"

"All right, yes," she said. Yes, she wanted him to know she had faith in him, never mind his past. Yes, she wanted to help him make something of himself after all. "I suppose you'll never be home now," she teased.

Nick just laughed and walked her to the bank, where she couldn't help wondering if the teller counting out the cash might think they were married or something. She handed Nick the bills. "And don't you go killing yourself on that thing." She hated the way she sounded. "They'll all blame me."

"They don't need to know," Nick said, "and don't you be telling them neither."

Walking through the park on her way home from downtown, Holly stopped at the wading pool to shift her shopping bags around. She'd bought some groceries and three summer dresses on sale, red, blue, yellow, like long t-shirts, which she planned to wear with her elastic black belt tight at the waist to show off her legs which she'd always liked, their pretty bony kneecaps and their slim smooth calves.

From the pool, she could see Gran stationed on her porch and wished for a way to sneak home without having to walk past her and hear her say yet again, "Worst summer in twenty years it's not the heat it's the humidity hard on them." Being a congenitally polite person, Holly could only nod and agree enthusiastically.

She and Nick had said little more than hello in over a week. He was working, he said, extra shifts at the gas station, going to his father's for dinner with Nicky, going to his mother's to watch movies on the new VCR, going to see his parole officer once a week. Holly could hear him racing in and out of the driveway on the motorcycle at all hours. Sometimes she was lying in bed reading and then she would tiptoe into her dark kitchen to watch him riding away. Sometimes it woke her up. Once she complained, just kidding, about the noise and from then on he wheeled the bike down the driveway and halfway to the corner before he started it. Or he'd coast in with the light off. So she never knew anymore when he was coming or going, at home or away.

He rode up behind her in the park on Frank's ten-speed, the spokes clicking. He said, "Well, I don't have to worry about him, she took him for all weekend." Holly felt cozy being able to decipher this code, which meant Nicky was staying with Vivian and Walter, as he often did lately. He practically lived there. Gran was insulted by this and complained about how spoiled he got there, staying up late, eating Smarties all day and ice cream. "I raised him for a year and a half," she told Holly. "Up all night and toilet-training too. He flushed a toy car one time, had to get a whole new toilet. I done all the work, now she comes home, thinks she can just take over."

Nick grunted as a police car cruised the perimeter of the park. "Hey you, I'm over here," he called, holding his arms out in front of him, hands back to back, miming being handcuffed. "They're always watching me now. Anything goes wrong around here, you watch, they'll be on my doorstep."

"Where'd you go Saturday?" he asked.

"Just out." Holly had gone to the show with a friend, female, from the college, and then bar-hopping.

"Heard you come home three in the morning for godsake."

"I saw your lights on, yes."

His cousin, Frank, came over one night with his ghetto blaster and a large tumbler of 100-proof Jack Daniels. Nick was at work. Frank was wearing his black Jack Daniels t-shirt with the sleeves ripped out to show off his tattoos: a prancing blue unicorn on the right biceps and *Frank loves Penny* in script on the left, but he was going to see about getting this one covered up or removed.

"Got any apple juice?" he asked Holly. "I like it with apple juice. Divvy it up, you have some too. She got it in the States." Gran had spent the previous weekend visiting her brother,

Ted, in Michigan where, she told Holly the night she returned, everything was better and cheaper than here. "'Cause they know how to stand up for themselves, those people," she said. "Not like here, we just take it all lying down, whatever they tell us. Price of coffee, I'll never drink it again. You watch."

Holly went into her kitchen and mixed up the juice. Frank fiddled with his tapes and cranked up Whitesnake: *Here I go again on my own/Down the only road I've ever known/Like a drifter/I was born to walk alone.* His girlfriend, Penny, who waited tables down at Subway Submarine, had recently left him for a drummer. So now Frank was renting two rooms with a kitchenette in Gran's basement and listening to love songs, loud.

They sipped their drinks, which were gruesome, and tapped their feet to the music, singing along. They could relate to the lyrics, the loneliness, both of them.

"He'll be jealous, he catches me sitting over here," Frank said.

Holly giggled.

"He thinks a lot of you, no really," he said.

"You'd never know it half the time."

"Oh, that's him. She says he changed since he got out this time, got God and all that. I don't see no change. He's always been the golden boy around here. Can't do no wrong far as she's concerned. He's mean to that kid, you know. Nicky loves me more than him. He don't do a thing around here. Won't even take out the garbage and her with her leg."

"I've noticed that," Holly agreed, cozy with conspiracy against Nick, who hadn't been over for nearly a week.

"It won't last long. He don't like me, I make him look bad. Here he is."

Nick on his motorcycle roared past them up the driveway and slammed the back door on his way into the house. They heard his helmet hit the floor. The screen door slammed again and they could hear him pounding on the punching ball out back. Holly, half drunk on the overproof whisky, found this rather amusing and flirted harmlessly in her short blue sun-dress with Frank all evening long till he went home to pass out.

Towards the end of August, Holly quit drinking and sat on the step angelically sipping her ginger ale right out of the can, so Nick would notice and know it wasn't spiked.

"I quit drinking," she tells him.

"Yeah sure," he snorts. "Till the next time."

"If you can do it, so can I."

"Maybe. My parole, I got no choice. Get caught drinking, back in for six months."

A woman in a pink sweatsuit jogs past with her breasts bouncing and her Walkman turned up so loud they can hear it like an insect.

"She'll get cancer," Nick says.

"What?"

"Jogging without a training bra'll cause cancer, you know."

"That's crazy!"

"Cherie said."

"She was kidding you."

"No way. It's true. She read it in a book."

When Holly goes inside for two more cans of pop, Nick nods. She can tell that he is pleased with her.

"The Lord He don't hold with drinking," he says. "Once me and my buddies sat down in that field over by the Pen all day and we were drinking a case of two-four just so those poor buggers in the yard they'd know what they were missing. Was when she lived up on Concession Street. Them guys always coming around the house looking for a party, drinking her rye, stealing her stuff. Then I did some time and she got hit by that car, drunk driver. In the hospital she was throwing bedpans at the doctors, you just ask her, till they let her out. That was my first time in, break and enter, that's all I ever done wrong. Got in with that bad crowd, don't see them no more. This guy I ratted on be out in three years, says he's coming to get me but I'm not worried, got God, my weights. Look at that."

Holly is surprised to see a raccoon ambling across the close end of the park, right here in the middle of the city. And sometimes in the morning there is the stink of skunk in the air.

Once she asked Nick why the squirrels here are black, when out west they were brown. And she still marvels at the sound of the cicadas, which she never heard in the west, a vibration like a plucked high wire, a sign of hot weather.

"Well, that's Alberta for you," Nick said, satisfied.

"Groundhogs last year," he says now.

Steve Winwood on the stereo is singing: *All the doors I closed one time/ Will open up again/I'll be back in the high life again.*

"I been in three times now but the Lord He forgives me."

Nick puts an arm around her with unusually obvious affection. "And He understands about a man needing a woman now and again too."

Holly has been waiting for just the right moment, this moment, to give him the card she is fingering fondly inside her sweater pocket. The size of a credit card, it is covered with tiny white printing on a shiny silver background, which reflects Nick's face as he leans close to the bug light to read.

The blue title in italics says *Footprints:*

One night a man had a dream.
He dreamed he was walking along the beach with the Lord
and across the sky there flashed scenes from his life.
In each scene there were two sets of footprints in the sand:
one belonging to him and the other to the Lord.
Looking back at the scenes,
the man saw that many times along the path of his life
there was only one set of footprints.

This bothered the man so he questioned the Lord.
"Lord, You said that once I decided to follow You,
You'd walk with me all the way.
But during the lowest and saddest times of my life,
there is only one set of footprints.
Why did You leave me when I needed You most?"
The Lord replied,
"My son, I love you and would never leave you.
In your times of trouble
when you see only one set of footprints,
it was then that I carried you."

Nick was telling Holly the story from jail about this guy who tried to cut off his thing, you know, his *thing*, with a plastic spoon, then a comb, and then finally he slammed it in a steel door. "It was those doors," he said, "those steel doors slamming all night long. It was those doors made me feel like I was being tortured. Never slept the whole time for the sound of those doors slamming. It's those doors I dream about, slamming."

Holly, horrified, asks, "Did he die? What happened to him?"

But Nick doesn't know. He can't remember and seems never to have wondered. This is not the point of the story.

They are camped out on the sofa bed in Holly's living room, which is the only room in the house cool enough (not very) to sleep in, for though the quickening evening darkness of September has moved the whole neighbourhood back inside most nights, the humidity still hangs and the air will not move.

They are watching a TV documentary called *In Search of Dracula* in which the narrator says, "Story-telling wards off vampires."

Nick says, "Garlic." He does not talk much about the Lord anymore.

Talking this night before they fall asleep in each other's arms, they discover that they both always wear pajamas for fear of having to get up in the middle of the night and run (Holly) or fight (Nick).

During this night they both dream, at different times, that someone is standing at the front door looking in at them. Close to morning, Holly gets up and pulls down the blind.

When Nick sneaks home across the driveway at 6 a.m., Holly can hear Gran hollering, "Where the hell have you been?" She goes into her bedroom and shuts the door so she cannot hear the details of the lengthy argument. All day long she wonders what he said.

Holly and Nick are lying on Gran's couch watching rock videos and she has her head in his lap. There is so much big furniture jammed into the little room that there is hardly space to walk around. On the wall facing Holly's house, there is a large velvet painting which, in the flickering television light, might be of horses rearing or of women dancing, but Holly keeps thinking it's a window and she catches herself looking over every few minutes, trying to see out. Nick is telling her about the new bunk beds Gran has ordered so he and Nicky won't be so crowded in their little bedroom. They are whispering for fear of waking Gran or the boy. None of his people, it appears, are to know about their relationship yet.

Nick says, "Don't get me wrong sometimes."

"What?" His thought processes are often hard to follow.

"Sometimes when I don't see you, don't get me wrong. I just don't want to get serious. After Cherie I know all about love, just don't want no part of it no more. It aches my mind."

Holly reaches up and strokes his face, which she loves, consoling him and not believing a word of it.

"Just gonna live here forever," Nick says, stretching. "Never pay no rent again."

"But how can you stand it? A grown man still sleeping in bunk beds. I could never live with my family now."

"But my people, they're different, let me do what I like. They're always trying to give me things. The bike. Now she wants to buy me a car. Camaro, I want a blue Camaro."

Holly is reading in bed when she hears Nick ride up. Over the sound of the bike there comes a delighted wild whooping.

Holly goes into her kitchen to peek out at him. He is already inside Gran's house where the kitchen light comes on. He leans against the sink with his back to the window, his helmet still on him like a huge insect head. He takes it off, bending forward so she can see his mouth moving but she can't hear the words: the screen is closed now against the cool night. The other person puts a small hand up on each of his shoulders and he kisses her.

They come back outside, the girl drunk and staggering around in the driveway until Nick steadies her tenderly. She is wearing blue jeans, a white t-shirt under a baggy black cardigan with a can of beer in each pocket. She is pointing at something in Holly's backyard and laughing her dizzy head off. Holly can see her clothesline reflected by moonlight in Gran's kitchen window. She has hung from it this morning her new summer dresses all in a row. In the window in the wind now, they flap and collide like decapitated bodies, headless chickens, hopeless. They will hang there for two days before they dry in this humidity and then they will be spotted with mildew which will never wash out.

Nick and the girl drink the beer. Then he wheels the bike down the driveway with her on the back clutching him, saying, "Are you sure about this?"

Holly goes back to bed, saying out loud, "So what? Who cares? I don't care what you do or who you do it with," goes back to reading her poetry books because classes have started.

A few minutes later she can hear sirens. They would be, she estimates, just to the far corner of the park by now, somewhere between the black cannon that points down Clergy Street and the monument to that dead minister who founded the church on the corner in 1893. She imagines them crumpled together on the cool grass, his head like an egg now inside the helmet and hers just flattened and still, like a plate.

He could end up back in jail, the fool, when they arrest him for violating his parole.

Or he could be dying even now, repenting as the scenes of his life flash like sheet lightning, promises out of the southern sky.

NONE OF THE ABOVE

(1987)

THE CITY is a conglomerate of oil-rainbowed bubbles, all of its unknown neighbourhoods dissolving one by one behind David and Belinda Boyce as they pass obliviously through on their way home in the five o'clock Friday rush-hour dark of early December. In other parts of the city,

(A) a lonely woman may be eating Kraft Dinner right out of the pot, standing there in her housecoat, watching *The Young and the Restless*, trying not to cry in her condo on Elm Street.

(B) an old woman may be lying dead in her bed-sitting room on Sixteenth Avenue, having been there four days, the newspapers piling up outside her door: maybe tomorrow someone will miss her or smell her.

(C) a desperate young woman may be holding up a liquor store at the corner of Centre and Tenth, making off with all the cash and two magnums of French champagne.

(D) a scorned woman may be slashing up the waterbed in a high-rise on Dalhousie Drive, stabbing her unfaithful husband twenty-six times in the back, letting his lover go naked and screaming and free through the puddles already leaking through to the apartment below.

(E) all of the above.

David Boyce is driving the old blue Pontiac, having stopped to pick up Belinda at the plant store where she works on his way from the pet store where he works. In the plant store, Belinda sells

(A) African violets.
(B) Wandering Jews.
(C) geraniums.
(D) rubber trees.
(E) cacti and succulents.

In the pet store, David sells

(A) guppies.
(B) parakeets.
(C) lizards.
(D) guinea pigs.
(E) pitbull puppies.

Belinda is

(A) beautiful.
(B) short.
(C) tired.
(D) young.
(E) too young to be so tired.

David is

(A) handsome.
(B) tall.
(C) smug.
(D) young.
(E) too young to be so smug.

Belinda is

(A) innocent.
(B) carefree.
(C) contented.
(D) lovable.
(E) only occasionally depressed.

David is

(A) responsible.
(B) hard-working.
(C) ambitious.
(D) lovable.
(E) only occasionally insensitive.

Tonight, December 8, it is

(A) windy.
(B) snowy.
(C) icy.
(D) twenty below.
(E) pretty miserable for this time of year.

David drives with extra care because Belinda beside him holds in her lap

(A) a baby.
(B) an aquarium.
(C) an angel food cake.
(D) a bouquet of rare orchids.
(E) a snowball melting all down her thighs.

David and Belinda (née Johnson), high-school sweethearts, were married the summer after graduation at 3 p.m. on Saturday, August 8, three years ago. At the time, they expected their linked lives to play out happy and long. So far, they are

(A) correct.
(B) mistaken.

(C) convinced.
(D) surprised.
(E) still waiting.

In their early twenties now, they are still living in the same city where they were both born. Their city, it seems to them, will always be
(A) solid.
(B) snug.
(C) friendly.
(D) comfortable.
(E) home.

They have never had, either one of them, the slightest desire to move to
(A) Toronto.
(B) Los Angeles.
(C) Indian Head, Saskatchewan.
(D) Amsterdam.
(E) Argentina.

With the generous help of their parents and the Bank of Montreal, they have been able to purchase and furnish a semi-detached home on Edelweiss Crescent in the new subdivision of
(A) Canyon Meadows.
(B) Silver Springs.
(C) Tuxedo Park.
(D) Greenview Estates.
(E) Briar Hill Heights.

In their new home, there is
(A) a 12-cup Philips Coffee Maker. Dial-a-brew system with showerhead design water spreader. Pause control

for one-cup convenience. "On" light and dust cover. Two-hour automatic shut-off if you forget! Drip reservoir in basket.

(B) a 20" Colour Television. Quick-view feature means a clear picture seconds after you turn the television on! Off-timer automatically turns off television at a predetermined time. Charcoal-grey styling adds the perfect modern touch to your home!

(C) a Proctor-Silex Broiler Oven. Will bake, broil, toast, and keep warm! Continuous-clean interior, large window, all-purpose bake pan, dual-weight oven rack, easy-clean crumb tray.

(D) a Sunbeam Electric Blanket with BodySensor feature. Personal Monitoring System monitors your entire body while you sleep, compensating for any temperature changes it senses! 80% polyester, 20% acrylic.

(E) a Water Pik Home Dental System. The Command Control Pik allows you to control the water flow! Includes oral irrigator, electric toothbrush, 4 colour-coded jet tips and 4 brushes.

They are also saving their money for

(A) wall-to-wall carpeting.
(B) a microwave oven.
(C) a CD player.
(D) a new car in the spring, maybe a Volvo or a Ford Mustang Cobra GT Convertible.
(E) a trip to Hawaii next winter or maybe to the West Edmonton Mall.

Having discussed the future at length, David and Belinda would like to have

(A) 12 children.
(B) 2 children.

(C) 0 children.
(D) a cat.
(E) a dog.

If they have a cat, she is sleeping like a sweater in the middle of the kitchen table when they get home. If they have a cat, her name is
(A) Puff.
(B) Tiger.
(C) Muffin.
(D) Bubbles.
(E) Bert.

If they have a dog named Rex, he is
(A) a cocker spaniel.
(B) a Doberman pinscher.
(C) a poodle.
(D) a chihuahua.
(E) not house-trained yet.

If they have a Doberman named Rex, he is watching for them loyally from his mat by the door. He greets them with exuberance and his jaws come shut with the sound of a wet handclap. While David has a beer and wrestles around with Rex, Belinda makes for their supper
(A) Stuffed Herbed Chicken Breasts with Vinegar Sauce.
(B) Steamed Broccoli Nouvelle.
(C) Baked Parmesan Rice with Mushrooms and Sautéed Almonds.
(D) Eggplant-Zucchini Salad.
(E) Perfect Apple Pie.

Over their meal, they talk amiably about
(A) how tender the chicken is, just delicious, done this way, also the broccoli.

(B) how glad they are it's finally Friday and they can just relax.
(C) how Belinda would really like to get her hair permed.
(D) how David has a nasty corn on his left baby toe.
(E) what they will do tomorrow.

Tomorrow being Saturday they will
(A) stay in bed all day.
(B) defrost the fridge.
(C) wallpaper the bathroom.
(D) watch football and drink beer.
(E) go shopping at the mall.

At the mall, they will buy
(A) a cookie jar shaped like a duck.
(B) a shower curtain with dolphins on it.
(C) mauve sheets.
(D) a shovel.
(E) a hand grenade.

Over their meal, they do not discuss
(A) the fact that David's younger sister, Andrea, has been arrested for shoplifting after stealing a blow dryer and a Rolling Stones tape from Woolworth's when she had $100 in her purse and had just come from her weekly session with the shrink.
(B) the fact that Ginny Andrews who works with Belinda at the plant store is having an abortion, her third, in the morning.
(C) how yesterday there was fighting all night next door, Al and Suzanne screaming, glass breaking, and something round and solid, but soft too, like a head or a cabbage, hitting the wall.
(D) Belinda's recurring nightmare in which she is chasing David around Edelweiss Crescent with an axe until he

stops dead in his tracks, turns around and shoots her, with a face on him like Bruce Springsteen.
(E) the threat of nuclear war which has permeated their whole young lives.

David and Belinda Boyce think of themselves as
(A) a lucky couple.
(B) an unlucky couple.
(C) a happy couple.
(D) an unhappy couple.
(E) they do not think of themselves.

After the dishes are done, Belinda puts on her terry cloth bathrobe which she bought last weekend at Woolworth's for $70. The bathrobe, which she loves, is the colour of
(A) peaches.
(B) peppermints.
(C) lilacs.
(D) her eyes.
(E) broken glass.

Curled up in the corner of the sectional, Belinda is
(A) watching *Miami Vice.*
(B) knitting a green sweater for David for Christmas.
(C) painting her toenails that great new colour called Red Alert.
(D) playing solitaire.
(E) reading her horoscope in the evening paper.

Belinda is
(A) a Virgo.
(B) a Cancer.
(C) a Libra.
(D) a Pisces.
(E) an Aquarius.

David is

(A) an Aries.
(B) a Taurus.
(C) a Leo.
(D) a Scorpio.
(E) a Sagittarius.

If Belinda is reading her horoscope, it says

(A) Influential people are less likely to support your ideas. Postpone entertaining a new alliance. Relaxing at home appeals more than a night on the town.
(B) You finally see the light at the end of the tunnel! Have faith in your talents and let other people handle their own problems.
(C) Your optimism is contagious today. You will be happiest with your family and pets.
(D) Anything can happen this weekend and probably will. You love surprises! Stay in touch with friends overseas. You may want to take a trip.
(E) You get a second chance and make the most of it! Your popularity continues to grow. Use wit but not sarcasm to make a point.

If Belinda is reading David's horoscope, it says

(A) Career demands begin to get to you. Take a long weekend and recoup. Someone may be trying to deceive you by withholding facts.
(B) Be careful not to pledge something you cannot afford to give. Real estate transactions look good. Speculative ventures, romance, and meetings with siblings are favoured.
(C) Partner is more sensitive to your ideas and needs. Long-term financial security should be a top priority now.
(D) You may have more than your usual work to cope with. Your ability to produce when under pressure will

impress an influential person. A family member's problems are not as serious as they seem.

(E) The world could be at your feet if you play your cards right. Get some exercise instead of a large lunch at noon.

This is like in high school when they played the Top Ten on the radio every night at 10 p.m. and, if Belinda could guess all ten songs right and in order, then the next day would be a good day. The next day

(A) they would not have to play basketball.
(B) Mrs. Sanderson, the biology teacher, would be away and they would not have to learn any more about those stupid fungi.
(C) they would have tacos for lunch in the cafeteria.
(D) her hair would look just right.
(E) David would walk her home after school, carrying her books and holding her hand.

This is like Belinda playing solitaire to pass the time when David isn't around and, if she beats the devil on the first try, tomorrow

(A) she will not have to make a funeral wreath.
(B) Mr. MacKay, her boss, will be in a good mood all day.
(C) the other girls from the plant store will invite her to lunch at Red Lobster.
(D) her hair will look just right.
(E) David will tell her he still loves her, without her having to say it first.

David does not appear to be around right now. He has

(A) gone to the basement to play with his model train set.
(B) gone next door to watch the hockey game with Al.
(C) gone out to walk the dog.

(D) gone to bed.
(E) gone.

Just before The National news comes on at ten o'clock, there is a knock at the back door. Not sure whether to answer it or not, Belinda turns on the outside light, temporarily blinding a man who has come to

(A) read the meter in the basement.
(B) demonstrate a new improved Electrolux vacuum cleaner.
(C) sell her a lifetime subscription to *Better Homes and Gardens.*
(D) mystify her with magic tricks, pulling parakeets out of a hat, plucking gold coins from her eyelids, turning purple orchids into flying fish.
(E) let her in on the meaning of life.

In the immaculate kitchen, the man says

(A) Thou shalt have no other gods before me.
(B) Thou shalt not make unto thee any graven image, or any likeness of any thing that is in heaven above, or that is in the earth beneath, or that is in the water under the earth: Thou shalt not bow down thyself to them, nor serve them: for I the Lord thy God am a jealous God, visiting the iniquity of the fathers upon the children unto the third and fourth generation of them that hate me: And showing mercy unto thousands of them that love me, and keep my commandments.
(C) Thou shalt not take the name of the Lord thy God in vain; for the Lord will not hold him guiltless that taketh His name in vain.
(D) Remember the sabbath day, to keep it holy. Six days shalt thou labour, and do all thy work: But the seventh day is the sabbath of the Lord thy God: in it thou shalt

not do any work, thou, nor thy son, nor thy daughter, thy manservant, nor thy maidservant, nor thy cattle, nor thy stranger that is within thy gates: For in six days the Lord made heaven and earth, the sea, and all that in them is, and rested the seventh day: wherefore the Lord blessed the sabbath day, and hallowed it.
(E) Honour thy father and thy mother: that thy days may be long upon the land which the Lord thy God giveth thee.

Belinda asks
(A) Who are you?
(B) Where have you come from?
(C) Why are you here?
(D) Am I guilty?
(E) What am I guilty of?

In the cosy living room, the man says
(A) Thou shalt not kill.
(B) Thou shalt not commit adultery.
(C) Thou shalt not steal.
(D) Thou shalt not bear false witness against thy neighbour.
(E) Thou shalt not covet thy neighbour's house, thou shalt not covet thy neighbour's wife, nor his manservant, not his maidservant, nor his ox, nor his ass, nor anything that is thy neighbour's.

Belinda says
(A) I believe you.
(B) I believe you.
(C) I believe you.
(D) Yes, I believe you.
(E) Yes, yes, I see what you mean.

The man leaves
(A) suddenly.
(B) silently.
(C) very carefully, stepping over the dog.
(D) satisfied.
(E) sanctified.

When David reappears about an hour later, Belinda is
(A) still sitting on the sectional still painting her toes.
(B) lying in bed with her head covered up.
(C) laughing.
(D) crying.
(E) levitating somewhere over the kitchen sink.

Belinda
(A) tells him.
(B) doesn't.
(C) tells him.
(D) doesn't.
(E) does.

If Belinda tells him, David says she must be
(A) crazy.
(B) drunk.
(C) dreaming.
(D) premenstrual.
(E) truly blessed.

Because of this night, the lives of David and Belinda Boyce are forever
(A) changed.
(B) unchanged.
(C) fulfilled.
(D) unfulfilled.

(E) forever finished for better or worse.

In her later life, Belinda Boyce will

(A) become manager of the plant store and proceed inconspicuously over the years to stock the shelves exclusively with thousands of Prayer Plants and Venus Fly Traps, until the place finally goes bankrupt and is replaced by a massage parlour.

(B) give birth to a charming cherubic child named Joshua, who will give true meaning to her heretofore shallow life.

(C) write a bestselling book about her blessing and go on *Phil Donahue* talking in tongues.

(D) do twenty-five years in the Prison for Women for hijacking a jumbo jet to Jerusalem on which the in-flight movie was *Oh God II.*

(E) die peacefully at the age of eighty-seven, sleeping between the mauve sheets in the master bedroom of the house on Edelweiss Crescent, never knowing what hit her.

In his later life, David Boyce will

(A) buy a Cadillac Fleetwood, GM Executive, V8 loaded, air conditioning, power windows, power steering, power brakes, cruise control, gold, and die in a twenty-seven-car pile-up on the 401.

(B) join the Hell's Angels and die in a gang war.

(C) buy a Kentucky Fried Chicken franchise and die in a grease fire.

(D) take up windsurfing and die in a tidal wave.

(E) suffer eternal unenlightened life.

In his later life, the man who came to the back door will become

(A) a television evangelist.

(B) a Rosicrucian.

(C) a family man.
(D) a mass murderer.
(E) the burning bush.

No matter what happens in the rest of their lives, tonight, in other parts of the city,

(A) a contented woman may be tucking in her babies in a bungalow on Amethyst Crescent, kissing their smooth fair foreheads, singing them a lullaby sweetly, the one about how when the bough breaks, the cradle will fall, and down will come baby, cradle and all.
(B) a carefree, only occasionally depressed, woman may be getting ready for bed on Baker Street, taking her face off with cool gobs of Noxzema, doing an Apricot Facial Scrub, brushing and flossing her pretty straight teeth, studying them closely in the mirror, so happy to see she hasn't changed a bit.
(C) an innocent woman may be down on her knees beside the brass four-poster waterbed on Francis Street, praying fervently for forgiveness.
(D) a tired, only occasionally peculiar, woman may be sitting at her typewriter in her study on Dunlop Street (the only room on the block with the lights still on, like a beacon in the night or, less obviously, an anchor), writing a story in which she tries, for no apparent reason, to make a connection between Christianity, astrology, and the Consumers Distributing catalogue.
(E) none of the above.

HOW MYRNA SURVIVES

(1987)

> They were all in their early thirties. An age at which it is sometimes hard to admit that what you are living is your life.
>
> — Alice Munro, "Accident" in *The Moons of Jupiter*

1. Myrna Lillian Waxman is thirty-two years old and lying on the couch all the cool afternoon. The couch is a cautious grey corduroy which wears well and doesn't show the dirt. Myrna has covered herself with a green-and-yellow quilt made by her distant cousin, Annette, before she was hit by a freight train at the level crossing a quarter-mile from her house, which she had travelled over twice a day for twenty years. On the wall above the couch there is a silk-screen print of footprints in the snow in which the bushes are black, the snow is blue, and the footprints, white, are those of a small desperate animal with only three legs.

There is a certain amount of guilt attached to sleeping in the daytime but Myrna has managed to convince herself that she needs or deserves it. She is letting her mind wander between waking and sleep, willing herself to sustain this surreal state for much longer than any normal person would, because this, she is convinced, is where her best ideas come from and where all of her problems are solved. (This may also happen, though less reliably, when she is having a bath or driving alone in the car.) In the end, though, she usually falls asleep anyway and dreams about sex or love or a staircase transformed into egg-shells beneath her bare feet, or maybe all three.

This habit of napping in the afternoon can be tricky for Myrna at this time of year, late autumn, because there is a certain quality of light at a certain advanced hour which she finds she must avoid waking up into. It is that time of the day when, normally, you would be going through rooms turning on lights without thinking about it, your husband (if you had one) would be driving home from work, and you would be stirring something savoury on the stove. It is a cold light in the late afternoon, and grey, sinking, heartless. It is almost fluorescent in the way it magnifies all of your flaws and failures till you barely recognize yourself. It is when you know for sure the day is over, you've had your chance and missed it, there is nothing to be done about it now, and so you go on into evening.

Before she lies down, Myrna puts her little travel alarm clock on the coffee table beside her and sets it so she can be safely up and doing something when the light, defeated, goes down and the day slops, or at least drains, out of her like blood. What she likes to be doing best is folding laundry.

She heaps her clean clothes on the couch, extracts each article (t-shirt, underwear, blue jeans, towels, that black-and-white flowered skirt with the elasticized waist which hangs so prettily and which she will wear out to dinner if anybody asks her) and smooths it out on the coffee table, taking the time to pick off the lint balls and appreciate the new-improved-fresh-scent of the detergent. She folds carefully and slowly, with calm concentration, depositing each item in its appropriate pile. While she folds, she thinks about her ex-roommate, Rose. She is teaching herself to do things the way Rose did them.

Rose, who could spend an hour folding and patting her sweaters, arranging them like woolly pillows in piles on the top shelf of her closet. Rose, who got up an hour early every morning to iron her clothes for work so that by the time Myrna came to, the kitchen was filled with the nurturing smells of coffee and hot cotton. Rose, who brought to every little thing she did such a serenity and single-mindedness that you just knew her mind was perfectly clear, healthy, and *good.*

Rose has since married and moved to Vancouver. Myrna hasn't heard from her in nearly a year. She automatically assumes this unnatural lapse to be somehow her fault but, as of yet, has done nothing to make amends.

Emulating Rose, arranging all her clean clothes in her clean closet, with every button buttoned and all the wrinkles shaken out, Myrna is filled with a distinct sense of accomplishment. She feels competent. She feels content. She feels like a good person for the time being and the dangerous hour has safely passed.

With the alarm clock set and the washing machine spinning sturdily in the basement, Myrna on the couch is thinking now, unaccountably, of when she was twenty-one, an undergraduate student in English Lit, engaged to marry Gordon Bates, a Business Admin major. Both she and Gord had a night class Thursdays from seven till ten. His was Advanced Accounting and hers was Creative Writing, her favourite. She was secretly in love with her professor, Dr. Diamond. Either good old Gord hadn't figured this out yet or, if he had, he wasn't letting it bother him.

Dr. Diamond (or Bernie, as he encouraged his students to call him—something which Myrna never could bring herself to do, this name being so colloquial or trivial, so unsuitable) was married to a dilettante sculptor named Jocelyn Bringhurst, who was always telling the story at university parties of how she'd once met Salvador Dali and Moon Dog at a coffeehouse in New York City in the sixties. Myrna cannot now remember who or what Moon Dog was anyway.

Dr. Diamond and Jocelyn Bringhurst had two small sons, Adrian and Damian, of whom Dr. Diamond often spoke at length, joyfully. One Thursday he brought them to the writing class when the babysitter unexpectedly broke her leg.

And where was Jocelyn? Never around when he needed her, Myrna supposed with satisfaction. And why had she kept her maiden name anyway?

The children played quietly in the corner of the classroom with their crayons and their little trucks, little angels. Myrna fantasized about how Dr. Diamond would finally come to his senses and leave Jocelyn, taking the children with him, of course, and she, Myrna, would bring them up beautifully.

After class each Thursday night, Gord would take Myrna down to Dino's Pizzeria for a couple of beer and a fifteen-inch double pepperoni with double cheese. The few nights they decided to be daring and order something different, Myrna went home feeling cheated, irritable, not even full yet. If they didn't go to Dino's, they went to the A&W for teenburgers or to Country Style Donuts for cinnamon crullers. These variations too left Myrna feeling unsatisfied and surly.

Over their food, Myrna and Gord talked about their respective classes: debits, credits, dialogue, description, and suspense. Dr. Diamond was a demanding teacher with impeccable literary standards and occasionally his sarcastic comments on her earnest efforts reduced the hopeful Myrna to tears over her pizza. Once he told her she was too normal to ever be a really good writer anyway, and she didn't drink enough either. Gord thought his Accounting prof was a bona fide idiot and so was always imbued with righteous anger after his class. So they had plenty to talk about while they ate, sucking back their beer and waving their hands around, energized but ineffectual. And then they would go home around midnight to their respective parents' houses, where they both still lived.

All of this was more or less unremarkable at the time and, Myrna realizes, probably still is. Being twenty-one was, in itself, unremarkable. And, if the truth were told, nothing had turned out the way Myrna thought it would. She'd gained twenty pounds but got an A in the course. The last night they had a party at Dr. Diamond's house instead of a regular class. They sat cross-legged in a circle on his green Persian rug, drinking dark rum and reading poetry tensely to each other. Myrna surreptitiously studied his bookshelves and snooped in the medicine chest and two kitchen cupboards. Dr. Diamond drove her home last and kissed her once, sideways in the car. A year later he left Jocelyn and married Maureen, a mousy graduate student in Renaissance Lit. Jocelyn got Adrian and Damian but Dr. Diamond and Maureen soon produced two more offspring of their own, Chloe and Cassandra.

Myrna and Gordon Bates never did get married. She lost interest somewhere around the time she was supposed to be choosing her china pattern for the Bridal Registry at Birks. Gord soon after became a card-carrying member of the Progressive Conservative Party and married an ex-beauty queen whose father owned a furniture store.

But knowing all this now does not cloud Myrna's sense of the state she had lived in then: that quality of twenty-oneness when absolutely everything was a promise, when her expectations were inchoate and unbounded, not yet unbearable, when there were just never enough hours in any given day, and sometimes she couldn't get to sleep at night for the sheer jumble of joy and the future working through her. This is a state of being which she is always trying now to get back, to get back *to*.

An image comes to her of her twenty-one-year-old self strolling down the street (any street in any weather) and she is thinking and thinking, always thinking, carrying a book bag, tossing her high head, and her posture is loose-limbed but perfect. This picture is like one of those in a child's colouring book where every object, including the cumulus clouds, is outlined in black and those pure Crayola colours all stay neatly inside the lines, absolute. Except you always have to leave the hands and faces white because there is never a good flesh colour in the crayon box.

Now at thirty-two Myrna feels, by comparison, muddied. She has to admit that sometimes she gets tired of herself. She has come or is coming to understand that her life can no longer be seen as a temporary condition. She has to admit that maybe her old friend, Jane, was right when she said, "It's not true that it gets easier as you get older. No. It only gets harder. Too much water under the bridge." Jane has now vanished southward, to California or Arizona, Myrna forgets which, so maybe that makes a difference.

Now Myrna has a sense of herself as accumulating day by day layer upon layer of residue or something like silt: half-remembered conversations, arguments, heartbreaks, friendships which faded for no good reason but can never be resumed now, things she was supposed to do but never got around to, promises broken like dishes or the blood vessels in her left cheek, sins she has committed but forgotten or else convinced herself they weren't so bad, yes, sins. It is like the bathroom floor with those tiny grouted tiles that she never can get clean and then there is the mildew growing on the window frame and the soap scum around the tub. But she is so tired and sometimes when she looks at that ground-in dirt, sometimes when she thinks of herself, she just wants to sob and gulp air. But even this seems like too much trouble—or too melodramatic anyway. Sometimes she just wants to scream and then sleep.

2. This is how Myrna survives.

3. Every morning Myrna wakes up early. She has a new PermaForm mattress on her queen-size bed which is so comfortable that she hates to get out of it. But she feels too guilty if she sleeps too late.

Every morning it is like waking up in a strange hotel room with all your clothes on and the phone is ringing. Every morning it takes her a few minutes to get her bearings, to determine that yes, she really lives here: yes, there is her ceramic cat mobile hung by the window, her Olivia Parker orchids art poster on the closet door which is safely shut against nightmares, her new quilt in a mauve and blue pattern of leaves and vines which she got last week half-price at The Bay and she carried it out to the car in her arms like a child. Every morning it takes her a few minutes to decide or remember what mood she's in today. Sometimes she feels really good, but if she lies there long enough, comfy or not, all the reasons (or excuses) why she shouldn't will come whining around again.

So she gets up and throws her old grey cardigan over her flannelette nightie, pulls on her paisley knee socks and her panda bear slippers. This crazy get-up makes her feel funky and self-assured, the kind of woman who can wear anything she damn well pleases and still look great, the kind of woman who thinks nothing of being twenty-five minutes late for everything, neither explaining nor apologizing, when she finally does show up, for her tardiness, her messy hair, or the cold sore on her upper lip. Myrna just wishes there was someone here to observe this disguise, but she also knows that she will die of embarrassment if anyone comes to the door, and she has never been late for anything in her life.

Over coffee and cigarettes at the kitchen table, Myrna reads and listens to the radio. She doesn't watch TV in the morning anymore because there is always the carnage on the Detroit cable news. There is always some young black kid getting shot dead by mistake when the gunman was really aiming at his own mother, the neo-Nazi next door, the pizza delivery man, or the pimp in the Cadillac idling at the stoplight. And the game show contestants always have names like Earl, Mabel, Flossie, and Melvin, and they don't have a care in the world. They want to say hi to all their friends watching back in

Boca Raton, Muscle Shoals, and Memphis. They get to guess the prices of Trident Sugarless Gum, Uncle Ben's Converted Rice, and a set of Lee Stick-on Fingernails, glamour length. They win big: refrigerators, golf carts, three-piece bedroom suites, or *a new car!* They are jumpy, so noisy they make Myrna want to cry or throw things.

So Myrna makes her morning list which, like most things, is a double-edged device, producing great feelings of accomplishment and/or guilt according to how many items are/aren't crossed off at the end of any given day. Myrna optimistically means to:

1. Bath and wash hair
2. Change bed
3. Letter to Rose
4. Bank
5. A&P: bread, milk, cheese, eggs, hamburger, kidney beans, frozen quiche, celery, onions, green pepper, mushrooms, sour cream, toilet paper, canned tomatoes
6. Work on story.

Against all odds, Myrna is a writer, and every morning, to prime the pump, she likes to read a few chapters of some book good enough to be inspiring but not *so* good as to induce paralysis with its shameless brilliance.

Over her third and fourth cups of coffee (a fresh ground blend of Brazilian and French Roast which she invented herself last week and is justly proud of, though no one else has ever tasted it), she makes notes of the ideas that have come to her lately from one place or another. Things like:

1. While dressing herself up for the date, she couldn't help but think about chickens.

2. The man at the bar in the black cowboy hat ordered up another round for the house. He liked to play the big shot. Nobody else's money was good around him.

3. I was pushing the stroller up to the A&P to get the baby some prunes and there was this ambulance coming towards us. It turned left at the lights, heading over to Rideau Street, and there was me, pushing the baby in the heat and hoping it was for you.

4. At moments like this, Dorothy's husband, Sven, would always say, "Kooks, Dotty. This whole world is full of kooks. What's the world coming to? That's what I'd like to know." And at moments like this, Dorothy would always wonder how she'd come to be living here in Houston, married to a man named Sven, of all things, and he's wearing a sombrero and never been anywhere near Sweden in his life.

Myrna fully intends to expand on these ideas later in the day. For now, she likes to get them down before she loses them. She likes the feel of her favourite pen in her hand first thing in the morning.

An odd phrase comes to mind and sticks, like a song or a name, knocking: it says, "All the length of . . ." Feeling playful and creatively eccentric, she writes:

1. All the length of the dead garden
   there were raspberry canes.

2. All the length of the clothesline
   there were pink baby clothes and beach towels.

3. All the length of the roof
   there were loose shingles slapping in the wind.

4. All the length of the street
   there were empty garbage cans, upended and rolling.

5. All the length of the stadium
   there were blonde cheerleaders waving red pom-poms.

6. All the length of the forest
   there were trees burnt black in the fire.

7. All the length of her arm
   there were bruises.

8. All the length of her life
   she was happy.

Myrna does not expect anything much to come of this exercise but it was fun, like flexing, and she calls it "Longing."

4. Myrna smokes too much.

5. Myrna drinks too much coffee.

6. Myrna has often been told she thinks too much.

7. Myrna waits for the mailman, who finally trudges up the driveway at 10:36 a.m., looking red in the face and grim. He leaves three bills, an envelope full of discount coupons for diapers and dog food, a flyer from Beaver Lumber where they have two-by-fours and padded toilet seats on special. Myrna is fed up.

8. She drives downtown with the window open and the rock-and-roll radio up full blast so the handsome young construc-

tion workers at the corner of Princess and Division will notice her and know she isn't exactly what she appears to be in her dark blue compact with her seatbelt on. She sings along loudly and puts a look on her face she thinks of as saucy.

9. She parks in the Marion Springer Memorial Lot on Queen Street which is out of the way but there is always a space. She walks the three blocks to her bank. It seems to be one of those days when every second person she passes has something wrong with them. There is a man with one arm, the empty sleeve of his white jacket pinned across his chest like a beauty queen's banner. There is a little girl with a bulging pocket of lumpy scar tissue on one side of her mouth and her left eye is three times as big as her right, protruding and watering, pointing right at Myrna. There is that smelly man she always sees, in greasy jeans and a lumberjack shirt, talking to himself and barking. There is a woman with Down syndrome riding in a shopping cart, wearing short white gloves and waving like the Queen, pushed along by a woman old enough to be her grandmother but who is probably her mother. Myrna knows that's how these things can happen because her own mother, on ugly occasions requiring excuses, apologies, or some vague kind of justification, often reminded her, "I was nearly forty when I had you. You're just lucky to be normal."

Standing in line in the bank, she tries to shake off the insidious fear these poor people have put in her. She's hoping she won't run into anyone she knows, someone who will corner her, and then she will actually have to smile at them and make some street small talk, as if she were happy to see them. She concentrates on not catching anyone's eye. By the time she gets up to the teller's wicket, she is able to make minor pleasantries about the weather and the mechanic in Hamilton who won $2.2 million in the 649 draw Saturday night.

10. In the A&P she gets out her list and loads up her cart, immensely enjoying the way the purchase of yellow toilet

paper, whole wheat bread, and a family-size can of kidney beans on sale can give her such a sense of self-worth. Standing in the checkout line, she feels confirmed in her pursuit (disguise) of normalcy (domesticity) and would like to point this out to the woman behind her, who is talking baby talk to her little girl in the cart which is filled with jars of baby food and a jumbo pack of ninety-six ultra-absorbent diapers.

Once Myrna was buying a fig tree along with her usual groceries and the woman behind her explained all about how it would need lots of water and lots of sun and then half its leaves would fall off anyway but this was nothing to worry about because a fig tree will just do that sometimes, shedding. And then it was such a beautiful plant, and only $14.99, that the woman went back and got one for herself, even though the last thing in the world she needed was another fig tree. Every time Myrna waters her fig tree now, she thinks about that woman.

Myrna waits her turn and chuckles at the tabloid headlines:

CHOCOHOLIC MOTHER GIVES BIRTH
TO SUGAR-COATED BABY

BRIDE'S STOMACH EXPLODES AT
WEDDING RECEPTION

79-YEAR-OLD PRIEST MAKES 15-YEAR-OLD
TRIPLETS PREGNANT.

The cashier seems pleased when Myrna fishes around in her wallet and quickly comes up with the exact change.

11. Myrna likes to take herself out to lunch. But she doesn't go to the Pizza Hut anymore because they always bring the food so fast that she thinks they feel sorry for her, having to eat lunch all alone. Either that or they want to get rid of her. She

gets so nervous eating there, what with all the good cheer and rushing around, that she's afraid she'll choke and terminally disgrace herself, face down in her food.

She doesn't go to Bonnie's Bistro anymore either because the last time she did, there was an elastic band in her french fries.

She doesn't go, at least not very often, to The Waterworks Café, which is a popular place where all the local artists, writers, musicians, and aspirants like to congregate. She does go there once in a while because every time she walks by, she feels like she's missing something.

The Waterworks is tastefully decorated in trendy pastels, mint green and dusty rose, with original artwork on the walls, oil paintings and silkscreen prints with price tags in the corners. They play eclectic music. The menu features soups, salads, pâté, a selection of items which can be attractively served on a croissant, and twenty-seven varieties of mineral water, domestic and imported, sparkling and still. It is a small place, meant to be intimate, but there is not even a decent space between the tables, so you are always bumping the back of your chair into the back of the chair of the person at the table behind you. And they are always bumping your chair just as you are trying to get a spoon full of hot soup (homemade minestrone, or cream of broccoli) up to your mouth.

The other patrons wander from table to table, carrying their cappuccino or Perrier, congratulating or commiserating. Myrna must be feeling impervious and relatively intelligent in order to go into The Waterworks because, once inside, she feels like an impostor or an intruder. She secretly yearns to be part of this group but knows she will never pull it off.

Myrna likes to have lunch at Martin's Gourmet Burger Palace where the efficient waitress named Donna brings her a coffee and says, "The usual?" while Myrna is still taking her coat off, arranging it on the back of her chair. She sits so she can see out the window. She has bought a lottery ticket before coming in and sits for a while with it in her hand, trying to decide if, when she scratches and wins, she will jump up and down screaming her head off, "I won! I won!" or if she will just sit there smiling gently, sure of herself, her secrets, and the future.

She reads *The New Yorker*, especially the "Goings On About Town," though she's never been there and doubts she ever will because she is afraid of big cities.

She observes the people at the next table, a party of five, three men and two women, drinking pear cider and wearing quiet office outfits. One young man in a grey trench coat passes around a blue binder with the title *Focus on Dermatology* on the cover. Myrna cannot imagine what these people are going to do with the rest of their lives, once this lunch is over. No matter how often she comes here, she never sees the same people twice.

Sometimes, by the time Donna brings her food (a mushroom and bacon burger with Caesar salad instead of fries), Myrna has got to feeling guilty for being there, wasting time when she should be home washing the floor, doing the laundry, cleaning that mildew from the bathroom windowsill because sometimes she thinks she can *smell* it. She should be at home *thinking*. Mostly, she should be at home *writing*. At the very least, she should be finishing up the rest of the things on her list because these are the parameters she has set for herself, these are the promises she must live up to, in order to feel justified, in order to wrest, wring, rake, rescue, resurrect order out of chaos, value out of worthlessness, or the tidal fear of it.

While in Martin's, she writes in a small hardcover notebook which she carries in her purse at all times. She writes about how the sight of Canada geese travelling across the sky in their V spring and fall always gives her a lump in her throat which she has never been able to figure out. But suddenly, in the act of writing it down, she sees that this natural phenomenon is an affirmation that all is right with the world, that things indeed are unfolding as they should. And the lump in her throat comes from the precious duplicity of simultaneously believing this and knowing that it's not true.

Myrna likes the image of herself writing in restaurants and, for a few minutes, everything makes sense.

Myrna leaves a good tip and waves at the waitress on her way out. She has seen this Donna several times on the street but they do not acknowledge each other, as if they keep a shameful secret between them, as if Myrna keeps having lunch at Martin's with somebody else's husband instead of alone.

12. Myrna doesn't have to eat lunch alone. There are always some women who try to befriend her and so she feels grateful, tries to encourage them, tries to be sociable, tries to be a good listener and tell them her troubles in return. But she finds as soon as she tells them one little thing—as soon as she tells them about the time she ran into her ex-lover, Peter, with a woman named Ingrid at The Calabash Bar when he'd said he was working and then she drank so many double Scotches while watching them slow-dance and laugh that she fell down on the corner of Barrie and Princess and there was a cop right there at the light and he picked her up, literally picked her up off the sidewalk, and took her home and she wanted him to put on the lights and the siren when they pulled into the driveway but he wouldn't—as soon as she tells these friendly women something like this, then they want to take over her whole life: they want her to tell them everything.

And then she feels guilty for not telling them about the time she got drunk on homemade red wine and smashed the telephone to smithereens with the empty bottle and then she threw up in the hallway and in the morning she couldn't remember doing either of these things but there was the phone in pieces, still plugged in, shards of green glass all over the kitchen, and there was the vomit on the hardwood floor. She just says how she doesn't drink alone anymore because she's heard it's a bad sign, and self-destructive.

She feels guilty for not telling them about how this morning just before dawn she had an erotic dream of such beauty and power that she woke up having an orgasm and felt good all day, about how walking to the A&P yesterday she couldn't remember what she was going to buy so she turned back and went home crying, about how last night she thought of the words *dim sum* and liked the sound of it so much that she ordered Chinese food for supper, let the chicken she'd defrosted yesterday just sit there and rot, and in the back of her fridge there is a pot of spaghetti sauce that's been there since August.

She compensates by telling them that she talks to herself when driving the car, orders pizza so often that they know her name and address as soon as she says hello, how she likes to sleep in the afternoon, how sometimes she goes to bed at eight o'clock, even in the summer when it's still light out, just because she's had enough of *this* day.

She says all these things in such a charmingly self-deprecating manner that these generous women invariably want to reciprocate. They tell her how they do these and similar silly things, but Myrna knows they're lying to save her feelings, to save her from thinking she's crazy.

13. The true art of telling stories on yourself, Myrna suspects, involves being able to rearrange, exaggerate, or denigrate the facts enough to make yourself look good or, failing that, blameless. This is called fiction.

When relating, for instance, the story of her visit to her parents out west last summer, she says how on the Friday night she thought she'd just walk down to The Cecil Hotel, which was close, and have a quick beer just because she hadn't been there for ten years nearly and was feeling nostalgic. She doesn't say how really she was climbing the walls of her parents' hot little bungalow, her mother was already repeating herself after only two days, her father was planted in the swivel chair, drinking a forty-ouncer of rum, staring out the bay window at nothing, and Myrna went storming out in an inexplicable rage which was never mentioned again.

At The Cecil (which hadn't changed much, was still a dive, overcrowded and vaguely criminal), she stood drinking beer at the bar until she caught the eye of a handsome black-bearded biker by the pool table who motioned her over, bought her a drink, said his name was Leonard but they called him "The Drake," pleasta meetcha. It turned out that the slim French woman playing pool like a shark was his girlfriend, Jacinte. Resting her heavy breasts on the table for the long shots, Jacinte was cleaning up at a buck a cue and proudly handing him her winnings after each game.

But Jacinte went home early because she had to work in the morning. Then Myrna was buying and The Drake was pumping her quarters into the jukebox and pulling up his black Harley-Davidson t-shirt to show her his tattoos. There was a lion, a wolf, a dragon, a cobra, and the omnipotent eagle. Myrna said, "I like a tattoo," and touched them.

The next thing she knew they were kissing at the table. The Drake was putting his whole tongue in her mouth and she was feeling invisible the way she always did when she was drunk: as if nobody could see what she was doing so she thought she could do anything. The Drake said how much he'd like to take her for a ride but he'd lost his licence for five years, vehicular manslaughter, and so now they had a car, which he called a cage, and Jacinte did the driving. He walked Myrna back to her parents' house, kissing and pleading, and when she tells this story, Myrna doesn't say how she just wanted to get rid of him. His tongue was too big, and rough like a cat's. She'd already got what she wanted, which had little to do with him in the first place.

Four days later she flew home and Brian, her lover at the time, met her at the airport with flowers and a bottle of pink champagne, which was romantic but not like him at all. At three in the morning her phone rang. It was The Drake calling to say he'd bought a bus ticket, he'd be there Sunday at eight. Then Jacinte grabbed the phone away from him, yelling, "Who the hell are you talking to? I'll kill you, I'll kill you!" Myrna hung up, unplugged the phone, put a butcher knife and the empty champagne bottle on the top shelf of her bedroom closet, not sure yet who she should be frightened of. Brian from the bed asked, "Didn't you tell him about me?"

Telling this story, Myrna says how she felt terrorized for weeks afterwards but that was the end of it, thank God. Except (she doesn't say this part) she told Brian that the biker had called her again, not once, but twice, when Brian wasn't there, was sleeping, Myrna suspected (and correctly), with another woman.

She doesn't say how she kept expecting to be punished but nothing ever happened, nothing changed, and she could still look herself in the eye in the bathroom mirror in the morning without flinching or cringing. This consummate failure of justice, poetic or otherwise, this failure of a call or a need for atonement to appear gave her a licence, she felt, to do whatever she wanted, because nothing made any real difference after all and you really could get away with things without being caught, damaged, or disfigured.

But of course this new lease on life was fleeting, and when considering whether to write a story about this story, she eventually abandoned the idea because whatever promises it contained (of violence, retribution, or morality) could be neither broken nor fulfilled in the end, not convincingly anyway.

14. Myrna doesn't pick up strange men in bars anymore. There is the fear of disease, of course, and the problem of breakfast: what to make without appearing too domestic or grateful, or whether to just stay in bed with her head covered up, waiting for him to comb his hair and leave.

There is the perennial problem with the ones you wish would stick around because you would like to spend the rest of your life (or at least the rest of the weekend) with them, so you offer coffee, an omelette, grapefruit, buttermilk pancakes, but he is shrugging on his jean jacket, edging towards the door at 6 a.m. because he has to go fishing, has to go rip the engine out of his truck, play baseball, move a piano, feed the dog, and you know you will never get him back into your bed again.

But the ones you never want to see ever again, not even in the grocery store by accident, the ones you will cross the street to avoid, are always calling and driving by your house and falling like feathers in love with you. They have no sense of humour, none of them. There is the way the bedroom begins to fill up with their long faces and the only thing left to do is redecorate or move.

15. Myrna is walking back to her car on Queen Street. At the busy corner of Queen and Clergy, a man with no legs is trying to manoeuvre his wheelchair over the curb up onto the sidewalk. His head lolls alarmingly to the left and the stumps of his thighs are wrapped in white bandages.

Myrna turns and walks in the other direction.

Her heart is beating so hard that the blood seems to be escaping the ventricles, filling up her whole chest cavity, hot and shameful, bubbling like soup all down to her knees.

She is swallowing and swallowing, like the time she was driving through a trailer park at night (she didn't know anyone who lived there, she was just cruising) and a cat ran out in front of her, green eyes likes marbles in her headlights, and after she hit it she just kept driving until she was home.

16. Myrna checks her answering machine as soon as she gets home. She is disappointed when there have been no messages but, on the other hand, she often doesn't feel up to returning the calls she does get, even when they're long-distance from people she hasn't talked to in years. Their phone numbers get accidentally erased.

Sometimes, feeling antisocial, frightened, or smug, she leaves the machine on even when she's home. In the instruction manual, this impersonation of absence is politely referred to as "Screening Your Calls". Eating supper, soaking in the bathtub, lying on the couch reading *The Unbearable Lightness of Being* by Milan Kundera, or watching *Family Ties* on TV, Myrna looks up and listens to disembodied voices speaking with false bravado into the machine: "Hi Myrna! It's just me! Haven't heard from you in ages! Just called to say hi! Call me back when you can!"

What she hates most are the hang-up calls when the machine faithfully records a click and then the dial tone or a maddening silence. Myrna plays back these calls over and over, trying to detect breathing, background music, or a sigh. Frustrating as they are, these mystery calls also fill her with exhilaration, with a premonition that someday soon somebody special is going to get through to her.

17. Myrna is sitting at the kitchen table just around suppertime. She is working on the crossword puzzle in the evening paper, discovering that she knows:

1. a 4-letter word for ACIDITY (1 Across)
2. an 8-letter word for IN AN ADULT FASHION (10 Down)
3. a 4-letter word for GR. CHEESE (68 Down).

But she has to look up in her crossword puzzle dictionary:

1. a 4-letter word for AVATAR OF VISHNU (94 Across)
2. a 4-letter word for CHIN. GELATIN (64 Across)
3. a 4-letter word for ONCE, ONCE (13 Across).

She is trying to decide if she should heat up the leftover chili from last night or should she just give in to temptation and order another pizza?

She is looking periodically over at the well-kept brick house across the street. She doesn't know these neighbours, still hasn't figured out who all lives there or what the connections are between them. One of them is a mailman who looks very handsome in his postal uniform, there is an older heavy-set couple who drive a blue Lincoln, a woman in a fur coat who comes over every day with or without a small child in a red snowsuit, there is a very old woman with long white hair who sits at the upstairs window in her nightgown (for a long time Myrna thought the old lady was watching her in *her* window but now she thinks she's watching TV). These neighbours are always juggling their cars around in the long driveway, backing out, pulling in, waving, honking, just driving away.

They have one of those pretty Tiffany lamps hung over the dining room table (at least Myrna thinks it's the dining room). The multicoloured light which it casts makes the whole house look safe and inviting. Inside, Myrna imagines, there would be a cosy warmth, good smells of supper, the sound of the television news coming quietly from another room, laughter. The older man sits at the table with his back to the window, reading the paper, sometimes shirtless even in the winter so that his broad white back looks like a pillow.

One day at The Bay Myrna bought herself a Tiffany lamp too, also a tablecloth printed with flat-faced pansies and long-necked pink gladioli, also one of those new wooden dishracks which looks like a book- or music-stand. She put these purchases on her charge card and hurried home with them. She ironed the tablecloth, laid it out, set up the dishrack, and hung the lamp above the table.

But later that evening, sitting under it doing another puzzle, she had to admit that she didn't *feel* any different. She supposed her house must *look* different from the outside, to someone walking by, walking the dog or taking the air, or having just had a fight with their husband/wife over who was supposed to take out the garbage and needing to get away for half an hour, trying to figure out why nothing ever went right in their lives—to someone just walking by like that, Myrna supposed the house might look now like a home for happy well-adjusted folks with children, pets, and dreams.

This gives her some small satisfaction but, sitting under the lamp, which sheds its colours, she imagines, down upon her lustrous black hair like rainbows or leaves, Myrna has to admit that she doesn't *feel* any different: she still doesn't feel like the people across the street.

18. After supper, Myrna does the dishes promptly, sweeps the floor, reads and watches TV at the same time, thinks about all the writing she will definitely do tomorrow, goes to bed early, and reads some more. She prefers a good fat hardcover, the weight of it expensive and significant in her hands. She does not like library books because they smell funny, the plastic jackets crinkle, and the pages feel coated and damp.

After she turns out the light, she curls up on her left side till she feels all warm and relaxed. Then she rolls over onto her right and falls asleep.

Sometimes she thinks about Rose, when they were roommates, announcing puffy-faced at breakfast, "I cried myself to sleep last night."

Myrna has never managed to cry herself to sleep. She has tried it the odd time when, at some suitably melancholy juncture, the idea seemed attractive enough in theory: the tragedy, the loneliness, the balled-up Kleenex all over the bed. But in practice she finds it impossible to sustain. For one thing, crying keeps her awake. And once she starts, she wants only to stop, to get up, eat, wash, smoke, something, anything to save herself at the brink. Because once she starts, she is afraid she will never be able to stop. She can only imagine poor Rose drifting off in mid-sob, waking up before the alarm with her fingers still in her mouth.

19. Myrna has never doubted that she will survive. Oh, there was that one time years ago when some man had dumped her and she was drunk and thinking she'd drive her car into the river. It was February, the ice was rotten, and she would sink down slowly like a horse to its knees, nose first and the windows open. But then she realized how drunk she was and, with her luck, she'd probably get picked up for impaired on her way to the river and it would be just too embarrassing, losing her licence like that. So she threw the clock, several heavy books, and her cowboy boots across the room and stayed where she was: in bed fully dressed, listening to his favourite song, and pounding her pillow and her thighs.

By the next morning, she was already laughing at herself, writing "A Fate Worse Than Death" in her notebook—which is what she would have called the story she might have written about the story someday.

But Myrna never thinks about that time anymore, she doesn't write or tell the story, and she does not remember the name of the man, the song, or the river.

20. This is just some of how Myrna survives.

TRICK QUESTIONS

(1989)

Only the most naïve of questions are truly serious. They are the questions with no answers. A question with no answer is a barrier that cannot be breached. In other words, it is questions with no answers that set the limits of human possibilities, describe the boundaries of human existence.

— Milan Kundera, *The Unbearable Lightness of Being*

The important thing about grass is that it is green. It grows, and is tender, with a sweet grassy smell. But the important thing about grass is that it is green.

The important thing about the sky is that it is always there. It is true that it is blue, and high, and full of clouds, and made of air. But the important thing about the sky is that it is always there

— Margaret Wise Brown, *The Important Book*

SAM was telling Janice an amusing anecdote from his recent trip to a conference in Oslo. On the flight home, he had been seated beside an obnoxious young man named Dirk, who, Sam said, did not know his ass from his cranium and hadn't the sense to shut up about it either. As they embarked on the first leg of the transatlantic trip, Sam was trying to read, sleep, or think with his eyes closed. But this Dirk was one of those unfortunate seat-mates who simply cannot settle themselves. He partook liberally of the free liquor served in first class, flirted with the stewardess every time she came within range, drummed his fingers maddeningly on the arm of his seat in time to whatever juvenile trash was blaring through his headphones, and tried repeatedly to engage Sam in meaningless conversation.

"Where are you from?"

"Where have you been?"

"What do you do for a living?"

Sam responded with vague one-word answers:

"Canada."

"Norway."

"Teach."

He kept his eyes closed and could only hope that the idiot would get the hint eventually.

After the meal had been served and then cleared away again, Dirk pulled a briefcase out from under his seat and placed it on his lap. Sam thought thankfully that finally he was going to get some peace and quiet.

But when the innocuous-looking briefcase had been sprung open, Dirk pulled from it, with a flourish like that of a magician pulling a rabbit from a hat, a contraption of tangled wires and Styrofoam balls in different sizes and colours. He fussed with it for a minute and then shoved it triumphantly under Sam's nose. It was a planetary model, and a primitive one at that, with the nine Styrofoam balls impaled upon the wires at various intervals, waving now like insect antennae.

Mars was painted red, of course, and the rings of Saturn were shaped in gold foil.

"What's wrong with this model?" Dirk challenged Sam.

"Pluto should be three blocks away," Sam said.

"That's right!" Dirk cried. "How did you know that?"

"What do you think I am?" Sam said. "Stupid?"

Now, to Janice, Sam said, "It was a trick question. You can ask things like that of your friends, but not of a total stranger on an airplane." Janice laughed with what Sam took to be intelligent appreciation.

They were in the kitchen: Janice at the stove stirring the spaghetti sauce, Sam at the table having a drink of single-malt Scotch, their ten-month-old daughter, Celeste, in her playpen in the middle of the room, flinging brightly coloured plastic blocks at her parents and crowing.

Technically, of course, Janice knew that Pluto was the most distant planet, placed at an educated guess of 6000 million kilometres from the sun. She could still recite the mnemonic device she'd learned in public school for remembering the planets in order: Man Very Early Made Jars Stand Up Nearly Perpendicular. It was only the M's, Mercury and Mars, that sometimes still got mixed up. She knew that Pluto had been found almost by accident in 1930 by Clyde Tombaugh and that it was believed to be a frozen world, totally encased in ice, possibly once a moon of Neptune that had somehow been flung out of its orbit, left to wander around the sun on its own.

But whenever they talked about Pluto, Janice pictured a grassy sweet-smelling planet populated by thousands of cartoon Pluto dogs, like the one from Mickey Mouse, with yellow fur, flapping black ears, and noses like black jelly beans. Lanky and clumsy with oversized feet and tangled-up legs, they went wiggling under white picket fences, tromping through pink flower beds, and tumbling headlong down soft green hillsides. So whenever they talked about Pluto (which was often enough in their household), Janice laughed.

Janice was Sam's second wife. Sam, a professor of astronomy at the university, was twenty-one years older than Janice, who was almost twenty-five. Sam had been divorced from his first wife, Solange, for only two months when he became involved with Janice.

The circumstances of their meeting and subsequent marriage were, as Sam put it, so trite that he had long ago begged Janice to please stop telling the story to everyone they met. She agreed. Guiltily. It was as if he knew (but how could he? he was intelligent, yes, but hardly omnipotent) about that time last fall on the crosstown bus when Janice, then six months pregnant and very pleased with herself, had told the whole story to the woman sitting next to her. She was a friendly, motherly sort of woman who was, in fact, on her way to the hospital to visit her daughter who had just given birth to twins. She held on her lap a wicker basket of fruit with two pink bows on top. She sat for ten whole minutes with her hand on Janice's belly, waiting to feel the baby kick. She predicted that it would be a girl because Janice was carrying high—or was it because she was carrying low? Either way, she was right. And when she got off at her stop, she gave Janice a big hug, an apple, and two perfect pears.

The fact of it was that Janice had been Sam's student. She had just returned then from an extended trek through Asia. She had taken a year off from university, where she had been studying a little bit of this, a little bit of that, in her first year:

English: When is *Beowulf* generally believed to have been written and by whom?

French: *Comment allez-vous?*

Geography: What is the principal export of Surinam?

Art History: What group of French painters was most intrigued by the science of light?

Developmental Psychology: At what age does a child normally realize that he is not the centre of the universe?

Like many people of her age and persuasions, Janice thought that travelling to another continent would simultaneously broaden her horizons and help her to focus, to *centre* herself. But when she returned, she was more unsettled than ever. She did not go back to university right away. Instead, she roamed around the city in her beautiful Asian garments, her Nepalese silver ankle bracelet tinkling its twelve tiny bells as she wandered in and out of specialty bookstores, Indian restaurants, and eastern import shops, buying incense sticks, patchouli oil, camel bells, and an annotated copy of *The Tibetan Book of the Dead*. It seemed that everyone she'd ever known or cared about had moved away.

Janice had always been subject to bouts of depression, which had begun to escalate in both depth and frequency. But she had the kind of small perky face, apple-cheeked and bright-eyed, that always looked happy no matter how bad she felt. So that even when she was positively "beside herself" (as Janice sometimes thought of her condition, picturing a clone-like creature weeping and wailing and carrying on right alongside of her more ordinary self, which continued all the while to perform the necessary manoeuvres of daily life), nobody even seemed to notice. It was this sunny little face of hers which Janice blamed for the fact that no one seemed to consider her capable of sorrow or serious thought.

Janice's real problem, she had decided while travelling, was not that she wasn't serious; it was just that she had always had trouble distinguishing between what was meaning*ful* and what was meaning*less*. So that her problem was not a lack of seriousness, but rather, of not ever knowing what should be taken *seriously*.

Finally, in September, she took a job at the Farmers' Market and a night course called "Astronomy for Amateurs." Five days a week she stood behind a table under a green canvas awning, selling organically grown carrots, apples, and spinach, fragrant peaches, and living lettuce with its roots in a clump of wet dirt in a clear plastic bag. She also sold real maple syrup and free-range eggs. Two nights a week, Tuesday and Thursday, she went to Sam's class.

It began when she took to joining Sam and several of her classmates for a beer in the pub afterwards. Soon she and Sam were sneaking away from the group early, going to another bar where they could be alone together. By Christmas, they were lovers—by one of those romantic quantum leaps which afterwards left Janice, in her new-found happiness, unable to retrace the steps they'd taken, to reconstruct the decisions they made, unable to remember even the simplest things:

When did they first kiss?

How did they get that first time from the bar to her bedroom, from the car to her bedroom, from the kitchen to her bedroom?

Did they, that first time, take their own clothes off or each other's?

When did they fall in love, before or after?

When Janice discovered, less than six months later, that she was pregnant, Sam (much to everyone's surprise, including hers) up and married her.

* * *

Getting ready for another faculty dinner in the third month of her pregnancy, Janice stood naked in front of the full-length bathroom mirror. Sam was still in the shower behind her and the steam was welling up over the plastic curtain, so that Janice had to keep wiping the mirror clear with a towel.

She was twisting and turning supplely, trying to see herself from all possible angles. Was she showing yet? Finally she turned her back to the big mirror and looked into the tiny one in her eyeshadow case, positioning it so she could get a look at her behind.

Sam had always gloried in her slim young body, her tiny waist, her prettily protruding hip-bones. He liked to have her stretch out flat on the bed and hold her breath so he could count her ribs. Sometimes, when he drank too much Scotch at faculty parties (as he might well do tonight), he would point out the finer details of her figure to his friends.

Sam stepped out of the shower and wrapped himself in a blue bath sheet. To his reflection in the misty mirror, Janice said, "Will you still love me when I'm fat?"

Sam considered this carefully. He knew enough by now about pregnant women and their dazzling hormones to know that Janice was just feeling sensitive and insecure.

"Well," he said finally, caressing her damp back, "you won't be *fat* exactly—you'll just be pregnant."

"But what *if*," Janice countered, "what if I *do* get fat someday? I mean, *real* fat. I mean, someday. Would you still love me then?"

Sam was cornered. "Well, no," he, being an honest man, felt he just had to admit. "No, I'm not sure I would."

While Janice lay face-down on the bed in her bathrobe and sobbed, she thought about a man she'd slept with in Tibet. His name was Gerry and he was yet another Canadian student on a tour of the east. She had first noticed him because the scars of adolescent acne on his cheeks and forehead were still so red and raised they looked painful. He had stringy greasy black hair and a scruffy goatee, but his brown eyes were soulful and kind. They undressed shyly on either side of the small foreign bed, having left the hostel where they'd met the week before and splurged on a real hotel room for the night. It was at that moment when Janice most betrayed herself for the sake of getting into bed with a man.

"Are you sure you want to do this?" she asked him. "I look really awful when I get up in the morning. Do you still want to sleep with me?" Now she was crying even harder, hating herself in retrospect for having said it and for having been so grateful when Gerry laughed and hugged her and stayed.

Sam was ignoring her now, rummaging through the dresser drawers, wondering aloud why nobody wears cufflinks anymore and humming. Janice went on crying and hating herself vigorously, also hating, for the first time, the fact that she was pregnant. She did not hate the baby, she hated the pregnancy.

She tried to console herself with the thought that for nine months at least, longer if she breast-fed, she wouldn't have to put up with having her period. That was an advantage, certainly. But then she remembered the time, early in their affair, when she had apologized to Sam for not wanting to make love because she had her period.

Sam said, "I knew you had it. I can always tell. I can even tell two or three days before it comes."

"Am I that crabby?" she asked.

"No, no, it's nothing like that," he said and refused to explain.

For days she bugged him and bugged him to tell her how he knew. Could he smell it? she wondered with horror. Could he smell the blood, the useless blood, the decaying blood dripping from between her legs?

Finally Sam tired of her persistence and said, "It's just that your mouth tastes different when I kiss you at that time of the month."

Janice, embarrassed and self-conscious, had no proof of this, one way or the other. It was one of those things she never asked even her best friend about. The next month, when the time came, she took to brushing her teeth obsessively, gargling with Extra Strength Listerine, chewing mints and cinnamon-flavoured gum. Sam was amused but exasperated, said he wished he'd never mentioned it in the first place. It wasn't a bad taste, he assured her, it wasn't bad at all, just different. But Janice never forgave him.

* * *

Janice had always liked children, and the birth of Celeste in early December brought out all of her suppressed maternal instincts and set them in full glorious swing. She realized that she had been longing for years to have someone she could legitimately mother. She had often been accused of trying to mother everyone she knew, adults, mostly men, who lapped it up for a while and then left because they felt suffocated. Mothering a real live baby was much more satisfying, she discovered, if only because a baby could never be loved too much.

After Celeste was born, Janice felt this part of her personality to be infinitely expandable and so, to indulge it even more, she set up an arrangement with several other mothers in the neighbourhood, forming a loose kind of babysitting exchange. When she and Sam had a dinner to attend or just needed an evening out once a month or so, one of these women would look after Celeste. Janice was always available to look after their children in return, often overnight. It was an unbalanced arrangement but Janice didn't mind.

Two or three nights a week, when Sam returned from the university, there would be a toddler or a half-grown child in the kitchen baking cookies with Janice and Celeste. Sometimes Sam would find them in the living room with the stereo turned up loud as they leapt and danced all around the coffee table and the bookcases, Janice leading the troupe at the top of her lungs with the turkey baster for a microphone and the soup-pot lid for a tambourine.

There had been no children in Sam's first marriage, to Solange, and so, at almost fifty years of age, he didn't really know whether he liked kids or not. They were certainly a rambunctious lot and their high-pitched voices seemed too often to become shrill and demanding. Their presence in the house seemed to fill every room at once with movement, bright noise and colours, projects and plans. Not to mention little trucks and wooden blocks that he was always tripping over. They hadn't been told in prenatal class about the way a baby would change every little thing in their previous serious lives. All they had been told was, "Breathe, breathe, breathe!" and that was certainly of no help to anyone now. He had trouble reconciling this constant commotion with his own intellectual preoccupations, with his image of himself as a bearded, learned man in a quiet book-lined room, smoking a pipe and nodding his large head with drowsy, dignified wisdom. But he had to admit that he loved to watch Janice with the children: the way she would get down on her knees to talk to them, the way she could understand everything they said even though it all sounded like gibberish to him, the way she could not pass by any one of them without touching, patting, or hugging some part of their compact bodies, the way her love came spilling out all around her.

He worried occasionally though that Janice was neglecting her intellect. He deeply mistrusted the vacant milky look that came into her eyes whenever she put Celeste to one of her engorged leaking breasts. He suspected that she watched game shows and soap operas, maybe even *Sesame Street*, while he was at work. He tried leaving selected academic books and articles on the back of the toilet, on the top of the TV, on the pillow of their perpetually unmade bed. But by the time Janice picked them up, it was only because they'd been lying around for so long they were covered with dust and sticky little fingerprints. The only book she ever read with any dedication at all these days was called *The Womanly Art of Breastfeeding*. She went out and bought a three-volume set of child-care manuals which answered all her questions about teething, feeding, sleeping, and gross motor development. At the end of each chapter there was a growth chart showing what the child should be able to do at any given age. These charts listed such developmental achievements as:

Looks in appropriate place when asked, "Where is daddy? Where is the ball? Where is baby?"

Uses trial-and-error method to discover new solutions to problems.

Pokes, bangs, pulls, turns, and twists everything within reach.

Over dinner Sam would try to engage Janice in meaningful discussion about Stephen Hawking's time concepts, the preposterous search for a tenth planet beyond Pluto, the quasar mystery, or the place of art in society. But Janice was always distracted, jumping up from the table to mash more carrots, get more milk, more apple juice, more ice cream. He tried once to tell Celeste that it was not necessary to scream bloody murder when one was hungry, because if that were the case, think what miserable places restaurants would be. But Celeste threw a forkful of zucchini at him and Janice just laughed indulgently and said, "Now you know why God made washing machines."

Of the neighbourhood children Janice looked after, Sam's favourite was an eight-year-old boy named Josh, who lived in a duplex at the end of the block. His parents were, as Sam put it, plain people: his father worked for the city, Public Works, and his mother was a salesclerk at Woolworth's downtown. Sam saw in young Josh an inquisitive, agile mind, hungering for all kinds of knowledge and much in need of guidance. Sam was secretly flattered by the fact that Josh seemed to prefer his company to Janice's patient nurturing.

While Janice cooked supper and tried to keep track of Celeste, who was just learning to walk, Sam and Josh would sit together in the living room or in Sam's study. Josh was a shy child, long-limbed and awkward, with bright brown eyes and a remarkably ugly haircut. He would sidle up to Sam and begin firing questions at him, one after the other, as if he'd been saving them up for days. And he listened to the answers too. Sam could barely conceal his delight as he pulled books from the shelves, flipped through back issues of scholarly journals, drew diagrams and charts, raising even more questions in his efforts to satisfy Josh's curiosity.

Sam treated even the simplest questions with the utmost seriousness. He understood that everything was equally important to Josh, who could not know yet the difference between trivia and truth, lightness and weight. There was an almost unbearable feeling of suspense around Josh as he waited for Sam's carefully considered answers.

"Why is the grass green?" Josh might ask.

"Why don't worms die when you cut them in half?"

"Why is Mars red?"

"Who invented ice cream?"

"How much does the Earth weigh?"

"Why is the sky blue?"

Janice in the kitchen had to laugh as she overhead Sam droning on in answer: "Not all skies are blue. The sky on Mars is pink. On the moon, it is black. Venus has a yellow sky. Sunlight is composed of a spectrum of colours. When it enters the Earth's atmosphere, it meets atoms and molecules of air. All of the colours except blue travel straight to the surface, but blue light bounces off these atoms and molecules. Because the blue bounces around, it eventually reaches us from all parts of the sky, not just straight from the sun, as the other colours do. Therefore, the sky looks blue. On the moon, there is no air, so the sky is black. Dust in the Martian atmosphere makes the sky pale orange or pink. Clouds on Venus make the sky yellow."

What, Janice wondered, did Sam expect a mere child to make of all this? There was plenty of room in a lifetime, she thought, to accumulate such information. Rather, it should be like telling them about the birds and the bees: you should only, as the child-care manuals advised, tell them as much as they could understand, otherwise they would be frightened and overwhelmed.

* * *

Which is not to say that life with Sam was a constant feast of intellectual stimulation or an endless barrage of braininess. Sometimes at dinner, instead of explaining (again!) how the weight of a planet might be measured or railing against a recent Letter to the Editor in the evening paper which tried to demonstrate the part witchcraft had played in the history of astronomy, sometimes Sam would just whine (yes, Janice had to admit it, he *whined*) about the petty politics of the department or the ungrateful illiterate ignoramuses passing themselves off as graduate students these days.

Sometimes whole evenings passed in which all the questions Sam asked were the same questions other men, other husbands, might well be asking other women, other wives, anywhere:

"Where are my socks?"

"What's for supper?"

"Why is the baby crying?"

"Why can't you make the baby stop crying?"

"Please, I'm so tired, would you please rub my back?"

* * *

Sam was still friends with his ex-wife, Solange. At first Janice found this unnatural and upsetting. She had never maintained a friendship with any of her former lovers because, once the romance was over, she invariably discovered that she didn't even *like* the guy, they had nothing in common (a discrepancy which could be overlooked in love perhaps, but certainly not in friendship), and in fact, she had to wince with embarrassment or outright revulsion whenever she thought about the time she'd wasted on the stupid guy or the look on his face as they climbed into bed.

But Solange was a gracious and generous woman who seemed to have nothing against Janice—after all, she and Sam were already divorced when Janice came along. But it was the layers of memory which Sam and Solange shared that Janice could not penetrate or duplicate. They did not deliberately exclude her from their reminiscences but she always felt left out. After Solange left, Janice would be petulant and childish (she knew she was being childish but could not stop herself), trying to trick Sam into saying that he loved her more than he'd ever loved Solange.

Eventually it occurred to Janice that it was hardly their fault for getting married the same year that she was born. And so what if they were off honeymooning in the Bahamas when she was cutting her top front teeth? So what if they were buying the limestone house when she was being potty-trained?

After Celeste was born, Solange confessed one afternoon to Janice that she had always wanted children but found she could not get pregnant. Janice decided she could afford to be sympathetic, and besides, Solange was even older than Sam and not very pretty. Janice vowed to try harder to rise above her own pettiness and, for the most part, she succeeded.

Solange came to their house once or twice a month and Janice no longer found it necessary to manufacture excuses to avoid her. Now, instead of having suddenly to go to the grocery store, visit a sick friend, or do the laundry in the basement, Janice was quite comfortable to sit and have coffee at the kitchen table with Sam and Solange. After twenty-three years of marriage, there were still many practical matters they needed to discuss.

The divorce had been amicable enough and, in the settlement, Solange got both the house and the car. The house was a hundred-year-old five-bedroom limestone building which Janice thought of as a mansion, but she struggled to master her resentment over the fact that she and Sam lived in a small stucco bungalow with tiny dark rooms and a wet basement. She knew better than to ask what on earth Solange needed with five bedrooms, a sunroom, and a walk-in pantry the size of Janice's kitchen and living room put together.

Solange had recently retired, but for the years of their marriage, she too had worked at the university, a professor of philosophy. Being a true intellectual totally immersed in academia, Solange had never much troubled herself with the trivia of daily living. Now she found running the household, not to mention the car too, a complicated and often overwhelming job. She came to Sam for help and advice. She could sit for hours at the kitchen table drinking coffee, asking questions, and taking notes.

"Should I buy radials or regular? Where should I buy them?"

"How often does the furnace need a new filter?"

"The toilet keeps running. Should I call a plumber?"

"What was the name of that piano tuner we always used to get?"

Janice would sit with them only half-listening, flipping through cookbooks and her recipe box, planning Sam's supper. Solange, as Sam often pointed out when she wasn't there and he and Janice were sitting down to yet another delicious and nutritious meal, was not much of a cook. Janice, on the other hand, was one of those enviable people who could throw any number of things together, toss in a little bit of this, a little bit of that, and produce a culinary delight night after night.

"Cooking, ah, cooking," Solange would sometimes sigh. She had already admitted that she went out for dinner almost every night, and when she did eat at home she favoured wieners and beans, Campbell's tomato soup, or those dehydrated dinners with a shelf-life of two years.

She began to collect cooking hints from Janice and some recipes that were supposed to be quick and easy: Skillet Spaghetti, Quick Western Rarebit, Chicken Dinner Omelette.

But there were always so many details to worry about:

"What's the difference between dicing and chopping?"

"Does this mean fresh peas, frozen peas, or canned?"

"How much is a pinch?"

“How do you do it?” she would ask Janice with envy. “I just don’t know how you do it.”

* * *

In January, at Sam’s suggestion, Janice enrolled in a painting course two nights a week. He said it would be good for her to get out of the house, to get away from Celeste sometimes. Janice could not make him understand that she didn’t *want* to get away from Celeste. Even on a bad day, when Celeste was teething and fussing and crying, Janice could think of nothing else she’d rather do than be with her, cuddling her and giving her ice cubes to suck on or a raw carrot to chew on. Sam did not know how many afternoons, while Celeste was napping, Janice would sit on the floor beside her crib, just listening to her shallow sweet breaths, wishing she would wake up.

In the end, Janice took the painting class because she thought it would be good for Sam to have some time alone with Celeste. Maybe he would come to feel it too: the joy and the fear of loving her so much, the joy which suffused everything Janice did now, the fear which would strike suddenly, paralyzing in its intensity, when she thought about Celeste getting sick, getting hurt, dying, when she heard on the radio stories of child abuse, Sudden Infant Death Syndrome, a two-year-old boy in Toronto whose mutilated body was found in a dumpster behind the corner store.

The painting instructor was a man named Réjean Simard who had earned a considerable reputation for himself with his oversized flamboyantly coloured still lifes of apples and oranges twelve inches across, wine bottles three feet high, salamis the size of torpedoes viewed through the glass window of a downtown deli so that they became mystical, pregnant, out of this world. He was most often described as an iconoclast, a compliment or an insult depending on who delivered it, a variable term of endearment, celebration, or disapproval.

During the first few classes, Janice found her mind wandering. She could not concentrate on the advantages and disadvantages of each medium which Réjean Simard enthusiastically explained to them. She could not get a grip on the differences between watercolour, oils, polymer, acrylics, pastels, and tempera, as he carefully and energetically demonstrated them. She was intimidated by her fellow classmates, who all seemed to know more about painting than she did. She felt just plain stupid. She could not think of anything that she wanted to paint. She was terrified when Réjean Simard said that the first question they must ask themselves was *why* they wanted to paint. He said the only way to find the answer was to look deep inside themselves, to uncover their own sensitivities, and then to train those sensitivities so that they became even stronger, even sharper, even more demanding. Then and only then could they hope to find their own true subject matter.

On class nights, Janice would lie awake afterwards in bed beside Sam with a sick feeling in her stomach and the growing certainty that she did not have a creative bone anywhere in her body. But she was too disappointed and embarrassed to admit it, even (or especially) to Sam. He could sleep through anything anyway and so had no idea of her recurring insomnia.

After Réjean Simard had covered the more mechanical aspects of the art form, he moved on to broader theoretical concepts which he called "the elements of art." He taught with a frenetic energy, always in motion, pacing dramatically and flinging his arms towards the back wall as if a gallery of great art hung there. He scrawled words and shapes across the blackboard so wildly that the chalk often broke in his fingers and bounced across the room. He pontificated in italics.

"Colour is *everywhere*," he said. "*We cannot escape it.* But what is it? *What is it?* Green. *What is green?* It is not enough to know why the grass is green. *What is green?*"

"In nature," he said, "*there is no such thing as a line.* Scientifically speaking, *no such thing.* But *how can we possibly* recreate nature, how can we reproduce the world, without lines? *We cannot.* We must have the horizon in order to *survive.*"

"What does the word *texture* mean?" he asked. "Even the dictionary *does not know.* The dictionary *does not know* what you think of when I say gravel, a brick wall, newly mown grass, *skin.*"

"*Your paintings must have balance,*" he said. "How many white daisies does it take to balance the weight of *one black ball*? How much blue sky does it take to balance the weight of *three tall trees? How can a mountain equal the sun*?"

Janice, finally, was inspired. Now, when all the other students were nodding into their notebooks, she was riveted. One night at coffee break she overheard two women muttering to each other:

"What is all this airy-fairy stuff?" asked the first.

"Yeah, really," said the other. "We didn't come here to think, we came here to paint."

Now, on class nights, Janice lay awake afterwards with her head full of pictures while Sam slept on beside her, flat on his back, snoring.

They had stretched their canvases now and they had finally started to paint. Réjean Simard would flit among them, swooping down on one easel after another, exclaiming, adjusting, occasionally drawing the whole class around one painting to have a closer look.

Janice began with a painting of eggs, three white eggs submerged in a glass bowl of water. The perfectly oval eggs and the slightly cloudy water were rendered in an opaque shimmering light so that the total effect was one of otherworldliness, a submerged universe complete in itself, elliptical and promising.

If Janice's eggs were derivative of Réjean's own work, he didn't seem to mind. "These eggs," he said, "are *more than eggs.* These eggs, in the act of imagining them, have become *important.* These eggs are *the truth.*"

Janice suspected the successful picture was little more than a happy accident but she was encouraged by Réjean's admiration and began to see things in the painting that she hadn't known were there in the first place.

Each student was required to complete one major painting for the course. The rest of the class was painting landscapes, flowers, their mothers, their cats. Janice stretched another canvas, a larger one, and began. She painted nine pregnant women in various poses, sitting, standing, lying flat on their backs, so that their big bellies were like planets emitting pure light and their shiny faces were like reflecting moons.

Réjean was impressed. "Beautiful," he said. "*Beautiful. Perfect. Power.*" He wanted to know where her vision had come from, but Janice couldn't tell him, could not remember.

"Ah yes," Réjean said softly, and rested his hand on her shoulder. Janice noticed for the first time his swarthy skin, his black flashing eyes, and the gentle strength of his broad shoulders inside his tight t-shirt.

When she took the painting home, Sam liked it too. Yes, he agreed, most definitely they must frame it and hang it in the living room. She was talented, yes, brilliant even, to have conceived of such a thing. "But," Sam said, "what does it mean?"

* * *

Josh's mother called to say she and her husband were going to a do at the Legion, one of his fellow employees was retiring, their other babysitter had come down with the flu, could Janice *please* keep Josh for the night? Janice agreed before she remembered that it was Wednesday, a class night. But she did not want to let Josh's parents down. They were such nice people. It took some convincing but finally Sam agreed that he was quite capable of looking after Celeste and Josh both for the evening. Yes, it would be all right, he finally conceded. There were some things he'd been researching anyway, for

Josh, the questions he'd asked last week about the rings of Saturn.

"Did you know," Sam asked her, "that although the rings of Saturn stretch over 65,000 km, they are only a few kilometres thick?"

"Yes, I knew that," Janice said.

"Distant stars shine right through them," Sam said, but Janice wasn't listening. She was putting on her red coat, lacing up her black winter boots.

"What time will you be home?" he asked plaintively as she went out into the snowy night.

"Don't worry," she said. "I'll come right back. I'll be home by 9:30."

That night's class was especially stimulating. They were talking about composition now, how a painting when completed would have become more than the sum of its parts. Réjean used the analogy of human beings being more than the sum of their parts too, so that if you mixed together all those things that make up a person—water, blood, bone, and skin—you still wouldn't have a person, you'd only have a big mucky mess. Janice could see exactly what he meant and she was imbued all evening with that rarely reached sensation of everything falling into place, absolutely everything, so that all of her questions had answers and the whole world felt friendly.

When the others said they were going for a drink after class and Réjean made a special point of inviting her along, Janice changed her mind about going straight home and went to call Sam. Just for an hour, to go to the pub for just one hour, an hour and a half at the most, that's all she wanted, surely he wouldn't complain, she wasn't really asking for much.

Réjean and the others waited in the foyer while she stood at the bank of telephones and dialled. She could see the snow still falling outside, the night through the glass doors looking black and white at the same time. Réjean wore a black beret (of course!) and a red wool scarf wrapped twice around his neck.

The phone was ringing, five times, six, seven, eight. She let it ring twenty times. She hung up and dialled again. No answer.

She rushed right past Réjean and the others still standing there smiling stupidly. "I can't come, I can't come!" she called as the snow fell on her face, her bare hands, down her naked neck.

She could not remember where she'd parked the car. She ran around the parking lot with the keys in her hand. There it was. The tires spun in the snow and then she fish-tailed away.

No answer. No answer. Where was Sam? Where were the children? The house was burning down. The house had burnt down to the ground. Someone was dead. They were all dead.

She hit the snow-covered caragana hedge as she skidded into the driveway. The house was still standing. The lights were on. Where were they? They were at the hospital. Someone was sick. Celeste was sick. Josh was sick. Someone was dead. They were all dead.

Sam was stretched out on the couch, flat on his back, snoring. The first thing Janice saw clearly was the bottoms of his feet propped up on the arm of the couch in those pathetic grey socks.

"Wake up, wake up! The children, the phone! If you couldn't even hear the phone, how could you hear the children if they cried? You stupid bastard, wake up!"

Sam stirred and grunted but did not open his eyes. "Sleeping," he muttered and started snoring again.

There was a half-empty glass of Scotch on the coffee table beside him.

Janice grabbed it and threw it in his face. She sank to her knees and sobbed into her red coat still covered with snow which was melting now and dripping to the floor all around her.

"What the hell—" Sam sputtered, struggling to sit up. "What the hell is going on here?"

"What the hell is going on here?" Janice sobbed.

The children heard nothing, slept on.

In bed an hour later, Janice was calmer. She'd had a glass of Scotch and a hot bath. Sam had rubbed her back and told her she was overreacting. She was chastened, ashamed now of her own bad behaviour. She curled against Sam's back like a child in her white cotton nightgown, her hair on the cool pillow still damp from her bath. She tried to match her breathing to Sam's, which was already becoming deeper and slower. Breathe, breathe, breathe.

"Please, will you talk to me?" she asked.

"Mmm."

"Do you love me?" she asked.

"Yes, of course."

"Do you *still* love me?"

"Yes, of course." Sam patted her patiently and sighed.

"Why do you love me?"

She kept asking different questions and getting the same answer. The children slept on and knew nothing.

LOVE IN THE TIME OF CLICHÉS

(1990)

. . . it was love at first sight . . .

SHORTLY AFTER Carmen falls irretrievably in love with Abraham, she notices that she is often at a loss for words. This is unusual for Carmen, who has been told many times that she's been blessed with the gift of the gab. She supposes that she inherited or appropriated this gift from her mother, Maureen. Most of Carmen's childhood memories feature the sound of Maureen's lilting voice running as an undercurrent through everything, the melodious background music to their daily lives.

There, for instance, was Carmen, already a devoutly practising insomniac at an early age, tossing and turning in her narrow bed till the sheets were twisted like seaweed round her ankles. She could hear her mother in the living room, talking to her father, Frank, who never said much in reply, who was in fact probably stretched out on the couch half-asleep, not even listening, but Maureen didn't seem to notice or mind much. Carmen was on the tip of being a teenager then and often coaxed herself to sleep with fantasies of what it would be like to have a man, a full-grown, not-too-hairy man beside her in the bed, a man who would sleep all night long with his arm around her waist, his hand between her legs, not caressing, just cradling and holding her close, quietly.

It was not until Carmen took on the surly self-absorbed silence of adolescence that she began to wish Maureen would just SHUT UP. She never had anything important to say anyway, Carmen fumed silently. Especially first thing in the morning, Maureen was just like a magpie: yack, yack, yack. She just loved the sound of her own voice, Carmen thought, and closed her long-suffering eyes while her oatmeal congealed.

It was almost ten years later, long after Carmen had surfaced from beneath the iceberg of adolescence, had finished university, moved away from home, and settled into her own eventual adult life, that she understood how her mother's sometimes manic loquaciousness might actually have been compensation for the fact that she *knew* she had nothing important to say or, if she did, for the fact that she was afraid to say it.

Now Carmen finds she can afford to be sympathetic and doesn't mind admitting that, in terms of volubility anyway, she is her mother's daughter. It is an inheritance which serves Carmen well, both in her teaching job and in her personal life.

She is often admired for her ability to talk to anyone about anything. She can talk to her students about their families (who don't understand them), their boyfriends (who are collectively uncooperative and afraid of commitment), their wardrobes (which must look stylish but not too studied), their hair (which must be easy to take care of and yet look perfect at all times). She can talk to her fellow English teachers about the existential commitment in *Macbeth*, the symbol of the green light in *The Great Gatsby*, and the passage of time in the novels of Virginia Woolf. She can even talk to people she doesn't particularly like about things she isn't the least bit interested in. She talks to the jocks about football, to the math teachers about sine, cosine, and tangent, to the cashier in the cafeteria about the occupational hazard of breaking your fingernails on the cash register drawer, and to the foreign students about the price of tea in China. She is seldom stuck for a snappy answer to anything.

She works hard during the week and goes to lots of parties on weekends. Usually the first to arrive and the last to leave, she can dance and dance and never get tired, drink and drink and never pass out or throw up. She is the legendary life of the party. Her friends marvel at her stamina, her energy, her irrepressible love of life. She is, someone once said admiringly, the kind of person you cannot ever imagine asleep.

They don't know the half of it. They don't know about the insomnia, Carmen waking up in a sweat (hot or cold or an indescribable combination of both) at 3:14 a.m., her heart pounding so hard she can see it trembling beneath her nightgown, and then she can't go back to sleep even though she has to get up for work at 6:30 a.m., so she lies there worrying about anything and everything that crosses her mind, watching the red numbers on the digital clock click inexorably over until morning.

Her friends don't know how she sits by herself for hours on end not doing anything, not listening to music or looking out the window or anything, but just sitting there, brooding and stewing and travelling further and further inside herself, trying to catch a glimpse of what is really in there.

They don't know how she often plays a game with herself when walking down the street: looking closely at total strangers and trying to imagine them making love—not necessarily to her, but to anyone. That woman there in the purple shorts, the one with the snotty-nosed toddler on a leash and the prune-faced baby screaming in the stroller. That man there in the three-piece suit with his neck bulging over his perfectly-knotted tie, his hair combed forward over his bald spot, a chunky gold wedding band on his third left finger. Could they ever really have been laughing and snuggling, naked and happy in their lovers' arms? There are, Carmen has discovered, a great many people who, despite all evidence to the contrary, cannot be imagined into love in any position. She is afraid that she has become one of them.

Carmen has had lovers, of course—lots of them, in fact. Too many lovers, some people (her mother) might say. But nothing has ever worked out. With the twenty/twenty hindsight acquired somewhere around her thirtieth birthday, Carmen can see these men now as a long and relatively listless line of losers. Not one of them, she sees now, could have changed her life even if she'd wanted them to. Once, in a fit of foolishness precipitated by a six-month dry spell and a bottle of wine, she sat down to make a list of them (in order of appearance, not importance). When she got halfway through, when she got to the veterinarian who, in his exuberance to get her into his waterbed, knocked over the hamster cage on the nightstand, killing the stupid smelly little thing, when she discovered that she couldn't even remember his name (Kevin? Karl? Keith?), she was so appalled and depressed that she went to bed, where, of course, she couldn't sleep for a long time anyway and then all of her dreams were dotted with furry little dead things.

Her friend, Lorraine, a woman with a similarly checkered and disappointing past, once sent Carmen a cute card that said: "A question every woman asks herself . . . Is it possible that I deserve the kind of men I attract?" So Carmen smiled wryly, said, "Yes, well, yes," and kept on wondering, kept on trying to convince herself that none of it mattered anyway, that she preferred to be alone anyway, that sex wasn't what it was cracked up to be anyway, was definitely not one of the basic human needs like food, water, and shelter. And what was all the fuss about anyway when there were so many more important things to be considered?

And sometimes she even manages to look fondly forward to spending the rest of her life alone. Sometimes, when she can embrace it from just the right angle, she is able to conjure an image of herself as very tall, very thin, standing very straight, wearing something white and willowy, feeling stoic and serene, untouched by human hands and so, unsullied, uncomplicated, and clean.

Carmen's friends misinterpret her liveliness as the result of a natural ebullient energy, when really it is the result of a persistent low-grade anxiety that escalates according to the situation at hand. Knowing that she has a party to go to on Friday night is enough to keep her going all week long. By Friday morning she is so keyed-up that all day at work she is thinking of it: of what she will wear (does she need a new shirt? a black one? new pants? a new hairdo?), of what she will say (did she tell that story about the hamster last week or what about the guy who told her she was pretty well-preserved for her age and then couldn't understand why she dumped him?), of what she will drink (beer makes her sloppy but affectionate and gregarious, Scotch leaves her lucid but brave), of who else might be there, of the music, the dancing, the sky going dark outside the windows and then maybe coming light again too, pinkish and pale, and she won't have to sleep (or try to) all night long.

Nobody knows that she is the first to arrive because, by that time, she can't take the anticipation a minute longer and has to swing into action before she explodes. And that she is the last to leave because, by that time, she can't bear to admit that the party is over and nothing has happened. (She is never quite sure what she is expecting to happen but she *is* sure that if it ever does, she'll know. This is akin to what her mother told her years ago when Carmen asked her how you know when you're really in love, and Maureen said, mysteriously, maddeningly, as all mothers do, "Oh, you'll know, you'll just *know*.")

So it is at a party, naturally enough, that Carmen first meets Abraham. A party thrown for no good reason other than that they are all mired in the backwater of mid-February and they just need to let loose. Carmen is wearing her tightest black jeans, her baggy hot-pink sweatshirt, and silver hoop earrings the size of saucers. Her hair, for once, has turned out just right and her black leather jacket, she thinks, adds just the right hint or promise of danger.

She has never seen Abraham before in her life (he is new in town, working in the English Department at the university, so she's been told) but as she watches him browsing through the tape collection, selecting one and then plugging it into the machine, she suddenly thinks, Now there's a man I'd like to have around all the time.

For about a minute and a half the fact that he has chosen her own favourite tape seems merely coincidental. Emmylou Harris sings, *I would walk all the way/From Boulder to Birmingham/If I thought I could see/I could see your face.*

When Abraham asks Carmen to dance and takes her in his arms, it all makes perfect and sudden sense.

* * *

. . . love makes the world go round . . .

It is exactly two weeks later that Carmen notices she is more and more often at a loss for words. Her friends are concerned at first. They think she is depressed. When they realize that she is just in love, they take to teasing her gently while she smiles stupidly (they call it "mooning") with the realization that Abraham is the only person in the whole world she wants to talk to or listen to anyway. Sometimes her friends complain that she's just no fun anymore.

She can feel herself beginning to shed the cynicism with which she has protected herself for years. It comes peeling off her in ragged sheets like sunburned skin. Sometimes it is embarrassing, like when she does get talkative and catches herself quite unconscionably running off at the mouth about a beautiful sunset, a perfect tree, or the precious light of a misty morning. Her friends take to rolling their eyes impatiently whenever she begins to wax poetic about how WONDERFUL everything is. They don't understand how loving Abraham is like getting new glasses which amplify and intensify everything so that even the colour of the clouds, the sound of the rain, and the taste of her chicken salad sandwich at lunch are magnificent and miraculous.

Abraham usually picks Carmen up after work and, as they drive through the familiar city streets, they joyfully point out landmarks and points of interest to each other. There is their favourite house on the corner of Dundas and Tait, the vine-covered brick one with the verandah, the dormers, the bay window through which they can see a stone fireplace, floor-to-ceiling bookshelves, and hanging plants everywhere. They are both thinking, Someday we'll have a house like that. Even though they see it every day, it never ceases to amaze them.

They comment happily on sleepy cats curled on porches or window ledges, frisky black squirrels, bright-eyed and bushy-tailed, chasing each other from branch to branch, rosy-cheeked children in pink snowsuits and bunny hats, plump lumpy snowmen with carrot noses and corncob pipes. The whole neighbourhood strikes them as happy and handsome, resplendent and promising, tangible proof of the power of love.

When they see a young couple kissing on the corner, the girl's face tilting up to meet the boy's lips, her naked throat an offering, tantalizing with trust, Carmen and Abraham feel tender and empowered and Carmen lays her head on his shoulder while they wait for the light to change and the boy on the corner buries his face in the girl's cold hair.

On Fridays they stop at The Brunswick Bar for a drink on the way home. At The Brunswick they hold hands across the table and share a plate of nachos with cheese.

One Friday afternoon in the car when both of them are singing along with the Top 40 AM radio love songs (*I had the time of my life/And I owe it all to you*), they notice that, much as this music used to seem sappy and naïve, it has lately become poignant and perceptive.

Suddenly they simultaneously realize that most of what has been coming out of their mouths these days is one massive love-soaked starry-eyed cliché.

They go directly to The Brunswick to talk it over. The bar, as usual on Friday afternoon, is crowded with other hard-working people celebrating the end of another busy week. Everyone feels exuberant: they're buying drinks for each other as fast as they can, laughing uproariously, taking off their jackets and ties, letting their hair down for a few happy hours. Abraham and Carmen are lucky enough to get their favourite table and they smile and nod at familiar faces as they make their way to the back corner by the window. It's a cold dark day with snow clouds piled like blankets in the northern sky. The fireplace is lit and the room closes cosily in around the orange-tinted light, the smell of wood smoke, the sound of jazz music.

They are disgruntled at first by their unsettling revelation. They have always thought of themselves as creative, original, sophisticated, and very amusing people. They look cautiously around The Brunswick wondering if anyone has noticed the change in them but been too polite to mention it. Today they consciously resist the urge to feed nachos to each other.

No wonder they can only talk to each other these days! How could they say such things to their friends, to their conscientious politically correct friends who are all wrapped up in the larger issues: the environment, the Third World, the nuclear arms race, poverty, pornography, abortion, AIDS, and injustice. Certainly their friends have their love lives too, but they seem to look upon these liaisons with practical, matter-of-fact eyes. They are careful never to neglect their work, their other friends, or their social consciences in favour of their loves and/or their lusts. They are mature, independent, self-sufficient, self-controlled, meticulously realistic people who would never let love get in the way of anything.

Before she fell in love with Abraham, Carmen was just like them. Not since one misguided juvenile moment in Grade Ten has she turned down an evening with her female friends in favour of staying home and waiting for the phone to ring. She once laughed out loud at a woman who kept a snapshot of her lover on the dashboard of her car when he was away travelling and thought it probably served this woman right when she ran out of gas because the picture was over the gas gauge. She used to sneer churlishly at couples who kissed on corners. She had, a scant six weeks ago, turned down a date with a man she had been interested in for ages because he invited her to go and see a band called The High Heels whose lyrics were notoriously sexist and, besides, there was a rally that same night for animal rights.

Abraham too admits that he once broke a hot date with a gorgeous lustful woman because he wanted to stay home and reread *Madame Bovary*. And that he had once ended a fairly serious relationship with a woman named Wanda because she said nuclear war was inevitable so what was the point in getting all worked up about it?

Now Carmen and Abraham, by comparison both to their friends and to their former selves, are either iconoclastic or insipid lovebirds.

They order more beer and consider the nature of clichés.

Carmen recalls an incident from Grade Eleven English class when, in a short essay on Dickens' *Great Expectations*, she used the phrase "the eyes are the windows of the soul" and referred to it as "that old cliché." Her teacher, Miss Crocker, had put a question mark in the margin and a comment saying she'd never heard that saying before. Even then Carmen was aghast and never trusted Miss Crocker again.

Abraham suggests that the reason clichés become clichés in the first place is because they are true and that's why they come so easily to mind. "So yes," he says, "there must be a great many people in the world who have skin white as snow, hair black as night, lips red as cherries, voices clear as bells, and eyes just like diamonds or stars."

Carmen frowns into her half-empty glass.

Abraham elaborates on his theory: "Certainly, all over the world there must be thousands, if not millions, of people who are smart as whips, quick as winks, busy as bees—"

Carmen catches the spirit and they trade clichés across the table like playing cards:

"—right as rain," she offers. "Nervous as cats, quiet as mice, happy as clams—"

"—wicked as witches, thick as bricks, crazy as loons, strong as bulls, big as houses—"

"—mad as hatters, sick as dogs, cold as ice—"

"—wise as owls, bald as billiard balls, weak as kittens, naked as jaybirds—"

"—hot as blazes—"

"—nutty as fruitcakes—"

"—slow as molasses in January—"

"—pretty as pictures—"

"—ugly as sin—"

"—as old as the hills."

"So what's wrong with that?" asks Abraham.

"And drunk as skunks too," Carmen adds, taking another sip. She is not quite convinced that clichés might actually be acceptable currency in intelligent conversation. "When was the last time you saw a drunk skunk?" she counters skeptically. She also points out that people who sleep like babies have obviously never had one. And those who insist they are happy as larks know next to nothing about the real secret lives of birds, about the pressures they're under, trying to get that nest built out of thin air, laying those eggs and then sitting on them for God knows how long, hatching the babies, feeding them, teaching them how to fly—and having to keep on singing the whole time too.

"But what about love?" Abraham asks. "What about 'I love you'? What about 'I love you like there's no tomorrow'?"

Their sheepish chagrin is replaced quickly enough by an amused relief at finding themselves finally able to indulge their nascent romanticism, a tendency they had convinced themselves was a shameful weakness to be forever monitored, suppressed, and camouflaged for their higher-minded friends, indeed for the entire modern world. They marvel now at their ability to say romantic things to each other without feeling embarrassed or self-conscious, without having to make fun of themselves for being in love. They congratulate themselves on their new-found ability to say such things over and over again with a straight face and without gagging.

"Next thing you know," Carmen warns, "we'll be reading romance novels. Our hearts will be pounding, our breasts will be heaving, our hands will be quivering. Even the tips of our fingers will be tingling and electrified. We will be throbbing all over the place."

They say to hell with the cynical high-minded modern world. They have been tempted (or trying) to fall in love like this all their lives. They have nothing to hide, they can wear their passion everywhere. They are immaculate lovers, shameless. They will never be ordinary people again.

* * *

... you are always on my mind ...

Abraham is coming over for a special dinner to celebrate their first-month anniversary. Carmen spends the whole day, Saturday, getting ready while Abraham puts in a few hours of work at the university. She gets up early and reads cookbooks.

Then she goes downtown to gather the ingredients for the meal, which will be a nourishing feast fit for a king. Abraham is a man who loves to eat and Carmen loves to cook.

At the A&P, Carmen hums along with the muzak (*. . . the girl from Ipanema goes walking . . .*) and grins when they play a mutilated instrumental version of "You Light Up My Life." She makes her way slowly up and down the aisles, instead of tearing through the whole store in ten minutes like she usually does. She reads labels and considers prices carefully, instead of grabbing items off the shelves with one hand while still pushing the cart with the other so that it never stops moving. She waits patiently behind an elderly woman who has left her cart blocking the cereal aisle and smiles sympathetically as the woman tries to decide between regular oatmeal and the new quick-cooking kind. (She is not happy to recall the time an innocent but unsteady old man tried to shuffle past her in the produce section and banged into her cart with his and she told him to fuck off.) She lovingly selects the zucchini, the onions, the green peppers, weighs them gently in each hand, caresses them intimately, then lays them down in the cart as if they were alive. She handpicks the mushrooms from the bulk bin instead of buying a pre-packaged plastic tub. She imagines them slippery and flavourful in Abraham's mouth. She is patient with the cashier who is new on the job and doesn't have the hang of the electronic scanner yet. She loves every minute of it.

On her way into the seafood store, she bumps into her friend, Debbie, from school. Debbie teaches Health. Debbie says she just read an article in *Popular Psychology* that said that over 75% of any given person's thoughts on any given day are about either food or sex. The article also said that the average person has seven sexual fantasies per day.

Carmen thinks, What? Is that all? Only seven?

Debbie says, "I don't believe it. Nobody has that many! I've never had that many. I must be one of those people who fantasize about hot fudge sundaes instead!" She heads for the Dairy Queen, chuckling.

In the seafood store, Carmen buys a whole pound of fresh jumbo shrimp with the shells still on. While the man behind the counter wraps them up, she tells him she's making a special dinner tonight for her lover and they'll just have to see if it's true what they say about seafood being an aphrodisiac. She isn't even embarrassed when the man stares at her as if she's gone straight out of her mind.

At a gift store, she buys two pale blue candles and two white porcelain candleholders. She imagines Abraham's tender face touched by their elegant light. At the flower shop, she buys a bouquet of dusty pink alstroemeria, arranged with graceful green ferns and white Baby's Breath. She imagines Abraham pressing his face close into them and sighing deeply. At the liquor store, she buys a bottle of brandy. She imagines Abraham lifting the glass to his full moist lips, tasting the wine as thoroughly as he will afterwards taste her nipples and the back of her neck.

She spends the whole afternoon chopping, slicing, and dicing, singing along with Emmylou: *I don't want to hear a sad story/Full of heartbreak and desire.* She puts together the zucchini and barley casserole, then the cold lentil salad. She has to consult *The Joy of Cooking* about how to clean the shrimp. The cookbook has instructions and a diagram: "Shelling is easy—a slight tug releases the body shell from the tail. De-vein using a small pointed knife or the end of a toothpick, as sketched. This is essential." In the diagram, two disembodied female hands lay a small black knife upon a plump shrimp that looks like a fat peapod. The procedure may be essential but it's not easy and it takes Carmen a long time to master this tugging and hacking, so that the blue veins come snapping out of the meat like elastic bands. She marinates the shrimp in olive oil, parsley, basil, wine, and garlic. There is garlic in everything because they love garlic and the smell of it in the warm kitchen is pungent.

Finally content with her efforts, she sits down to read the newspaper and wait for Abraham. She recognizes that, short of an apron and bare feet, the whole scene is a cliché. *The way to a man's heart . . .*

"The way to a man's heart," she used to like to quip for her friends, "is an unmarked minefield." Or: is a barbed wire fence, an electric one at that. Is a shot in the dark. Is a roller-coaster ride to hell. At the time she thought she was vastly amusing. Now she feels sorry for her former self.

"Contentment," she used to say, "is for cows."

"Patience," she used to say, "is a virgin."

In the newspaper, she reads the story of two lovers reunited finally and forever after seventeen years and her eyes mist over lightly with sweet warm tears.

And so it is in the power of true love to liberate all emotions unequivocally and without restraint. It is no longer necessary to deny your emotional excesses. No longer necessary to pretend you have something in your eye when you cry at the long-distance commercials on television. No longer necessary to try and convince anyone, not even yourself, that you stopped believing in "happily ever after" around the same time you got smart about Santa Claus and the Easter Bunny. It is no longer necessary to keep your heart in check and your passion under control. You can be as flagrant and ecstatic as you have always wanted to be.

Abraham arrives with more flowers, white wine, and a chocolate cheesecake for dessert. They kiss for a long time in the doorway, stranded on the stairs.

"My lover," Carmen says, "my lover." The mere sound of the word lets loose a voluptuous leaping in her heart, her stomach, or some hitherto unknown, unexercised internal organ. The other beautiful feast will just have to wait.

* * *

. . . I can't live if living is without you . . .

In the morning they make love again. Carmen is above him, her hands on his shoulders, his tongue licking her breasts, his hands squeezing her buttocks as she moves on him in small circles, his long thin fingers sliding in and out of all her moist places, beads of sweat and her long hair falling into her eyes, into his, and when she comes he says, "I love you, I love you." He says he loves the way she looks right at him when she comes, the way she comes *into* him rather than away, the way she doesn't go off to some other planet where he can no longer reach her. And he is right, she is not transported; rather, she is transformed. In his innocent arms she becomes the person she has always hoped to be.

Everywhere their bodies are like mouths, slippery and warm, brimming with nerve endings and succulent taste buds.

Abraham holds her there on top of him. She rests her wet face on his wet chest and she can feel his heart beating against her forehead like a pulse in her own brain. When he says, "I want to hold you like this forever," she can feel the words as much as hear them. Even if she were deaf, she would know what he was saying. They stretch out side by side face-down on the big bed and take turns tracing words with their fingertips on each other's bare backs and then trying to guess what they are. They make words like "hope," "love," "forever," "hearts," "sweethearts." Even if they were blind, they would dwell in the language of love.

Abraham says it's his turn to make breakfast. Carmen gets to luxuriate in her own laziness, lolling around in the messy bed, the smell of their lovemaking still on the sheets, the smell of his hair still on the pillow. While Abraham clatters around in the kitchen, she tries smelling her own skin, her arms, the crook of her elbow, tries to catch that smell of herself which Abraham is always saying he loves so much. Except for a possible hint of garlic from last night's meal still on her hands, she cannot smell anything special. This is akin, she supposes, to not being able to tickle yourself—why can't you?

If she sprawls crossways on the bed and leans over the edge, she can just see Abraham in the kitchen at the stove. The sight of him stirring and tasting, bare-chested in his blue jeans, leaves her weak-kneed with pleasure.

She comes into the kitchen in her pink chenille housecoat which makes her feel like an irresistible if slightly dissolute movie queen from the fifties. Dishing up their hot porridge, Abraham tells her that she looks glamorous. The sash of the housecoat comes loose as she sits down at the table. Abraham smiles at her brown nipples that look like another pair of eyes, blinking with surprise at the light.

"There is," he says, laughing, "a fine line between sordid and glamorous."

Porridge is something that Carmen would never make for herself (if only because it would remind her of those mornings when she was busy hating her mother, Maureen, who was rambling on about the virtues of a hot breakfast while Carmen's oatmeal turned to concrete in her bowl). But cooked up now by Abraham, it is the best thing she has ever eaten. And when he expounds on the virtues of a hot breakfast, she is touched by his loving concern for her health.

From the kitchen window, they watch the empty Sunday morning street. It has rained heavily all night and now the temperature is dropping quickly, freezing the rain as it falls, forming a skin of ice on everything in sight. It is springtime, or it should be. Carmen thinks again of Maureen who, whenever the weather was unusual, said it was because of those damned Russians out in space always shooting at the moon. An occasional car slides past the house, windshield wipers flapping ineffectually, ferrying intrepid men in rumpled suits and devout women in subdued hats to worship at the churches of their choice. They laugh, but not unkindly, at the woman from next door making her way down the treacherous sidewalk with a box of salt in her hand, sprinkling it on the ice in front of her as she inches along.

They decide it is a good day to be decadent. They close up all the curtains again, put a little brandy in their coffee, and carry their cups into the living room. They've got classical music on the stereo, Beethoven's "Ode to Joy": *O friends, no more these sounds!/let us sing more cheerful songs,/more full of joy!*

They're curled up on the chesterfield like luxurious cats and the hanging lamp in the corner drops a circle of yellow light down around them like a tent. They take turns reading poetry to each other.

The day unravels in slow motion around them and they know in their hearts how beautiful they truly are.

By mid-afternoon it is still raining and they are still nestled there in each other's arms. Abraham is dozing and Carmen is suspended somewhere between thinking and dreaming, all of her borders blurred. Now that she has at last learned how to love, she worries sometimes about how much now she has to lose.

As if from a great snow-covered stony height, she feels Abraham's fingers go limp and fall away from hers. Her eyes snap open.

To look into the future and not see them together is like going blind.

In his sleep, Abraham tucks his hand between her legs where it is furry and moist and he sighs.

* * *

... wish you were here ...

In August, Carmen goes home to visit her parents for two weeks. Abraham drives her to the airport where they re-enact the time-honoured scene, hugging and promising while Carmen hides her teary eyes in his neck. At the last minute, Abraham tucks the Emmylou Harris tape into her purse, and says, "Reinforcements."

The small plane gaining altitude after takeoff fishtails like a car skidding on the ice in slow motion. Carmen, who does not like flying at the best of times, is praying silently at the top of her lungs, praying to a God she is not sure she believes in but whom she is not averse to invoking when she thinks it might help, praying, Please don't let me die now, not now, not now when I'm in love. But then, sinking back into her seat, she thinks, Oh well, all right then, go ahead, at least I won't have died without learning how to love.

But of course she doesn't die. She smiles gratefully at the calm competent stewardess and tries to enjoy the flight. The man in the seat beside her is headfirst in his briefcase, avoiding her glance, clearly not interested in making conversation. She looks out the window.

The sight of the familiar countryside falling away from her at odd angles as the plane continues to climb is mesmerizing. She is already writing a letter to Abraham in her head. She must remember to tell him about these lakes like the little mirrors on that embroidered Indian bag she used to carry, about these trees like broccoli, too green to be true, about this highway like an artery, these country roads like veins. She relaxes and closes her eyes. The two women in front of her are gossiping in shrill but thrilled voices, using words like "odious," "flagrant," "screaming," and "wild-eyed." Over the drone of the plane, nothing they are saying connects. There is another voice, a pretty voice in her own head, running as the soothing undercurrent through everything. It takes her a minute to realize it is the voice of Emmylou, singing.

As Carmen drifts further away, the voice in her head becomes that of Maureen superimposed upon a picture of Carmen in her sandbox, mucking around with a yellow plastic shovel and a little red pail while her mother leaned against the white picket fence, chatting with the neighbour lady, Mrs. Lutz, who smiled and nodded knowingly as Maureen considered at length the possibilities of the weather, the problems of the old wringer washing machine (which once got a good grip on her left hand and flattened all four fingers), and what would become of the Watson house now that the Widow Watson had finally passed on, poor old thing? Mrs. Lutz was poking around in her big garden while they talked, handing Maureen vegetables over the fence: waxy green cucumbers, plump red tomatoes, crisp orange carrots with the dirt still on them. Maureen carried them into the house cradled in her apron as if they were alive. Carmen didn't mind being left alone in the yard. Not until she heard the sound of a train on the track at the end of the street and as it bore down on her, she ran the whole length of the yard screaming, banged the screen door open and flew into her mother's safe arms in the safe yellow kitchen.

Maureen and Frank are waiting at the airport and Carmen is surprised at the lump that rises in her throat when Maureen takes her in her arms. For a minute, Carmen thinks Maureen is wearing little white gloves, wrist-length, the kind she would have been wearing twenty years ago with her white-feathered hat with the veil. But no, it's just that Maureen's skin is so white that her hands look disembodied, as if hung from the sleeves of her fancy black blouse. Her father, Frank, pats her gently on the back.

Maureen talks all the way home in the car, while Frank drives smiling, and Carmen marvels, as she does every year, at how nothing and everything has changed: how the street looks the same but wider and the houses look the same too but smaller and cleaner.

Maureen's kitchen hasn't changed either: there is the same flooring (white with gold swirls), the same arborite kitchenette set (blue with black specks), Maureen's collection of little ceramic animals and birds gathered from boxes of Red Rose tea and arranged on the windowsill above the sink, Carmen's Grade Twelve school picture still stuck to the fridge with an owl magnet.

But this year, Carmen finds she does not immediately turn back into a seething sixteen-year-old the minute she steps into the house. This time, as she lays her suitcase down on her old bed, she is still a grown woman with a good job. She is still a happy woman with a photograph of Abraham in the gold locket at her throat. It is an antique locket that Maureen gave her when she left home and so it is engraved in delicate curling script with Maureen's initials instead of her own. She has never worn it before and now, with Abraham's picture inside, the locket is a potent talisman that will protect her from all sadness, all evil, despair. Abraham's spirit will not desert her. Whenever the ache of loneliness surges up into her throat so that she can feel it like a second pulse, she rubs the gold locket between her thumb and forefinger until it is warm, warm as his hands on her cheeks when he kisses her closed eyelids, warm as the sound of his voice in the dark.

This time, too, Maureen and Frank seem to sense the change in her and, indeed, they treat her like an adult instead of like a seething sixteen-year-old. She finds she can even afford this time to remember scenes from those tortured adolescent years with a nostalgic fondness for her own plaintive perpetual whining ("Stop treating me like a child!") and for Maureen's condescending triumphant reasoning ("Then stop acting like one!")

She can sit there at the table eating a pressed ham and Kraft processed cheese sandwich on white bread, drinking Lone Star beer right out of the can, skimming through Frank's *National Enquirer* and Maureen's *True Romances*, listening to Frank suck his teeth while Maureen complains about the new people next door who never mow their grass and what will become of this neighbourhood anyway? She can sit there calmly without hating them at all. She can think with amusement: Ah, the life I left behind!

She can even look at the fake fireplace in the living room (plaster of Paris painted like bricks which Maureen was always touching up with a piece of grey chalk when the paint got chipped and there is a revolving orange lightbulb below the metal grate which is filled with charcoal briquets) without cringing or wishing she could take a sledgehammer to the damn thing.

She can think of Abraham's face between her naked trembling thighs and she can hear him whispering her name when she comes. For once in her life, she does not feel guilty about anything, least of all about growing up.

And so the lovers, the true lovers, may become at long last generous and genuine, capable of expanding in all directions at once without ever losing track of themselves. All memories are bearable, all dreams are possible, and the future feels like a very fine thing full of truth and spirit and tender power.

* * *

... the minutes pass like hours ...

On the third day of her visit, Carmen goes to bed early because the time will not pass. She has always had a problem with time. As a child, she was always trying to coax or trick the hours into hurrying up because there was always something she could hardly wait for and Maureen was always warning her, "Girl, you're wishing your life away."

Now she lies awake in the half-dark watching the numbers on the digital clock and listening to the Emmylou Harris tape.

She can hear her mother in the kitchen, talking on the phone to her sister, Giselle.

Carmen can picture Maureen perched on the stool by the phone, twirling the coiled cord with one hand and doodling all over the phone book with the other. Maureen and Giselle are having the same conversation they had twenty years ago while Carmen struggled with her math homework and eavesdropped. They would talk on about shopping, cooking, their respective aches and pains, some program they'd both watched on TV and hated or loved.

Often they would reminisce about giving birth: Giselle to her two boys and Maureen to Carmen, who is an only child. Childbirth, Carmen discovered while eavesdropping, is something that mothers never tire of talking about, no matter how many years have by then intervened. They love to tell each other the numbers again and again, slipping them back and forth like the balls on an abacus: hours in labour, hours in the delivery room, minutes between contractions, how many pushes before the head popped out like a pumpkin. It is a competition of sorts to see who has suffered the most pain and indignity and survived. It is also proof that those who say you won't remember the pain are lying.

Sometimes they talked about their own childhoods and how they hated each other when they were kids: "Do you remember when you broke the teapot over my head? Do you remember when I tried to stick your head down the hole in the outhouse?" It was a wonder they hadn't killed each other. They laughed and laughed and left red lipstick all over their respective receivers. When Maureen hung up, she looked flushed and girlish again.

Tonight, after she hangs up, she taps on Carmen's door and slips into the dark room. "That's pretty music," she says and curls up on the bed with Carmen. She is wearing her chenille housecoat which falls half-open to reveal a shiny white slip with spaghetti straps and Carmen can see just the top of her mother's breasts which are beautiful and luminous like the inside of seashells.

They wiggle around on the bed until they are both sitting propped against the headboard with the pillows behind them. Carmen lays her head against her mother's shoulder and tells her all about Abraham. She tells her how he is kind, sensitive, intelligent, funny, warm, wise, healthy, peaceful, passionate, serious, generous, gentle, beautiful, and strong. How he is the man she'd almost given up hoping to meet, how he is the man she has had in her heart all along. She shows Maureen his picture in the locket.

Her father seems to have graciously accepted the fact that he can inhabit only the fringes of this moment and she can hear him paddling around in the kitchen in his slippers, humming and making cocoa and toast.

As she talks, Carmen feels like she has been doing this all her life. But the truth is she has not told her mother anything important since the time Mickey Roach kissed her on the mouth at recess and Carmen punched him in the nose.

Years later, there was the time Reg Henderson took her out to the airport parking lot where all the would-be lovers used to go and she let him touch her small breasts under her sweater and there was a tickling between her legs and she wanted him to touch her there but then she pushed him off her and felt sick to her stomach with loving it and hating it. She was crying when she got home and her hair was a mess and of course Maureen was waiting up for her but when she tried to talk to her, Maureen said, "I don't want to hear about it," and then she went to bed, leaving Carmen alone in the dark living room, trying to make sense of herself.

Years later still, there was the time Carmen called home long-distance and she was telling Maureen about the trip to Toronto she'd made that weekend with her boyfriend, Terry, and how their hotel room was so elegant, an oak four-poster bed with curtains and everything, and Maureen said, "I don't want to hear about it", and Carmen, in a flash of futile anger, said, "What the hell do you think I do out here—knit?" But Maureen was already talking about the new wallpaper they'd hung in the bathroom and Carmen couldn't get another word in edgewise.

Now Carmen tells her mother that Abraham is the best lover she has ever had and Maureen doesn't even flinch. She doesn't laugh or change the subject either. She is silent and then she says, "Yes," and her voice is smiling.

They talk about Abraham for two hours straight and the time passes so slowly that missing him is exquisite.

* * *

. . . I'm so lonesome I could cry . . .

Long after Maureen and Frank have gone to bed, Carmen is still awake. Listening to her parents giggling and whispering in bed, it occurs to her for the first time that they are in love, still in love.

When the phone on the night table rings, it is Abraham.

"I miss you," he says and his voice is rich.

"When you get home," he says, "I want to make love to you until you pass out."

"I've been reading about lions," he says, "who have been known to make love eighty times a day, and this," he says, "is something to strive for."

The sound of his voice in the dark makes her wet.

After Carmen hangs up, she thinks about a summer evening at Black Bridge Falls when they had been swimming, were sitting afterwards on the high grassy bank in their bathing suits, just watching the river flow. Carmen pushed him gently back onto the grass, pulled down his bathing suit, and took him into her mouth and he moaned and arched up towards her.

In the dark bedroom now, she pretends the cool sheets against her naked body are his skin against hers and she strokes her breasts until the nipples grow hard and she touches herself just the way he touches her and she imagines him watching her as she slides her own fingers in and out slowly, so slowly. But when she comes, she cries.

Falling asleep finally, she realizes that the man in the original memory was not Abraham at all, but Jason Campbell whom she dated ten years ago. And in real life, when she tugged at the waist of his bathing suit, Jason brushed her hand away as if it were an insect and said, "Don't do that. Someone will see. Are you crazy?"

And so it is in the power of true love to alter everyone and everything that has gone before. All of your former lovers, it seems, are reduced to stand-ins, replaced now in your memories by the figure of the beloved. All of their lips have become his. All of their lips were his all along.

The thought of Abraham is so much with her that often she can't tell whether she's thinking of him or not. She knows this sounds crazy. But he is so much inside of her, that even when she is consciously thinking of other things, she is always aware too of his presence, or now of his absence, which is everywhere. She thinks of all the places they can touch each other when she gets home. They can turn each other inside out.

* * *

. . . I love you like October . . .

Autumn is their favourite season, when the sky is cool blue and the air is a tonic, sharp and invigorating after the humid muzzle of the summer heat. On Saturday, they go walking through the neighbourhood just at that hour when the lights have been lit but the curtains are still open and all the houses are emitting snug squares of yellow light into the deepening afternoon. Carmen knows that half the people inside those houses may well be bored to tears or hollering at each other but they look so contented from the outside that, when she walked like this before she met Abraham, she would be enveloped by a sickening liquid envy running through her like vinegar and, at the sight of lovers walking hand in hand, she would be swamped by a self-pity so caustic that it left her clenching her fists in pure rage, white-knuckled.

Now she and Abraham walk down to the park at the corner which has been abandoned these cool days by all but the faithful: a woman in a camel-hair coat walking her Cocker Spaniel, a group of half-grown boys in rubber boots and too-small sweaters playing hockey with a ball where the rink will be, another pair of lovers on a green wooden bench eating chocolate doughnuts with their mittens on.

Carmen and Abraham leave the paved pathways and shuffle through the fallen leaves piled so high in places that they are up to their knees and the colours fall away in front of them like noisy surf. They lie down together and the crispy leaves envelop them. As they put their arms around each other, a woman alone walks past, stares, and then averts her eyes. Carmen recognizes this woman as her own former self, fighting her way through another serious Saturday, jamming her fists into her pockets and heading home still alone, with the wasteland of another Sunday yet to come.

On the way home, they gather leaves, carefully selecting the best ones from among the millions under their feet: red, orange, yellow, one maple leaf gone so dark it looks black. At home, Carmen arranges the leaves on lengths of wax paper, places them between sheets of old newspaper, and then presses the whole package beneath the thick volumes of the Encyclopedia Britannica.

Abraham, in the living room, is putting on a tape: *The last time I felt like this/I was in the wilderness/And the canyon was on fire/And I stood on the mountain/In the night/And I watched it burn/I watched it burn/I watched it burn.*

As Carmen watches him from the doorway, he turns for a moment back into the stranger she met at the party, the man she knew nothing about, the man who could change her life if she let him.

At such a moment, unknowingly observed, the beloved becomes a singular distant miracle, a transcendent untouchable star. At such a moment, the lover is illuminated by the impossibility of love and of loss, galvanized by the immutable possibility of both. At this moment, the lovers may believe they are immortal.

Carmen goes up behind him and drapes her arm around his shoulders, nuzzling her face into his neck. "You smell like the leaves," she says. "You smell like October." He says this is the nicest thing anyone has ever said to him.

* * *

. . . I love you like a child . . .

In the dream, Carmen and Abraham are standing naked face to face but when she reaches out to stroke his neck, the rise of his breastbone, the curve of his hips, he feels like a blank wall covered with glossy white paint.

In the dream, Carmen is pregnant, her round belly slick with sweat and luminous, the way Maureen's breasts were luminous, glistening like mother-of-pearl.

In the dream, Maureen is dead, laid out in a glass coffin covered with flowers and pendulous fruit. The funeral parlour is filled with singing strangers. Maureen says, "Listen. Can you hear me? Listen. Can you hear the sound of my eyes closing, the sound of my breath in your body, the sound of your head coming out from between my legs? Can you hear the singing? Can you hear the celebration?"

When Carmen wakes up sobbing, Abraham takes her in his arms and he says, "Cry, just cry. It's all right to cry."

In his arms like a child, she must give over her fear, all fear all grieving all trust all power, and she must deliver it there into his purified arms. And here is all the faith in the world, all the trust in tomorrow, and the possibility of finding and losing everything, and the rocking of a soul, these souls ecstatic in such sorrow such joy the attainment of all and every extraordinary life.

She is lying face-down on the big bed and he rubs her neck her shoulders, his hands drawing wordless circles into the small of her back, his tongue on her buttocks and the backs of her thighs.

She moves beneath him slowly so slowly and the sweetness runs out of her over his long fingers between her legs between her opening legs inside of her aching where she is aching and he slides in and slides in and slides in moving together sweating and he rubs his wet chest against her trembling back his teeth are on her neck and they are silent so silent they have never loved before in such excellent silence only breath and breathing they are only breathing the room is full of them and she can feel the hot liquid spurting into her and they are blossoms opening in an instant in what could be forever flowers unfurling the petals like pale skin encompassing all time and they are opening each other opening themselves to the world and there is room enough inside at last for everything room enough for all life new life and the serious suddenness of love and there can be no word for this or if there is a word and if they ever find it there will be nothing left to say and they are moaning and laughing and they will never be ordinary people again.

AS FAR AS IT GOES

(1990)

JANE'S LOVER Daniel has decided he is going to tell his wife on Thursday night. He is going to tell her the whole story. He is finally going to tell her the truth. He actually made the decision last Friday but due to extenuating circumstances (friends coming for the weekend, a conference which Anna, his wife, has to attend, then a dinner party they planned weeks ago), he couldn't see his way clear to telling her the truth until Thursday.

On Thursday afternoon Jane has a staff meeting at work. She calls Daniel from the office just beforehand and tries to be strong and supportive on the phone. No one can guess what will happen once Anna knows. Daniel says he is just on his way to the liquor store for some whisky because he figures Anna will probably need it. Jane doesn't hear a single word that is said at the staff meeting and is grateful that no one seems to expect her to contribute.

After the meeting she goes and picks up her son Nicholas at the daycare. Back home she orders a pizza for supper because she feels too rattled to cook. She eats standing up beside the sink which Nicholas thinks is very funny. She puts him to bed early because his innocent exuberance is making her feel irritable, which in turn makes her feel selfish and guilty, and in the end she cannot concentrate on him at all. She is extremely anxious but it is an exciting invigorating kind of anxiety. She cannot imagine how Daniel will begin the conversation but she is pretty sure that by the end of it Anna will throw him out.

Jane spends the rest of Thursday evening sitting at the kitchen table looking out the window at the rain. She can just picture Daniel coming up her driveway in the dark, his duffle bag in one hand and his heart in the other. She drinks three bottles of imported beer and listens to the classical music radio station. It isn't so much that she's big on classical music—in fact, she knows almost nothing about it—it's just that she finds she can no longer listen to songs with words. All the tapes she owns, all the Top 40 songs, all the golden oldies, are far too laden with love, too fraught with implication and intimacy or the inevitable lack thereof. She remembers her friend Deborah telling her that when she was breaking up with her husband years ago she found she could no longer tolerate bright colours. She just wanted to live in a world of black and white and grey. Jane thinks she would like to live now in a world without lyrics.

At ten o'clock she turns the phone up as loud as it will go and then she goes to bed.

Surprisingly she sleeps very well.

* * *

Although she is off work on Friday, Jane gets up at six o'clock as usual and takes Nicholas to the daycare. She intends to do some work at home but as the morning wears on with still no word, she has to admit that she is accomplishing absolutely nothing. She cannot settle herself to anything. She wants to go out for a walk, having heard repeatedly from her more health-conscious friends, including Daniel himself, that physical exercise is the best antidote to anxiety. But she is afraid to leave the house in case Daniel calls or comes by. Finally after lunch she has to go out for more cigarettes. Although she'll only be gone for fifteen minutes, she turns on her answering machine and tapes a note to the back door: *Gone to the corner store. Back in a few minutes. Please wait.*

She walks to the store and back as quickly as she can, having forgotten her umbrella, so that by the time she gets home her jacket is soaked through and her hair is hanging in strings that are dripping all over the kitchen floor. The note is still there, flapping soggily in the rising wind.

The afternoon passes somehow. Forever afterwards she will be unable to remember a single thing she did during those interminable hours.

At five o'clock she goes to get Nicholas, once again leaving a note and turning on the answering machine. They pick up Chinese food on the way home because she is still too jumpy to cook.

When they get back, Jane fairly pounces on the answering machine because the red light is flashing to indicate that a message has been recorded. But it is just her friend Deborah calling to see if Jane wants to go out for a drink later. Deborah's daughter Karen will stay with Nicholas. Jane calls Deborah right back and says thanks but no thanks, she thinks she should stay close to home, she promised Daniel that she would be there whenever he needed her. Deborah sighs and says she understands. Jane suspects that Deborah is tired of hearing about Daniel and their difficulties anyway. She can see Deborah's eyes glazing over as soon as she starts telling her the latest episode, upset, or hopeful sign. Of course Deborah still listens, giving advice and trying to cheer her up, but Jane can sense her impatience with the whole story. Deborah is just waiting now for Jane to snap out of it and get back to normal. But Jane cannot imagine when or how that will happen. Jane can barely remember what "normal" means.

After supper Jane shows Nicholas how to build a castle with his Lego and then she helps him finish putting the stickers into his new Sticker Dictionary:

A is for apple. An apple is a round fruit that grows on trees. A juicy red apple is delicious to eat.

B is for banana. A banana is a curved yellow fruit. The monkey ate the banana, peel and all. . . .

At eight o'clock she says, "It's time to find a clean pair of pajamas and get into bed."

Nicholas says, "What's a pair?"

Jane explains that a pair means two, like a pair of shoes or a pair of socks. Two people are a pair. Three people are a triangle. Three people are a torment. But of course she doesn't tell him this part.

Nicholas grins suddenly and says, "Oh I get it! Two is a pear and one is an apple."

Jane tucks him in and goes back to her vigil at the kitchen table. She can't sit in the living room because she cannot let herself think about the times she and Daniel made love there on the soft pink couch, lying there afterwards curled up naked and marvelling how well all parts of their bodies fit together. The kitchen is a slightly more neutral territory although it too can become crowded with memories of meals they cooked together: feeding each other mushrooms fried in butter, crisp steamed broccoli, tender chunks of beef plucked from the bubbling stroganoff, kissing at the stove with the food fragrant all around them while Nicholas got underfoot and sang. Perhaps because she's lost her appetite now, these memories are easier to avoid.

The wind is rising and the rain pours down. Nicholas calls out to her in a panicky voice, "Mom, will it thunder?"

Jane says, "No, don't worry, it won't thunder."

Satisfied, Nicholas sings a few rounds of the song he's just learned at daycare: "Row row row your boat/Gently down the stream/Merrily merrily merrily/Life is but a dream," and then he goes to sleep. Briefly Jane envies how easily and totally he can be reassured.

Again she spends the evening waiting, but still there is no word from Daniel. She cannot decide what this might mean. The possibilities seem to expand exponentially as the darkness falls slowly down the wet street.

* * *

On Saturday morning Jane wakes up feeling ambitious and energetic in spite of herself. While Nicholas watches cartoons, she whips up a batch of baking soda biscuits with cheese and they eat them still warm with lots of butter and a bowl of fresh strawberries. After breakfast she washes down the kitchen walls, a job she's been meaning to get at for nearly six months. The water in the bucket turns brown with accumulated grime and nicotine. Nicholas mucks happily around in the soapy water until his shirt and pants are soaked.

Jane is just folding the third load of laundry around noon when Daniel appears at her back door with a half-empty bottle of whisky in his hand. It is still raining, it has been raining for three days, and in the porch she strokes the cold droplets from his forehead and rests her cheek against his wet hair.

They sit down at the kitchen table and Daniel tells her the whole story while Nicholas obligingly takes a nap.

Yes, he told Anna everything. No, she didn't throw him out. She doesn't know what she wants to do now. Neither does he.

He is taking small sips of whisky straight from the bottle.

All he knows for sure is that it is up to Anna for now. If she wants him to leave, he will leave. If she wants him to stay, he will stay and try to work things out.

This is not at all what Jane was expecting.

"Are you saying then," she asks calmly, "that it's over?"

Daniel says, "Yes."

Jane takes a drink from the bottle.

Daniel says, "What else can I do?"

* * *

It is Saturday night but Jane is lucky enough to find a babysitter at the last minute. Deborah's daughter Karen can't come but her friend Connie will do it. Nicholas loves Connie and waits anxiously at the window for her to arrive, with his new Batman cards spread out on the kitchen table and the Lego castle cradled in his lap.

After Connie gets there, Jane takes a taxi downtown to her favourite pub, Carlyle's. She is pretty much a regular at Carlyle's and Stuart, the bartender, is a good friend. In fact, Jane and Stuart slept together once about two months ago, on a night when she had temporarily lost sight of the hope which had sustained her all those months and had succumbed to a tidal wave of whisky-magnified despair, feeling sure that Daniel would never be able to tell Anna the truth, let alone leave her. Stuart was in a similar state that night, having temporarily admitted that Andrea, the woman he loved, was not ever going to love him back.

In fact, it was this mutual romantic misery that formed the basis of Jane and Stuart's friendship in the first place. They had passed many hours together at Carlyle's, one on either side of the stand-up bar, Stuart serving and sipping, Jane drinking one beer after another, as they bemoaned their respective fates, tried to become insightful and decisive, tried in vain to stop loving the people they did so truly love. They were a great comfort to each other.

Jane never once told Stuart he was stupid for loving a woman who would never love him back and Stuart never once told Jane she was an idiot for getting involved with a married man. They took each other's errors in judgement for granted so that there was no need for justification or self-defense. Whenever Jane would say, "That's it, I've had it, it's finished, I will *never* see him again," Stuart would say, "Yes, you're right, yes, this is the right thing to do." When Jane would come in the very next night and say, "I love him, I can wait, I'll wait for however long it takes," Stuart would say, "Yes, you're right, yes, this is the right thing to do."

But after they spent the night together, they found they were tense with each other, maybe even a little hostile, not knowing anymore what to say. All the ease had gone out of them. A week later they got together for lunch and discovered with great relief that all they really wanted from each other was friendship because certainly neither one of them was in any kind of emotional shape to be starting something new. And so they slipped gratefully back into their former positions, passing the beer and their pain back and forth across the well-polished bar between them like beads on an abacus, both of their dark curly heads bending in above their bottomless glasses, both of their faces flushing rosy with emotion or alcohol or both, all of their big brown eyes shining with heartache and hope once again.

On this particular Saturday night, Stuart is more than willing to sympathize. He listens generously, nodding or shaking his head at the appropriate junctures, letting Jane tell him the whole story, even letting her tell him again all the parts of the story she's already told him before. He buys her several double whiskies and has a few himself because Andrea has once again told him that she does not love him and he is starting to believe her. By eleven o'clock they are both half-drunk and repeating themselves, laughing at things that aren't very funny, especially at their own steadfast stupidity. Stuart is making fun of Andrea and Jane is making fun of Daniel, even while reflecting that the person she is always telling Stuart about is not at all like the *real* Daniel, not at all like the man she loves, and afterwards she always feels a little ashamed of herself.

At midnight Stuart phones a taxi and Jane goes home. After she pays Connie for the babysitting, she checks on Nicholas who is sleeping peacefully with Batman in one hand and a blue-and-white garbage truck in the other. At the sight of his long dark curls tumbling across the white pillowcase, his long dark eyelashes so still upon his smooth pink cheeks, her eyes fill with tears of love and fear. She rests one hand lightly on his chest and feels him breathing deeply. She remembers asking Deborah, whose daughter is fourteen, when you stop this nightly checking to see if your child is still breathing and, laughing, Deborah said, "When they move away from home, I guess."

In the living room, Jane puts Daniel's favourite tape on the stereo, sits cross-legged on the floor, and presses her ear to the speaker, singing along and sobbing at the top of her lungs. Then she dials Daniel's number and hangs up when Anna sleepily says, "Hello?" An hour later she calls again and there is no answer so she supposes they have wisely unplugged their phone. She goes to bed wondering what ever happened to her self-respect. It is still raining.

* * *

In the morning she has a headache and an upset stomach. Even the coffee doesn't taste right. Smoking is out of the question. From within the shroud of her hangover, everything in the house looks cheap and flimsy, sour, soiled. There are toys and comic books spread everywhere. The kitchen smells funny and there seems to be a film of sand all over the linoleum. The sink is full of dirty glasses and on the counter sits the grease-stained pizza box, the Styrofoam Chinese food containers, the empty green beer bottles, a half-eaten strawberry and three hard baking soda biscuits. Beside the fridge is the bucket she used to wash the walls, still full of cold brown water with crumbs and clots of hair floating on top. Next to the bucket is the laundry basket piled high with clean but now wrinkled clothes, little socks and silky underwear dangling over the sides.

Sitting down to a bowl of Corn Flakes (which is the best Jane can manage this morning), Nicholas says, "Mommy, your hair's a mess. Have you got the flu?"

She takes Aspirins along with her vitamins and slips a surreptitious shot of whisky into her coffee to steady her hands, if not her nerves.

First she calls the bus depot and finds out what time the next bus leaves. Then she calls the office and tells them she is sick and will be taking a few days off. They say that's fine, there's a lot of flu going around. Then she calls the daycare and tells them she and Nicholas are taking a little holiday. They say that's wonderful, sounds like a lot of fun, have a good time.

Without paying much attention, she packs the overnight bag, plucking items out of the laundry basket and tossing them in. She presses Nicholas's teddy bear pajamas to her nose and inhales the clean comforts of laundry soap and flannelette. Nicholas helps her pack, busily rounding up three race cars, a black-and-white kitten he calls Tiger, and the Sticker Dictionary.

"Will you buy me a new toy when we get there?" he asks.

"Yes," Jane says.

"Promise?"

"Yes, I promise," Jane says. At that moment she realizes she would promise him anything if it would make him keep on loving her.

What she really wants is to vanish without a trace but she thinks better of it at the last minute and calls Deborah at work so she won't worry. Deborah says she thinks getting away for a few days is a great idea. Jane isn't so sure but she can't think of anything else to do. Deborah recommends a bed-and-breakfast place she's heard is very nice and reasonably priced, although she's never stayed there herself.

Then Jane calls a taxi while Nicholas jumps all around the kitchen in excitement, his trust in the inherent joy of adventure winning out for once over his often timid nature.

When the taxi arrives, Jane locks up the house behind her without leaving a note. She hasn't turned on the answering machine either and, with a determined sense of vengeful freedom, she imagines the telephone ringing off the hook into the empty house. Daniel, desperate, might even come to the door and stand there knocking stupidly for hours while she has gone on with her life. She will finally be beyond him.

The taxi driver is jovial and friendly, a burly red-bearded man who complains cheerfully about the rain and the rotten drivers in this city. Jane is silent but Nicholas strikes up a joyful chatter with this congenial man. The driver carries their bag into the bus station, wishes them good luck on their trip, and seems to be looking at Jane with curious concern. His genuine kindness makes her want to scream, "Don't be nice to me, I can't stand it!" She is holding herself together so tightly she is afraid that if he even so much as puts a hand on her shoulder out of that warm kindness, she will sink to her knees, sobbing and pounding her fists on the concrete floor, ending up face-down and howling amidst the cigarette butts and the crumpled candy wrappers. She does not want to cry in front of Nicholas because, the few times she has, it terrified him so much that he ran around the house in circles, rushing at her and then rushing away before she could touch him.

But she longs to tell this taxi driver that her life has just never turned out the way she thought it would. Sometimes she thinks she understands why. Sometimes she thinks it is fate, other times she thinks it is all her own damn fault. Either way, here she is at thirty-five stuck in the present, unable to think of the past because it is too painful, filled as it is with memories of Daniel, unable to think of the future because it is unimaginable without him. Sometimes everything about her own life seems an insoluble and unbearable mystery. Here she is at thirty-five thinking that taxi drivers and bartenders might well be the only people in the world who are likely to listen, let alone understand: virtual strangers who will be satisfied with hearing her sad story as far as it goes or as far as she cares to tell it.

At the ticket counter, Nicholas perches on the overnight bag while the officious agent asks her, "Where are you going? When are you returning? How old is the child?" until Jane feels herself to be under suspicion, scrutinized and found wanting. What does she look like: a kidnapper, a criminal, an escapee from an insane asylum, some other kind of desperado, wild-eyed and on the lam? Probably, and can he tell by looking at her that she is an adulteress, a woman whose lover has just dumped her, a full-grown woman running away from home for the first time in her life? Her hands shake as she hands him the money and can't he see that all she wants now is to be invisible?

She and Nicholas settle themselves into two seats in the smoking section. Nicholas chatters on in his excitement:

"When will we get on the bus?"

"How will we know which bus is our bus?"

"Will it be a big bus or a little bus?"

"How will the bus driver know where we're going?"

"When I grow up, I'm going to be a bus driver."

Jane answers his questions absentmindedly and smokes.

"What time is it now?" he asks and Jane realizes she has forgotten her watch.

Across from them, a pleasant-looking young man with sandy-coloured hair and a red windbreaker reads the newspaper. She studies the headlines backwards and compulsively feels for their tickets in her jacket pocket.

A woman in a fringed black leather vest and knee-high black boots is pacing the length of the waiting room. There are chains across the back of her vest and a dozen or more silver bracelets on her left arm so that she jingles insistently as she walks. Everyone notices her and then pointedly ignores her and the woman begins humming loudly as if she enjoys this kind of reverse attention. Nicholas, of course, is watching every move she makes. Jane thinks of the time he broke out in horrible lumpy hives and while they waited in the crowded emergency room, two armed guards led in a prisoner with one arm in a makeshift sling and a lopsided bandage wrapped round his head. The prisoner's legs were tied together with a short thick chain that clanked as he shuffled between the guards to an empty seat. Everyone else in the waiting room became suddenly intent upon their magazines, their injuries, their fingernails. Nicholas slipped out of his chair, went over to the toy box, and selected a blue plastic boat. Then he walked over to the prisoner and handed him the boat, saying, "Here you go, mister."

"Thanks, kid," said the man in chains, "you just made my day."

Jane, whenever she tells this story, feels a misty-eyed motherly pride in Nicholas's generous innocence and she does not want to worry yet about the future dangers it may lead him to.

Now the woman in the leather vest pauses at the bubble-shaped candy dispenser in the corner, puts in a quarter, and holds her hand to the mouth of the machine which obediently spits out jelly beans like coins from a slot machine. She walks towards them and puts the jelly beans straight into Nicholas' small hands. Then she walks away still humming, with no expression on her face. Nicholas, taking such a gesture for granted, makes no comment and pops the candies one by one into his mouth until they are all gone.

* * *

Their bus is called. They find a seat near the back and Jane helps Nicholas take off his jacket and get settled by the window. The young man with the newspaper sits across the aisle, two seats up, and goes on with his reading. Jane does not see the woman in the leather vest get on. Directly across from them is an elderly woman in a mauve dress who pulls a tangle of knitting out of a shopping bag and sets to work immediately, smiling fondly down at her own nimble fingers. She is soon joined by a younger woman in a grey jogging suit, very pale and quite overweight, with long limp hair and noticeably crooked teeth. She is talking when she sits down and she keeps on talking, telling the older woman, Jane supposes, her whole life story. Her voice gets louder and Jane hears her say, "Yes, he's a great ex-husband and he was a wonderful boyfriend. It was just the husband part he was lousy at."

Jane turns back to Nicholas who has taken his little metal race cars out of the bag at their feet and is driving them all over the rain-streaked window. The bus lumbers out of the station.

Nicholas is happily occupied with the passing scenery and his toys so Jane sits very still with her hand on his leg and her eyes closed, hoping that no one will talk to her. At odd moments, when the driver shifts and the roar of the engine lets up, disembodied voices come to her from various unidentifiable regions of the bus.

A man's voice: "Remember that old guy down the block when we lived on Union Street?"

An adolescent boy's voice: "Yeah?"

Man's voice: "They found him last week, dead in his bed."

Boy's voice: "Wow! I remember him. He was the one used to sit in his car in the driveway and drink all night. Wow!"

Woman's voice: "If I never see her again, it will be too soon."

Man's voice: "She used to come to our house and get drunk and take all her clothes off."

Woman's voice: "As if she had anything anybody would ever want to see."

Man's voice: "Well, that was years ago. She wasn't so bad."

Another woman's voice: "Have you told your husband yet?"

Another woman's voice: "I'm going to visit my sister."

Another woman's voice: "I was in labour for twenty-eight hours with the first one."

Another woman's voice: "My fourth one came out so fast all the doctor had to do was catch her."

Another woman's voice: "I've never cared for cashews myself."

Intermittently Nicholas needs to know once again how much longer it will take to get there, how does the bus driver know how to get there, and once they get there, where are they going to sleep? Jane answers him gently, still with her eyes closed and her seat pushed back, sternly willing herself to be patient, be calm, he doesn't mean to be a pest, he doesn't mean to be insensitive to her need for silence, he just can't help himself, being only four and not yet fully aware of the fact that he is not the only important person in the world. Finally he is lulled to sleep by the monotonous motion of the bus and the dull grey rain around it.

Jane does not sleep, but hangs there instead in some kind of catatonic abeyance, all of the stuffing knocked out of her, certain that she could not move a single muscle even if she tried. She does not try, for fear of finding herself paralyzed, bolted to the bottom of this itchy rust-coloured bus seat for all eternity. She feels she has been and will be hurtling down this black highway in this silver bus in this damn rain forever and forever.

Jane is not thinking, she is empty, she is sitting, just sitting, and she is not thinking about Daniel.

She is not thinking about the look on his face whenever he told her he loved her. She is not thinking about the feel of his head on her shoulder, his arms around her waist, while they waltzed in her living room one night after Nicholas was asleep. She is not thinking about the smell of his bare skin.

She is not thinking about Daniel lying even now in Anna's aggrieved but forgiving arms. She is not thinking about Daniel dying even now in Anna's enduring arms.

She opens her eyes as they enter the outskirts of the city and the bus begins to pick its surprisingly agile way through the building afternoon traffic. Nicholas is roused by all the jerks of stopping and starting and comes awake instantly bright-eyed and lively, asking, "Where are we now? What time is it now?" and Jane remembers that she has forgotten her watch and how can you know where you are when you don't know what time it is?

She sighs and begins to gather up their belongings. Now that it's over, the bus trip seems to have simultaneously taken days and days and yet no more than five minutes. What is it about time, this amoeba, this protoplasmic oozing entity, which enables it to expand and contract seemingly at will so that an hour has no verifiable length after all and a minute is merely a subjective experience which can never be measured, compared or satisfactorily retrieved? What is it about time, like sex or happiness, that it can never be quite rightly remembered and so must be endlessly repeated in order to be verified, in order to achieve, however fleetingly, some semblance of reality?

The bus pulls into the station and everyone gets off and disperses throughout the waiting room, intent once again upon their own private lives. Now that they have arrived, Jane finds herself perceiving everything in profuse and lavish detail, so that each small thing which would seem meaningless if left to its own devices is now rendered significant and noteworthy, as if backlit, shimmering with suggestion and resonance. All of the mundane objects that fall into and then out of her line of vision take on the inert but intense hyperacuity of a painting. She is not thinking though of the painting in Daniel's dining room, a reproduction of "Young Woman with a Slip" by Christopher Pratt: the back of a woman in her underwear, a slip in her left hand, standing in front of a white dresser in a beige room, her face in the mirror, eyes cast down to the open top drawer, her hair the colour of the wallpaper and the hardwood floor. She is not thinking of how when she said the woman in the painting looked a little like Anna, Daniel said he couldn't see the resemblance.

If on the bus she was a zombie, now she is a conduit. She remembers an odd man who accosted her once on the street near her house. He fixed her in his lunatic gaze and said, "I receive but I don't transmit." She hurried home then, locked the door behind her, and sat in her warm sunny kitchen seeking safety. She never saw the man again but she often thinks of him when she is lonely and fearful and sometimes he still surfaces in her dreams.

* * *

With Nicholas in one hand and their bag in the other, Jane finds her way to a blue taxi waiting at the stand out front. The driver sighs and flips the meter on when she gives him the address of the Gasthaus Wolfenschiessen which Deborah recommended. It is a long ride and they are all silent, Nicholas peering with delight out the back window at the tall buildings, the street cars, and a black-and-white dog chasing a bus.

The cab driver drops them in the street in the rain in front of a large grey stone building flying the red-and-white Swiss flag, the Red Cross emblem in reverse, the ensign of the land of neutrality. Long deep windows are flanked by white wooden shutters featuring heart-shaped gingerbread cutouts and there are many cheerful red window-boxes filled with red geraniums.

Jane leads Nicholas into the little lobby only to discover that the inside glass door is locked. She peers at the hand-lettered sign: "For information pick up white telephone."

As Jane presses the receiver to her ear, a sprightly, accented female voice says, "Good afternoon, may I help you?"

"Yes," Jane says, "I'm looking for a room for myself and my son," and as if by the wonder of modern technology, the voice is instantly embodied as a blue-eyed blonde woman in a peasant blouse and a dirndl skirt with a brass ring of keys the size of a saucer in her hand.

She leads them down a dark-panelled hallway. "I'll show you the room, it's the last one left," she says.

"Fine," Jane says, thinking, Fucking Heidi, torn between hating or hugging this amiable fresh-faced woman. Heidi jangles her keys and opens the last door on the left. Jane peers into a high-ceilinged room with two pine beds with puffy duvets in red-and-white gingham covers, a small wooden table with one chair, white walls decorated with travel posters featuring snow-capped mountains, picturesque wooden chalets, black-and-white cows, and rosy-cheeked revellers grinning in their lederhosen while hoisting hefty beer steins. There is even one poster extolling the exports of Switzerland: shiny golden wheels of cheese the size of automobile tires, chunks of glossy brown chocolate like bricks, music boxes, cuckoo clocks, and a dozen or more precision watches.

"Fine," Jane says.

Heidi leads them back down the hallway and then down a narrow flight of stairs to the basement which appears to be her home. She takes them into her cozy compact kitchen and performs the necessary paperwork.

"How long will you be staying?" she asks.

"Just one night," Jane says, although she has not thought this through beforehand.

"Wonderful," the woman says. "Just a little holiday, just the two of you, how very nice," she says encouragingly and Jane does not say, "Mind your own business, Heidi." She is not thinking about the plan she and Daniel made just last week to sneak away sometime to an inn in the Laurentians they'd heard about. She is not thinking about how the next morning, still carried away with their fantasy, she actually called the inn and made inquiries about rates and reservations. She is not thinking about what it would have been like to sleep a whole night in his arms.

She holds Nicholas firmly by the hand as he tries to pull away from her, pointing into the living room where two small children are watching cartoons in the dark. Heidi shows them the large windowless dining room where breakfast will be served. Heidi seems pleased when Jane pays cash up front.

Nicholas whines all the way back up the stairs but is placated when he sees that they have a TV set too. He flips through the channels (twice as many as they have at home!) while Jane unpacks their things, discovering she has brought six pairs of underwear, four shirts but only one pair of pants for him, and three pairs of jeans, only one t-shirt and no nightgown for herself. It is not until after she has arranged everything carefully in the pine-scented wardrobe and opened all the blinds that she notices the No Smoking signs and the fact that the bathroom is back down the hall.

First she calls Stuart at Carlyle's to let him know where she is—they'd planned to have lunch together tomorrow. He is pleasantly surprised to hear she's run off and he says, "Yes, you're right, yes, this is the right thing to do." He tells her that Andrea has agreed to go out for dinner with him. He is jubilant and Jane is genuinely happy for him.

Then she calls Deborah to let her know they arrived safely and are already settled in. Deborah says she will pick them up at the bus station when they get home.

Jane actually knows three or four people who live in this city but she has no intention of calling them. She does not want to be anywhere near anyone who knows anything about her.

And in this city there are a great many cultural attractions: nationally known museums, internationally renowned art galleries, famous and important historical sites, archives and libraries. But she has no intention of visiting any of them. She does not want to be educated, enlightened, or engaged in intelligent conversation. All she wants is time to think, although already she is coming to the realization that there are more things she *doesn't* want to think about than things she does.

* * *

"Let's go for a walk," Jane says.

"Hooray, hooray," cries Nicholas and rushes to the door.

They head up a side street and turn onto what appears to be a main thoroughfare. Jane smokes while they walk and keeps careful track of their route so they can find their way back. These streets could be the downtown streets of any medium-sized city anywhere, Jane thinks, as they pass discount drugstores with their windows completely covered by sale price signs in black and yellow, fashion boutiques with anorexic faceless mannequins displaying fluorescent Spandex sportswear, smoke shops with racks of French, Italian, Japanese and Greek language newspapers out front, video arcades with neon signs and darkened doorways revealing the backs of many adolescent boys hunched over row upon row of flashing beeping boinging machines.

As in every such neighbourhood, there are bedraggled-looking panhandlers, old men talking to themselves and scratching their crotches, clots of strangers waiting for a bus, three young boys on skateboards slaloming around the alarmed others with their headphones on, a young man listening to rap music on his ghetto blaster and bopping on the curb, a couple all in black with both their heads shaved, and two blue-haired matrons right behind them clucking their tongues and saying, "Isn't that disgusting?"

Nobody notices Jane who is, after all, nothing more than an ordinary woman in designer jeans and a peach cotton shirt, a perfectly ordinary mother walking through the city with her cute little boy by the hand.

"I'm starved," Nicholas announces. "I'm starved for spaghetti." Although since Daniel's visit yesterday at noon, Jane thought she would never eat (or sleep or smile or hope or make love) again, she too is suddenly ravenous.

They walk until they come to an Italian restaurant called Guido's. A woman in a white blouse and a short black skirt shows them to a tiny table for two in the corner. At four in the afternoon the place is empty except for the staff, all women wearing white blouses and short black skirts who are hanging around the cash register, waiting for the Sunday dinner rush, straightening piles of plasticized menus, replenishing dishes of pink and green mints, smoking, drinking coffee, and telling each other outrageous and involved tales of their dates the night before.

Jane orders a child's portion of spaghetti and a glass of milk for Nicholas, cannelloni and a half-litre of white house wine for herself.

"How does it feel," she asks Nicholas while they wait for their food, "to be running away from home with your very own mother?"

He considers this for a moment and says seriously, "Not bad."

"You're lucky, you know," Jane says. "Most kids have to run away from home all by themselves."

Nicholas of course cannot quite appreciate the humour of this but Jane is getting into the mischievous spirit of their little adventure.

When the waitress brings the food, Jane says, "We're running away from home," and giggles.

"That's nice," the waitress says flatly and Jane feels stupid.

She concentrates on cutting up Nicholas' spaghetti. She is not thinking about the time she and Daniel managed to sneak out for a fancy dinner at Darby's, a new restaurant on the other side of town, and on the way there, she said, "If I start cutting up your meat, just tell me to snap out of it," and he held her and hugged her, laughing, right there on the street. She is not thinking about how a thick fog came in off the lake while they were inside the restaurant (for nearly three hours!) and when they stepped back outside, they stepped into a different world and, shielded by the moist and opaque silence, they walked down the street holding hands. She is not thinking that they had been sleeping together for six months by that time but dinner at Darby's was their first real date. She is not thinking that, as it turns out, dinner at Darby's was their only real date.

By the time Nicholas has finished mucking around with his spaghetti, dunking his garlic bread into his milk, and dropping his fork on the floor three times, Guido's is beginning to fill up and Jane is anxious to leave. She feels conspicuous surrounded by so many smiling handsome couples, so many pretty young women in groups laughing and shining with all their hopes ahead of them, so many happy families folding up strollers, asking for high chairs, pulling bibs out of diaper bags, and admiring their angelic offspring. She thinks the waitress, who now seems to be avoiding them, is probably warning the other patrons to watch out for the weirdo who says she's running away from home. Her wine is all gone and she just wants to get the hell out of there. She realizes that while she waits for the bill she is clenching and unclenching her fists with impatience.

* * *

Back at the Gasthaus Wolfenschiessen, they turn on the TV and stretch out on their beds. Nicholas sprawls on his stomach with his chin propped in his hands, intent on an educational program, one of those gruesome nature shows where you get to watch the mommy and daddy raise their ugly hairless babies up to be cute furry tumbling bundles and then you get to watch one of the more adventurous little ones wander away and get eaten by a hyena. Jane curls up on her side with the book she brought, open but unread beside her. It is not until an hour later when Nicholas wakes her asking to go to the bathroom that she realizes she has fallen fast asleep. At home she is such a light sleeper that she can never nap when Nicholas is home or when the TV is on. At home she is almost always awake half the night.

They step into the shadowy hallway. A French-language TV program is blaring from the open door of the room across the way. Jane can see just the bottom half of the bed: the same red-and-white gingham duvet cover as they have, and on it the lower legs and feet of a man in grey dress pants and black socks. One pant leg is hitched up a ways and she can see a skinny white leg sprouting curly black hairs.

The small bathroom is spotless except for a long red hair in the sink and an empty pack of matches from a hotel in Halifax on the back of the toilet.

When Nicholas is finished, they go back to their room and read from the Sticker Dictionary for a while:

F is for fist. A fist is a tightly closed hand. Sometimes you hit a ball with your fist.

H is for hand. A hand is the part of the body at the end of the arm. Your hand has five fingers.

T is for turtle. A turtle is an animal with a hard shell on its back. Turtles move very slowly . . .

* * *

Then they are hungry again and Jane remembers a Mexican place they passed on their way to the Italian place so they set out for some tacos. It is still raining, it has been raining for so long now that it doesn't matter anymore. A person can get used to almost anything, Jane thinks as they pass the same drugstores, the same arcades, the same panhandlers, the same shaved couple in black with two different blue-haired matrons clucking along behind them. A person can get used to anything, even wet feet, Jane thinks, even this sadness which begins somewhere in the stomach and then expands to fill the space available so that now even her hands seem to be aching and useless. Supposedly, it was the human species' ability to adapt that enabled the race to prevail and survive in the first place. Supposedly, being able to get used to anything is a positive attribute but Jane wonders if it might not be instead some kind of trap which can keep a person from going forward, taking steps, making a decision, a difference or an irrevocable choice. Perhaps the dividing line between "getting used to" and "putting up with" is merely a matter of semantics.

When they get to the Mexican place, which is called Mexicali Mama's, they are shown to a table at the back. The place is crowded, the music is loud (but thankfully not especially Mexican), and the walls are liberally hung with sombreros, serapes, and brightly coloured piñatas. Jane sits facing a wall covered with tinted mirrors and so spends the whole time taking sneak peeks at her own face, compulsively checking to assure herself that no, she doesn't look nearly as bad as she feels . . . another look . . . oh yes she does, even worse, straggly hair, mottled skin, and bags under her eyes like bruises . . . another look . . . yes, she is still there, still here, still there, where?

A sympathetic-looking waiter brings the menu, takes their order, brings their tacos, one with hot sauce, one without, a Coke for Nicholas, a draft for Jane, and a clean ashtray too.

Nicholas likes the look of the piñatas and after Jane explains what they're for and how they work, he says, "Next time we run away from home, let's go to Mexico, okay Mom?"

At a table to Jane's right there is a man in a black turtleneck and blue jeans who promptly pulls a spiral notebook from his knapsack and begins to write in it while alternately sipping his beer and staring softly off into space. Jane tries briefly to distract herself but he is exactly the type of man she is invariably attracted to. She stares. He is a man who at first glance looks a little like Daniel and who, at second glance, strikes her as someone she could spend the rest of her life with quite nicely. He has fine features, olive skin, full lips, and dark curly hair.

She hasn't said two words to this man, does not even know what language he might return those two words in, but he looks French, whatever that means. She has to admit that this man hasn't even noticed her. And yet here she is wondering what his name is, what music does he like, what books does he read, what is his favourite film of all time, favourite colour, favourite season, favourite food, what's he like in bed and can he cook? Here she is imagining him right into her house, here she is cleaning out the spare bedroom so he will have a place to write (for he must be a writer, intent as he is on scribbling in that tattered notebook). Here she is: falling face-first into a fantasy world once again.

Then he is joined by a blonde woman dressed exactly as he is, except that her black turtleneck is adorned with several brightly coloured scarves, fringed and shot through with glinting silver threads, draped aesthetically around her neck and shoulders in a debonair style which Jane has sometimes attempted but never mastered. (She has a whole drawer full of similar scarves, testament to those attempts, but whenever she tries wearing them again, she just feels strangled and stupid, and whenever she catches a glimpse of herself decked out that way, she thinks, Who the hell is that? and the scarf, silver threads and all, ends up in a ball at the bottom of her purse.)

This blonde woman sits down gracefully and immediately she and the handsome man fall deep into an animated, intense, no doubt fascinating conversation (yes, they are French). Their heads bend in together and they often reach across the table to touch each other's expressive hands. They exude the enviable aura of two people who have been together for years, who will stay happily together forever and end up looking alike when they are old. Jane feels desolated, deserted, and completely ridiculous.

But then she thinks perhaps she should congratulate herself on being able to fantasize about this man at all. Perhaps it is a good sign, perhaps there is hope after all. But then again perhaps it is a bad sign, perhaps it just means that she hasn't learned a damn thing, will never ever learn, is doomed forever to falling in love with oblivious unavailable brown-eyed men.

She and Nicholas leave before the French couple (who seem to have settled in for the evening—they have menus now, more beer, the woman is bringing *her* spiral notebook out of *her* knapsack and also some intellectual-looking books which she is passing across to the handsome man) and Jane forgets about them the minute she leaves the restaurant with Nicholas by the hand.

* * *

Back at the Gasthaus Wolfenschiessen, they get ready for bed right away, Nicholas into his teddy bear pajamas and Jane into her t-shirt because she's brought nothing else. She tucks Nicholas into his bed and then she is going to read in hers but he complains that her lamp is keeping him awake. So she turns it off and lies flat on her back in the dark room with her hands behind her head, staring up to where the ceiling would have been if she could have seen it.

For once she is not waiting for anything. For once she is not waiting for the phone to ring or a knock at the door. She is not thinking about Daniel. She is not doing any of those things that she always does at home.

She is not willing him with all her might to call or come over. Not wondering what he is doing at this very minute while she is eating/drinking/sleeping all alone, while she is listening to songs without words and wanting him, always wanting him. She is not picturing him at home with Anna, at a movie with Anna, out for dinner with Anna, walking hand in hand with Anna, going downtown dancing with Anna and all their happily married friends.

For once she is not replaying the last conversation they had in which he told her once again how much he loved her, how he was in just as much agony as she was but how he couldn't tell Anna the truth, not yet, how he couldn't hurt Anna that much, not yet, how Anna would probably die if he left her.

For once she is not rehearsing the next conversation they will have in which she will tell him how much she loves him, how no one, not even Anna, could ever love him as much as she does, how if they were together they would surely have the very best that life has to offer, how lots of people have broken up and lived.

For once she is not even wishing that he would just get hit by a bus and be done with it.

She is just lying there, just lying there and listening. To the traffic swishing through the street in the rain, to the sirens from the fire station just around the corner, to the murmuring of passersby, to high heels clicking on the concrete, a solitary set of footsteps fast receding into the rain. She is just lying there breathing in the smell of the rain on the asphalt, the smell of her son, that precious heart-breaking scent which all sleeping children seem to give off. Just lying there inhaling the detergent-edged odour of the soft gingham duvet cover which forever afterwards she will imagine is what all of Switzerland smells like. Knowing full well that if she ever goes there (knowing full well that she will never go there), she is bound to be disappointed because the country will smell just like any other country anywhere.

She knows she'll never be able to fall asleep without having her favourite cigarette of the day, the last one. At home every night she has it at the kitchen table, the red dot of the lit end glowing into the dark while she thinks of everything she has and hasn't done today, everything she should and probably won't do tomorrow, and what on earth is going to become of her in the end?

Now she gets up and opens a window. It will only come up about six inches and then it gets stuck. She tries the others and they are no better. She drags the single chair over to the open window and sits down. She lights the cigarette and then rests the left side of her head on the wide windowsill and blows the smoke out through the screen. With every puff she is expecting an alarm to go off, expecting Heidi to come marching down the hall (having traded her dirndl skirt and peasant blouse for a brown SS uniform and knee-high lace-up boots), expecting the door to be broken down and a machine gun to be trained on her law-breaking mouth. She was brought up to obey authority, including crossing guards, librarians, and all manner of signs: No Parking, No Spitting, No Loitering, No Overnight Camping, No Speeding, NO SMOKING.

Every time she hears footsteps coming down the street, she pulls her head back in from the screen like a turtle and prays that none of these strangers scuttling past under their big black umbrellas will see her smoke coming out the window, think the building is burning, and run for the fire department around the corner.

All in all, she does not enjoy one puff of this cigarette but she smokes it all the way to the filter and then uses the empty tinfoil-lined half of the package as an ashtray for the butt.

She is not thinking of all the times she promised Daniel she would quit smoking even though she knew she never would, even though she knew it would kill her in the end. She is not thinking of all the times she ran for the toothpaste when she saw him coming up her street, how she brushed her teeth madly while he knocked so he wouldn't smell it on her. She is not thinking of how every time after they made love Daniel had to have a shower so Anna wouldn't smell it on him. She is not thinking how all along she knew that what they were doing was wrong, dangerous, doomed, how many times she tried to stop but how she couldn't help herself, even though she knew that either way, loving him or leaving him, it would kill some part of her in the end.

She goes back to bed.

* * *

In the night she is roused several times by the fire sirens and also she thinks she hears singing, some thumping, a loud male voice pontificating in a foreign language, beer cans popping, footsteps in the hallway, a hand on her doorknob, a voice in her ear.

In the morning they wake up early (how early Jane can't say for sure, being without her watch and unable to locate a TV channel that gives the time) and when they venture out of their room, there is no evidence of a disturbance, a party, or a crime. There is only a red-haired woman in a blue bathrobe striding down the hallway with a towel and a bottle of shampoo. She beats them to the bathroom and glares at them triumphantly as she slams the door behind her.

They wait anxiously for their turn, Nicholas bouncing from one foot to the other and clutching himself, Jane perched gingerly on the side of his bed, feeling something warm leaking out of her, horrified to think she's lost control of her bladder and will have to spend the rest of her life wearing adult-sized diapers.

In the bathroom at last, she sees that it is not urine but blood pouring out of her with a vengeance she hasn't experienced since she was thirteen in Geography class giving her report on apartheid in South Africa, wearing a light pink skirt of course, and feeling sure she would die of shame right there in front of Mr. Dawson, all her friends and Stephen Soanes, the boy she'd been in love with for three whole weeks. Now she washes herself and folds a clean white washcloth into a thick absorbent pad and places it between her legs.

After they are dressed, she and Nicholas go down to the basement for breakfast. Heidi, in a shiny emerald green dress more suitable for evening attire than breakfast, shows them to one of the square white pine tables with which the windowless room is crowded. The placemats and napkins are red-

and-white gingham and there are more travel posters on the pine-panelled walls. Heidi makes a little fuss over Nicholas who instantly becomes shy and uncommunicative, ducking his head and refusing to answer any of her perky questions.

Some of the other guests are already eating, singly or in pairs, reading newspapers, studying maps of the city, asking Heidi for directions to the museums, the galleries, the provincial archives. Heidi is flitting between the tables, dispensing such valuable information along with tiny glasses of fresh-squeezed orange juice and endless refills of rich black coffee.

She brings a plump round loaf of bread, still warm and cradled in a white wicker basket, to their table. She whips out a small ceramic board and lops off several slices of white cheese. She comes back with a huge crockery bowl of some Swiss specialty (Jane doesn't catch the name) which appears to be a combination of oatmeal, yogurt, and chunks of fresh fruit. She holds a spoonful of this mixture right under Nicholas' nose and tries to tempt him to taste it.

Nicholas says, "Oh yuck," and asks for Corn Flakes instead. He eats two bowls full while Jane sips her coffee, feels her blood flowing into the wadded washcloth, and wishes she could smoke. She asks Heidi for directions to the nearest shopping centre. It turns out that there is a lovely new one just two blocks west. She tells Heidi they'll be back to get their things before checkout time.

* * *

Out on the street, Jane tries to determine which way is west. She has a chronically unreliable sense of direction. She is the kind of person who has to turn a map upside down to figure out where she is. She almost always has a sense that she is facing west, an intuition that is only occasionally correct. Whenever she is travelling, be it by train, plane, bus or car, she always has the unshakeable sensation that she is heading westward. She left the city where she grew up, where she lived for twenty-one years in fact, still wondering why the main street was divided into East and West sections when it had always seemed to her to be running north and south.

After two false starts, she gets them headed in the right direction and the shopping centre, a massive conglomeration of concrete, steel, and copper-tinted glass, turns out to be exactly where it's supposed to be, wedged between two office towers which seem to be made of miles of glass, giant panes streaked now with rain (it is starting again) and the feeble morning light.

"Ice cubes," Nicholas says, looking up at the towers. "They look just like ice cubes." As they go up the stairs leading into the shopping centre, he catches a glimpse of his reflection in one of the ground floor windows. He waves at himself and says, "Look, Mommy, there I am, stuck inside the ice cube. Look, Mommy, I'm melting."

It is early and the centre is nearly empty, a vast shiny cavern full of fluorescent lights, dead air, anesthetizing muzak and acres of over-priced merchandise prominently displayed and demanding to be bought. Some of the stores aren't even open yet. Sleepy clerks are straggling in, unlocking glass doors, pushing back floor-to-ceiling fences made of black iron bars that disappear into slots in the walls. They are turning the "Closed" signs to "Open" and firing up the cash registers in preparation for another exhausting day of conspicuous consumerism.

Much to Nicholas' chagrin, the toy store isn't open yet so they go across to the drugstore instead. Jane buys a box of sanitary napkins and a new wristwatch that she selects from a locked revolving glass case on the cosmetics counter. The clerk patiently shows her several styles (they are all on sale for $39.99) and Jane finally chooses the plainest one: white face, black Roman numerals, black leather band. The clerk tries to interest her in a tube of Really Red lipstick, a compact which contains sixteen different colours of eye shadow including the ever-popular silver with sparkles, a minuscule jar of face cream which costs as much as the watch and will make her look ten years younger in only one week. Jane says, "Thanks, but no thanks," and straps the watch on right then and there and wears it out of the store. She thinks about shopping with her mother and how, no matter what they bought, shoes, sunglasses, barrettes, a new jacket, her mother would never let her put it on until they were back home, how her mother wouldn't even let her look in the bags on the bus.

Jane never has liked shopping, has never quite been able to fathom the comfort it seems to bring to some of the women at work: the ones who tell her at coffee break what they bought at the mall last night, describing every little thing and then describing all the things they didn't buy but wanted to; these women who can quite without conscience spend $300 on a new tablecloth and feel happy every time they use it, twice a year, Christmas and Easter, and how are they ever going to get along without that $900 teak table it would look so good on, they just have to have it, they *have* to. At home Jane and Nicholas eat off plastic placemats with Big Bird on them and the kitchen table has an empty cigarette pack wedged under one leg to keep it level. Jane is used to it, she says she likes it that way.

Now Nicholas says he needs a chocolate bar, a licorice pipe, a bag of sour candies shaped like Teenage Mutant Ninja Turtles. He settles for a package of sugarless gum (of course Jane doesn't tell him that it's sugarless).

They head across to the toy store which is finally open. Nicholas has a hard time deciding between a puppet meant to resemble an elephant but looking more like a grey alligator and a race car guaranteed to do wheelies on a dime. He carries both of these toys around the store with him while he checks just to be sure he isn't missing something better. Finally, with a little prodding, he decides to get the puppet and reluctantly puts the race car back on the shelf. He whines a bit but Jane says, "One thing, just one, not both," and he gives up.

They leave the shopping centre, Nicholas with the elephant puppet on his hand pretending to bite off his own nose, Jane with the watch on her wrist wondering if maybe she should have bought the red one instead. Nicholas engages the puppet in a long conversation about Batman and Spiderman and the relative merits of each. He's forgotten all about the race car already, the choice that he didn't make, Jane thinks, no longer relevant or regrettable.

* * *

Back at the Gasthaus Wolfenschiessen, Jane takes their clothes out of the wardrobe and packs them neatly into the overnight bag. She calls Deborah to tell her they'll be on the next bus. She calls a taxi to take them to the station. Since the room is already paid for, she puts the key on the bed and leaves without saying goodbye to Heidi. They get to the station just in time to board their bus.

Forever afterwards Jane will be unable to remember a single thing about the return trip.

Deborah is there at the other end, waiting just like she said she would be. Jane cries briefly when Deborah puts her arms around her and says, "Don't worry, it will be all right," which is all a person is wanting to hear half the time anyway, but why does it always make you cry? Deborah drops them off at home. She can't stay, she has to get back to work.

Nicholas is glad to be back and rushes to his bedroom, eager to introduce the elephant puppet to all his other toys. Jane unpacks the overnight bag and then spends the rest of the afternoon cleaning up the house.

She puts away the toys and the comic books. She washes all the dirty glasses and throws away the grease-stained pizza box, the Styrofoam Chinese food containers, the half-eaten strawberry and the three hard baking soda biscuits. She puts the empty green beer bottles in the case. She empties the bucket she used to wash the walls and puts it back under the sink. She folds the clean but now wrinkled clothes and puts the laundry basket back in the basement. The phone rings a couple of times but she doesn't answer it. Nicholas thinks this is very funny and he says, "Go away, phone, we're busy."

She makes a simple supper of bacon, scrambled eggs and toast with Deborah's homemade strawberry jam. She cleans up again and then she gives Nicholas a bath. He wants to take the elephant puppet in with him but Jane convinces him that the elephant doesn't know how to swim. He takes in Batman and three empty yogurt containers instead. Jane sits on the toilet seat and supervises while Nicholas tries to drown Batman and splashes water all over the floor in the process. She shampoos his hair carefully (he hates this part) and helps him out of the tub.

He stands on the bathmat and pretends he's so cold that his teeth are chattering. Jane dries him off with the big soft towel. As she rubs the thick terry cloth over his pale skin, his thin shoulders, the ridges of his little ribs, she realizes that this is the first time in a long time that she has seen him, really seen him. She realizes that this is the first time in a long time that the presence of Daniel, the all-pervasive obsession of loving Daniel, has not stood like a pane of lightly frosted glass between her and the rest of the world, between her and her very own child, between her and her very own self.

She helps Nicholas put on his pajamas and then she hugs him hard and he laughs when the water from his hair gets all over her blouse.

After the bath, they curl up on the couch with a big bowl of buttered popcorn between them and Nicholas wants to read from the Sticker Dictionary again:

C is for cloud. A cloud is white and fluffy, way up high in the sky. Clouds move quickly in the wind and sometimes they bring rain.

E is for elephant. An elephant is a large grey animal with a trunk. We fed peanuts to the elephant at the zoo.

Q is for question. A question is what you ask in order to learn something. A question has an answer.

X is for x-ray. An x-ray is a picture that shows the inside of the body. The x-ray showed that my foot was broken.

When Jane is tucking Nicholas into his bed, he informs her that he doesn't want to be a bus driver when he grows up anymore. "Now," he says, "now I want to be a beautiful cloud. Maybe you can be one too." And Jane supposes she should have expected as much from a child whose first word, after "Mama," was "light."

After Nicholas falls asleep, Jane pours herself a glass of whisky. She puts on a tape, opens the back door, and sits down on the single concrete step. The weather is warmer but still wet. She plants her bare feet squarely in a big brown puddle and the rainwater is soft and sweet-smelling. She is singing along with the music which is so loud that she can only hope the neighbours like it too.

In the pause between songs, she can hear the telephone ringing inside the house. She knows it must be Daniel. No one else would be calling this late. She thinks about answering it but doesn't. It occurs to her that all she wants to say to him now is: Look.

Look at me.

Look at the face of my son sleeping and dreaming of clouds.

Look at the face of your wife sleeping beside you, dreaming of a happy life.

Look at all of us.

Look at what we have done.

She paddles her feet in the puddle and it occurs to her that in the morning their lives will get back to normal. She will take

Nicholas to the daycare where they will ask, "How was your little holiday?" and she will say it was wonderful. In the morning she will go back to work and they will ask, "How are you feeling?" and she will say she is fine, just fine.

It occurs to her that as far as it goes, this might be the whole story. As far as it goes, this might be the end, this might be the truth.

PUBLISHING HISTORY

The date given after the title of each story is the year in which it was written. The publishing history of the stories is as follows:

"The Diary of Glory Maxwell": *The Muskeg Review*, Thunder Bay, Ontario, February 1975.

"Body Number 15": *Descant*, Toronto, Ontario, August 1976.

"The Climb": *Canadian Fiction Magazine*, Vancouver, B.C., April 1976.

"Bright Wire": *Nebula #8: Four New Writers*, North Bay, Ontario, April 1979.

"Waiting": *Quarry Magazine*, Kingston, Ontario, July 1979; *Frogs and Other Stories*, Quarry Press, 1986; *Hockey Night in Canada and Other Stories*, Quarry Press, 1991.

"To Whom It May Concern": *Branching Out*, Edmonton, Alberta, September 1976.

"An Evening in Two Voices": *Nebula #8: Four New Writers*, North Bay, Ontario, April 1979.

"Prophecies": *Harvest*, Willowdale, Ontario, December 1979.

"The Gate": *Canadian Author & Bookman*, Welland, Ontario, January 1983; *Pure Fiction: The Okanagan Short Story Award Winners*, ed., Geoff Hancock, Fitzhenry & Whiteside, 1986; *The Man of My Dreams*, Macmillan of Canada, 1990.

"Notes for A Travelogue": *Frogs and Other Stories*, Quarry Press, 1986; *Hockey Night in Canada and Other Stories*, Quarry Press, 1991.

"Crimes of Passion": *The Old Dance: Love Stories of One Kind or Another*, ed., Bonnie Burnard, Coteau Books, October 1986; *Hockey Night in Canada*, Quarry Press, 1987; *Hockey Night in Canada and Other Stories*, Quarry Press, 1991.

"Histories": *Matrix*, Lennoxville, Quebec, January 1981; *Frogs and Other Stories*, Quarry Press, 1986; *Hockey Night in Canada and Other Stories*, Quarry Press, 1991.

"First Things First": *Quarry Magazine*, Kingston, Ontario, December 1984; *Frogs and Other Stories*, Quarry Press, 1986; *Hockey Night in Canada and Other Stories*, Quarry Press, 1991.

"The Long Way Home": *Frogs and Other Stories*, Quarry Press, 1986; *Hockey Night in Canada and Other Stories*, Quarry Press, 1991.

"What We Want": *CBC Radio, Alberta Anthology*, Edmonton, Alberta, excerpt, September 1983; *Coming Attractions 2*, eds. David Helwig and Sandra Martin, Oberon Press, 1984; *Women and Words: The Anthology*, Harbour Publishing, excerpt, November 1984; *Hockey Night in Canada*, Quarry Press, 1987; *The Man of My Dreams*, Macmillan of Canada, 1990.

"Life Sentences": *Double Bond: An Anthology of Prairie Women's Fiction*, ed. Caroline Heath, Fifth House, October 1984; *Hockey Night in Canada*, Quarry Press, 1987; *Hockey Night in Canada and Other Stories*, Quarry Press, 1991; "Condanna A Vita" (Italian)

Altre Terre: Raconti Contemporanii Del Canada Anglofono, ed. Branko Gorjup, Supernova, Venice, Italy, 1996.

"True or False": *Frogs and Other Stories,* Quarry Press, 1986; *Hockey Night in Canada and Other Stories,* Quarry Press, 1991.

"She Wants to Tell Me": *Quarry Magazine*, Kingston, Ontario, April 1987; *Hockey Night in Canada,* Quarry Press, 1987; *Hockey Night in Canada and Other Stories,* Quarry Press, 1991; *The Penguin Anthology of Stories by Canadian Women*, ed. Denise Chong, Viking Penguin Canada, November 1997.

"His People": *Prism International*, Vancouver, B.C., September 1988; *The Man of My Dreams,* Macmillan of Canada, 1990.

"None of the Above": *The Man of My Dreams,* Macmillan of Canada, 1990.

"How Myrna Survives": *The New Quarterly*, Waterloo, Ontario, January 1989; *The Man of My Dreams,* Macmillan of Canada, 1990; *Written In Stone: A Kingston Reader*, eds. Mary Alice Downie and M.A. Thompson, excerpt, Quarry Press, October 1993.

"Trick Questions": *The Man of My Dreams,* Macmillan of Canada, 1990.

"Love in the Time of Clichés": *90 Best Canadian Stories*, eds. David Helwig and Maggie Helwig, Oberon Press, October 1990; *The Second Gates of Paradise: The Anthology of Erotic Short Fiction*, ed. Alberto Manguel, Macfarlane Walter & Ross, November 1994.

"As Far As It Goes": *Canadian Fiction Magazine,* Toronto, Ontario, October 1991.